BEST NEW AMERICAN VOICES 2001

BEST NEW AMERICAN VOICES 2001

GUEST EDITOR
Charles Baxter

SERIES EDITORS
John Kulka and Natalie Danford

A Harvest Original • Harcourt, Inc.
San Diego   New York   London

CONTENTS

PREFACE

Best New American Voices is an annual story anthology that introduces new writers. Its purpose and scope are different from those of other story anthologies: Few of the names in the table of contents of *Best New American Voices 2001* are familiar, and many of our contributors are publishing for the first time in these pages.

As series editors, we do not look to magazines and literary quarterlies for story nominations. Instead, we solicit nominations from arts organizations like the Banff Centre for the Arts and the PEN Prison Writing Committee, from summer writing conferences like Bread Loaf and Sewanee, from community workshops like those held at the 92nd Street Y in New York City, and from the many hundreds of graduate writing programs associated with North American universities.

Each year we ask program directors to forward to us the best stories submitted to workshop instructors during the previous year. For *Best New American Voices 2001* we received in total about 350 pre-screened nominations from about 150 different writing programs. Many of these programs are selective and rightly famous training grounds for our best new talents. Consider, for example, the Stanford program. In a recent letter to us, Tobias Wolff, the program director there, indicated that last year only five writers of 658 applicants were accepted as fiction fellows into the Stanford program. The University of Iowa, another of our participants, has without question produced some of America's finest writers of the previous century: Flannery O'Connor, Raymond Carver, Andre Dubus, Wallace Stegner, and T. C. Boyle, to name just a few. All of the writers included here stand in very good company.

Guest editor Charles Baxter has selected seventeen stories from this year's finalists for inclusion in *Best New American Voices 2001*. His selections make for a diverse, multicultural anthology. As Baxter notes in his introduction, much of the energy in these stories comes from a "meeting of cultures: gay and straight, black and white, domestic and foreign." The young authors included here have different concerns and writing styles, but they share the same general observation about life in the twenty-first century: multiculturalism as sociological *fact*. What these writers also share are skill and talent.

We would like to extend thanks to Charles Baxter for his careful reading of the manuscripts, for his enthusiasm for this project, and for his excellent editorial suggestions regarding the stories in this volume. To the many writers, directors, teachers, and panel judges who help to make this series a continuing success we extend heartfelt thanks and congratulations. To name just a few others: We thank our editor André Bernard for his patience, counsel, and understanding; Meredith Phillips at Harcourt, Inc. for her constant attention to details; Lisa Lucas in the Harcourt contracts department for the obvious and maybe not so obvious; Margie Rogers, deputy managing editor at Harcourt, for her unflagging efforts; and our families and friends for their support.

—John Kulka and Natalie Danford

INTRODUCTION

Charles Baxter

Many writers whose phone numbers are still listed in the directory, as mine is, may have a story similar to the one that follows. A few months ago, I received a call from a person with a gruff-sounding voice who left his name and number on the answering machine. He said that I should get in touch with him and, somewhat against my better judgment, I eventually called him back. After we had introduced ourselves, he told me that he had a great story, a terrific story, and that *I should write it.* When I put him on notice that I didn't write other people's stories, only my own, he explained to me that what I had just said to him was a crying shame and that surely I must be running out of material by now. A bit irritably, I asked him what he meant by that. "Well," he said, "if you're writing your own stories, they must just about be used up. The things you've done and seen, you know. Your experiences."

No, I told him, when I said *my stories*, I was referring to stories that I had imagined, not stories that I had actually lived. The stories that I could imagine were not used up, not by a long shot.

"Too bad for you," he said. "Having to imagine things all day."

The call was not going well, I could see that. "So," I said, "what's your great story?"

"I was in the Navy," he said. "I saw a lot of what was going on."

"What stuff?"

"Well," he said, "I'm not about to give it away."

"Why don't you write your story yourself?" I asked.

"I don't have the time," he said. "I'm awfully busy."

The call limped to its conclusion, and we wished each other good-bye, and that, at least for a while, was that. Nevertheless, I thought often of my phantom phone caller while I was editing this selection of stories, for some obvious and perhaps less obvious reasons.

E. B. White observed (and many other writers have agreed in so many words) that all writing is an act of faith. But it is particularly an act of faith for young writers, writers getting their start, many of them unrewarded with prizes, contracts, awards, acclaim, publication, and even the encouragement of their relatives and friends. To begin with, there are the rejection slips (my own personal favorite: *"Dear Mr. Baxter: These stories have it too much their own way. One longs for more negativity in the façon"*), the doubts, the occasional visits from the Fraud Police. Then there is contemporary American culture itself, which does not exactly encourage the production of literary works and certainly does not encourage writers to take their own sweet time over the job. No wonder my caller thought someone else could write his story for him. In this context, one thinks of a revision of an old epigram: "As for our stories, our servants will write them for us."

But no: The servants will not do it. Only the person in possession of the story can write the story. This truth seems obvious, but its long-term consequences are far from obvious to nonwriters. If there is a literary masterpiece written by a ghostwriter (unless you count the Bible), I have yet to see it. Finally it makes little or no difference whether the writer has lived the story or just imagined it; either way, the writer must experience the story internally, in the heart and the soul, if it is going to come alive. The writer must give the story some of his or her own life.

Each one of the stories in this anthology—the one you hold in your hands—is an act of faith. Each one was written by someone who, as my caller said, had "to imagine things" all day and who was not too busy to write those things down, one by one, patiently, painstakingly. And each story—I like to think—has something precious in it, a gift given away, worthy of a commitment of the writer's time, and yours.

I chose the selections in this anthology from a group of finalists forwarded to me by the series editors, John Kulka and Natalie Danford. Of course, I have certain biases. Everyone does. The short story form, because of its necessary brevity, typically deals with impulsive (as opposed to long-considered and decisive) actions as part of its traditional subject matter, and I like the intensity of stories in which some character or other indulges in such an impulse. I also tend to admire stories in which strangers find themselves together, and stories in which an unusual or even unknown world is evoked. My own tastes move in the direction of narratives that manage somehow to combine the familiar and the strange so that the world of the tale is recognizable and unrecognizable at once. All this is simply to say that I admire fiction in which the very definition of what is "real" is stretched, or, to use another metaphor, is brought to a line that demarks the real and may even cross over it. Arnold Schoenberg once said that there was plenty of music still to be written in the key of

C major, and there are plenty of stories left that cunningly test our sense of what is real and what isn't.

Jean Rhys once said that she liked fiction that "takes you away," and the vehicle for that taking, that flight, is the plot, which, as Aristotle was one of the first to observe, is the last technical skill young writers acquire. After all's said, the story has to take you somewhere, even when the protagonist is going nowhere in particular. *Especially* when the protagonist is going nowhere in particular.

The surprise for me—and perhaps it shouldn't have been a surprise—in reading through these stories was the degree to which these narratives found their energy in the meeting of cultures: gay and straight, domestic and foreign, a recombination of the familiar and the unfamiliar, as if the International theme, as Henry James once called it, had staged a great comeback 100 years after he identified it, and in its new form had somehow become subsumed into the whole issue of cultural diversity. And I was also struck by the subtlety and depth of those stories with gay/lesbian subjects or subtexts, as if it had taken a new generation of writers to take this material for granted (in the best sense), to be calm about it, before treating it in such a way that it might really be made visible again in its newest forms. The combination of these two sources made me think of Paul Bowles, who might have served as the godfather of this entire collection, though none of these writers has his particular ferocity in the service of punishing innocence.

Often it is easier for a writer in midlife to love the work of writers who have gone before than of those who will come after. The authors included here are the writers who will be around when those of my generation are no longer on the scene. But literature is not an endurance contest or a sack race, as my fellow Michigan writer Jim Harrison once said, and I confess that I loved much of what I found here for its courage, its formal daring, its ambition, even a kind of writerly heroism. After so many have described the "typical" writing program story (complacent, domestic, middle class), a sympathetic reader will discover that these stories thrive on extremity rather than the middle way, and that furthermore these writers are probably more ambitious and daring than those whose work you might have encountered in magazines during the fifties and early sixties. The world in *these* stories is vivid and very wide and often quite heart-stoppingly dangerous, even when the formal properties of the story are traditional; there's a worldliness in them that startled me.

Among the many stories here with international themes, where one culture views itself through the lens of another, are Christina Milletti's beautifully modulated "Villa of the Veiled Lady," in which various layers of an ancient civilization seem to have been peeled back for exposure, and Kira Salak's "Beheadings," with its extraordinarily hushed ending, in which time almost seems to have stopped. Ha-yun Jung's "Our Lady of the Height" deals with trauma and its aftermath, and its ending, too, takes great risks, and in my judgment rises to the astonishing challenge it has set itself. Lidija S. Canovic's "Bats" is an entirely remarkable story about Bosnia and its airborne domestic terrors, while Zoey Byrd's "Of Cabbages," a story that uses Korea as a setting for its central dramatic tragedy, made the small hairs on the back of my neck stand up straight with its ubiquitous cabbages and its calm advice to mourners about talking to the dead: *"Be polite and firm as if speaking to a child."*

Several of the stories here have a headlong narrative energy that signals the writer's confidence in the story and its ability to hold the stage: I defy any reader to stop reading Julie Orringer's "Pilgrims" once past the second or third paragraph, or to predict where the story will go, or how on earth it will end. Patrick Ryan's "Before Las Blancas" is about speed and sex and violation, and like its protagonists, it moves so quickly through its heat-oppressed milieu that you may not notice how complex its seemingly simple narrative has become. Both these stories have the virtue of visionary scene writing, as does Amanda Davis's gracefully parabolic "louisiana loses its cricket hum." The limits of the real are very pleasingly tested in that story, as they are in Lysley A. Tenorio's "Superassassin" and Matthew Pitt's "The Mean," which manages in one story to mingle marijuana, mathematics, cancer, and chimpanzees (did I mention the punks in the zoo?) as the base materials of propulsive narrative elaboration.

Another one of the features of these stories that pleased me was the ability of many of these writers to shift the tone within a scene: Jeb Livingood in "Oh, Albany, My Love," Susanna Daniel in "We Are Cartographers," and Erin Flanagan in "Intervention" are utterly expert in their abilities to mingle painful material with comic moments that deepen rather than deflect the central conflict. Antoine Wilson's "Home, James, and Don't Spare the Horses" keeps you guessing about strategies and levels and tones, about the genuine and the fake, and the thin line between the horrifying and the comic.

Raymond Carver once wrote that "Writing is trouble, make no mistake, for everyone involved, and who needs trouble?" But then he went on to say—this was in one of his last essays—that now and then lightning strikes, sometimes early in a writer's life, sometimes late. The lightning follows no particular pattern—there's no justice in it, of course. But for the lightning to strike at all, you have to stand out in the rain for a while, just stand there, while everyone around you is running for shelter.

Having made all these claims for the stories that I have included, I want to insist that, finally, to cite Jean Rhys again, they took me away. From the air-conditioned doghouse in Timothy Westmoreland's "Darkening of the World" to the bent light fixture in Roompa

Bhattacharyya's "Loss," to the toxic shores of the Pocahontas in Whitney Davis's "The Sharp Light of Trespassers," they gave me the pleasure of astonishment and understanding, along with the feeling that the writer had stayed out in the rain, believing the lightning would strike. This anthology stands as evidence that it did.

BEST NEW AMERICAN VOICES 2001

JULIE ORRINGER

Stanford University

PILGRIMS

It was Thanksgiving day and hot, because this was New Orleans; they were driving uptown to have dinner with strangers. Ella pushed at her loose tooth with the tip of her tongue and fanned her legs with the hem of her velvet dress. On the seat beside her, Benjamin fidgeted with his shirt buttons. He had worn his Pilgrim costume, brown shorts and a white shirt and yellow paper buckles taped to his shoes. In the front seat their father drove without a word, while their mother dozed against the window glass. She wore a blue dress and a strand of jade beads and a knit cotton hat beneath which she was bald.

Three months earlier Ella's father had explained what chemotherapy was and how it would make her mother better. He had even taken Ella to the hospital once when her mother had a treatment. She remembered it like a filmstrip from school, a series of connected images she wished she didn't have to watch: her mother with an IV needle in her arm, the steady drip from the bag of orange liquid, her father speaking softly to himself as he paced the room, her mother shaking so hard she had to be tied down.

At night Ella and her brother tapped a secret code against the wall that separated their rooms: one knock, I'm afraid; two knocks, don't worry; three knocks, are you still awake? four, come quick. And then there was the Emergency Signal, a stream of knocks that kept on coming, which meant her brother could hear their mother and father crying in their bedroom. If it went on for more than a minute Ella would give four knocks, and her brother would run to her room and crawl under the covers.

There were changes in the house, healing rituals that required Ella's mother to go outside and embrace trees or lie facedown on the grass. Sometimes she did a kind of Asian dance that looked like karate. She ate bean paste and Japanese vegetables, or sticky brown rice wrapped in seaweed. And now they were going to have dinner with people they had never met, people who ate seaweed and brown rice every day of their lives.

They drove through the Garden District, where Spanish moss hung like beards from the trees. Once during Mardi Gras, Ella had ridden a trolley here with her brother and grandmother, down to the French Quarter where they'd eaten beignets at Café du Monde. She wished she were sitting in one of those wrought-iron chairs and shaking powdered sugar onto a beignet. How much better than to be surrounded by strangers, eating food that tasted like the bottom of the sea.

They turned onto a side street, and her father studied the directions. "It should be at the end of this block," he said.

Ella's mother shifted in her seat. "Where are we?" she asked, her voice dreamy with painkillers.

"Almost there," said Ella's father.

They pulled to the curb in front of a white house with sagging porches and a trampled lawn. Vines covered the walls and moss grew thick and green between the roof slates. Under the porte cochere stood a beat-up Honda and a Volkswagen with mismatched side panels. A faded Big Wheel lay on its side on the walk.

"Come on," their father said, and gave them a tired smile. "Time for fun." He got out of the car and opened the doors for Ella and her mother, sweeping his arm chauffeurlike as they climbed out.

Beside the front door was a tarnished doorbell in the shape of a lion's head. "Push it," her father said. Ella pushed. A sound like church bells echoed inside the house.

Then the door swung open and there was Mister Kaplan, a tall man with wiry orange hair and big dry-looking teeth. He shook hands with Ella's parents, so long and vigorously it seemed to Ella he might as well say *congratulations.*

"And you must be Ben and Ella," he said, bending down.

Ella gave a mute nod. Her brother kicked at the doorjamb.

"Well, come on in," he said. "I have a tree castle out back."

Benjamin's face came up, twisted with skepticism. "A what?"

"The kids are back there. They'll show you," he said.

"What an interesting foyer," their mother said. She bent down to look at the brass animals on the floor, a turtle and a jackal and a llama. Next to the animals stood a blue vase full of rusty metal flowers. A crystal chandelier dangled from the ceiling, its arms hung with dozens of God's-eyes and tiny plastic babies from Mardi Gras king cakes. On a low wooden shelf against the wall, pair after pair of canvas sandals and sneakers and Birkenstocks were piled in a heap. A crayoned sign above it said SHOES OFF NOW!

Ella looked down at her feet. She was wearing her new patent-leather Mary Janes.

"Your socks are nice, too," her father said and touched her shoulder. He stepped out of his own brown loafers and set them on top of the pile. Then he knelt before Ella's mother and removed her pumps. "Shoes off," he said to Ella and Ben.

"Even me?" Ben said. He looked down at his paper buckles.

Their father took off Ben's shoes and removed the paper buckles, tape intact. Then he pressed one buckle onto each of Ben's socks. "There," he said.

Ben looked as if he might cry.

"Everyone's in the kitchen," Mister Kaplan said. "We're all cooking."

"Marvelous," said Ella's mother. "We love to cook."

They followed him down a cavern of a hall, its walls decorated with sepia-toned photographs of children and parents, all of them staring stone-faced from their gilt frames. They passed a sweep of stairs, and a room with nothing in it but straw mats and pictures of blue Indian goddesses sitting on beds of cloud.

"What's that room?" Benjamin said.

"Meditation room," Mister Kaplan said, as if it were as commonplace as a den.

The kitchen smelled of roasting squash and baked apples and spices. There was an old brick oven and a stove with so many burners it looked as if it had been stolen from a restaurant. At the kitchen table men and women with long hair and loose clothes sliced vegetables or stirred things into bowls. Some of them wore knitted hats like her mother, their skin dull gray, their eyes purple-shaded underneath. To Ella it seemed they could be relatives of her mother's, shameful cousins recently discovered.

A tall woman with a green scarf around her waist came over and embraced Ella's mother, then bent down to hug Ella and Benjamin. She smelled of smoky perfume. Her wide eyes skewed in different directions as if she were watching two movies projected into opposite corners of the room. Ella did not know how to look at her.

"We're so happy you decided to come," the woman said. "I'm Delilah, Eddy's sister."

"Who's Eddy?" said Ben.

"Mister Kaplan," their father said.

"We use our real names here," Delilah said. "No one is a mister."

She led their parents over to the long table and put utensils into their hands. Their mother was to mix oats into a pastry crust, and their father to chop carrots, something Ella had never seen him do. He looked around in panic, then hunched over and began cutting a carrot into clumsy pieces. He kept glancing at the man to his left, a bearded man with a shaved head, as if to make sure he was doing it right.

Delilah gave Ella and Benjamin hard cookies that tasted like burned rice. It seemed Ella would have to chew forever. Her loose tooth waggled in its socket.

"The kids are all out back," Delilah said. "There's plenty of time to play before dinner."

"What kids?" Benjamin asked.

"You'll see," said Delilah. She tilted her head at Ella, one of her eyes moving over Ella's velvet dress. "Here's a little trick I learned when I was a girl," she said. In one swift movement she took the back hem of the dress, brought it up between Ella's knees, and tucked it into the sash. "Now you're wearing shorts," she said.

Ella didn't feel like she was wearing shorts. As soon as Delilah turned away, she pulled her skirt out of her sash and let it fall around her legs.

The wooden deck outside was cluttered with Tinkertoys and clay flowerpots and Little Golden Books. Ella heard children screaming and laughing nearby. As she and Benjamin moved to the edge of the deck there was a rustle in the bushes, and a skinny boy leaped out and pointed a suction-cup arrow at them. He stood there breathing hard, his hair full of leaves, his chest bare. "You're on duty," he said.

"Me?" Benjamin said.

"Yes, you," the boy said. "Both of you." He motioned them off the porch with his arrow and took them around the side of the house. There, built into the side of a sprawling oak, was the biggest, most sophisticated treehouse Ella had ever seen. There were tiny rooms of sagging plywood, and rope ladders hanging down from doors, and a telescope and a fireman's pole and a red net full of leaves. From one wide platform—almost as high as the top of the house— it seemed you could jump down onto a huge trampoline. Even higher was a kind of crow's nest, a little circular platform built around the trunk. A red-painted sign on the railing read DAGNER! Ella could hear the other children screaming but she couldn't see them. A collie dog barked crazily, staring up at the tree.

"Take off your socks! That's an order," the skinny boy said.

Benjamin glanced at Ella as if to ask if this were okay. Ella shrugged. It seemed ridiculous to walk around outside in socks. She bent and peeled off her anklets. Benjamin carefully removed his Pilgrim buckles and put them in his pocket, then sat down and took off his socks. The skinny boy grabbed the socks from their hands and tucked them into the waistband of his shorts.

The mud was thick and cold between Ella's toes, and pecan shells bit her feet as the boy herded them toward the treehouse. He prodded Ella toward a ladder of prickly looking rope. When she stepped onto the first rung, the ladder swung toward the tree and her toes banged against the trunk. The skinny boy laughed.

"Go on," he said. "Hurry up. And no whining."

The rope burned her hands and feet as she ascended. The ladder seemed to go on forever. Ben followed below, making the rope buck and sway as they climbed. At the top there was a small square opening, and Ella thrust both her arms inside and pulled herself into a dark coop. As she stood, her head knocked against something dangling from the ceiling on a length of string. It was a bird's skull, no bigger than a walnut. Dozens of others hung from the ceiling around her. Benjamin huddled at her side.

"Sick," he said.

"Don't look," Ella said.

The suction-cup arrow came up through the hole in the floor.

"Keep going," said the boy. "You're not there yet."

"Go where?" Ella said.

"Through the wall."

Ella brushed the skulls out of her way and leveled her shoulder against one of the walls. It creaked open like a door. Outside, a tree limb as thick as her torso extended up to another plywood box, this one much larger than the first. Ella dropped to her knees and crawled upward. Benjamin followed.

Apparently this was the hostage room. Four kids stood in the semidarkness, wide-eyed and still as sculptures, each bound at the ankles and wrists with vine handcuffs. Two of the kids, a boy and a girl, were so skinny that Ella could see the outlines of bones in their arms and legs. Their hair was patchy and ragged, their eyes black and almond shaped. In the corner, a white-haired boy in purple overalls whimpered softly to himself. And at the center of the room a girl Benjamin's age stood tied to the tree trunk with brown string. She had the same wild gray eyes and leafy hair as the boy with the arrows.

"It's mine, it's *my* treehouse," she said as Ella stared at her.

"Is Mister Kaplan your dad?" Benjamin said.

"My dat-*tee*," the girl corrected him.

"Where's your mom?"

"She died," said the girl, and looked him fiercely in the eye.

Benjamin sucked in his breath and glanced at Ella.

Ella wanted to hit this girl. She bent down close to the girl's face, making her eyes small and mean. "If this is so your treehouse," Ella said, "then how come you're tied up?"

"It's *jail,*" the girl spat. "In jail you get tied up."

"We could untie you," said Benjamin. He tugged at one of her bonds.

The girl opened her mouth and let out a scream so shrill Ella's eardrums buzzed. Once, as her father had pulled into the driveway at night, he had trapped a rabbit by the leg beneath the wheel of his car; the rabbit had made a sound like that. Benjamin dropped the string and moved against Ella, and the children with ragged hair laughed and jumped on the platform until it crackled and groaned. The boy in purple overalls cried in his corner.

Benjamin put his lips to Ella's ear. "I don't understand it here," he whispered.

There was a scuffle at the door, and the skinny boy stepped into the hostage room. "All right," he said. "Who gets killed?"

"Kill those kids, Peter," the girl said, pointing to Benjamin and Ella.

"Us?" Benjamin said.

"Who do you think?" said the boy.

He poked them in the back with his suction-cup arrow and moved them toward the tree trunk, where rough boards formed a ladder to the next level. Ella and Benjamin climbed until they had reached a narrow platform, and then Peter pushed them to the edge. Ella looked down at the trampoline. It was a longer drop than the high dive at the public pool. She looked over her shoulder and Peter glared at her. Down below the collie barked and barked, his black nose pointed up at them.

Benjamin took Ella's hand and closed his eyes. Then Peter shoved them from behind, and they stumbled forward into space.

There was a moment of terrifying emptiness, nothing but air beneath Ella's feet. She could hear the collie's bark getting closer as she fell. She slammed into the trampoline knees first, then flew, shrieking, back up into the air. When she hit the trampoline a second time, Benjamin's head knocked against her chin. He stood up rubbing his head, and Ella tasted salt in her mouth. Her loose tooth had slipped its roots. She spat it into her palm and studied its jagged edge.

"Move," Peter called from above. The boy in purple overalls was just climbing up onto the platform. Peter pulled him forward until his toes curled over the edge.

"I lost my tooth!" Ella yelled.

"Get off!"

Benjamin scrambled off the trampoline. Ella crawled to the edge, the tooth gleaming and red-rimmed between her fingers, and then the trampoline lurched with the weight of the boy in purple overalls. The tooth flew from her hand and into the bushes, too small to make a sound when it hit.

When she burst into the house crying, blood streaming from her mouth, the long-haired men and women dropped their mixing spoons and went to her. She twisted away from them, looking frantically for her mother and father, but they were nowhere to be seen. Her throat ached with crying. There was no way to explain that she wasn't hurt, that she was upset because her tooth was gone, and because everything about that house made her want to run away and hide. The adults, their faces creased with worry, pulled her to the sink and held her mouth open. The woman with skewed eyes, Delilah, pressed a tissue against the space where her tooth had been. Ella could smell onion and apples on her hands.

"The time was right," she said. "The new tooth's already coming in."

"Whose is she?" one of the men asked.

Delilah told him the names of Ella's parents. It was strange to hear those familiar words, *Ann* and *Gary,* in the mouths of these long-haired strangers.

"Your mother is upstairs," Delilah said, her eyes swiveling toward some distant hidden room. "She felt a little swimmy-headed. Your dad just brought her some special tea. Maybe we should let her rest, hm?"

Ella slipped out from beneath Delilah's hand and ran to the hall, remembering the stairway she'd seen earlier. There it was before her, a curve of glossy steps leading to nowhere she knew. Her mother's cough drifted down from one of the bedroom doors. Ella put a foot onto the first stair, feeling the eyes of the adults on her back. No one said anything to stop her. After a moment, she began to climb.

In the upstairs hallway toys and kids' shoes lay strewn across the floor, and crumpled pants and shirts and dresses lay in a musty-smelling heap. Two naked Barbies sprawled in a frying pan. A record player sat in the middle of the hall, its vacant turntable spinning. Ella stepped over the cord and went into the first room, a small room with a sleeping bag on the bare mattress ticking. In a cage on the nightstand, a white rat scrabbled at a cardboard tube. A finger-painted sign above the bed said CLARIES ROOM. Her mother's cough rose again from down the hall, and she turned and ran toward the sound.

In a room whose blue walls and curtains made everything look as if it were underwater, her mother lay pale and coughing on a bed piled high with pillows. Her father sat on the edge of the bed, his hands raised in the air, thumbs hooked together and palms spread wide. For a moment Ella had no idea what he was doing. Then she saw the shadow of her father's hands against the wall, in the light of a blue-shaded lamp. A shock of relief went through her.

"Tweet, tweet," Ella said.

"Right," her father said. "A birdie."

Ella's mother turned toward her and smiled, more awake, more like her real self than earlier. "Do another one, Gary," she said.

Ella's father twisted his hands into a new shape in the air.

"A dog?" Ella said.

"A fish!" said her mother.

"No," he said, and adjusted his hands. "It's a horsie, see?"

"A horsie?" said Ella's mother. "With fins?"

That made Ella laugh a little.

"Hey," her mother said. "Come here, you. Smile again."

Ella did as she was told.

"What's that? You lost your tooth!"

"It's gone," Ella said. She climbed onto the bed to explain, but as she flopped down on the mattress her mother's face contracted with pain.

"Please don't bounce," her mother said. She touched the place where her surgery had been.

Ella's father gave her a stern look and lifted her off the bed. "Your mom's sleepy," he said. "You should run back downstairs now."

"She's always sleepy," Ella said, looking down at her muddy feet. She thought of her tooth lying out in the weeds, and how she'd have nothing to put under her pillow for the tooth fairy.

Her mother began to cry.

Ella's father went to the window and stared down into the yard, his breath fogging the glass. "Go ahead, Ella," he said. "We just need a few minutes."

"My tooth," Ella said. She knew she should leave, but couldn't.

"It'll grow back bigger and stronger," her father said.

She could see he didn't understand what had happened. If only her mother would stop crying she could explain everything. In the blue light her mother looked cold and far away, pressed under the weight of tons of water.

"I'll be down soon," her mother said, sniffling. "Go out and play."

Ella opened her mouth to form some protest, but no words came out.

"Go on, now," her father said.

"It fell in a bush!" she wailed, then turned and ran downstairs.

The other children had come in by then. Her brother stood in line at the downstairs bathroom to wash before dinner, comparing fingernail dirt with the boy in purple overalls. Hands deep in the pockets of her velvet dress, Ella wandered through the echoing hall into a room lined from floor to ceiling with books. Many of the titles were in other languages, some even written in different alphabets. She recognized *D'Aulaire's Book of Greek Myths* and *The Riverside Shakespeare* and *Grimm's Fairy Tales*. Scattered around on small tables and decorative stands were tiny human figurines with animal heads—horseman, giraffe-man, panther-man. On one table sat an Egyptian beetle made of milky green stone, and beside him a real beetle, shiny as metal, who flew at Ella's face when she reached to touch his shell. She batted him away with the back of her hand.

And then, just above where the beetle had fallen, Ella saw a shelf without any books at all. It was low, the height of her knees, with a frayed blue scarf pinned against its back wall. Burned-down candles stood on either side of a black lacquer box, and on top of this box stood a glass filled with red water.

Ella reached for the glass, and someone behind her screamed.

She turned around. Clarie stood in the doorway, dress unbuttoned at one shoulder, face smeared with mud.

"Don't touch that," she said.

Ella took a step back. "I wasn't going to."

Clarie's eyes seemed to ignite as she bent down and took the glass in both hands. She held it near a lamp, so the light shone through it and cast a red oval upon the wall.

"It's my mother," she said.

For dinner there was a roasted dome of something that looked like meat but wasn't. It was springy and steaming and when Mister Kaplan cut it open Ella could see that it was stuffed with rice and yams. Benjamin tried to hide under the table, but their father pulled him up by the arms and set him in his place. He prodded his wedge of roast until it slid onto the tablecloth. Then he began to cry quietly.

"The kids aren't vegetarian," their father said, in apology to the men and women at the table. He picked up the slice of roast with his fingers and put it back on Ben's plate. The other men and women held their forks motionless above their own plates, looking at Ella's mother and father with pity.

"Look, Ben," said Delilah. "It's called seitan. Wheat gluten. The other kids love it."

The boy and girl with almond-shaped eyes and ragged hair stopped in midchew. The girl looked at Benjamin and narrowed her eyes.

"I don't eat gluten," Benjamin said.

"Come on, now," their father said. "It's great."

Ella's mother pressed her fingers against her temples. She hadn't touched her own dinner. Ella, sitting beside her, took a bite of wheat gluten. It was almost like meat, firm and savory, and the stuffing was flavored with forest-smelling spices. As she glanced around the table she thought of the picture of the First Thanksgiving on the bulletin board at school: the smiling Pilgrims eating turkey and squash, the stern-faced Native Americans looking as if they knew the worst was yet to come. Who among them that night were the Native Americans?

Who were the Pilgrims? The dark old house was like a wilderness around them, the wind sighing through its rooms.

"I jumped on the trampoline," said the boy with ragged hair, pulling on the sleeve of the woman next to him. "That boy did a flip." He pointed at Peter, who was smashing rice against his plate with his thumb. "He tied his sister to the tree."

Mister Kaplan set down his fork. He looked sideways at Peter, his mouth pressed into a stern line. "I told you never to do that again," he said. He sounded angry, but his voice was quiet, almost a whisper.

"She made me!" Peter said, and plunged a spoon into his baked squash.

Mister Kaplan's eyes went glossy and faraway. He stared off at the blank wall above Ella's mother's head, drifting away from the noise and chatter of the dinner table. Next to him Delilah shuttled her mismatched eyes back and forth. Ella's mother straightened in her chair.

"Ed," she called softly.

Mister Kaplan blinked hard and looked at her.

"Tell us about your tai chi class."

"What?" he said.

"Your tai chi class."

"You know, I don't really want to talk right now," he said. He pushed back his chair and went into the kitchen. There was the sound of water, and then the clink of dishes in the sink. Delilah shook her head. The other adults looked down at their plates. Ella's mother wiped the corners of her mouth with her napkin and crossed her arms over her chest.

"Does anyone want more rice?" Ella's father asked, holding the bowl aloft.

"I think we're all thinking about Lena," said the man with the shaved head.

"I know I am," said Delilah.

"Infinity to infinity," said the man. "Dust into star."

The men and women looked at each other, their eyes carrying some message Ella couldn't understand. They clasped each other's hands and bent their heads. "Infinity to infinity," they repeated. "Dust into star."

"Matter into energy," said the man. "Identity into oneness."

"Matter into energy," everyone said. Ella glanced at her father, whose jaw was set hard, unmoving. Her mother's lips formed the words, but no sound came out. Ella thought of the usual Thanksgivings at her Uncle Bon's, where everyone talked and laughed at the table and they ate turkey and dressing and sweet potatoes with marshmallows melted on top. She closed her eyes and held her breath, filling her chest with a tightness that felt like magic power. If she tried hard enough could she transport them all, her mother and father, Benjamin and herself, to that other time? She held her breath until it seemed she would explode, then let it out in a rush. She opened her eyes. Nothing had changed. Peter kicked the table leg, and the collie, crouched beside Clarie's chair, whimpered his unease. Ella could see Clarie's hand on his collar, her knuckles bloodless as stones.

Mister Kaplan returned with a platter of baked apples. He cleared his throat, and everyone turned to look at him. "Guess what we forgot," he said. "I spent nearly an hour peeling these things." He held the platter aloft, waiting.

"Who wants some nice baked apples?" he said. "Baked apples. I peeled them."

No one said a word.

After dinner the adults drifted into the room with the straw mats and Indian goddesses. Ella understood that the children were not invited, but she lingered in the doorway to see what would happen. Mister Kaplan bent over a tiny brass dish and held a match to a black cone. A wisp of smoke curled toward the ceiling, and after a moment Ella smelled a dusty, flowery scent. Her mother and father and the rest of the adults sat cross-legged on the floor, not touching each other. A low hum began to fill the room like something with weight and substance. Ella saw her father raise an eyebrow at her mother, as if to ask if these people were serious. But her mother's shoulders were bent in meditation, her mouth open with the drone of the mantra, and Ella's father sighed and let his head fall forward.

Someone pinched Ella's shoulder and she turned around. Peter stood behind her, his eyes narrow. "Come on," he said. "You're supposed to help clean up."

In the kitchen the children stacked dirty dishes on the counter and ran water in the sink. The boy and girl with almond eyes climbed up onto a wide wooden step stool and began to scrub dishes. Peter scraped all the scraps into an aluminum pan and gave it to Clarie, who set it on the floor near the dog's water dish. The collie fell at the leftover food with sounds that made Ella sick to her stomach. Clarie stood next to him and stroked his tail.

Then Benjamin came into the kitchen carrying the glass of red water. "Somebody forgot this under the table," he said.

Again there was the dying-rabbit screech. Clarie batted her palms against the sides of her head. "No!" she shrieked. "Put it down!"

Benjamin's eyes went wide, and he set the glass on the kitchen counter. "I don't want it," he said.

The boy in purple overalls squinted at the glass. "Looks like Kool-Aid," he said.

"She gets all crazy," said Peter. "Watch." Peter lifted the glass high into the air, and Clarie ran toward him. "You can't have it," he said.

Clarie jumped up and down in fury, her hands flapping like limp rags. Her mouth opened but no sound came out. Then she curled her fingers into claws and scratched at Peter's arms and chest until he twisted away. He ran across the kitchen and onto the deck, holding the glass aloft, and Clarie followed him, screaming.

The ragged-haired brother and sister looked at each other, arms gloved in white bubbles. In one quick movement they were off the stool, shaking suds around the kitchen. "Come on!" said the boy. "Let's go watch!"

Benjamin grabbed Ella's hand and pulled her toward the screen door. The children pushed out onto the deck and then ran toward the tree castle, where Clarie and her brother were climbing the first rope ladder. It was dark now, and floodlights on the roof of the house illuminated the entire castle, its rooms silver-gray and ghostly, its ropes and nets swaying in a rising breeze. The children gathered on the grass near the trampoline.

Peter held the glass as he climbed, the red water sloshing against its sides. "Come and get it," he crooned. He reached the first room, and they heard the wall-door scrape against the trunk as he pushed it open. Then he moved out onto the oak limb, agile as the siamang monkeys Ella had seen at the zoo. He might as well have had a tail.

Clarie crawled behind him, her hands scrabbling at the bark. Peter howled at the sky as he reached the hostage room.

Benjamin moved toward Ella and pressed his head against her arm. "I want to go home," he said.

"Shh," Ella said. "We can't."

High above, Peter climbed onto the platform from which they had jumped earlier. Still holding the glass, he pulled himself up the tree trunk to the crow's nest. High up on that small, railed platform, where the tree branches became thin and sparse, he stopped. Below him Clarie scrambled onto the jumping platform. She looked out across the yard as if unsure of where he had gone. "Up here," Peter said, holding the glass high.

Ella could hear Clarie grunting as she pulled herself up into the crow's nest. She stood and reached for the glass, her face a small moon in the dark. A few acorns scuttled off the crow's nest platform.

"Give it!" she cried again.

Peter stood looking at her for a moment in the dark. "You really want it?"

"Peter!"

He swept the glass through the air. The water flew out in an arc, ruby-colored against the glare of the floodlights. Clarie leaned out as if to catch it between her fingers, and with a splintering crack she broke through the railing. Her dress fluttered silently as she fell, and her white hands grasped at the air. There was a quiet instant, the soft sound of water falling on grass. Then, with a shock Ella felt in the soles of her feet, Clarie hit the ground. The girl with the ragged hair screamed.

Clarie lay beside the trampoline, still as sleep, her neck bent at an impossible angle. Ella wanted to look away, but couldn't. The other children, even Benjamin, moved to where Clarie lay and circled around, some calling her name, some just looking. Peter slid down the fireman's pole and stumbled across the lawn toward his sister. He pushed Benjamin aside. With one toe he nudged Clarie's shoulder, then knelt and rolled her over. A bare bone glistened from her wrist. The boy in purple overalls threw up onto the grass.

Ella turned and ran toward the house. She banged the screen door open and skidded across the kitchen floor into the hall. At the doorway of the meditation room she stopped, breathing hard. The parents sat just as she had left them, eyes closed, mouths open slightly, their sound beating like a living thing, their thumbs and forefingers circled into perfect O's. She could smell the heat of them rising in the room and mingling with the scent of the incense. Her father's chin rested on his chest as if he had fallen asleep. Beside him her mother looked drained of blood, her skin so white she seemed almost holy.

"Mom," Ella whispered. "Mom."

Ella's mother turned slightly and opened her eyes. For a moment she seemed between two worlds, her eyes unfocused and distant. Then she blinked and looked at Ella. She shook her head no.

"Please," Ella said, but her mother closed her eyes again. Ella stood there for a long time watching her, but she didn't move or speak. Finally Ella turned and went back outside.

By the time she reached the tree castle Peter had dragged Clarie halfway across the lawn. He turned his eyes on Ella, and she stared back at him. The sound of the mantra continued unbroken from the house. Peter hoisted Clarie again under the arms and dragged her to the bushes, her bare feet bumping over the grass. Then he rolled her over until she was hidden in shadow. He pulled her dress down so it covered her thighs, and turned her head toward the fence that bordered the backyard.

"Get some leaves and stuff," he said. "We have to cover her."

Ella would not move. She took Benjamin's hand, but he pulled away from her and wandered across the lawn, pulling up handfuls of grass. She watched the children pick up twigs, Spanish moss, leaves, anything they could find. The boy in purple overalls gathered cedar bark from a flower bed, and Peter dragged fallen branches out of the underbrush near the fence. They scattered everything they found over Clarie's body. In five minutes they had covered her entirely.

"Go back inside," Peter said. "If anyone cries or says anything, I'll kill them."

Ella turned to go, and that was when she saw her tooth, a tiny white pebble in the weeds. She picked it up and rubbed it clean.

Then she knelt beside Clarie, clearing away moss and leaves until she found Clarie's hand. She dropped the tooth into the palm and closed the fingers around it. A shiver spread through her chest, and she covered the hand again. Then she put her arm around Benjamin and they all went back inside. Drawn by the sound of the chanting, they wandered into the hall. All around them hung the yellow photographs, the stony men and women and children looking down at them with sad and knowing eyes. In an oval of black velvet one girl in a white dress held the string of a wooden duck, her lips open as if she were about to speak. Her eyes had the wildness of Clarie's eyes, her legs the same bowed curve.

At last there was a rustle from the meditation room, and the adults drifted out into the hall. They blinked at the light and rubbed their elbows and knees. Ella's mother and father linked arms and moved toward their children. Benjamin gave a hiccup. His eyes looked strange, the pupils huge, the whites flat and dry. Their mother noticed right away. "We'd better get going," she said to Ella's father. "Ben's tired."

She went into the foyer and pulled their shoes from the pile. Mister Kaplan followed, looking around in bewilderment, as if he could not believe people were leaving. He patted Benjamin on the head and asked Ella's mother if she wanted to take some leftover food. Ella's mother shook her head no. Her father thanked Mister Kaplan for his hospitality. Somewhere toward the back of the house the dog began to bark, a crazy, high-pitched bark as if the world were ending. Ella pulled Benjamin, barefoot, through the front door, and her parents followed them to the car.

All the way past the rows of live oaks, past the cemetery where the little tombs stood like grounded boats, past the low, flat shotgun houses with their flaking roofs, Benjamin sat rigid on the backseat and cried without a sound. Ella felt the sobs leaving his chest in waves of hot air. She closed her eyes and followed the car in her mind down the streets that led to their house, until it seemed they had driven past their house long ago and were moving on to a place where strange beds awaited them, where they would fall asleep thinking of dark forests and wake to the lives of strangers.

TIMOTHY A. WESTMORELAND

Open Road Writing Workshops

DARKENING OF THE WORLD

Sometimes I wake myself up laughing. Dim light cuts into the room from between the curtains, where they fail to meet. I hear Pork snoring, the noise echoing down the hall. The exposed wood floors carry the sound. I don't know what I laugh about. But I recognize the voice, I know it is mine, and I lift into waking easily. When this happens, and it happens more often now, I am unable to drift back to sleep. I listen for the sound of Pork's dachshund, Heidegger, at his water bowl, lapping water. I measure his steps, his nails on the linoleum in the kitchen, the rickety noise of his wicker basket as he settles himself down. This is winter and Pork says he can't afford to insulate and heat Heidegger's doghouse. Summer is a different story. Summer, Heidegger has a house. The house is antebellum style, two story, columns and balustrade. The mullioned windows open and close.

Pork is good with his hands. He built the house himself with tempered glass, double-paned, to keep in the cool air. He's air-conditioned it with the motor from an old refrigerator, having adjusted the thermostat. On cool evenings he turns the air off and opens the screened windows. He turns on the ceiling fan, made from a floor model he purchased at Wal-Mart. Heidegger can come and go as he pleases, the door to the house swings shut, a rubber seal sucking tight to keep in the coolness.

In the morning Pork stands in front of the stove in his boxers, cooking up sausage. He talks to Heidegger.

"How was your night?" he asks Heidegger. He does this in a high, unnatural voice.

I sit at the table with coffee and watch. Heidegger begins to wag his tail.

"How was your night?" Pork repeats, this time higher.

Heidegger wags his tail more, spins, darts from the kitchen to the living room. I can hear him running in tight circles. Then he does figure eights. He runs back into the kitchen, skids to a stop at Pork's feet.

"You're my love-dog," Pork says. He forks a patty of sausage and feeds it to Heidegger. What the dachshund doesn't get off the fork, Pork eats. Pork eats with the same fork as Heidegger.

"You're a sick man," I say.

Pork sits down in front of me. He looks at me.

"Not sleeping well?" he says. "Still laughing yourself awake. I hear you."

"Sorry," I say. "I don't know what it means."

"Darkening of the world," Pork says. He shakes his head, takes a bite of sausage, chews. "Darkening of the world." He gets up and goes to the stove where he has more sausage cooking.

Pork sells bowling supplies for a living, but when he was in school he studied philosophy. He sees everything in terms of philosophy. His work ethic, his dog, his love life, my not sleeping all provide him with philosophical investigations, all come down to some kind of reasoning. He's a reasonable man. I like him. But I don't understand him.

"What do you mean, 'darkening of the world'?" I ask. I take a sip of coffee and stare at him. He flips the patties he's cooking and turns to me.

"You have fallen out of Being," he says. "Being with a capital 'B.'"

"I have," I say, as if I understand.

Pork takes the sausage off the skillet and puts it onto a paper towel. He flips the patties, drying both sides. Reaching into the cupboard, he takes out a saucer and sets it on the counter. Heidegger stands at his feet, eyeing each move Pork makes. He sniffs the air.

"You work at the paper mill," he says turning to me, "but you have stopped understanding."

Pork brings the saucer to the table and sits down in front of me. He reaches over and takes my coffee cup. He takes a swallow.

"And this is serious?" I ask. After Pork sets my coffee cup in front of me, I push it back across the table to him.

"Very," he says. "Very." He forks a patty of sausage and takes a bite. Heidegger sits at his feet.

"What does it mean?" I ask.

"You're caught up in the minutia," he says. "Making paper. The people around you. You're forfeiting yourself, your realization of your potential."

"What are you saying?"

"You need some dread," he says, finishing off my coffee. "Some real nothingness."

I run the barking drum and the chipper at a paper mill in Miller's Falls. In winter it is cold and in summer it is hot. It's never just right. I take the timber, cut it down to size, turn it into something usable.

All day long I have nothing to think about. Today, I a
what Pork has told me at breakfast. I consider my pote
not much there. I can run a few machines and I know h
paper. Blank sheets of paper that someone else can fill up v   ideas.
It's not much, but without me some people would become desperate.

By lunchtime, I feel pretty good about myself. I'm convinced I'm
doing something important. That without me Pork wouldn't have his
books to read. Then I think, maybe I should stop. Maybe we all
should stop what we're doing. Then people like Pork would understand dread. We'd throw a wrench in their notion of Becoming. Then
the lunch whistle sounds and I go back to work. I need the pay.

I work all day and then come home to find Pork on the couch
napping. Heidegger is curled up by his chest, resting his long nose
over Pork's neck. When I come into the living room Heidegger opens
his eyes, watches every move I make. It's as if he's guarding Pork and
I think if I make the slightest questionable move, he'll come off the
couch and latch on to me. I go to the kitchen and get a dog biscuit.
I return and give it to him, hoping crumbs will trickle into Pork's ear
or something.

I switch on the table lamp at the end of the couch. It is late March
and, though light is lasting later into the evening, I know it will be
dark when Pork wakes. Too exhausted to eat, I climb the stairs and
go to my room where I fall into bed, boots and all. I fall asleep easily,
quietly.

I am laughing. Suddenly, I am awake and covered in a light sweat.
The room is bright, lit by moonlight angling between the open curtains. The room seems barren, vast. It's as if it is covered in a blanket
of light snow. Downstairs I hear the television going. The evening
news is playing. Outside my window, down in the yard, I hear muted
voices. I raise myself, walk over, and look.

Pork and his girlfriend, Sheila, are standing apart, tossing an old baseball glove back and forth. Heidegger runs in the snow between them. He barks and leaps. Sheila laughs. The moonlight is bright on the snow. It casts the jagged shadows of trees all about Pork and Sheila. As Sheila throws I notice how thin and beautiful she is. Pork is heavyset. I don't see how the two of them got together. Pork throws the glove to her. She catches it and bends down. Heidegger runs to her and leaps into her arms. He takes the glove in his mouth and shakes it. Both Sheila and Pork are laughing. I open the window and feel the cold air come in. I feel the sweat drying on my skin and a chill down my back.

"Hey guys," I yell down to them.

Sheila turns. "Strawberry!" she says. "Come down and join us."

"Hey, Straw," Pork says. "We've got a hint of spring in the air. Come out."

I shut the window and go downstairs to get my coat.

Standing in the yard, I can see out across the large lawn that fog is beginning to rise. An unnatural warmth has settled in. I walk up to Sheila and give her a hug. She kisses me on the cheek.

"How'd you sleep?" Sheila asks. I can tell Pork has told her about my laughing.

"Okay," I say.

"Went for a walk in the woods," Pork says. "Snow's still too deep for Heidegger in areas. We carried him."

"Yeah."

"You should have come," Sheila offers.

"Yeah," Pork says. "You need to get away from forfeiture."

Sheila hands me Heidegger. He wriggles in my arms, leans up and licks my chin. A bank of fog is headed across the yard, blowing toward us.

"Get off that," Sheila says to Pork. "Don't listen to him," she says, leaning into his chest.

Suddenly we are standing in the fog. Light from the moon spreads through the air. It floods out the windows of the house. We can hardly see each other for the glare. Our breath is visible, suspended before us.

"Let's go in and have a drink," Pork says. I can see his words hanging in the air.

"Let's," Sheila says.

We go inside and shed our coats. Pork goes to the cupboard and gets three glasses. He pours us each a gin and tonic. Heidegger laps water from his bowl, then shuffles into the den to settle on the couch. The three of us follow his lead.

"You laugh in your sleep?" Sheila asks. Heidegger sits between Pork and her. His head is on Pork's lap.

"I've started to," I say.

"How strange," she says. "That's never happened to me." She runs her hand down Heidegger's back. "What do you suppose it's all about?"

"I don't know," I say. "Pork claims it's a symptom of my falling out of Being."

"Pork always thinks that," she says. She takes a sip of her drink.

"It is," Pork says. "We are cast into the world of Being. We appropriate that world. If we fail to find ourselves in it, if we don't see our finite consciousness in connection to the future and the past, we fall out of Being."

"And that makes me laugh?" I say.

"Yes," Pork says. "You need a sense of dread. A sense of Being toward death. It wakes you up, except in a positive way."

"Laughter isn't a good thing?" Sheila says.

"Not in this case," Pork says. "Straw has no sense of himself in the world. He makes paper. That's it. It's a gadget that has consumed him. He worries too much about others."

"Pork," Sheila says. "Sometimes you worry me."

"You think that death will motivate me?" I say. "You think I'll sleep better, won't wake myself laughing, if I worry about death a little?"

"Yes," Pork says. He holds his glass down. Heidegger lifts his head and licks the moisture that is dripping down its side.

"I won't sleep at all if I worry about such things."

"Let's go to bed," Sheila says. "Let's all go to bed before this gets out of hand."

Pork seems happy with this suggestion. He picks up Heidegger and heads up the stairs. Sheila reaches over and pats my leg.

"Get some sleep," she says. She follows Pork up the stairs.

I go to my room and undress. I slip under the sheets and lie on my back. I try to think forward, to a time when I am dead. I consider what this house will be like and who will live in it. All I can imagine is that I will die soon. That Sheila and Pork will live here. I imagine them forgetting that I ever lived here. I hear their conversations, daily, about all kinds of things. But they don't include me. I can't stand these thoughts and I imagine what it was like before I was born. This is easier. I think of the World Wars. I think of my mother and father, both still alive. I see the house where I grew up, my mother and father living inside, having dinner and breakfast. This is easier. It helps me see how I came to be here in this bed. I think of this bed. I think of my childhood bed. Then I fall to sleep.

It is summer now. It has been three months and I still wake myself up laughing. Pork goes on the road selling supplies to bowling alleys during the summer months. This leaves me to take care of Heidegger. Since summer began there has been a drought, a forest fire, and I have been laid off from the mill. It is temporary, they say. Just until the timber becomes available from out of area. I don't mind. I have all day in the house with Heidegger, though mostly he stays out in his own air-conditioned antebellum. Afternoons, I doze on the couch. I have taken to reading *Being and Time*. Pork's copy is marked with notes. I can only take a few pages at a time, maybe ten or twenty a day. I don't feel good about what I am reading.

Late one afternoon I awake without laughter. From the shadows I know it must be about five. The heat of the day has just passed. I'm used to seeing Heidegger on the carpet when I wake up this late. He comes in to share the couch with me sometimes. Sometimes he stretches out on the floor just below me. He is gray muzzled, old, and he sleeps like an old dog. He snores. But the room is quiet. So I get up and go to the window to look out. I don't see him in the yard. I think he must be in his house, or down the street playing with the neighborhood kids. I decide I will walk down after dinner and collect him. He's not supposed to wander. Pork has put up a short, white picket fence—really used for garden and flower bed boundaries—but sometimes Heidegger gets it in his head to jump the fence.

I scoot into the kitchen to cook dinner. I slice and chop bell pepper and carrot, press garlic, peel and dice onion, all to make stir-fry. I feel good about using my hands. All afternoon with nothing to do, I miss the mill. This kind of work, cutting and chopping in the kitchen, frees me. But for some reason Heidegger is on my mind. I have fed and watered him, turned on his air conditioner and ceiling fan. I stop what I'm doing and go back to the window. His windows are down. He's either cool inside or down the street playing along the creek bed with the kids. He'll come home caked in cool mud. I'll have to hose him down and scrub him with a towel. I go outside.

The heat is oppressive. It clings to my shirt and pants as soon as I walk out the door. It has been like this for weeks. The news is on the radio and television, everything about the forest fire, the heat, the disaster area we are becoming. I consider Pork to be lucky, traveling and all. He calls on occasion to check on Heidegger.

I take the water hose in my hand and turn on the flow at the spigot. I begin to water the flowers Pork has planted along Heidegger's fence row. The news has called for water conservation. But I think this little will not amount to much.

"Heidegger!" I call as I spray the honeysuckle. Pork has planted it hoping for hummingbirds. I point the water away from Heidegger's house, toward the fuchsia. The bee balm and petunias are all but dead. I lay the hose down in their bed to give them a deep soaking. I knock on the second-story roof. "Heide!" I yell. "Come on out."

His house is quiet. The air conditioner has cycled off. Inside I can hear the hum of the ceiling fan. I peek through a second-floor window, but don't see him.

"Heidegger!" I yell, directing my call with my hands. I am hoping the kids will bring him up from the creek so that I don't have to hunt them down. I hear them whooping it up down by the water. Since the drought there is only a trickle, which pools where the beavers have dammed it. I have warned the kids that Heidegger will give a beaver a run for its money, that they should be careful and keep an eye on him. Considering rabies and all, though I don't know if that's a worry, I fret when Heidegger is away. Pork says it's fine. Over the phone he says, "Let him enjoy himself, he's a dog."

Leaving the hose running on low, I decide to go in and cook up the vegetables I've cut. Cool air greets my face and I breathe in heavily. I hate to warm up the house by cooking. But my not working all day somehow builds up a ravenous hunger in me. I put some oil in the pan and heat it up. Flipping on the vent over the stove, I spill the carrots, peppers, onions into the pan. Steam rises. I stand back from the hissing pan for a moment. While I stir the vegetables, I consider what I have read that day. Being toward death. The notion that by placing ourselves in the context of history, time, we see our beginning, our end, and the dread that arises moves us to appropriation of the world, of seeing ourselves in the world. It is a practical idea as I understand it. It's reasonable. I sprinkle water into the pan. It hisses and smoke rises. Turning down the heat, I cover the pan.

Heidegger's food is in a plastic wastebasket on the back porch. I lift the lid and fill his bowl. I leave it on the kitchen floor, step off the porch into the heat, and look toward Heidegger's house. Through a front window I gather sight of brown-black fur. Heidegger is in his house, sleeping. Going to the window, I peek inside, tap on the glass. Heidegger moves a little, then settles back in. I tap on the glass again and he ignores me.

"Heidegger!" I call as I rap on the window nearest him. "Hey boy," I say. "Come out."

He doesn't move. He sleeps more these days; his age is beginning to slow him down. Pork says it's part of the process. He says Heidegger is beginning to look distinguished. Like an old southern gentleman, he says.

Open palmed, I slap the glass. "Heide," I yell. "Wake up." I notice the glass is warm and Heidegger doesn't move. I listen. The air conditioner hasn't cycled back on. I feel the window nearest Heidegger and then the other, the opposite side of the door. They are warm. Jesus, I think, he must be hot in there. I lean over and push open the door. It's resistant, the seal locked tight. The door opens and a wave of heat pours out. It reaches up to my face, into my eyes. It's blistering, as if coming up off asphalt, with a chemical smell—the paint, the plastic frames of the windows, the rubber seal on the door. The ceiling fan is still working, but it is just pushing around the unbearable heat and smell. There is something else on the air. Something living. It is the musty scent of warm fur, urine, dog shit, all that has been baked for hours. Heidegger has messed his house, has lain in his own stench in this convected heat, the sunlight intensified through the glass, the white interior walls radiating back and forth, undulating, the trapped energy. I catch him by his hind legs. I feel shit caked to them. I drag him out of the house, out onto the porch, and then pick him up and carry him to the lawn.

He is still breathing. Taking shallow, quick breaths, his eyes are unfocused, distant. I turn the spigot on full and take the hose from the flower bed. Around Heidegger's eyes and along his mouth and gums there is something dry and powdery. The water is cool and I pour it over his body. He doesn't resist. His eyes move, following my movements.

"Jesus," I say. "What the fuck happened?" I bathe his face with water. I wipe it away from his eyes. I run my hand over his body. It is unbelievably warm. A smell, something that I cannot describe, rises. It is sweet, sickly. "Heidegger," I say. "Oh Heidegger."

I carry him inside the house and lay him on the couch. His body is limp. A stain spreads out on the fabric, taking on the larger shape of his body. For a moment, Heidegger's breathing slows. I go to the kitchen and get ice, wrap it in dish towels. I lay the towels down around his belly. I lift his head and put an ice pack down. He rests on it. His eyes close. He is calm. His breathing seems better.

I sit back and watch. A few minutes pass and then Heidegger gasps. He lifts his head and his tail, curling his body upward at both ends. He sucks at air convulsively, rapidly, one, two, three times. Then he lays out flat again. His eyes are wild. A mucus comes from his nose. I get close to his face, kiss the side of it, and I stare into his eyes.

He is wanting. It's as if he tries to talk. He whines and leans his face close to my lowered head. I hold his face in my hands. I stare into his eyes and for a moment I imagine I am him, that I am having his thoughts.

There is a gnawing, tugging in my chest. A beating fills my head. I cannot hear for the beating in my chest. Heat throbs, cuts into my body, as hot as the pavement on the hottest days. I feel as if I am falling. I cannot hold my eyes open. I am afraid to close my eyes. His flesh is warm against mine. I will close my eyes for a moment. The beating in my chest is easier. It becomes lighter, less painful. I take a deep, long breath. The burning in my head eases. I hear the throbbing as it eases. He touches against my face. I will close my eyes. Sleep is deep, black. My chest rises. It rises. Then falls. I am falling, without fear.

The moon is bright, near full. The lights are on in Heidegger's house and they spread out on the ground before me. The earth is soft, soggy from where I left the water on. The edge of the bee balm and petunia bed are tender and make for easy digging. I dig, exposing the blackened soil. Heidegger's body is still warm, yielding. I lay him in the ground and cover him. I go inside and climb the stairs to my bedroom. Undressing in front of the window I can see out to where Heidegger is buried. Light cast from his house illuminates a small cross I've made from a piece of leftover clapboard. I leave the light burning. It is a comfort. I go to sleep and sleep late into the next morning.

Pork stands holding Heidegger's blanket. His face is red, swollen. He is silent for a moment. Heidegger is still visible on the couch as a stain, his shape outlined by the water that has dried there.

"Why didn't you let him lie in state?" Pork asks. "You could have wrapped him in his blanket."

"I don't know," I say. "I thought it would be best . . ." I don't know how to finish this sentence. Outside the window, Sheila is standing over Heidegger's grave.

"Damn it, Straw," Pork says. "You should've kept an eye out. It's a fucking machine. A compressor. You can't trust machines." Pork is getting angry. He sits down on the couch. He places his hand on the stain. "I have to see him," he says. "I have to see him."

"You can't," I say to Pork.

"I can just see him over there," Pork says. He points to an open area of the carpet. "Running those figure eights."

"I'm sorry," I say. "I'm really sorry. I did what I could."

"It wasn't enough," he says. "You could have let him lie in state. It would have been fine for a day."

I am standing up, looking down at Pork. He sits on the couch with his arms crossed. He looks at Heidegger's shape crusted on the cushion next to him. I think we'll never get rid of the stain. It will stay with us. I don't know what to do. I don't know what to say. There is no saying what one feels when it's grief that's on you. I'm grieving just like Pork.

"You're going to help me," Pork says, finally. "I'm going to see him one last time."

"I can't," I say.

"What do you mean?" he says.

"I just can't," I say.

"You killed Heidegger," he says. "You buried him without me. You're going to help me dig him up."

"You're getting irrational."

"I have to see him."

"You don't want to do that," I say, calmly. I want to comfort him.

"You're going to have to face it one day," Pork says. "You are so fucking weak." He stands up and looks at me face-to-face. "You know it?" he asks. "I've got to see him."

Pork slams the door on his way out. I see him give Sheila a hug before he takes the shovel in his hand and begins to dig. The ground is hard and dusty. The sun has been beating down all morning. It's been beating down for as long as I can remember. It's as if I can't remember anything. Pork shovels. The earth comes up in clots. Heidegger's cross is laying off to the side. Pork has pulled it from the ground.

Sheila stands back with her hands over her mouth. She is red faced and crying. It's as if it's her child. Pork stabs at the earth. He kicks the shovel down into the dust. He is careful, making a much larger hole than I dug.

Pork works for twenty minutes while I watch him from inside. I cannot go out and help him. It's just not in me. I can't imagine how Heidegger will look. I can't bear the thought of the sight of him. Pork's body is rising and falling heavily. His shirt sticks to his back with sweat. It makes a runnel straight down the middle of his back. Moisture drips from his chin. His face is wet.

I watch him lift soil from around the edges of the ground he has broken. He falls to his knees and begins to use his hands to push away dirt, forming a mound along the far edge of the grave. Pork stops for a moment. He looks up at Sheila. She kneels beside him. Pork leans over and lifts Heidegger's body from the ground. The body is swollen and rigid. Pork lifts him to his face, kisses him along the side of his head. He cradles Heidegger in his arms and rocks him. Sheila is leaning back, sobbing. Pork's large body rises and falls. He is trembling, shaking with grief. He holds Heidegger to his chest. I can see flies hovering in the air. Pork leans his head back for a moment and shakes from side to side. He heaves, bending over. All I can imagine is the smell and how it must feel having it so close to my body. I can almost taste it. It is in my mouth, watering. My stomach turns, gurgles. I breathe out a heavy sigh. Something rises, in the heaviness of my stomach. It overcomes me. I begin to laugh, quietly. But it builds from within me and I cannot control myself. It builds, rises, becomes impossible for me to silence. Pork and Sheila turn, holding Heidegger, staring blankly. I am laughing uncontrollably.

LYSLEY A. TENORIO

Wisconsin Institute for Creative Writing

SUPERASSASSIN

September 1958. Coast City, California. The noble alien Abin Sur, protector of sector 2814 of our galaxy, crash-lands on Earth. Buried beneath the rubble of his spacecraft, he uses his last flicker of energy to summon test pilot Hal Jordan and offers him the fabled Ring of Power, a weapon created by the Guardians of Oa. With his dying breath Abin Sur asks, "Will you be my successor, Hal Jordan? Will you swear to use this ring to uphold justice throughout the universe?" "I swear it," Jordan promises. He slips the ring onto his finger, and takes the Guardians' Oath:

> *In brightest day, in blackest night*
> *No evil shall escape my sight*
> *Let those who worship evil's might*
> *Beware my power—Green Lantern's Light!*

For nearly four decades Hal Jordan will save the universe on countless occasions as the Green Lantern, establishing himself as one of Earth's greatest champions. But in the 1990s, just years from the new millennium, his intentions and heroism become questionable. By 1994 he has turned on the Guardians and become the most powerful villain in the galaxy. The question remains: Did the Green Lantern die a villain or a hero? This question has stumped historians in recent years. This essay will retrace the history of the Green Lantern, and conclude once and for

Black ink gashes my paper when Brandon DeStefano swipes it from beneath the point of my pen. "May I?" he asks. His eyes rush side to side over my words. "Listen to this crazy shit," he tells Tenzil Jones, his best friend. Brandon reads my paper to Tenzil in what is supposed to be my voice, adding an accent that isn't mine. Then he looks up at me, shaking his head in disapproval. "It's supposed to be about a real person in history, freak. What's wrong with you?"

"Hey," Tenzil whispers from behind me, "maybe I'll do mine on the Tooth Fairy."

I don't waste my time with talk. I put my hand out for the paper's return. Brandon makes sure that Mr. Cosgrove isn't looking and then crumples my paper, hurling it at me like a grenade. It hits my face and falls dead to the ground. *"Ka-pow!"* Brandon says, pointing his finger at me like a gun. "Why didn't you use your power ring to stop it?" Tenzil holds up his palm, and the two high-five each other, as if they've accomplished some great feat of teamwork.

"You are no Dynamic Duo," I tell them.

"What?" Brandon asks.

"You are"—I lean into him, aligning my eyes with his—"no Dynamic Duo." I say each word slowly, every syllable getting equal time. It's not my place to make terrible truths easier to hear; all I do is reveal them.

Suddenly Tenzil's finger flicks my ear, fast and hard. My neck jerks, my back stiffens. I feel the heat just below my right temple. "You're whacked, man," he says.

I know better than to tell Mr. Cosgrove. Not because I'm afraid; I just prefer another kind of justice.

I pick up my essay from the floor, pulling at opposite corners to undo the crumpled mass. It's wrinkled, like old skin, so I rub it between my hands, up and down until my palms burn from friction. When the page is smooth, I continue to write, even after the bell rings and the classroom has emptied. Only when Mr. Cosgrove starts locking up windows and shutting miniblinds do I stop.

"Mr. Cosgrove?" He can't hear me above his whistling, so I say his name again.

"What? Oh, sorry." He turns to me. "Didn't realize you were still here."

"I know." I start erasing the chalkboard for him.

"I just wanted to tell you that I'm excited about this assignment. I think I'll learn a lot from this."

He nods. "I'm sure you will."

"I used to hate your class, this subject."

"History changes," he says, smiling.

"And I used to hate you."

For four seconds Mr. Cosgrove is silent. Then he says, "I guess we change, too, depending on how you look at things." He looks me in the eyes, smiling, and I think he means it.

"Right." I wipe chalk dust from my shirt and offer to help him with the windows, but he says they've been done, and explains that he needs to get home soon. I grab my backpack from my chair, and before I leave I tell him that his class is my favorite, the only one that's useful in the real world.

———

Long before the heckling from classmates and neighborhood children, the questioning stares from old churchwomen, and long, long before I knew the true story of my father, I was aware of the strange mutant abilities that my body possesses: Though my skin is fair, I never burn in the sun, can barely manage a midsummer tan. When seasons change, so does the color of my hair, back and forth from brown to black. Despite my roundish face I have a unique bone structure that captures both shadow and light in just the right places, so that in the proper lighting my face can be startling. And my eyes—somewhere between slanted gashes and perfect ovals—are of two colors: The right is as brown as wet earth, and the left is jet-black, a perfect obsidian orb. I keep them behind slightly tinted eyeglasses.

Fifteen years ago, at the moment of my spawning, no one could have guessed the potency of my hybridity.

"What are you goofing about now?" Luc asks me. He is quick to interrupt my meditations, dismissing them as daydreams. He shoots a rubber band at me from across the table. It bounces off my right lens. When I tell him to quit, to stop or I will kill him, I am shushed by the librarian, who frowns at me like an archenemy whose plans I have just foiled. "You're zoning out again," Luc says, sliding his grammar book over to me. "You said you would help me, so help." Though Luc is the most intelligent and perceptive student in the ninth grade (and the only other person I've ever known who is able to comprehend the theories of an antimatter universe), his counselor insists that he take ESL classes. His English, standardized testing says, is not up to speed. In grade school they said the same thing about me. I knew the words—I had a tenth-grade vocabulary by the time I was eight. I just chose not to speak.

We muddle through the textbook examples of passive voice, and I even devise my own exercises, in comic-book format. *"Superman has been killed mercilessly by me," proclaimed Doomsday.* But today I am in no mood to be a champion of standard written English. "Later," I promise. Luc shrugs his shoulders, thinking that I have given up, that surrendering is a possibility. So I rescue the moment by suggesting "Dystopia?" and his frown morphs into a smile. In a flash we cram books into our backpacks, slip on our raincoats, and pull hoods over our heads. As we exit the library, the words *psychos, faggots,* and *losers* reach us from behind study carrels. Luc and I stop to face our accusers, giving them looks that we will substantiate when the time is right. Then we are out the library door, off the campus, and under the afternoon drizzle. We stand at the bus stop, two secret heroes on the fringes of winter, waiting for the sun, any source of rejuvenation, just one outbound bus away from here and into the city.

Dystopia Comics is the only all-used-comic-book store in Daly City. Most stores file their back issues away in neat alphabetized rows, each one sealed in a plastic bag with rigid backing. But Dystopia lives up to its name. Comics are stuffed into shoddy cardboard boxes, and Luc and I spend hours rummaging through bin after bin. We always win in the end: In the past half hour Luc has found issues of *Justice League* and *Sandman,* even a water-damaged issue of *The Watchmen,* and I've started a small stack of old issues of *Green Lantern,* precisely what I need for my research. I sometimes think that Luc and I possess an extra sense, an instinct for finding small treasures among the slightly torn and the discarded.

"Closing time," a husky voice mutters from behind and above me. I do a quick one-eighty, fists clenched and ready. I face the cashier, who stands just inches away from me. His globular, fleshy belly is even closer, oozing over the elastic waistband of his Bermuda shorts. "If you're going to read it, then buy it."

I give Luc the signal and then shift my eyes back to the cashier. "Pardon me, sir," I say, "but your volume is infringing upon my space."

He blinks. "My what?"

"The amount of space your cubic units are occupying."

He blinks again. "So?" Already I've confused him, thrown him off, and all he can do is point to the clock. "Just hurry it up, all right?"

My eye catches the exposed belly once more. With the proper serrated edge I could carve into the flesh, cut a tunnel right through it.

I smile at the mass before me. "Let's go, Luc."

We walk out the door and turn the corner into a narrow alley. We crouch down to the ground, shielded between Dumpsters, and Luc unzips his backpack. From between textbooks and folders he pulls out our stack of comics and gives me my half. "Distract him longer next time," he says. "He almost turned around too soon."

"No back talk from the sidekick." I tuck my comics away in the secret pocket of my backpack.

The rain has stopped, but we don our hoods anyway. We proceed into the street, outside the crosswalk lines, defying the blinking red hand before us. "Nice work," I tell Luc. "See you tomorrow, oh seven hundred hours."

"Oh seven hundred hours," he confirms.

On sad nights my mother listens to her 45 rpm of "Johnny Angel" over and over again until she passes out. Tonight is going to be one of those nights. Before I can even lock the door behind me, she starts screaming, asking where I've been. "Nowhere," I tell her. "Just out."

"And what should I do if something happened to you out there?" she asks, one hand on her hip, the other tugging at the neckline of her LAS VEGAS sweatshirt. "What should I do then?" She takes heavy, staggered breaths and begins to empty out the kitchen cupboards, throwing food we need over the fire escape, weeping, uttering profanities about men and why they are the way they are.

I give her five quick shots of Johnnie Walker and put her to bed. I take off her shoes, pull the sheets over her, and press replay on her turntable. She puts her arms around my neck and pulls my face to hers, telling me what a good boy I've been. "Don't you change," she whispers. I can feel the tears on her lips wetting my ear.

"Go to sleep, Mom," I whisper. I pull down the shades, shutting out the last bits of daylight.

She got left again. I knew my mother was feeling hopeful this time around. This guy lasted almost four weeks.

When I warn her, she tells me I'm crazy, so this time I kept quiet. But I saw it coming. Her strategy was faulty: She had been making domestic offerings—a home-cooked meal of lumpia and pinakbet, Filipino delicacies she calls her love potions. But they lack any magical properties. Her men always see the food as alien and weird, a little too far from home. So they take what they want and then vanish. "Ride a rocket to the moon, that's fine," she once slurred to some guy on the phone, "but baby, baby, won't you please come back?" It was my twelfth birthday party, but I wasn't the one who wanted him there. I took the receiver from her hands. "Accidents happen, bastard," I warned, "so watch your back." She grabbed the phone, hit me with it, and then apologized for my rudeness. But he'd already hung up.

Mom's messed-up universe started with one bad star: a nine-month marriage to the man who was my father. He brought her to the States, a living knickknack from his military days. Their union, brief as it was, spawned me and all my biological peculiarities. "You're like Aquaman," Luc said when I told him the story. "Cool." But Aquaman's mother was a mermaid, his father a human being.

Nothing is human within the man who was my father. He disappeared from her life just hours before I was born. What I imagine, what I've even dreamed, is that he is a sinister breed of assassin, with white hair, white skin, and white eyes, invading alien streets, sent to find and fuck my mother and then finish her off. When she is drunk, she talks about my origin, sticking the sick story in my head, panel after panel after panel.

And then she'll break in half, Johnny Angel and Johnnie Walker to the rescue. But I forgive her. Like all heroes, she needs her Fortress of Solitude, her Paradise Island, any place tucked away from the evil in the world. Not to worry: I keep a lookout.

From 1958 to 1965 the Green Lantern thwarts villains from every quadrant of the galaxy. At the end of the sixties he is ordered by the Guardians to return home, to uphold good on Earth. For the first time he encounters evils that the Guardians themselves cannot defeat: racism, poverty, overpopulation. "Ironic," he thinks in Green Lantern #187, *carrying the dead body of a black man beaten by racist thugs, "with my power ring I can drain an entire ocean, shrink an entire galaxy to the size of a penny. Yet hatred and human cruelty are still impervious to it!"*

This is a turning point in the Green Lantern's history. Though many claim it is the defining experience of his career, I will argue that it distracted him from his primary objective: the upholding and protection of justice at the galactic level. This paper will show that his return to Earth was a mistake, one we would pay for decades later.

Rain dots my paper, so I put it inside. I'm wet but warm, wrapped up in a black Army-issue blanket. I remain on the fire escape.

I can hear mothers' voices screaming for their kids to come in, old homeless men arguing for space beneath an awning. Ten minutes later and twenty yards beyond, a teenager holds a knife against an old woman's neck while his friend rummages through her purse. When they're done, they shove her to the ground, light their cigarettes, and walk away.

Nourished by the elements, bloated with stars, our universe is still a hungry one; even I can feel it. So why did the Guardians send him back? With our region of space abounding in alien threats, why did the Green Lantern return? I was resistant at first, but I'm beginning to see the point of the assignment: *This is the inquiry of history,* just like Mr. Cosgrove says. It changes when the perspective changes. It's too late to repair the as-is of planet Earth. In the end we're the residue that the Green Lantern's ring can't penetrate.

Drizzle turns to storm, but I'll sit here for another hour before I go in.

This morning I knock on my mother's door, three times, but she's out cold. She's already late for work, so I go into her bedroom and lay her pink waitress uniform on a chair. I whisper good-bye and then leave for school.

Luc meets me on the corner. "Ready?" I ask.

He opens his backpack. "It's all here."

"Good," I nod. "Let's go."

We have our enemies. Today Luc and I will deliver Brandon DeStefano to justice.

Last week we were reading comics at lunch on the football field bleachers when Brandon and Tenzil walked by. "It's Luc the Gook!" Brandon screamed. I gave him the finger, and Luc told him to run along with the other nonsentients. "Non*what*?" Brandon said, climbing up toward us, bleacher by bleacher. "I don't understand Korean, gook." Then Tenzil reached from behind and snatched Luc's comic (an almost valuable issue of *Swamp Thing* #12) right out of his hands. He tossed it to Brandon, who stuffed it down the back of his pants, farted on it, and then dropped it in a puddle beneath the bleachers. "Freaks," he said. Then they walked toward the lunch courtyard, a trail of sinister *ha-ha-ha*s ricocheting behind them.

Luc went down to rescue the comic, but I kept Brandon in my eye when I noticed that something about him wasn't quite right: His head started twitching, shoulder and ear crashing against each other. His spine arched him forward and back, forward and back, each vertebra breaking through skin until the body was no more. Then, in a sudden flash of light, Brandon DeStefano became The Gas, a force able to release methane-based emissions powerful enough to stun an enemy or wipe out an entire planet. Luc and I vowed revenge, and I intend to get it every time I can.

We get to school early, while the boys' locker room is still empty. We find The Gas's locker, and in seventy-four seconds Luc picks the lock. I pull the impostor Right Guard deodorant from my backpack and make the switch.

Later, when PE is over, Luc and I dress quickly, taking position by our lockers. We keep an eye out for The Gas, who has just emerged from the showers. He comes closer and closer but pays us no mind. In regular street clothes we are anonymous, merely mortal men.

The Gas dries himself off and reaches into his locker for his deodorant. He shakes the can once, twice, and removes the cap. He raises his arm above his head, positioning the Right Guard at his armpit. Before he can spray, Luc and I vanish.

The Gas has no idea of the power that's about to befall him; no one ever does. But this is how I like it. First my enemies underestimate me; then I smash them.

"Do you think it'll heal?" On this team Luc is the conscience.

"No one has ever died from a scorched armpit," I tell him, stashing another swiped teacher's edition in my locker. He knows I speak the truth. I don't say things just to be reassuring.

The final bell rings. By tomorrow morning we'll hear snippets of talk here and there about the incident. Campus security will circulate in homerooms and PE classes, spouting the same refrain: If we work together, we can prevent this from happening again.

Feeble heroism from the crooked authorities. This is what they said last time and the time before that, and no one suspected our true identities then. "We ought to celebrate," I decide. "Meet me at Kingpin Donuts before school tomorrow."

Luc stares into my eyes as if he means to challenge me. "You said you would change the deodorant into spray paint, not a blowtorch," he whispers. "You said you wouldn't do that anymore."

"Shut up." I slam my locker shut. "We're done for today. Go home."

After school I check on my mother at the restaurant. I take my station on an adjacent rooftop, over what was once a tropical-fish store. I would stop in after school just to watch the fish, tracing their paths with my finger. I liked the bubble aquariums best—the fish looked airborne, flying around in their Plexiglas globes like lovely winged mutants. Four months ago the store was bombed (by a Filipino gang, the newspapers suspected), and the next day I walked by to find half the storefront missing, the floor blanketed with aquarium shards. I entered and walked among the ruins, the crunch of glass beneath my feet. Beams of morning light seeped through broken windows and cracks in the wall, teleporting me to a kaleidoscopic world: ruby- and sapphire- and emerald-colored fish lay on the ground, lifeless, but still reflecting the brilliant sun in each tiny scale. I took out my lunch, threw away the sandwich, and stashed as many fish as I could fit into the Ziploc bag. Had they been alive, I would have been carrying nearly four hundred dollars worth of fish; dead, they were worth nothing. I didn't care. I took them home and kept them tucked away for three months, behind the ice trays and TV dinners, and took them out late at night to look at them. Bathed in freezer light, they were like life-giving stones, alien and cold. When Mom found them, their color had finally faded, and she flushed them down the toilet.

The store remains vacant, but the roof is sturdy, and my vantage point is good. From up here I can see down into the restaurant, beyond the gaudy-lettered window, which reads BARRY ALLEN's though the owners are a Vietnamese couple by the name of Ngoc-Tran. "They probably needed something catchier, for business purposes," Luc said, explaining why they used the name. "Koreans do it all the time."

So do superheroes.

The last of the afternoon regulars finally leaves, and my mother takes a cigarette break at a corner booth. She stares out at the street, taking greedy drags of a Marlboro. She exhales smoke against the window, and it dances before her face like some sort of phantom lover that I can see, too. I often catch my mother in these moments, a sad woman in pink, looking into nothing, waiting. "That's how I met your father," she once confessed in a stupor. She was one of Manila Rosie's Beauties, the best dancing girls the Navy boys could find in the city. "And I was your daddy's favorite," she said. After a two-week courtship he proposed to my mother, promising her citizenship in the U.S.A. "United Stars of America" is what she called it. I have had longing dreams about this incarnation of my mother, seeing her asleep and afloat in outer space, the constellations reforming themselves around her. I try to locate this part of her in myself, to isolate it from all the other stuff.

Then suddenly, from nowhere, a man in a uniform invades the picture. He sits down at her booth, lights my mother another cigarette, lights his own. They begin to talk. I don't need to hear what they're saying; I can read the words, frame by frame. My mother laughs, her hand over her breast, as if she is gasping for air. She is weakening.

Oh, stop! You're too much, do you know that? she says, giggling.

He tosses his head back, his shoulders bouncing up and down, up and down, laughing at his own jokes with a villain's arrogance. Then he grabs my mother's hand and brings it close to his face. He is acquainting himself with my mother's biology, remembering the texture of her skin, her scent. *My little tropical gardenia,* he says to her. But his thoughts betray him. *So easy* bubbles from his head. *This bitch will be so easy.*

I'm too far and high up above. There's no way to warn her in time, no hope for a last-minute rescue.

Having discussed the Green Lantern's shift in crime-fighting focus, this paper will now examine its consequences. In 1976 the Green Lantern returns to the stars. This is a difficult time for him. Realizing that he is unable to wipe out the societal ills of the era, he falters in his ability to wield the power ring. He is summoned to Oa, where the Guardians put him on trial and consider finding a replacement. The following dialogue is an excerpt from that trial:

"Perhaps Abin Sur was mistaken in selecting you, Hal Jordan."

"Please, Guardians. Allow me to prove myself worthy of the ring. Allow me to be your champion once more."

The world jerks to a stop, and my pencil slips from my hands. I pick it up from the littered bus floor. "Brake more gently next time, please!" I shout to the bus driver. Baldie shoots me a look from his extended rearview mirror.

He does it again at the next stop. "Hey!" I rise from my seat. "I said brake more gently next time!" I walk toward the front. "Did you hear me?" Baldie ignores me and slams on the brakes at the light. I keep him in my eye as I fight gravity, but I lose my footing; I fall. Just as quickly I'm up again, and I almost manage to dig the point of my pencil into his arm, but two of his henchmen passengers force me off before I can make contact with his skin. I walk the rest of the way home against traffic so loud that it smothers and suffocates the battle cries in my head.

When I call, Luc's grandmother picks up the phone. I don't bother identifying myself; she always drops the receiver at the sound of my voice, and I have to wait two or three minutes until Luc finds out it's for him. To his grandmother, I'm The Filipino, the mutant friend who is too different for her to speak with, too weird to be allowed to come over.

Luc finally picks up, and I tell him what happened. "Just breathe for a sec," he says, competing with loud kitchen noises in the background. "It'll be fine."

"He had to be stopped," I explain. "He's putting other lives at risk. Better the driver die than a busload of innocents." If I have to be the one to do it, then I'll do it.

Luc understands the good of my intentions and says so. "But it's over now. You kept all those passengers safe."

"Let's hope."

Then Luc says he's sorry but he has to go, his mother needs to call his aunt about a Korean variety show on cable. "No problemo," I say, "and thanks again, old chum." I wait for the click on his end and then I hang up.

With my mother at the restaurant, I have time to work in my lab. I can construct bombs and explosives, but these require the proper chemicals and materials, and I can use the bathroom for only so many hours in a day before my mother becomes suspicious. When she pounds on the door, asking what I am doing, I tell her nothing, to please give me five or ten minutes. She guesses that I am masturbating and tells me to stop. I tell her okay.

My favorite weapon is my slingshot. I stole it from a high-quality sporting goods store six months back: lightweight, aerodynamic, potential of elasticity twenty times as great as the average sling. It angers me how a lesser comic like *Dennis the Menace* has reduced the slingshot to a mischief-making toy kept in a child's back pocket. People forget that David killed Goliath with a slingshot. With the proper ammunition I could kill from afar, too.

But I am at work on what I hope will be the greatest addition to my arsenal. Centuries ago Filipino warriors created the yo-yo as a weapon, emitting from their hands stone-heavy objects at the ends of twenty-foot-long ropes. They learned to hunt with it, to kill. Eventually the yo-yo immigrated to America. The story goes that a traveling salesman named Duncan saw one and introduced it to the country as a new hobby, a toy to pass the time.

I intend to get it back.

I will fuse my native ingenuity with modern technology to create a weapon of deadly hybridity. My yo-yo will be of marble, attached to string at least fifty feet long, so that even from rooftops I can stun my enemies far, far below. My father, too, had weapons. In the framed photo my mother keeps on her bureau, he holds a rifle in one hand, my mother in the other.

Suddenly I hear movement in the apartment. "Come out here!" my mother shouts, pounding on the bathroom door. "Come out and meet my new friend!"

"You're early! Hold on a sec!" I stash everything behind the toilet paper under the sink, hiding it next to the Windex and Lysol.

I open the door and find my mother standing before me, her head resting dreamily on his arm. "Honey," she says, smiling at me, "this is Lex. He's our mailman. We met today at the restaurant."

At least six feet tall, Lex towers over my mother and over me. He is well-postured, undoubtedly strong and agile. His uniform shows a badge of a bald eagle, and another badge tells me that he has proudly delivered U.S. mail for five years. "Hey, champ," he says. He fixes his eyes, as blue and sharp as lasers, on me. Five milky-white fingers reach out.

Armed with addresses and zip codes, Lex can track down anyone, anywhere. If my mother and I were to escape, he could follow the trail of our forwarding address to find us. It's the extra sense, the instinct, of a hunter.

Villain.

But I accept his challenge and take his hand. I tilt my head down just a bit, so that my glasses slide down the bridge of my nose. "Nice to meet you," I say with a smile. Lex does a double take at my non-matching eyes. Already I have the upper hand.

My mother and Lex want privacy, so tonight I'm a bedroom shut-in. But I can still hear them laughing, dancing clumsily around the front room to old Motown love songs. Luckily, I have the ability to phase out any and all distractions, to teleport my thoughts, even my senses, elsewhere. I believe this is another of my mutant abilities, the active residue of my father's genetic imprint. It's the power he used on Mom and me.

I use that power tonight. I have homework to do.

I research, going through issue after old issue of *Green Lantern*. Already I feel like the Green Lantern's biographer. I recognize the earnestness of the early years, when he is made up of simple, clean strokes of a pen, when the green of his costume is bright and the black is bold, and the villains are easy to tell from the heroes. In the sixties he is more weathered, and in the seventies the battle scars are painfully obvious in the inking of his musculature: The mementos of victories are also the reminders of loved ones lost. I feel sad for him, for all the time he's been forced to see.

And now I'm at that difficult point in my project where his status as a hero comes into question. "It's where history stops becoming fact," Mr. Cosgrove would say, "and you have to choose what's true and what isn't."

Brought to Oa, he stands before a jury of Guardians, on trial for abusing his power, for attempting to alter history to save his city and the woman he loved. *"Hal Jordan, Green Lantern of sector 2814, for misuse of the power of Oa, you are hereby asked to surrender the ring to us,"* they say. Half of Hal Jordan's face fills the next panel, and his rage is clear even behind the mask. Next is a Guardian's bony, blue-skinned hand reaching out, palm open. *"You will surrender the ring, Hal Jordan,"* he says.

"THE RING!" five voices echo through the same voice bubble.

And then Hal Jordan's face, the mask, one eye, and nothing. Only a frightening flash of green.

I take the bottom corner of the page between my fingers. I turn the page slowly, knowing what comes next: an exploding sky, fallen emerald towers, the lifeless bodies of Guardians long thought to be immortal scattered among the debris. *"Traitor!"* one accuses with his dying breath. But Hal Jordan admits nothing, denies nothing. He takes their rings, all of them, and explodes into space, Earthbound, a furious green light trailing behind him.

History is to be interpreted; that's the rule. What makes me so angry is that the decision has already been made for us. The cover's depiction of Hal Jordan proves the bias: His eyebrows are sharp-pointed arches, his lips stretch in a sinister grin, and behind the mask his eyes are vacant, blank with madness and power. It's the face of a villain, the kind I've seen a million times.

But consider what Hal Jordan has seen. Consider the burden he bears: *He got there too late.* He got there in time only to see his city wiped out by an enemy he couldn't defeat. You don't recover from that; you fix it. If I could rewrite the comic, I'd do the same.

The following pages are panels of green: He wipes out a building in the background, *KRAZAAKK!,* one in the foreground, *BLA-ZAAAM!* He destroys another, and another. Then—*crash!*—something made of glass falls to the floor in the living room. I hear my mother and Lex whirling around to the music, bumping into book-shelves and walls, causing fragile things to fall. They laugh through loud kisses.

"Could you please be quiet out there?" They don't answer. "Would you be quiet, please?" Still nothing, only the soft sounds of my mother being taken yet again. "Be quiet."

At 2:43 A.M. I wake from weird dreams. Dehydrated and dizzy, I get a glass of milk. On the way back to my room I peek through my mother's half-closed door. She's curled up in Lex's arms; the sheets are wrapped around their bodies, binding them together. In her sleep her hands still clamp around his neck.

I walk toward them, silent in bare feet, invisible in the blue glow of the digital clock. I stand at the foot of the bed, watching their bod-ies just barely rise from breath. If I wanted to, I could crawl in be-tween them, my head in the circle of my mother's arms, my knee rammed into Lex's balls.

My mother mumbles something in her sleep, taking quick breaths, and slowly she turns away from Lex. I go to her. I can feel her pupils shift side to side beneath the skin of her eyelids, and I press down on them just enough until the panic in her head subsides. I move a strand of black hair away from her face, looping it slowly around my finger.

I float to the other side of the bed, over to Lex. In the moonlight he is even paler, and the stubble on his chin is like metallic bristles against my knuckles. I kneel next to him and set my head down beside his. I can see my mother's lipstick smeared along his neck, trailing down to the center of his chest. It's the residue of what she thinks is love, and I can imagine my mother kissing him, just inches above the spot where the heart should be. I lay my palm flat on that spot, just barely touching skin. I can feel the life beating inside him. Maybe this is how my father felt. "What do you want from us?" I whisper to him. "Who sent you here?" But like my mother, he is drowned in sleep or just passed out.

So I test him. I tip my almost-empty glass, letting a tiny drop of milk fall onto his ear. The white liquid dot slides from the outer edge and vanishes into the black hole of his ear canal. His neck and shoulders jerk, lightning quick. Then he is still again. "Assassin," I say. I return to the kitchen to wash my glass.

We have not seen The Gas for almost two weeks since the battle. At lunch Luc and I split up, eavesdropping on conversations, trying to piece together the fate of our nemesis.

After school we regroup on the library roof. "I heard Suzy Cheerleader talking to one of the vice-principals," Luc says. "Brandon's in the hospital."

"The Gas will be fine," I tell him, staring out onto the campus quad. We stay low, speaking in whispers.

"Did you hear me? He's in the hospital now. His arm needs some sort of operation. Skin grafts or something. What did you put in that thing anyway?"

Skin grafts. Then the body of my enemy is mutating as well. Fascinating. "Mercury fulminate, chloride of azode, some other chemicals. The usual."

I keep an eye out until I finally spot Tenzil, blanketing the school with his propaganda. I blame Tenzil, an ally of The Gas, for our corrupt student government. As vice-president, he's the person who rejected my proposal for a school trip to the San Francisco Comic Book Convention, and gave my money to varsity track instead.

I pull the yo-yo from my bag. "What the hell is that?" Luc asks.

"Quiet." This moment requires silence and the utmost precision.

Tenzil comes closer as I loop the string round and round my finger until I've cut off circulation. I raise my hand over the edge. But suddenly Luc grabs my wrist. "Don't," he says, trying to bring me back.

I take a quick foot to his stomach, freeing myself from his clutches. "If we don't get him, he'll get us."

"What are you talking about?" Luc asks, as if he doesn't already know. He rises from the ground and reaches for my wrist again, but he's too slow: I snap my hand forward, letting go the yo-yo for its spectacular debut.

Marble-heavy, the double disk drops straight to the ground. But Tenzil is gone, and the yo-yo dangles at the string's end, lifeless, refusing to wind its way back up to me. "Where is he?" I say. "Where the fuck did he go?" I crane my neck over the edge, scanning the quad, the locker bay, anywhere someone might hide from me. But Tenzil is nowhere to be found. "Traitor," I accuse Luc. "This is your fault." But when I turn, he, too, is gone. I take a quick inventory of the rooftop. No traces.

I run through the campus, taking down Tenzil's posters and flyers. I return to the roof, where I tear them into a pile of tiny pieces. Then

I scoop them up and throw them to the sky, letting them fall like ashes on the spot where the chalk outline of Tenzil Jones's body should have been. I want to mourn today's loss.

I keep no school ID, have no driver's permit. I tossed my Social Security card once I had committed the number to memory. If I have no money, then there's nothing in my wallet. I have my anonymity to keep me safe.

Today my wallet is empty but I'm hungry, so I stop by Ollie's Market on the way home. Ollie stands behind the counter, a sixty-something grump in a dirty undershirt, venting his frustrations on his customers. At his side is Sasha the Amputee, Ollie's half retriever, half something else. Sasha's right hind leg was the only casualty of the last holdup, which Ollie swears, despite the ski masks, was done by Filipino gangsters. "Filipinos!" he curses to the air. "Stealing this and stealing that!"

He makes this so easy.

My mutant biology hides that part of me he would fear. It is, after all, layered with the skin of my father, fused with that of my mother, and it gives me chameleonic powers. Ollie continues complaining and accusing, unaware that a shape-shifter stands before him. I tell him I know exactly how he feels, that they really can't be trusted, that they're a dangerous and deadly breed, and I keep Ollie in my eye, drowning out his sound as my hand fingers its way to the minirack of candy bars at my side.

But Sasha sees. The mutt snarls, her snout pointed at me, accusing me. *Go ahead,* I dare her. *Hobble after me and you'll lose another, you damaged bitch.* Mission accomplished, I tell Ollie good-bye, and press my heel onto Sasha's front paw as I walk out the door. She lets out a pathetic yelp. "Sorry." I smile at Ollie, petting the dog's head.

I exit the store and make a sharp right into an alleyway. I walk through and cross a four-way intersection diagonally, dodging cars and buses. I make a left, a right, and another right. I round corner after corner until the geometry of the city swallows me whole and it's safe for me to eat.

The shades are drawn when I enter our apartment. I hear movement from the bedroom. "Mom?"

I open her door. "Mom." She's on the floor, lying on her side. Laid out beside her is my father's uniform, still wrapped in plastic on a wire hanger. She reaches out to it, moving her thumb back and forth over a shiny gold button.

I give her a shot of whiskey. I pour her another and then another, and she goes on about how Lex doesn't love her, that the evil in men will always kill her, more and more slowly each time. "All the time. All the time this happens. Tell your father to stop it, please." She weeps into my chest, clinging to my shirt. Streaks of blood stain her hands. She's been cutting herself again.

An orphaned boy sees a bat flying through a window. The last son of Krypton dreams of the afterglow of his dead home world. All heroes have their omens; this blood will be mine.

"I will," I tell her. "I swear it." But she cannot hear my oath.

In conclusion, he is no longer the Green Lantern. With a final surge of power, Hal Jordan transforms himself into Parallax, a master of space and dimension, wielder of the greatest power ever known. His only agenda: to destroy time, to interrupt for good the linearity of history. With one hand he will knock past, present, and future out of order; he will be the judge of who may live, who will die, and who will never have existed at all. Time will move forward, time will move back, until it collides with itself, until what is left is the Zero Hour, and all that has gone wrong can finally be set right.

Villains and heroes don't ask for the power they're given: Destiny, Fate, and Luck drop it on us like a star, and we have no choice but to use it.

It's due tomorrow, but fuck the paper. Tonight I must enter the fray.

I paint black around my eyes, like a domino mask, erasing the traces of who I am.

Mother's future slips into Mother's past as I don my father's uniform jacket. It fits perfectly; I never knew our bodies were the same. Gold buttons sparkle on my chest, badges adorn my arms. To the collar I attach a cape, a long piece of cloth light enough that it does not impede my speed, dark enough that it keeps me wrapped in night shadows. All superassassins rely on the darkness.

I place my ammunition—segments of aluminum pipe filled with impact-sensitive explosives—in a tiny suede pouch attached to my belt. I secure the slingshot in my front belt loop; the yo-yo I keep in an oversized pocket on my pant leg.

Midnight strikes. I climb out the window, descend the fire escape, and run through the city, staying in back alleys and unlit streets. I keep an eye out for any and all enemies who dare to venture into the night. Though they are many and I am one, I will fight this battle alone. I have no need for Luc anymore. Sidekicks are extraneous; they give up the fight too easily. Robin was killed off for a reason after all.

I make my way to the abandoned projects. I enter through the back, and blast open the door to the stairwell. I fly up seven, eight, nine flights. I need to go higher.

Fourteen, fifteen, sixteen flights. I must go higher.

I reach the roof. I walk along its perimeter, to be sure I am alone. Night wind howls all around, blowing my cape behind me like a black ghost in tow.

I peer over the edge; the city itself has become a grid. Black streets and white sidewalks crisscross, framing city blocks like tiny pictures, a page of panels with too many scenes. But somewhere in all of this I know my enemy lurks, waiting for me to strike, daring me to cross the white borders and enter the battle. I will wait for him every night if I have to.

I take out the slingshot. I load the ammunition and pull back the sling. I aim, ready at any moment to let go.

CHRISTINA MILLETTI

University at Albany, SUNY

VILLA OF THE VEILED LADY

In August, the sun hovered above the ruins of Herculaneum. The heat was fierce, the earth parched. Only dragonflies swarmed the streets of the city that was once buried in ash. As Alice approached the gates to the site, an old man in a booth waved her over.

"We close at five," he said as he sold her a map and a ticket. Then he pointed her down a cobbled street that had ruts worn by wheels in the stones.

Although Alice heard the clatter of hand tools off in the distance where the digging continued, the excavated center of the city was quiet, still even. Studying her map, she left the main thoroughfare and followed the side streets to the southeastern corner of town. It was old homes, a dead life, that she wanted to see—the broken walls built from paper and dust, spent embers, tiny insects, and sand.

In the long moment of the late afternoon heat, the distance Alice traveled to get to the ruins was of little consequence to her. Where she began was implicit—a green suburb of Philadelphia where they still tip the postmen—but her home, her town and circle of friends were no longer *of* her journey. She had left them behind, made an exchange of the past—a past that would likely become her future— for a present that was unknown. For three weeks she rode the trains, sometimes rented a Vespa, traveled from big toe to ankle, up the calf of the Italian countryside. Perhaps when she arrived in Milan—perhaps then she would go home. For now, just a few things mattered: where she ate dinner, where she slept for the night, where she would head off to in the morning. There were too many places to trek through, to eat through, to buy tickets to see. For Alice, time seemed scarce, so she'd begun to hoard it. The past couldn't be changed; the future would take care of itself. For now—for the present—Alice would *see* (that was her duty). She wanted to see more than anything else. Her guidebook with its maps and suggestions was everything; it was precious to her. There was little to do at home.

Alice was young. She had time on her hands, but she was not, as they say, independent. She was, in other words, that new breed of American—part of an overoptioned middle class, full of investment portfolio chatter, although her parents, with whom she still lived, continued to reside in their familiar, split-level home.

Today, Alice was tired. She'd had it. For hours, she walked through the ruins, through homes and temples, baths, ball courts and toilets, even sat for a time on a listing block of seat at the omnitheater. She hadn't seen everything, but she'd seen enough, and the sun, still high and bright—enormous over the excavation all day—was fading, not in strength, but against the tick of the clock. Soon, the groundskeepers would call her in, round her up, expel her with the rest of the flaggers out into the streets of the city above the city: the modern-day Ercolano which, like a grown child standing over an elderly parent, overlooked the site of the ruins.

Outside the building archaeologists had named House of the Stags (for the stag sculptures unearthed inside), Alice found a bench and sat on it. She was hot, she needed to rest, and her canteen was filled with stale water. She sipped it anyway, then spat in the dust. At first, the dry earth refused to absorb it. But then with an almost perceptible sigh of irritation, the earth seemed to relent. When she looked back a few moments later, the damp sand was already dry.

"Hello?"

Though Alice knew no one, had met no one, knew of no one who might look for her among the ruins, she sat up and looked around.

"*Signorina?*"

It was the same voice, neither soft nor loud, friendly nor urgent. After a moment, she found it, *him,* hidden among stone gray and shadow in the half-light of the building's portico.

"Me?" Alice said, rubbing her eyes as if to see him more clearly. He was leaning against a column, had propped himself there as comfortably as if the House of the Stags were his own home. From just a few feet away, she could smell his cigar. He was sucking on it, letting a perilous tumbler of ash grow at its tip just above a thick kerchief loosely tied at his neck.

He was watching her watch him; he was a patient man. Clearly, he wasn't a tourist.

Alice called out to him again.

"Me?" She pointed to her shirt to emphasize her meaning. It was soaked, she realized, thinking, not for the first time, that the sun and the city were in hostile collusion against the curious visitor—the sun sapping from tourists the fluids the long-dead city needed to bring life back to the parched buildings and dusty streets, an urbanity buried in ash. After all, much like its sister city Pompeii, which Alice had toured just one day earlier, Herculaneum had been built beneath an active volcano that, long ago and since again, had erupted with catastrophic force over the cities in its shade. While much of Pompeii had been unearthed, Herculaneum—a small town in comparison—still remained largely concealed. As Alice had read, the pyroclastic blanket that interred the city was as hard as concrete. For diggers, it was tough going. They were hampered not only by the solid matrix of ash and mud, but also by the complaints of the locals in the city above who threw chestnuts and chastised them whenever a modern building was imploded to make way for the past.

The man at last emerged from the doorway, his hands turned up as though in supplication. He stopped just a few feet away, rocked back on his heels. At first, she thought he was nervous—there was a peculiar excitement about him. Yet he was all motion without actual movement. He was silent, still. There was little plot to him, Alice decided as she looked him over. He didn't make her uneasy; she didn't feel wary, even though she noticed he wore calfskin pants in the heat.

"Come," he said at last, adding, as though he had carefully chosen his words (or perhaps his translation of them), "I show you something you like."

Turning his back, he walked a few feet away, then looked over his shoulder. He was surprised, Alice realized, that she hadn't followed, that she had remained, feet stretched out before her, resting on the bench.

"Come come," he said, clapping his hands. He was perturbed, there was no other word for it. Alice couldn't help it—she laughed.

"What's your name?" she asked.

He bowed. "In Italian," he said, "they call me Apollinaro. In English, they say Tebel. They are two different names—not the same name in two different tongues. Always, however, my last name is Vos." He could hold a conversation, it seemed, even with half of his tongue wrapped around a cigar.

"My mother, you see, she was English, the people who raised me, from New Ercolano, the city above." He sighed. "The story is complicated and not complicated at all."

"Vos," she said. "That's an English name, too?"

"A Welsh name," he said. "My father is not known."

She considered. "What should I call you then?"

"Whatever you like." Again he bowed, not from the waist, but by waving his arm out in an arc as though he were wearing a cape.

Alice—reflecting on Romans and being in Rome, at least an ancient Roman city—made her decision without effort. "Apollinaro," she said, "I'm afraid I can't come." She tapped the watch on her wrist. "It's almost time to leave."

Apollinaro stepped toward her, took the cigar from his mouth, and put a silencing finger across his lips. "True," he said. "But you see here," he pulled a ring of keys out of his pocket. "I have the ways in and out." He sat next to her on the bench. He looked very serious.

"I watch you today," he said. "You like to look at things. Let me show you what they keep hidden here." He took her hand and stood up, pulling her with him. "You will like it," he said. "For you, I make a guarantee." Apollinaro thumped his chest, but in doing so knocked some of the ash into his kerchief. He cursed and let go of her hand. He swiped at his neck and loose ash was suddenly around them in the air.

Under how much ash had this street once been buried, Alice wondered. And now this capful of it rose softly, almost gently, between them.

She looked back at Apollinaro. He was watching her; he'd gone very still. Then, reaching out, he took her hand again in both of his. His grip was damp but tough. She guessed it would be cool if not for the heat. And there was a strength he had not used.

"Okay," Alice said, trying to look him hard in the eye. "But no funny stuff."

"No funny stuff," he agreed. Surprising herself, Alice believed him.

At first they walked slowly away from the House of the Stags toward the edge of the city, away from the forum and baths, the shops and patrician homes, always toward the outskirts, the edge of the excavation and the steep hills of its perimeter which made the old Roman site look, from the city above, as though it had been built in a crater, as though it were a lunar resort spackled together with a mortar of cheese.

Apollinaro wasn't tall but he was taller than Alice, and though at first he picked a pace that suited her stride, he quickly forgot and began to let out his length. Soon she was jogging slowly behind him just to keep up, so she wouldn't lose him among the new digging sites through which they wove—in and out—even the ones that had been blocked off and through which, smiling, he led her so they could swiftly get to the particular site he wanted to show her: a squat but sprawling building in front of which a wheelbarrow and shovels had been left behind. A bucket and some brushes sat by one doorway, a canteen on its head against a wall. Evidently, the workers had left for the day; not one of them could be seen.

Unconcerned, Apollinaro grabbed her hand and pulled her through the doorway, into the shaded concourse of a massive hall.

"Here," he explained, "a place for many shops." He flourished his arm as if—right at that very moment—he had discovered the building himself.

"An arcade?" Alice asked as she looked around.

He nodded and began to pull her from shop to shop inside the hall, pointing at a jug still filled with grain, at a nearby hearth where a copper pot hung, a thick chain securing it level over an iron grate in the floor. In another shop they found a loom and a press and the remains of several baskets inside of which corroded bolts of fabric, scorched rope, and yarn seemed still to await purchase. Farther inside, a baker's oven and loaves of bread lined up on a shelf for display.

"I said you will like," he smiled as she walked around making soft sounds of pleasure, kicking up dust as she hurried along, bending here and there to get a better view of the grain and the fabric, of how delicately the eruption had encased the arcade and preserved its contents, while other buildings, some nearby, had been stripped, had become nothing more than ember, beam, and tottering stone.

"Amazing," she said and reached out to trace the outline of a fish a long-dead baker had drawn into the crust of a loaf on his counter. Quickly Apollinaro grabbed her hand, rapped her fingers with his own.

"Only for looking," he said. "You remember."

Alice nodded and began to pull her hand from his, but he had already released it. Now, he took her by the arm and led her back outside the marketplace. Around the backside of the building they tripped over loose dirt and digging equipment, scaffolding not yet erected or already dismantled. At last he stopped in front of a low window into which he leaned, then pulled himself through. Once he had righted himself, he leaned back out and reached for her hand. The window, apparently, was the only entrance into an otherwise sealed-off room. Earth and dense packed mud still blocked a doorway off to her left.

Alice gave him her hand and scrambled in after him. At first the room was dark, far too dark for her to see as she strained her eyes. But Apollinaro quickly sparked his lighter, let the flame curl high and bright above the fist he closed tightly around it. They walked together across the room until they stood in front of a small pedestal of hard mud that revealed the shape of a crib, a cradle perhaps. As Apollinaro leaned over it, Alice followed the path of the flame. Inside there was a pile of tiny bones, the ashen outline of an infant. The baby must have been carbonized, completely burned by the molten mud that had filled the room. How strange that other bodies had been preserved, soldiers and citizens, even pets, choked by the burning ash, the gases, which rained down in the streets, their bodies later wrapped in a blanket of pumice and mud so that, centuries later, their pain didn't yet seem spent. The bones still clutched hair and clawed at the ground, tore at eyes in disbelief. Yet this infant had been reduced to nothing more than a trace in its bed, an outline perhaps of what could have been: a mark for the future of a long dead past which had meaning—right then at that moment—only when Alice stood over it and looked down.

"Let's go," she said, suddenly shaken. He nodded, and it seemed to Alice as he gave her his hand, helped her back out through the window that, like her, Apollinaro let out a sigh of relief.

Her guide was quiet as they returned to the path toward the perimeter of the ruins. And though he stuffed his hands in his pockets, let the cigar seem to breathe for him as the air around Alice choked with its haze, he looked surprisingly stern in his outrageous getup. For a moment she could see the Brit in him, the imprint of the mother beneath his more olive nature. At last he said, "My friend, there were no more bones in that house."

Alice wasn't sure what he meant, but presently it came to her.

"You think the child was left behind?"

Apollinaro nodded. And Alice fell silent, too.

After a time, the path they walked on began to sway uphill, a steady grade toward the banks of the perimeter. It was a gentle rise at first, but when she looked back at the excavation behind them—below them, in fact—she realized just how far they'd climbed. He'd brought her to a graveyard. Around them, the tops of columns rose from the ground like footstools. The tips of rooftops marked the burial place of homes still hidden below, perhaps with their owners inside.

Beyond, steep walls encircled the ruins. Above, the high-rise slums of New Ercolano perched on the edge of the crater. They were scheduled for demolition, Apollinaro explained. But Alice could still see laundry pinned to lines between the tenements; the residents had not yet moved.

Apollinaro guided her toward a large structure whose topmost floor had been hollowed out of earth, though the bottom levels—a first and second floor—clearly were still buried. The building was surrounded by iron pikes with a thick blue rope strung through them. Warning signs hung from the rope, cautioning curious wanderers from entry.

Apollinaro spat a bit of cigar onto the ground.

"Not to worry you," he said, dismissing the signs. "Only for the babies." With that, he slid through a window much like before, stamping his feet inside the room to reassure Alice as she waited outside that the ancient floor was safe.

"Come come," he called to her. "This house is special." He extended his hand through the window, knocked a stone from the crumbling sill that skittered to Alice's feet. "Good girl," he said when she took his hand anyway and climbed onto the ledge. But before she could jump down next to him, he put a hand on her knee, stopped her from moving. "Wait," he said. "Give me the feet." Alice was perplexed. "Come come," he said again. Awkwardly, she swung around so that she could sit on the sill with her feet dangling toward him.

"No funny stuff," he comforted her as he started removing her shoes. "I put the shoes right here. Next to mine, you see?" He pointed at the pairs of shoes he lined up neatly and smiled. "We leave no traces, we walk gently, we must." Then he winked and she tried to smile, but for the first time she felt cautious, inexplicably nervous.

"You feel it, too?" he said seeing her face curl up. "You are not the first. The diggers, they feel the same way in this house. No one is

knowing why." He shrugged. "This house, they think it will fall."
(He thumped her hand when he felt her start.) "It is good *now*," he
assured her. "Later, when they must do more digging, there is the
problem. For now," he said, "it is like rock." He stamped his feet. It
was true, the room felt like a cave—sturdy, reliable, with the smell of
wet, old stone and dead things that have become dust.

Apollinaro sighed. "Later, when they begin to dig, they will build
this house again stone by stone. But it's never the same, I see it over
and over. It's the same house with the same parts, but never the same
house again." He looked at her. "The feeling you feel when you come
in this house, the feeling even *you* had, that will be gone. The house is
gone, and all that's left are its stones." He took a deep breath, ran his
hand through the air as if touching a fresco revealed there. "It's never
like this again," he said smiling sadly. "A one-time opportunity, eh?"

Alice smiled back and took the hand that he offered. How lucky
she'd been to get in his way. The tour they were on wasn't for her, she
now realized; it was for him. She was merely a guest—there could be
no tour after all without one. So she relaxed, began to enjoy the
somewhat musty view.

"A one-time opportunity," she agreed nodding seriously as he
helped her down from the sill.

The room into which they climbed was an anteroom, a small cu-
bicle off a much larger one that itself led out to the open air—onto
a covered terrace supported by columns off which many other rooms
had likewise been built on a rectangular plan. Each room had a view
of the city and also overlooked an internal garden. An atrium perhaps. Alice could only guess.

On the wall of the larger room, frescoes had been preserved largely
intact, though a large corner section had disappeared as if it had
been peeled away. At its center, there was a woman. She was wearing
white—a diaphanous gown that suggested the curves of her breasts,

her belly, beneath it. There was a veil over her face, a drapery made of the same fabric so that there was only the hint of dark hair loose to the shoulder, a strong nose, dark eyes staring out. Alice sensed that the veiled lady wasn't smiling beneath all the fabric. Yet she wasn't unhappy—it seemed, rather, as if she were patiently waiting. The veiled lady had waited for many things, Alice guessed, not just for the artisan who portrayed her with care to finish the work over which he clearly had labored. The veil and the gown fell to her ankles. Just below the hem, however, there was a pair of lovely bare feet, their pink toes pointing out as though her body weighed lightly on them.

"She is in every room," Apollinaro said softly. "In each room painted different, but painted the same."

"She's beautiful," Alice said.

"Come come." Her guide took her hand and pulled her out to the terrace, and slowly they began to walk through the rooms. In the next one, the veiled lady was sitting and washing her feet, her gown bunched up at her knees, so that the lower part of her calves were also revealed. In the room beyond that, she was resting on one hip on a pillow as she played a Roman game of knucklebones. Again she was covered, only her feet could be seen, but this time there was also one delicate hand, the fingers curled back to reveal the knucklebone pieces she'd shaken like dice in her palm. In the next fresco she was resting, one arm thrown back and under her head, her knees bent, feet pointing away from the painter. In another, she quietly looked off through a window. Elsewhere, she poured wine in a cup. Each painting was different, but Apollinaro was right. They were the same. It was the same woman, wearing the same opaque veils. In each painting her face was concealed, but she always looked back at the painter, directly out of the fresco at the people who saw her. She was staring out at her life as though through a mirror. As if the ruins were the fresco, charred rock, the still life. As though she still had a presence, a life of her own, if not life as such.

"Who is she?" Alice asked Apollinaro, her hand on his arm as they both studied the frescoes.

"No one knows," he said. "But the diggers, they call her Antonia."

"I feel like she's watching me."

Apollinaro patted her hand. "Yes," he said simply. That was all.

He took her hand in his and they walked into the corner room, which, unlike the others, had been badly damaged by flows of mud. The tile had buckled in waves, and one wall sloped toward them as though a giant had leaned against it until the mortar and stone gave beneath its weight. The sun shone through a window. There were no frescoes on the walls.

"Oh my," Alice said.

On the floor of the room, an outline of a body had been drawn in chalk over the roll and buckle of tile. The chalk itself had been left in the corner, tossed aside and forgotten.

Apollinaro came to a halt. "I was not thinking," he said. "I could not know it still was here."

"What happened?" she asked.

"A sad story."

She urged him on. "Please tell me."

"One month ago," he began, "the diggers came here to work. Instead they found their friend there on the floor, the *carabinieri*, the police, standing over his body, while a woman—a woman who was not his wife—wept in the corner. There was an investigation. It was the police who made the chalk picture. But what was to prove when all was to see? The digger's heart simply gave out. So the wife found out about the young woman, her dead husband. Both of them in one day."

"How awful." Alice shook her head.

"The girl's name was Antonia," he said. "So the diggers, they named the veiled lady for her. You see, the day that he died, the girl had a look: angry and sad at the same time." Apollinaro shook his head. "That's how the diggers think the veiled lady's face must be under all her veils. Why else would a painter hide her face? They think it is too sorrowful to see."

Alice nodded, and Apollinaro walked slowly out of the room, left her alone over the chalk drawing of a man—a stout man it seemed—who had curled up on his side, thrown one arm out as he died. The other must have been over his chest, over his heart when it failed.

After a time, Alice followed after her guide and found him next door, by the painting that portrayed the veiled lady asleep. Apollinaro was standing very still in front of it, his hands out as if he could lift the veil, peel back a layer of paint, reveal her face at last. Still breathing the dusty cigar and sweating in his calfskin pants, he looked large and sad, though Alice couldn't say why. It wasn't from loss, she slowly decided; there was more. Perhaps the inconceivability of losing.

"She means something to you," Alice said after a time, after he'd closed his face down, let the warm emotion retreat when he felt her join him in the room.

He didn't answer her directly. "Do you think she looks like the diggers say? Full of sorrow under her veils?"

Alice thought for a moment. "When I first saw her," she told him, "I thought she simply looked patient, as though she were waiting, but for what I couldn't say. I think she's watching us, though, not hiding from our view."

Apollinaro turned and took her hand. "Just so," he said squeezing it. Then he sighed. "But the diggers, they tend to be stubborn, you can't change their minds once they have been set. They know stone," he went on, "and so like stone they are." He smiled, rapped his skull lightly with his fist. Alice laughed because he wanted her to, though she didn't think he believed what he said.

"You're not a digger yourself, then?"

"No," he said. "The man who raised me, he still works here even though he is too old. The men let him come and sit on the rocks, use the small brushes to clean up pieces that won't be damaged if he drops them."

"How kind," she said.

Apollinaro grunted. "If he stays home, he just gets older. It is much better this way."

Alice laughed softly and he smiled.

"You are very nice for an American," he said.

"And you," she said taking his arm as though she'd known him much longer than just an hour, "are fortunate to be more Italian than Brit."

He smiled but looked sad, and unexpectedly Alice felt very small.

"I'm sorry," she said. "I didn't intend to be cruel."

Apollinaro pushed at her shoulder gently. "No worries," he said. "You are probably right." He looked back at the painting. And together they fell into the ancient silence that protected the ruins, its stale air of ash and earth, of the paint that had crumbled off the old walls where insects fed in the dark. The veiled lady had looked over it all—silent, unseen, and always alone. Alice felt a sudden immanence—of herself and the lady there in the room, of Apollinaro standing beside her, and, not so far away, of the room where the digger had died, where his woman had cried over him in the dirt. Alice went very still and closed her eyes, trying to make them all align as if they were a single point in her mind—a point of time within the time of the ruins, because, at that moment, as she stood in the villa with Apollinaro beside her wearing leather and ash, she felt as though she might feel time itself, or at least sense its shape—where she was *in time,* and where Apollinaro and the veiled lady were, not so far away, in relation to her in time's scheme.

"She seems so familiar," Alice said slowly, carefully, watching his reaction. "Like a woman we'd each like to know at some point in our lives."

For the first time Apollinaro studied her not as a host looking at a guest, but like a man with a past, a history guarded by custom. He even looked a bit fierce as he dug his toe into the dirt, and suddenly Alice was sad that she had broken the air with her voice. It was a rare thing to feel silence lap at one's body like warm water over a stone.

Her curiosity—her desire to know the rest of his story—was presupposed, she saw. He assumed she would try to pry his memories, his feelings, from him simply because they were part of her own adventure. And he was right. It was the American in her, Alice decided, and she tried to let it go, let the silence fill her again, fill them both like empty patterns in the dust. All around her, she thought, the stones, the villa, and its veiled lady, too: they were ancient, and they were the same. She and the veiled lady and Apollinaro standing right by her. They were ancient and new; they were the same. It was just a matter of perspective, she thought. Of seeing it all together against the same shape, of making the shape *fit* one's perspective.

There was a certainty Alice often sensed, but which came over her at inconvenient times. When, for instance, she walked by an old man on the sidewalk bending toward his destination, stuttering from one shoe to the next without any help, without even the hope of support. It was the same feeling she had when she sat near a woman eating her supper alone: that a small gesture could be everything—that an offered arm, a word spoken simply, could be everything in itself. Of course she'd never done much about it, never given her arm or said the word; there was always some place to be, some future to make. And she lived, after all, in a city.

"Wait here," she said to her guide, moving before she could stop. She returned quickly to the corner room where the digger had died. In the west, the sun was setting beyond the horizon of the two cities, the one new, the other old, though they both bore the same name. The sun was retrieving its last stiff rays from the window, recoiling its light from the leftover chalk she'd seen cast off to the side. Quickly, she picked it up. When she returned, Apollinaro was still standing with his hands in his pockets looking up at the woman in veils.

"Lay down," she told him.

"Scusi?" he said.

"Trust me," she said. "Lay down."

Perplexed, Apollinaro squatted down on his haunches, then rolled onto his back with a soft grunt. He rested his head on the back of one arm, put the cigar in his mouth, and, looking up, blew a smoke circle which rose up around her as she bent over him and looked down.

"Now what?" he said.

"Hush," she said, then kicked at his boots to make him spread his legs apart. Instead, he just squinted and puffed. "Come come," she said clapping her hands much as he had not long ago and, sighing, he did as she asked.

Alice bent down at his side and pressed the chalk hard into the dirt. Slowly she drew a line around him: down his side, around his heel, up his leg, and, quickly, from one thigh to the next, down to the heel, around and alongside his torso, into the pit of his arm, and around the point of the elbow he had thrust out behind him, along the curve of his head, taking into account the curls of his hair, back down his neck, around and down until line met line and the chalk shape completely enclosed him. Alice stood over Apollinaro and looked at her picture of him and how the two overlapped. Not bad, she thought, and gave him her hand so that when he stood he wouldn't mess up her work.

Carefully, he got up and stepped out of the image as though he had cut himself from the earth. He walked around it, encircled his image with another pattern of feet. Then he stepped back, looked at the two together—the painting of the veiled lady and the chalk image Alice had drawn in the dirt—the one on the wall, the other in earth, two figures waiting together.

"Do you like it?" she asked.

He smiled. "You think it will bring me luck?"

"Yes." She had no doubt.

Quietly, he accepted her gift. He forgave her as he bent and kissed the warm air above her knuckles just as, not a moment before, he had touched the fresco of the veiled lady without touching it at all.

"Thank you," he said softly and looked at her, then beyond her at the light retreating from the hall. Glancing down at his watch, Apollinaro stepped quickly from the room.

"It is late," he said, retreating, and he gestured for her to follow. "The sun has set. We must go now before the darkness." There was urgency in his voice.

Alice stood quickly and he pulled her from the room, back to their shoes, then over the sill and out of the window. She kept up with him as they loped down the hill and toward the center of the excavation. She kept up even as the light went gray—as the ruins and the sky became the same—and she lost all sense of the horizon. Past the House of the Papyri and the House of the Gem they ran together, past the forum and baths and the marketplace. They ran from the dark which, like a slow rain of ash, began to obscure the light as if it wanted to trap them. Perhaps turn them to stone. Add new citizens to a dead city. They were sweating when they arrived at the gates, as even the last streaks of gray disappeared from the sky as they can do only over the Mediterranean Sea—with a sudden exasperation.

"Good," he said. "We are safe."

Quietly, he unlocked the gates and they walked into the street that led up the hill to the city above. She could hear music and cars over the dead patience behind them which sounded, she thought, like the moon.

Alice was tired. And as she looked over her shoulder at the gate behind them—the caged shadow it threw over stone and weed—Apollinaro took her hand. He began to lead her up the hill. Toward the noise above.

He was dusty, she noticed, looking down at his hand. His shoes, his pants, even his hair—all of him covered in the fine loose sand that swept through the ruins. Yet his sweat still smelled like ash.

"When do you go home?" he asked, as they stopped at the base of the road. It was pitted, steep, and crosshatched with tread marks where rental cars driven by tourists had skidded and come to a halt.

Apollinaro waited, but not for long. "Come, come," he said. His voice was soft but urgent as he began to lead her again toward a worn path by the road. Beneath a lone cypress tree she stopped him, and turned to look back to the ruins. Peering into the darkness, Alice imagined she could see the villa off in the distance: The veiled lady was still patient inside.

"I'll be going soon," she said.

This time, Alice gave him her hand.

ERIN FLANAGAN

University of Nebraska, Lincoln

INTERVENTION

Harry's mom calls early Saturday morning to tell us she's planning an intervention for Gerald. This will be the third one in three years, and she is convinced it's the one that's going to stick.

"Tell her I'm not here," he hisses. "Tell her I'm out." I point to the clock by the bed: 6:43. How much does he think his mother is willing to believe? He grabs his stomach and pantomimes convulsions. He wants me to say he's not feeling well, and I contemplate telling her it's something serious, like a ruptured lung, broken bones, something that would have her on the next flight to Minneapolis, to teach Harry a lesson about forcing me to lie. I try to listen to Judith on the other end—something about a predicament and Gerald being a loose cannon in the air. He's been on leave from United for five months after a prolonged recovery from back surgery and will return to the skies in the next few weeks.

"Kate," she says again, "I am convinced there is a problem." There is nothing Judith loves more than a problem. Harry is out of the room now and I hear him brushing his teeth. She tells me how Gerald fell asleep on his boat two nights ago, "drunk as a skunk," with his head cocked back and a highball in his hand. Three sets of neighbors saw him before someone thought to call the police, convinced Gerald was dead. "It's a disgrace," Judith says. I hear the water stop in the bathroom. It starts up again with splashing, and Harry hums while washing his face. "You tell Harry that I've got it planned for next Friday and I expect him to be there. Gerald gets home around 5:30 from his physical therapy, and I want everyone in that house by 5:00." It sounds like a birthday party. She says nothing about whether I am invited. "This is it," she says. "You tell Harry his father needs him." Judith hangs up without saying good-bye; she likes the drama of such actions.

Harry comes back in the room with his face clean and his hair every which way. "Your mother's planning another intervention for your dad," I tell him. He comes over and puts his hand on my breast; I can smell his toothpaste. "She wants you there by 5:00 on Friday."

"I'm not flying to Myrtle Beach for another intervention," he says, but I know he will go.

At Harry's college graduation party Gerald got plowed and sang Janis Joplin's "Mercedes Benz" a cappella before the band had even finished setting up. I hadn't met his parents before; they lived in South Carolina and we were in Minneapolis. Judith had worn wool slacks and a sweater even though it was May and the weather was in the eighties.

Judith and I sat at a table together and I tried talking to her about adult topics such as political reform and the tax bill, things she dismissed with a wave of her hand. She was an intimidating Southern lady who until that week had never been north of the Mason-Dixon line. The tables were covered in maroon paper and I ripped off small sheets, tore them in my lap. She wore Shalimar and didn't seem to sweat. Harry came over with his tie wrapped around his head, two beers in his hand, and told her, "Kate and I got a place, it's right in the city. You can see Lake Calhoun from the bathroom window."

She turned her overwhelming, coiffed hairdo toward me and looked at my left hand—now streaked with maroon dye—where there obviously wasn't a ring. "Gerald and I didn't spend one night together before that wedding," she said. "You just don't do that kind of thing in the South. Kids these days have no sense of propriety."

I tried looking her in the eye but settled for the vicinity of her forehead. "Harry loves me," I told her, and it was true. He'd said so, out loud, for the first time two weeks ago before we signed the lease.

Judith turned away from me and watched the band do a horrible rendition of "Crocodile Rock," her clean hands crossed in her lap.

A week later they'd had the first intervention. Harry had gone home for two weeks with his parents before starting his job as a copywriter at McElliott and Jordan. When he got back he told me it'd been "fun."

"How can an intervention be fun?" I asked. He started unpacking his suitcase, dumping most of his clothes down our new laundry chute that led to the basement, then sticking his head in to watch them drop. "What do you mean by 'fun'?"

"You need to know my mother," he said. "She can plan the hell out of anything but it never goes how she wants. Dad ended up leaving with half the people to go bowling, and we didn't get home until after 2:00."

"*You* left the intervention to go bowling?"

"Well, you know," he said. "It *was* more fun." He turned to me and smiled. I knew somehow his actions reflected badly on me.

Harry doesn't call Judith back until Monday, by which time she has left three messages and sent a telegram. "I didn't even know they had these anymore," Harry says, holding the paper from Western Union in his hand. The yellow slip looks like a warning, a threat, a sign of danger, something imminent. I know this is the effect Judith is going for and she's hit the mark. "You need to call her," I tell him, and I hand him the phone.

He comes out of the bedroom fifteen minutes later with a defeated look on his face. "You're going, aren't you?" I say.

He tells me how Judith harangued him into it, used all kinds of familial guilt and coercion. There are relatives coming from as far away as Seattle. "We'll go down on Wednesday, hang out and relax for a few days."

"Your mom wants me there?" I ask. "She said that?"

"Hon, she's excited to see us."

I tell my women's group that meets every Tuesday evening at a coffee shop with framed Georgia O'Keeffe posters that Judith doesn't believe Harry and I should be living together. Her main argument against cohabitation has been a series of clichés, you shouldn't jump off a bridge just because your friends are doing it or don't put the cart before the horse. I tell my group these sayings belong where they originated—back in an earlier century. This is just the sort of quip I prepare beforehand to sound witty and off-the-cuff. There are four of us who meet: Jane, who is divorced with two children and runs a day care; Sarah, who's nineteen, a college student, and a lesbian; Martha, whose husband left her for a girl working the counter at an adult video arcade; and me. After college, many of my friends moved away with husbands or careers while I stayed with Harry and a job managing the gift shop at the Natural History Museum, where I'd worked part-time since I was a sophomore. In college I'd been lucky to find something even remotely related to my geology degree, but now the rocks we sold as paperweights and the eagle feathers we sold as bookmarks only seem silly and depressing.

Telling myself it was something of a joke, I answered an ad in the paper ten months ago. *Women's Lives, Women's Issues: The Evolving Role of the Female Experience.* When the group started we gave only our first names to retain a level of anonymity, although now I know everyone's last name and have sent Christmas cards to their home addresses.

When we began meeting, our agenda was to discuss important issues affecting women today. Issues such as independence, equal pay, and a modern version of equality that celebrates our differences. These are not the issues we discuss. We all cried when Jane's daughter told Jane she'd lost her virginity at the age of fourteen. We watched pornos with Martha and laughed to think what her husband had gotten himself into. We have talked about shoe sales and crow's feet, and we have talked about survival. I like this set of women even though none of us can imagine the others' lives, and we are far from where we assumed we would end up.

At group they tell me I'm doing the right thing by living with a man first. Harry and I have been together for four years now and own furniture together, although we still rent. I wonder about their notions of living with Harry "first" when there's been no indication of what might be second. Martha tells me to write my name in all my books and CDs just in case. "When Gary left he took my Motown collection. I'd been working on that collection a lot longer than my marriage." She smiles. "Harder, too." She says after a breakup it's important to retain a sense of humor, and I wonder if, like my quips about independence, her remarks are planned beforehand.

When I tell them Harry is taking me to Myrtle Beach, they agree this is a positive sign. Jane says it is "important movement toward resolution." Even four years into the relationship, I am constantly looking for signs.

I lie to my boss and tell her there's a family emergency, something with a close aunt, rather than my boyfriend's father. Weary of all the excuses she gets from college kids and high school students, she tells me to be back no later than Monday, that the days missed should be recorded either as vacation time or without pay.

Martha comes over to help me pack. She lies on her stomach, her knees bent with her feet in the air, tracing the design on the bedspread as I load the suitcase. "Is Harry's dad sick?" she asks.

"I don't know," I tell her. "I can't discern how much of this is Gerald or just Judith overreacting again." I say it with an air of knowing, like Judith is someone I've dealt with closely for years. "She tends to do that," I add.

"Why is it mothers-in-law are like that?" I don't correct her. "Jesus, Gary's mom used to come over and steal vegetables out of the garden while I was at work. I hated that. She could have bought them at the store if she'd wanted them. I would have given her the money if she needed it."

I come out of the closet with a black cocktail dress and khaki shorts; I have no idea how to dress for an intervention. "What happened," I say, "between you and Gary? I mean, why do you think he left?"

Martha continues tracing with her eyes focused on the pattern. "I don't know, Kate. I think about it sometimes, not so much anymore, and I'm not sure if I ever really come up with anything. It just seems like something I should have been able to make work." She looks up as if startled. "I think he was lucky to have me."

I start folding Harry's boxers and putting them in the suitcase, counting out undershirts for the number of days we'll be gone. "I miss that, you know," Martha says, and she waves her hand toward the suitcase and looks away. Though I would never admit it to my women's group, there is a comfort—almost a smugness—in having these tasks to do.

Gerald and Judith meet us at the airport Wednesday evening. He's wearing Bermuda shorts and a U of M sweatshirt, while Judith is dressed in summer linen. Harry runs to them with a "whoop!" hugs them both, and says, "I brought Kate. She's been dying to see Myrtle Beach," and I'm angry, yet not surprised.

Gerald hugs me and says, "Damn glad you could make it, Katie," while Judith looks at me severely. I can smell sweetness on his breath, something like rum and curaçao.

Judith drives the twenty minutes back to their house, Gerald beside her and Harry and me in the backseat. Gerald stays turned around for most of the trip, talking to us about changes in the airlines, the price of gasoline, what he likes best about his new boat. I see Judith's mouth stiffen, and I remember it was there that the need for the intervention originated, with Gerald passed out on the boat. "She's got a dead rise of eighteen degrees," he says and leans over to pinch Judith's thigh.

Their house is by the ocean, and though the water is not visible in the darkness, I can smell the salty air the moment I get out of the car. "Welcome home, son," Gerald says, and I hear his voice crack. Harry warned me his father gets emotional over such things, and I wonder how much of it is the drinking.

Gerald and Harry bring in our bags. As we get closer to the house Judith says, "Gerald, put Kate's bags in Missy's old room." She's afraid Harry and I will put up a fight about wanting to sleep together. It occurs to me there's about as much chance of Harry standing up to his mother about this as there was of his not coming in the first place.

"Righto!" Gerald says and hauls the bags through the front door. The foyer itself is intimidating. Sprawling staircase, hardwood floors, a living room that seems the size of a street block. It is considerably more adult than the townhouse where we live, with its small breakfast bar and all-white walls we're not allowed to paint. Harry hightails it up the stairs after his father and leaves Judith to show me silently to my room.

After I unpack I find Harry alone and ask him why he didn't tell his parents I was coming, when he'd led me to believe that they knew. We are in his room, which is still covered with posters from his childhood—a red Corvette, the Beastie Boys, a ludicrous picture of the Go-Gos straddling a motorcycle. "How could you not tell them?" I ask.

"Kate, check this out!" He hands me a Rubik's Cube.

"How could you not tell them?" I am conscious of my voice rising and check myself, not wanting Judith and Gerald to hear us arguing.

He puts his hands on my shoulders and I wince; the right one is bruised from Gerald's bear hug. "I just figured they'd know you were coming, seeing as we're together and all."

"That's not good enough, Harry."

"Well, then maybe I just wanted to give them a chance to get to know you since you've only met them a few times."

"Nope," I say.

"How about, I told them and they forgot?" He smiles impishly.

I set down the Rubik's Cube and cross my arms. "Harry, why am I here? Why did you lie to me?"

This change in approach has caught him off guard. "I didn't tell them because I didn't want my mother to say you weren't invited."

I blink a few times, try to recover from his honesty. "Okay, but why am I here?"

He smiles a sinister grin and I can tell he's preparing a bullshit answer. "No, Harry, why? You owe me that."

His face goes as candid as a child's. "Kate, I couldn't do this alone," he says, and I pull him into my arms.

When we've finished unpacking, Gerald takes us down to the boat to show us the ocean, as if water were something we don't have back in Minnesota, back in the land of ten thousand lakes. Gerald climbs into the boat. "Katie, set your ass right here," he says and slaps the vinyl passenger seat, laughing at the sound his hand makes against the quietude of the ocean.

I climb in next to him; Harry gets into the seat behind me.

"Now this here's an Exciter 270 with 135 horsepower per engine." Gerald takes a sip of his gin and tonic. "Yamaha!" he says, then slouches an arm against the back of my seat and gives me a wink. "Purrs like a woman."

"Jesus, Dad," Harry says, pushing his arm away. I'm not offended, even though I'm already planning to fake indignation when I tell my women's group. There is something childish in Gerald's fumbling— maybe it's the Southern accent—that paints him as harmless. "It's a nice-looking boat," Harry says.

Gerald sits up and puts his hands in his lap, cupping his drink. "I'd take 'er out for a spin but your mother won't give me the keys." He laughs. He knows nothing about the upcoming intervention. "She says I'm on probation after the incident." He raises his hands to make quotation marks around the word *incident*. We sit for a few moments and listen to the waves. Gerald's ice clinks when he takes a drink and I wonder if it has occurred to Harry that his father may have a serious problem.

Gerald barks out a laugh and says, "Listen to this!" hitting the horn with his fist. The sound is quacky and high in the darkness. It sounds like something a girl would win at a carnival. "Pussiest horn ever!" he roars. "Boat came with four life jackets and a damn good stereo. You'd think they could throw in a decent horn. Neighbors make fun of me as far out as Buxton Bay. It's a goddamn embarrassment."

Harry's in the backseat laughing, and Gerald joins in.

That night Harry sneaks into my room as I knew he would. "I can't get to sleep without you," he says. "I hate being in the dark without you."

I take this as proof that Harry loves me. We snuggle in the twin bed, our arms intertwined in a hug, Harry's sweet breath on my cheek. "This is every junior high boy's wet dream," he says, "sneaking in to have sex with your girlfriend when your parents are next door." He laughs softly and wraps his leg around my hip, begins stroking my hair.

"Does your mom usually like your girlfriends?" I say. It's embarrassing to refer to myself as Harry's "girlfriend" when we've been together for so many years. It seems stupid and childish, but I am afraid to use an adult term like "lover."

"God no," Harry says. "She's hated every one of them, ever since Becky Shinkle in the third grade."

"What was she like?"

"Jesus, she was something," he says. "Feathered hair, big brown eyes, the teacher always gave her stickers for her penmanship." He sighs. "I thought we'd be together forever."

"Why didn't your mother like her?"

"I can't remember why, I just know she didn't. Maybe her dad was a Northerner."

"Maybe she was threatened," I say.

"By what, her penmanship?"

"Just threatened."

Harry slips his hand under my T-shirt. "I've seen your penmanship, Kate. My mother has nothing to worry about."

In the morning I wake up alone, Harry having snuck out sometime around 3:00 A.M. so as not to upset Judith. Despite the sex, I am still angry at Harry for having lied to me, and now for abandoning me. When I come into the kitchen, Harry looks up from the paper and smiles, tells me he's had a brainstorm.

"Where's your mom?"

"Thursdays I think she's got some book club. Now really, hon, this is a great idea!"

"Why didn't you stay last night?"

He rolls his eyes. "Dad's gonna love this!"

After breakfast, Harry and I go to a store called Dave's Rock Shock to buy "a horn with balls." That's how Harry describes the horn he's looking for. The clerk is seventeen if a day and greets me as ma'am; this reference makes perfect sense to him. They sell issues of *Low Rider* in a rack by the cash register.

Gerald will be at the airline all afternoon filling out paperwork for his return, and Harry gets the keys to the boat from Judith. She's kept them in her pants pocket for two weeks now, out of Gerald's reach. "I don't know what you're doing," she says, "but if you screw up his toy that father of yours is going to kill you."

In the boat, Harry leans under the driver's seat and fidgets with the wires. It is beyond me how he knows to do this. He feels confident he can install a horn into a piece of high-powered machinery without the aid of directions. I stand on the dock, passing him tools and feeling helpless. "Harry," I say, "do you think your mother likes me?"

He grunts under the seat. "What does it matter if she likes you?"

"I want her to. I want to make a good impression."

"Sometimes I think she doesn't even like me." He hands me two wires and the plastic horn he has removed from the boat.

"No, Har, she likes you." I squeeze the horn and it honks, inconsequentially, in my hand. "She loves you. You're her son."

He comes out from under the seat with a smudge of grease on his cheek. He looks even younger than the clerk at the audio store. "I aggravate her," he says. "On purpose. I like to see her get riled up and take care of things." He smiles and looks as innocent as sugar.

"Do you love me, Harry?" I have the tools in my hands, ready to pass him what he might need next.

"Yeah, I love you," he says. He snorts like it's a dumb question he's not willing to put too much thought into. Like telling me how much he loves the Minnesota Gophers.

"Why?"

He puts down the new horn and stares at me; the sun's hitting my face, and I can't see his eyes. The squinting makes me realize my expression must be a scowl. "How could I not, Kate? You're so good to me." He swats me with the rag he used to wipe the grease from his face. "You take care of me."

"Well, then Harry, why do you think I love you?"

He seems bemused and is silenced by this question. I feel like we are getting dangerously close to something. For a few moments we stare at each other and I can feel the muscles in my stomach contract, feel the heat of the day against my skin. It's as if the last four years have been leading up to this moment, although, of course, that isn't the case. Harry suddenly jumps out of the boat and does a manic version of the Charleston, legs and arms flailing, dissipating the moment. "Is that it?" he says, slightly out of breath with his hands on his knees.

In another minute we would have gone too far to turn back without answers, and I am hesitant, this time, to nod in agreement.

———

When Gerald comes home, Harry tells him there's a problem with the boat—something with the stereo, possibly the equalizer. "Hell's bells!" Gerald says and the four of us tramp down to the dock.

We all climb in—me in the back with Judith, Harry up front with his father. "It's just a funny noise it's been making," Harry says. "Something loud, like the bass is out of control." He tries unsuccessfully to look serious about the situation.

Gerald stops for a moment and turns toward the rest of us. "Does anyone know how much I paid for this boat?" he says. "Does anyone have any idea?"

"Sixteen thousand," Judith says.

"That's right!" Gerald says. He points his finger in the air. "This Yamaha's a pain in my ass!"

"Dad, look at the radio." Harry's hands pass over the stereo buttons, over the equalizer, and land on the horn, which he presses before his father knows what he has done.

Gerald's head remains still, cocked at an angle, as he listens to the cacophonous horn. It is deep and resonant and unexpected after the useless horn that came with the boat. It's so loud Gerald looks around after a moment to see if perhaps it was another boat. "Jesus H. Christ!" Gerald says and Harry throws his head back, claps his hands, moves over to hit the horn again. "Jesus H. Christ!" They are slapping each other's hands away as they compete to hit the horn.

Judith starts to smile, rolls her eyes to the front seat, and winks. "That Gerald's a big goof," she says, and she seems happy with this diagnosis.

The next afternoon, the day of the intervention, people start arriving as early as 3:00; they've come from as far as Albuquerque and Des Moines. Judith tells me she's invited around thirty but she isn't expecting that much of a turnout. "People have things to do on the weekend, especially on such short notice." She rearranges crackers on a plate. "Bowling leagues, golf tournaments. I'm hoping for around twenty."

"What about an interventionist?" I say. "Isn't it supposed to be a small group?"

Judith waves her hand. "Gerald's got a lot of friends who would feel left out if I didn't invite them. Some go back as far as his Marine days. His family alone could fill a stadium."

"What about an interventionist?"

Judith looks at me. She is carrying a pitcher of orange juice and a pitcher of cranberry juice, both with masking tape bearing the word *nonalcoholic.* "Kate, this is my third intervention for the man. Do you really think I don't know what I'm doing by now?" She stands for a moment, the pitchers suspended. "Because there is a problem, Katie. Don't you think?"

I take the orange juice from her hand and touch her lightly on the arm. "There's a problem, Judith," I tell her and she smiles wanly at me before heading toward the living room.

When Harry returns around 4:00 from jogging, there are close to fifteen people milling about. He runs up and hugs his uncle Reggie, bows mockingly to his aunt Gertrude. A man in dress blues comes up, slaps him on the back, tells him he remembers when he was knee high to a grasshopper, and calls him a pissant.

I follow Harry, who runs buoyantly through the foyer and up the stairs to the bathroom. He strips and climbs in the shower. "Harry," I say, "I don't like the looks of this. I don't think this is going to go well."

He sticks his head out from the curtain, his hair gelled up like a shark's fin with shampoo. "Dickerson gave me my first beer when I was eight," he says. "He's been my dad's best friend forever. He wasn't able to make it to the first two and I bet Dad's gonna shit when he sees him."

"Harry, what about the intervention—what about the point of all this?"

"Kate, don't worry. My mom's got a handle on it."

By 5:00 the living room is packed. Judith has set up a buffet table with sodas and juices, little sausages. In a delicate silk pantsuit, she circulates with a tray of hors d'oeuvres. "Gerald's going to be home in about twenty-five minutes and he'll know something's up if he sees you all through the window." Half the people are banished to the kitchen; I don't point out the rows of cars lining the streets. When I offer to help, Judith hands me a tray.

By the time Gerald's Explorer swerves into the driveway, I'm on my second round of stuffed mushrooms and we're out of orange juice. He opens the front door and sees a crowd mingling in the living room. "Hell's bells!" he says, taking a look around. "Gertie? What the hell's going on here? Why aren't you in Tulsa?"

Judith gets up from the couch and walks toward Gerald, touches him on the arm. "Gerald," she says. "We're here to discuss your problem."

Gerald turns his head and looks at her, surveys the room again. "Marty Carlson? I don't think I've seen you since '95."

Judith takes a step. "Gerald, we're here for you."

A rumble has started in the kitchen and out bursts Dickerson singing "Semper Fi." He runs into Gerald from a tackling position, almost knocks him to the floor. "Jesus H. Christ!" Gerald yells. "Jesus H. Christ!" He and Dickerson slap each other on the back while Judith watches from across the room where she has jumped to avoid being tackled.

Harry sits next to me on the love seat with his arm around my shoulders. "You approve of this," I say. "You think this is okay."

"Hon, they haven't seen each other in a decade. Dick's been overseas with his third wife and just got back to the States."

I look toward his mother in the corner. She has recovered and stands straight with her chin forward, but the tray of canapés hangs limply from her hand. "There's a problem, Gerald," she says. "This is serious. Don't you understand that this is serious?"

Dickerson escapes Gerald's headlock, puts up his hands as if he is going to mime his way out of a box, and backs up. "Don't make the little lady mad," he tells Gerald. "Remember that time she cut all your trousers?" He smirks on one side of his face. "She means business." I remember Harry telling me the story of Judith and Gerald as newlyweds, how in the service she cut the inseams of all Gerald's pants to keep him from going to the Officer's Club one night.

Gerald turns toward Judith. "Jude, the last thing I want to do is make you mad, especially after you threw me this party."

She sighs. "It's not a party, Gerald. It's an intervention. We're here because you drink and because I love you."

Judith looks as close to helpless as I ever expect to see her. Gerald lifts his hand, takes one of the canapés from her tray, places it in his mouth, and makes yummy noises as if he is tempting a child to eat. His arm encircles her waist. "My wife's a goddamn gem!" he yells, and Judith nestles her face into his armpit as he tousles her stiff hair and kisses her on the lips.

Harry laughs, "Get a room."

"Knee high to a grasshopper!" Dickerson howls.

I wonder if Harry realizes why his mother does this, why she throws interventions that she knows will have no effect on his father's drinking, although it's obviously a problem. I look up and see she has already been dismissed as Gerald charges again for Dickerson. She looks forlorn in the middle of the room—her hair flattened on one side from the weight of Gerald's chest—as the guests mingle about her.

When the buffet table is almost empty, it comes out that one of the neighbors was in the Third Battalion and the men lunge for the door, heading to his house for a "real drink." Before Gerald leaves, he comes over and puts his arm around Judith, says, "Sugar drawers! I'll be home by midnight!" When he leaves he swats her ass, and she doesn't turn toward him. Compared to the faces of the party guests, her profile looks tightened, resigned, as she walks toward the kitchen.

Harry stands when the other men head for the door. "Don't do it, Harry," I say. "You can't do this to your mother."

He turns around. "This one lasted an hour longer than the second one," he says.

"Don't Harry. You can't desert her."

He leans over to kiss me and I pull away. "Come on, Kate. It's not that big a deal. Dickerson's been MIA for the last decade of my dad's life. I want to be there." He is starting to whine and I stand up, feeling an ultimatum coming, although even before I speak I wonder if it will be an empty threat, one I'm not willing to follow through.

"Harry, I'm telling you in all seriousness, do not leave this intervention." It seems a joke now even to call it that. "I won't be here when you get back, I mean it."

Harry looks at his feet, over at his mother, scratches his head. He looks much like he did the day before out in the sunshine, working on the boat. "Kate, I won't be gone long," he says, and smiles a pleading sort of smile as he turns for the door.

By 10:00 the house is empty. I bring the paper plates into the kitchen, wrap the hors d'oeuvres in Saran Wrap, and put them in the fridge. Judith has been missing for close to an hour and I find her out on the boat in the darkness. I tentatively put my foot on the passenger seat and the waves create the disconcerting feeling that I am suspended somewhere between solidity and the unknown. I sit down next to her, wondering if she has been crying, and I look straight ahead rather than directly at her face.

"I shouldn't have invited Dickerson," she says. "Dickerson was my big mistake." She is quiet for a moment before declaring, dramatically, "I sometimes wonder if that man even loves me."

"I don't think that's the issue," I say and am surprised to find I believe it. Before I can think I tell her, "He just loves that you try so damn hard." She snorts, and I glance over at her, surprised by the indelicate noise. She puts her hand to her face and covers her nose, but I can see her smiling. She snorts again, and I feel brave. "What it is, Judith, is that more than anything, he wants you to *keep* trying. He wants you to keep planning these damn things so he can know you care, but he doesn't ever want to change."

She turns her body toward me and I can see the traces of tears on her face. "Do you think that's it?" she asks, and I nod—I do. She turns forward again for a moment and I see her relax, staring at the water lapping against the boat. I'm getting used to the feeling now, the disjointedness of not being on the land. "And what about Harry?" she asks. "What does he want?" I am caught off guard by this question and remain silent, thinking about Harry and his sweet teenage smile. His gift to his father and the innocent, childish belief that everything will mend by itself.

"And what about you?" Judith asks.

I turn to my potential mother-in-law, who thirty years earlier had the spunk to cut the crotch out of her husband's uniform and now sits alone waiting for him to come back from where he shouldn't be in the first place. It's so easy for me to catapult myself that many years into the future, into a silk pantsuit and an identical marriage, Harry's pants hanging whole and unchallenged in the bedroom closet. He will come home tonight, chagrined and apologetic, and I will take him in my arms as I did the night before last. It seems inevitable now, and I wonder when Judith realized the same—at the first intervention, at the altar, on the bedroom floor of the officers' housing with a pair of scissors and a thirty-four-inch waistband in her hands.

It is now I hear it: the horn, breaking through the silence. A deep, steady sound louder than anything I can remember. It's like a foghorn, or a god, or a godlike foghorn, calling us home from sea. I look at Judith; the sound seems to have surprised her also, although her hand is on the horn and she's pressed it on purpose. It seems out of character for her, and out of character for the small size of the boat and the silence of the ocean. She begins to smile, and she blows the horn again. I feel the unsteady boat shake from the force of the blast, although we are secured to the dock by ropes underwater; we aren't going anywhere. I cover her hand with my own, press, and wait for the horn to sound into the night. I sit and wait for something more than just the inevitable echo to resound back.

HA-YUN JUNG

Emerson College

﹏

OUR LADY OF THE HEIGHT

On August 15, 1998, my husband was released from his 0.75-*pyong* prison cell after five years, eight months, and two days. Or so his mother told me; I had not continued my daily count after the first thousand. He stepped out to the streets from behind the faded emerald green steel gates, his face pale and placid like a monk's, and looked up at the overcast sky as if it were too bright for him. Though I was standing only several meters from him, our daughter, Na-yung, by my side with a bouquet of yellow chrysanthemums, their petals withering in the heat, he didn't seem to know which way to set his foot.

"Mr. Yun Ik-ho, could we have a picture with your family?" Reporters approached and camera shutters began to go off. The TV news that night would air a two-minute segment on the presidential pardon marking the fifty-third anniversary of Korea's liberation from Japan, and announce a long list of names—of septuagenarian spies from the North, alleged Communist agitators, labor activists, student saboteurs. People would barely recall any of these names the following morning.

Na-yung held out the flowers and my husband's cheeks brushed against mine in a quick, awkward embrace, his skin dry and rough, as if all his bodily fluids had long seeped out of him. It was the first time we touched, in five years, eight months, and two days.

The train is approaching the Gare SNCF in Belfort. We left Zurich three hours ago and crossed the French-Swiss border, into the region of Franche-Comté—the Free County. I take down my suitcase from the rack above my head. My husband sits across from me with his shoulder pressed to the window. That's how he sits or stands anywhere, like he's stuck to a wall or a corner. He is traveling with only a sports bag, now tucked neatly beneath his left elbow, but my luggage is heavy and inconvenient. It's one of those old-fashioned suitcases that weighs a ton even when it's empty. I open it and look for my wool scarf because it is snowing outside. One of the locks on the suitcase has been a nuisance since we arrived in Europe and I struggle to close it, but the metallic clicking does not sound right. With the banging of my hand, something springs out and falls to the floor, rolling under the seats. It must be a hook or a small attachment for the lock. I kneel down and peer underneath, but I don't even know what I'm looking for. All this time, my husband takes no notice; he seems captivated by the whirlwind of snowflakes. The first snowfall he has greeted outside of prison.

On his first night home, I put on the only nightdress I own, a silky long-sleeve too warm for the weather, because I felt I should, out of etiquette. He turned out the lights and we lay still for a while, then he pulled me to lie on my side and buried his head between my breasts. "Your smell ... it's too sweet ... it makes me dizzy," he said and fell asleep, abruptly, like a candle blown out with a forceful breath. He did not wake up for an entire day. And now we are on our first-ever overseas trip. We still have not had sex.

Belfort is a town locked inside centuries-old fortifications and citadels. I guess people find them beautiful. The taxi driver is taking us through the *vielle ville,* past a gargantuan carving of a reclining lion, a moss-covered château, and the ruddy façade of a cathedral. The snow has stopped, but the air is still filled with the damp, gray gloom that's been hanging over us throughout the trip. I suspect the driver is hiking the fare by taking the long way around, but my husband is pleased to see the historical attractions.

"That is the Belfort Lion," he says, "Frédéric Bartholdi's monument commemorating the fort's successful defense during the Franco-Prussian War of 1870. Since medieval times this region has gone through numerous invasions, and Belfort is its proud and brave garrison town. Since the French claimed it in the Thirty Years War, it has expanded and modified its fortresses, and has managed to guard itself."

His time in solitary confinement has turned Yun Ik-ho, the man once known as the eloquent theoretician of the progressive labor movement, into an encyclopedia. Surrounded by cement walls with barely enough room to stretch his body, he spent his time doing nothing but reading, everything from Buddhist scriptures to deconstructionist criticism. He has traveled around the world, following each destination with the tip of his index finger on maps and guidebooks. The letters I received from him, marked at the bottom of each page with a purple "Censored" stamp, gradually turned into long lists of books and periodicals. And now he speaks only of facts, clear-cut and indisputable.

Looking out the window on my side, I nod, only slightly.

All the information he provides me about Belfort does not make the town charming for me. The old stone walls are overbearing and make the entire scenery appear dark and oppressed. Even the street names suggest militant determination: Place de la Résistance, Rue des Armes, Avenue Général Leclerc. It feels like the whole town is obsessed with the duty to guard, to protect, to push away penetrating forces. Still, my husband goes on and on about the Maginot Line and Nazi bombings, and again I am tempted into the wicked fantasy that I've been nurturing since we arrived in Europe. About leaving my suitcase and this man behind—in the café, the Kunsthaus, or the airless pension room—and going off by myself, his passport, plane ticket, all our travelers' checks and marks and francs stuffed into my purse. Perhaps I wouldn't be thinking such things if we had brought Na-yung along. I have never been separated from her for more than a day.

The taxi stops at the deep corner of a cul-de-sac, about ten minutes from the town center, past rolling hills and roads lined with poplar trees. Compared to Switzerland, the landscape on this side of the Jura mountains is more verdant, although the weather is similarly chilling and sunless. We get out in front of a two-story cottage with an off-white finish and orange shutters on square windows, familiar from old photos that I have dug up in my research for this trip. The driver opens the trunk and I remember the broken lock on my suitcase. I decide to carry it in my arms, lest it burst open on the ground, which is muddy with a thin, melting layer of snow. My husband, with his bag strapped across his chest, stands with his back to the house and looks around the street and the hazy hills that stretch beyond the valley. I clasp my hands tightly around the suitcase and start toward the house.

At that moment, the front door opens and Madame Sohn steps out, wearing a benign smile. A spacious garden, looking dead and dry, stands between us, but I can see that her petite features are grace-ful, full of gentle pride. I had recognized that aura even in her mug shot, taken a quarter century ago by the South Korean intelligence agency. Already, I am intimidated by her presence.

The so-called European Student Ring incident was a fabricated espi-onage case during the 1970s that involved some fifty Koreans in Germany and Switzerland. A typical tactic of the Park Chung Hee regime, the crackdown helped keep antigovernment sentiments under control halfway through the dictator's third term in office, during which he declared himself president for life. Like the other students, scholars, and artists involved, the Zurich-based painter Sohn Se-in and his wife were kidnapped in the middle of the night and flown back to Seoul, where they were found guilty of participat-ing in North Korea's scheme to infiltrate the intelligentsia of the South through their envoys in the Eastern bloc. Their story is not much different from our own, only my husband and I were not in-ternationally renowned artists, just exhausted unionists in Seoul's Kuro Industrial Complex, where chimneys spit out black smoke and soot all day and, more often than not, into the night. And because our case was of far lesser political impact, I, being the wife, was re-leased on parole and sent home to take care of Na-yung, unlike Madame Sohn.

Times have changed now, I guess. The dissident who narrowly es-caped being murdered by Park Chung Hee's men is our newly elected president. Former leaders of the socialist movement have become minor celebrities, appearing on TV debate shows and even PC ads. Once-banned protest songs are used in campaign commercials dur-ing election season.

During that time of change and progress, while my husband sat inside his cell with his books, I wrote articles for *Women's Life*—never had the privilege of even thinking about doing any serious writing. I got paid by the printed page and had to grab anything that came my way—the surefire grapefruit-and-egg diet, retro-style home decoration tips, the best-selling writer who'd given birth out of wedlock. Some months, when my car broke down or Na-yung had to go see a doctor or my husband asked for an expensive imported hardcover, I had to make up sex counseling Q&As and "true-life" stories for the brown pages at the end of the book—"The kinkier the better," the editor would say, every time.

Unlike me, my husband was eager to take this assignment when the *Weekly Sisa* offered to pay us to travel to Europe, though not in luxury, and carry out interviews with those formerly accused as part of the European Student Ring. For me, there was nothing inspiring about the picture: the two of us in Europe, in the dead of winter, listening to stories of pain and survival. Besides, the magazine approached us, not on my behalf, but because having Yun Ik-ho, the freed activist, carry out the interview provides an interesting angle.

We've met with eleven people so far in Berlin and Zurich and my husband has rarely spoken, just sitting there with kind, calm eyes, like a priest in a confession booth. Belfort is our last stop before our flight departs from Zurich two days from now. He hasn't opened his mouth since we began our talk with Madame Sohn. He sits at the far end of the sofa, attached to the armrest.

"Looking back now, it all seems like a joke, almost," Madame Sohn says, her Korean still carrying a heavy dialect of the southern provinces. "The North Korean diplomats would treat us to dinner and encourage my husband's use of traditional motifs in his paintings." Her smile faded once we settled down with cups of tea in her living room, the air filled with the aroma of bean paste soup simmering in the kitchen. It is the smell of home, which I feel has been out of my grasp for a long time.

When the magazine approached her for the interview, Madame Sohn invited us to spend the night at the house, saying there were too many rooms for one person anyway. Upon our arrival, she took us upstairs to the guest bedroom, with a bed that seemed much smaller than the queen-sized ones in hotels and pensions, then she showed us the rest of the house. On the first floor, the late master's studio was preserved as it was when he was alive, the easels strewn about, palettes and brushes neatly arranged on the sturdy, rectangular table, its surface caked with dry patches of oil paint. One corner had been turned into a shrine of sorts, with a framed black-and-white photo of the painter—his face handsome, his smile childish, his hair like Albert Einstein's—and incense burning in a bronze pot filled with sand from his hometown on Korea's southwestern coast.

"What about the accusations that Mr. Sohn received money from the North for his exhibitions?" I ask.

"Those stories had all been made up even before our arrest," Madame Sohn answers, her tone firm, though slightly quivering. "The investigators pushed a fake statement into my face, saying my husband had confessed to everything. When I denied it, the tortures began. I stood naked in an unheated room, my eyes blindfolded, freezing-cold water splashing down from above my head every five minutes. It got worse every day. They gave up only when I fainted, hanging upside down, the water pouring into my nostrils. But when the trial began, they presented those statements as evidence anyway. It took only a day to find all of us guilty."

All this, of course, I already know, or can assume.

My husband pours himself another cup of green tea from the teapot and holds it up to his face with both hands, peering into the celadon teacup like a dazed fool. The vapor from the hot liquid steams up his glasses and it looks like he's hiding behind a thick haze.

"Could you tell us about your decision not to attend the National Museum exhibition?" I ask Madame Sohn, who glances at my husband for a moment.

She and her husband had not been able to return to Korea after their release—that was when they came to settle here in Belfort—but the new government recently proposed to lift Madame Sohn's persona non grata status, so that she could be present at the first Sohn Se-in retrospective in Seoul this spring. She had flatly refused.

"We've been offered such deals before. The so-called civilian governments want us to come back, to promote their support of human rights. But we demand a formal apology for the espionage case and for our names to be cleared of the charges. There is no reason for those conditions to change, although they probably thought, 'Of course that old crank will accept, now that her husband's dead.'"

Madame Sohn's face is old and full of deep wrinkles around her crescent-shaped eyes and straight mouth, which she wears like proud war wounds, no attempt to hide them with makeup. She appears ten years older than her age, because she does not dye her white hair, held together in a loose ponytail. Her face, her frankness, the way she still uses "us" and "we" in every sentence, all seem to suggest that she's a woman who has no regrets about the life she lived as the good wife—no misgiving, no blame. The kind of woman who makes me feel inadequate and wrong.

My own makeup feels thick and sticky in the warmth of this house. Seoul is a city where women cannot stand to walk around with bare faces, without a dab of color on the lips, without covering up the spots and the flaws. I have become one of those women, though I am not sure when.

The tape recorder is reeling in silence and the sun has set outside.

I turn off the machine, suddenly tired. My husband looks as if he's sleeping with his eyes open. I thank Madame Sohn for the interview, and her hospitality.

"I think it's wonderfully romantic that you're taking this trip together—reunited after so long! Have you been able to make time to see some sights?" she asks, putting our empty cups on a tray.

In fact, we have been going through the whole tourist routine between interviews—the Brandenburg Tor, the Nikolai Quarter, Christmas lights on Bahnhofstrasse, and all sorts of museums, large and small. Our itinerary consists of only two major cities and Belfort, and my husband has been scrutinizing the attractions in his guidebooks, from A to Z. We go and see them so that he may mark the checklist in his mind. I am relieved that the last leg of our journey has taken us to a remote town—whose famous forts we have already passed through.

To my surprise, my husband nods at Madame Sohn's question. She looks straight into his face with a glimmering, understanding gaze, making no effort to contain her joy at having made a connection.

"I feel bad that I've dragged you all the way out here, where there really isn't much to see. But my husband and I found it comforting here, deep in the 'Free County,' surrounded by the serene hills," she says, leaning toward us across the coffee table.

"Actually, there's something I'd like to see..." my husband says. My head does a ninety-degree turn. He hasn't mentioned anything to me, and we are scheduled to leave on the train for Zurich in the morning.

"Oh, you must mean the forts?" Madame Sohn asks.

"Well, no, it's not here, but near here...in Ronchamps..."

For a moment, Madame Sohn does not seem to make out his words. Then her face brightens. "Ah, Ronchamps." In her mouth, the word becomes an elaborate parade of beautiful, unpronounceable nasal syllables. "Yes, of course—la Chapelle Notre-Dame-du-Haut. A breathtaking place. You must see it."

"But we really should leave early in the morning," I protest.

"Ah, *c'est dommage*. It's only half an hour from here," Madame Sohn says. She's glancing at my husband, who's looking at me. I'm staring at the teacups, but I can feel him looking at me, pleading with his eyes.

"Please, let me help you with dinner." I reach for the tray and start carrying it to the kitchen. The two of them stay seated, for a moment, then Madame Sohn follows me to the sink. She hands me a plate of marinated *pulkogi* from the refrigerator and a pair of wooden chopsticks, then heats up a pan.

"Ji-won, if you could take care of that for me while I set the table and get the soup and rice ready," she says. I am grateful that she is wise enough to drop the Ronchamps issue. "I hope you don't mind my calling you by name. It's a very pretty name—I'd definitely prefer it to Mrs. Yun, if it were mine. What characters do you use for it?"

"'Ji,' meaning 'to know,' and 'won,' meaning 'garden.'"

"Garden of wisdom," she says, looking up from the flatware drawer.

"That's what it means," I answer, but it strikes me that my name no longer seems to reflect who I am but rather the person I wish to become. The beef slices are beginning to sizzle in the pan, curling into brown, gnarled clumps, and I turn them over. Madame Sohn is standing next to me, with silver chopsticks and spoons.

"I was a bit concerned, talking about torture. Perhaps I went too much into detail. Mr. Yun seemed shaken, listening to me. I apologize, I should have thought ahead," she says. Her eyes tell me she is being earnest, but I feel intruded upon, almost insulted. I hadn't noticed anything; I didn't even look his way.

"It's all right," I say, stammering. The words do not feel right.

Madame Sohn rests her hand on my shoulder for the briefest moment, then briskly walks out to the dining table. Finally alone, I sigh, and lift my eyes up from the stove, to the window facing the sink. Nothing but stark darkness outside.

Over dinner and wine we talk, intermittently, about Na-yung, the new president, the other people we've interviewed, then Sohn Se-in's paintings, which somehow leads to Le Corbusier, an abstract painter himself, whom Sohn admired, and so we are back to discussing the chapel at Ronchamps—the architect's masterpiece, it turns out. Madame Sohn provides us with up-close impressions of the building, while my husband fills in the factual details, the materials used, the history of the site, the controversy stirred up by the outrageous design. He is not drinking—he never does anymore—but I am, and I think, in my drunken impatience and irritability, these two people are conspiring to send me up on that hill, to that Chapel of Our-Lady-of-the-Height. And I think, well, then I'll go, if only to stop all this talking about it. There's nothing waiting for us in Zurich anyway except our flight the day after tomorrow. So it's settled, we're spending another night here.

"Excellent," Madame Sohn says.

"*Très bien,*" I say, wishing I weren't so drunk.

My husband, of course, says nothing. I can't even tell if he's pleased.

Forty is the age of *pulhok,* an age free from temptations. That's what we were taught in school, learning the writings of Confucius. But he's the man who emphasized hierarchical order between the king and his subjects, between parents and children, between husbands and wives. And I will be turning forty in a couple of weeks, when the New Year arrives, but I am not free from anything. Right now, lying in bed, I am tempted to sneak downstairs and pour myself another glass of wine, only I'm not sure if Madame Sohn is asleep yet. My husband is curled up in a tight ball on his side of the bed—we pulled out the night table on his side and pushed the bed against the wall, which is the way he needs it—and his breathing is steady and quiet.

My husband's arrest came at a time when we had begun to talk about leaving the factories. We'd been there for five years and married for three, our daughter just past her second birthday. To join the working class, we lived with borrowed names and forged IDs that concealed our college-educated backgrounds—"employed under camouflage" was the term we used. But the year Na-yung was born, the Berlin Wall came down. The consequences of an event that happened halfway around the world were alarming. With the decline of Communism, the progressive socialist movement in Korea became a faltering cause. We had stayed behind in Kuro-dong longer than other colleagues and before we could make up our minds whether wanting a better environment for our daughter was a selfish act, my husband, on his way home from a late shift on the hi-fi stereo speaker assembly line, was taken away and accused as a North Korea sympathizer, a spy.

A week ago we were in Berlin, where the wall no longer stands. Street vendors were still selling remnants of the wall—small, hard, insignificant scraps of cement.

I would try, during the following five years, to make it to Tapkol Park where the Families of the Politically Oppressed group held its weekly rally wearing purple scarves. I tried to remember to come home early on the days when my mother-in-law was pickling a month's supply of kimchi. And to make the five-hour drive to Sunchon every month with Na-yung for a four-minute visit, the three of us staring into the fiberglass partition.

But there would be evenings when I couldn't bear to head back to the crammed apartment fifteen subway stops and a twenty-minute bus ride from downtown, to find Na-yung asleep in front of the TV, sucking her thumb, and my mother-in-law lying on the heated *ondol* floor without bothering with the lights, crying, "My poor baby, my poor son." On those nights, I drank—it's always too easy to find someone to drink with—and sometimes there would be men, friend of a friend, friend of a colleague, friend of a stranger, who'd stay on later than anyone else. At some seedy inn in the back alleys of Chongno or Shinchon, we paid a half-rate—for people who don't, can't, spend the night—and went up to a room only slightly larger than my husband's cell. There would be a knock on the door, the innkeeper carrying a tray with a stainless steel kettle of barley tea and a roll of toilet paper, watching as we wrote down our fake names and citizen registration numbers in the guest book. Then it was done very quickly, and I'd be out on the street filled with drunks arguing, vomiting, crying into public phones, where I'd hold up my hand to catch a bullet taxi, which promised the fastest ride out of Seoul's past-midnight hours.

I feel my husband tossing on his side of this small bed. Perhaps we are both only pretending to be asleep. Perhaps he's thinking about Madame Sohn hanging by a rope tied around her ankle, unconscious, in a basement room with no windows. Perhaps he's recalling the things that they did to him—a wooden bar striking his back over and over, a heavy, wet towel pressing down his nose and mouth until he couldn't breathe, a crate full of investigation papers crashing down on his penis, stretched out on the table in front of him as if it were no longer a part of his body. He has never told me these things; these are things that have happened to others and which, I imagine, might have happened to him.

I climb out of bed and tiptoe downstairs. I take the cordless phone into the kitchen and dial for the operator. Her voice is coarse, thick with accent. It is early morning in Seoul, before Na-yung leaves for school. I want to run my fingers through her fine, light hair, feel her warm head on my shoulder, hear her say, "*Umma,* my pinky hurts," "I don't like my lunch," "I miss you." But the collect call doesn't go through. The woman on the other end didn't seem to understand and she has hung up, the operator tells me.

At the bottom of Bourlemont Hill, as the taxi turns onto Rue de la Chapelle, my husband insists we get out. Ronchamps is tiny, the town centered around three blocks of traditional businesses—the baker, the sausage maker, the tobacco shop. We start walking uphill and the paved road is steep, hard, and cold beneath my feet. The sun should be directly over our heads now, but after a few hours of hazy sunlight earlier the clouds quickly gathered and covered up the sky, as they always seem to do.

As we proceed, we soon lose sight of any trace of town life and both sides of the road are lined with shrubs and trees, some green, some naked—various types of conifers, with their comblike leaves and needles, and many deciduous trees, some still holding onto their color, a remnant of a brighter season. I walk with my hands dipped in my coat pockets. My husband's gloved hands are held together behind his back, resting on his bony hips like an old man's. His eyes are roaming among the trees, attempting to match each one with the names drifting in his mind. Poplar, holly, silver birch, weeping willow, he announces. We walk surrounded by a landscape deprived of warmth and sunlight, but of course, these trees have no fear, no despair about making it through the winter. They do not make an effort; they simply bear it, standing upright.

The hike goes on, endlessly. It's becoming too strenuous for me to keep in rhythm with my husband, now walking several meters ahead of me. I call to him and ask how far we have to go, without disguising my irascible tone. He turns to me and waits for me to catch up with him. "The chapel sits 472 meters above sea level," he says, look-ing up, as if he can see it beyond the forests. "Take your time," he says, almost in a whisper, and starts up again. I stand still, catching my breath, wondering if I should turn back before I go too far. The height seems unreachable to me. I could just turn the other way and keep going, down the hill. Then I see my husband, his legs stagger-ing, the new pair of black leather shoes he got for this trip soiled with mud and dust. His feet are probably not used to them yet—flat-soled white rubber *komushin* are the only shoes allowed in prison. Perhaps the skin at the back of his heels is grazed and blistered. I take a step toward him and start walking again, trying to remember what his bare feet look like.

By the time I reach the summit, I am faint in the head, as if my blood is not circulating fast enough to keep up with my breathing. I feel a tight, heavy pull in my hamstrings and drops of sweat cling to the hair around my ears. My husband is waiting by the gate to the chapel grounds holding two tickets. When he sees me, he points to the vast whiteness beyond the gate.

I do not recognize right away that this is the chapel, for it is not like a church at all. There is nothing that resembles the extravagance of the Romanesque-Gothic cathedrals we've seen in Europe. From afar it looks like a mammoth hybrid of abstract shapes, slanting this way and that, put together for display on top of the hill. There is nothing that distracts the eye here, only the sky and the green grass. As we approach, I see that the little rectangular holes scattered on the wall facing us are colored-glass windows and the white plaster façade is covered with a marvelous gray roof that looks something like a giant stingray reaching for the sky. Then I recall Madame Sohn and my husband talking about this bizarre design, that the architect's in-spiration for the roof was a crab's shell. But now my husband does not open his mouth. He stands in front of the main entrance, a door made up of eight panels of steel, painted with playful images in red and yellow and jade green. He breathes in, then places his right hand upon the painting of a huge blue, open hand and pushes the door. I follow.

Once the door closes behind us, it seems completely dark inside for a moment. I feel a chill at the tip of my nose. There is nothing here, really, but the altar with a plain cross and rows of wooden benches on untreated concrete floors for the congregation; everything seems to have been stripped to its bare, austere bones. My legs are shaking, the muscles begging for rest. I take a seat at the far end of the row. There is a young man, blond, sitting several rows in front of me, carrying a large backpack and looking up at the slanted ceiling in awe. Two children, a boy and a girl, follow their parents around, hopping and galloping, climbing into the recesses in the wall to touch the colorful windows. On a better day the sun would penetrate into the chapel through these openings, small and large, and make up a grand mosaic of light in this grim interior. But today the windows on the white walls reveal only slices of a colorless sky.

Then I see the Virgin Mary. This is her place, la Chapelle Notre-Dame-du-Haut. She stands like an antique doll, inside a glass box fitted into one of the windows above the altar, small and paltry. Religion is something ungraspable to me, the miracle of faith, of redemption—but this sad figurine seems human, womanly. My feet and hips feel numb from the cold air rising from the concrete. Simple paintings of flowers, stars, birds—childish in their lightness, their spirit of play—decorate the windows. The word *marie* is also painted on many of them, in script handwriting, like a teenager's scribbling of his first girlfriend's name in a corner of his notebook. It is this sense of freedom that I find comforting in this humble sanctuary, this unadorned openness—not its exterior grandeur, not the sacred height of the hill on which it sits.

I stand and look around. The other tourists have left now and I don't see my husband, though I haven't seen him go out the door. I walk across to the wall on the opposite end of the altar. To my left, there is a space enclosed with a curvilinear wall, fading light flowing in from the skylight. It appears to be a place for individual meditation, with a mini-altar in the center. I follow the wall to the right, which turns into a dim corridor, at the corner of which seems to be another small altar, darker than the first one. As I make a turn to step onto this oval-shaped space, I nearly bump into someone's face. I let out a scream.

It is my husband, his back pressed tight against the wall, his hands desperately wrapped around his upper arms. I try not to appear shaken, but I wish I hadn't seen him like this.

"You startled me," I say, as I look away and walk to the other side of the altar.

He does not say anything. His breathing is getting rough. I am beginning to feel afraid. I start heading toward the corridor, taking casual steps.

"I'm sorry. I didn't mean to scare you," he says, almost inaudibly.

I stop and turn around. He hasn't moved at all. His eyes are full of confusion.

"This space, it reminds me of my cell," he says, staring into the wall behind me.

I feel I should step closer to him, but I can't. "You're out of prison now. You're a free man."

"Am I?" he says, as if his words are draining all his energy. Then slowly, he looks up, toward the skylight, so high above our heads, letting in too little light.

"But I feel comfortable here. Freer than I've felt anywhere out of prison," he says. Then suddenly, he laughs—a loud, empty laugh. The sound echoes around the walls. "Pathetic, don't you think?"

He keeps laughing, his arms still crossed on his chest, his mouth open wide. I wish he would stop. I'm scared that if he goes on, he might end up crying. I take a few steps forward and stand in front of him, resting my weight on the altar. The cement feels like ice, the chill crawling up my arm, down my spine. Slowly, my husband's laughter fades. He drops his arms and looks into my eyes—his entire face seems to be collapsing, giving in to weakness. I recognize it, instantly. Then I realize that if I held up my arm right now, I would be able to touch him.

Madame Sohn seems saddened to see us leave, but we must catch the first train to Zurich to arrive at the airport in time for our flight. The day's first light is spreading across the sky, somewhere behind the thick clouds. The three of us stand outside the house, waiting for the taxi. My suitcase with the broken lock stands in the doorway.

Last night, as I was packing, Madame Sohn came into the room and asked if I wanted some rope or heavy-duty tape to secure the luggage. Perhaps that would have been a wise thing to do, but I said that it was okay, that I might as well carry it on the plane. Then she asked what I thought of the chapel and I didn't know what to answer. A look of concern and curiosity appeared in her eyes and she said, "Is everything all right? Did something happen?" And I had to smile and tell her that the chapel was breathtaking, as she had said.

I do not know, not yet, if something did happen up there.

The taxi arrives and my husband shakes Madame Sohn's hand. Then she turns to me and we embrace. Her strength, her will, her loneliness overwhelm me, but I hold her frail shoulders for a long time. "I hope we can see each other in Korea, soon," I say. I see tears in her eyes, but she smiles, and says she'd like that.

We are heading east, to the Gare in Belfort and I notice that a narrow sliver of light has opened up along the distant horizon before us. Red and orange rays peek out onto the rambling landscape, as if to tease the trees on the hills, reminding them that this bright, warm light is always there behind the gray clouds, even if they can't feel it. That small gift from the sun lingers on, until we make a turn and move into the town, the fortresses taking a blurred shape in my vision.

JEB LIVINGOOD

University of Virginia

⁓

OH, ALBANY, MY LOVE

Michelle tells her children to call us both uncle—Uncle Philip and Uncle Allen—and I can see the momentary confusion in their faces. But then her little boy nods a sleepy nod and the daughter starts pulling Allen's suitcase toward the hallway stairs. The wheels squeak.

"You're in my room," she says.

The little girl's name is Laura and she wants to move the luggage by herself. Allen, with more craft and subtlety than I'm used to, lifts one of the side handles to keep the wheels from scraping along the steps. He's tall and very gaunt and has to stoop as he climbs so that Laura doesn't realize he's carrying most of the weight. There's a small grin on his face. I've never really seen him with kids before and find his sudden playfulness amusing. Allen is full of surprises today.

We've been driving all afternoon and evening, fighting traffic and tolls, trying to reach Albany at a reasonable hour. Even so, it's well past nine and we're road-weary and a little tense. We've come for the midwinter Festival, a gathering of artists and crafters at the convention center downtown. I've convinced Allen that the show will give him some much-needed exposure and that it's also a good excuse to visit Michelle and Jon Prentice, his old college friends. My reasons are also selfish. I wanted to get out of Alexandria. Allen hasn't felt much inspiration lately, and our weekends have become pretty sullen because of it. I thought a change of scenery might do us both some good.

Michelle bends down to pick up Porter, the little boy, and he rests his chin on her shoulder. His eyes are puffy, red-rimmed. He's been sick all week.

"Where's Daddy?" he asks.

Michelle begins to rock him back and forth.

"Home soon," she answers.

Michelle has lovely brown hair that falls to her shoulders, the strands haphazard, almost abandoned, and a thin, elegant face. It's a beauty that's enhanced by nervousness. Her head tilts slightly forward, her expression timid, doubtful, like she still can't accept attention. I think she's one of those women who blossomed late in life—the awkward girl from high school who turns heads at the ten-year reunion.

I tell her that Allen and I can still get a hotel room, that we're worried about the late notice.

"Don't be silly," she says. "You're like family."

We exchange a few more pleasantries, mostly about how nice it is to finally meet. Then Porter lets out a sigh and thumps his head against Michelle's neck. It's time for bed. Michelle begins to rub her fingers between his shoulder blades, stroking the aches away.

When I say good night and go upstairs, Laura is helping Allen put his clothes in a drawer. Her room is narrow and warm, with a radiator clicking underneath a picture window. Laura sees my suitcase, looks back at her small blue dresser, and very matter-of-factly says,

"This will never do." Almost seven, she has china-doll eyes but can already frown like an adolescent. Allen is smiling and shaking his head.

He says, "Thanks, Laura. We'll manage."

The Prentices' house is an old but very small Victorian with only one full bathroom. We have to wait for Laura and Porter and Michelle to finish washing up before we can get settled. The pipes rattle in the walls every time the water comes on. Allen lies back on the bed, really a futon couch, and closes his eyes. I fall down next to him. The hard mattress is wonderful, and Michelle has spread flannel sheets and fluffed the comforter. We hear a few cars outside, the hiss of tires on salted streets. A pair of voices drifts up from the sidewalk, two women talking, their feet crunching in day-old snow. When I stare at the ceiling, the square light fixture in the center, it feels like everything is moving again, like I'm still on the road.

"Stars," Allen says, pointing up.

There are small glow-in-the-dark stickers on the plaster. A child's room. We will sleep beneath Orion, Cassiopeia, and the Big Dipper.

I say, "You didn't tell me Michelle was so pretty."

Allen closes his eyes again. "You've seen pictures," he says.

"But she looks different in person."

As if in answer to my fears, Allen reaches over and pats my hand. "No need to be jealous," he tells me. His fingers are rough, callused from using stone chisels and sanding papers. It's as though his skin absorbs the work, becomes a part of it. But there's also something comforting in his motion—Allen's hand touching mine—and it's all the more pleasurable in its absent, half-conscious movement, the way his fingers trace the back of my wrist. It's a wonderfully lulling sensation and we listen to the house grow quiet, the rooms turn silent and still.

The next morning, I park our rental car in a downtown garage and we spend twenty minutes trying to find the convention center. The

Rockefeller Empire State Plaza is a massive underground construction of tunnel and stone. Broad corridors and black-flecked floors lead to agency buildings, the state capitol, food courts. It's the mall to end all malls—a maze of corridors and side passages. Men and women in suits and skirts hustle around us, their voices echoing against marble. Signs point in every direction. There are so many letters and instructions that we quickly become overwhelmed and can't tell where anything is.

"My god," Allen says, "it's *Logan's Run*."

A man at a coffee concession tells us how to find the registration area. When we pick up our packet, we see that our booth assignment is 234. The high number feels like a bad omen. A map directs us to a bunch of metal doors. Through them, in an enormous convention hall with four tiered levels, we find our booth, on the lowest level and almost tucked in the corner. The dregs. There are ten other booths on our level—more late registrants—none of them set very close to ours. To our left, a man with a wheelchair is selling aluminum wind chimes; to our right, two women are setting up birdhouses made from PVC piping. They've posted a small sign that reads FREE COOKIES! They have frumpy woolen clothes and wire-rimmed glasses and look as prim and proper as church ladies.

"Oh, screw this," Allen says.

Allen is a sculptor. He makes hands mostly, abstract shapes of fingers and wrists, which he carves from soapstone. For almost five years he's been trying to capture an entire life in fifteen pounds of rock: desire, grief, love, envy. He says that all the human emotions exist within the lines of a palm, the bend of a thumb. I don't know. What I do know is that Allen could earn a lot more money using his lathe to make a few soapstone sushi bowls and trivets. Practical, moderately inexpensive things that crafty housewives might like. The sort of things that actually sell. He wouldn't have to do a lot of them, just

enough to pocket some extra cash. It's not that we need the money—
I make enough doing computer work to support both of us—but
Allen would feel better, like he was contributing.

I get him calmed down and find a dolly for his sculptures. Then I
give him the keys to the rental car and say I'll get breakfast if he gets
the hands. At first, he shakes his head like he's not going to go.

"Look," I say. "We're here."

He glares at me, his eyes brimming with contempt. "Hell," he
says.

While he's gone I pull our table out a bit, so it's a little more visible. Then I go back to the main hall for bagels and coffee. In about
an hour we have Allen's sculptures arrayed on the table, swirls of
taupe fabric around them, and we set out a basket of flyers about his
studio. I tape up a banner with Allen's Web site address behind us:
www.handscrafted.com.

We don't get much business, but that's par for the course. We've
done a lot of shows like this and have sold only two sculptures. Both
times Allen rode a high for a week or so, charging back to the studio
for more work, but soon his fighting edge wore off. He starts doing
the math and realizes how much effort he puts in for what is returned. It all gets pretty grisly. He's had some shows at private Washington galleries and he's sold a few hands to tourists passing through
the Torpedo Factory in Old Town. Mostly though, it's drought.
Desert and drought.

The only thing helping us today is the church ladies. The word
about their cookies is spreading. A steady stream of artists and festi-
valgoers comes to their table, forced, however nicely, to listen to
an orderly presentation on the durability of PVC before they get a
cookie. We've seen the women sell some birdhouses. A couple of
people have drifted by our table, picked up the flyers.

One man, dressed nicely but also wearing a withered face and a frown, asks what Allen's smaller sculptures are going for.

Allen looks up from the travel book he's reading. "Five hundred," he says, a little too much irritation in his voice.

The man coughs and thanks us and hurries away.

"You're a lousy salesman," I say.

Allen answers, "Location, location, location."

He goes back to reading his travel book and blows a few strands of hair out of his left eye. Like me, he's going gray, but he's blond and hides it better, has a sort of natural highlight. He's also let his hair get long again; its slight wave has come back. Allen says it takes a few years off. Recently, we've both started feeling a little worn, like two old homebodies, and though we've made the occasional trip to Dupont Circle and some of our haunts in Arlington, most weekends we get a video, maybe walk to a neighborhood restaurant. We still have friends over, occasionally head downtown for drinks. But almost anything involving a *plan,* an *effort,* feels like too much. It's all become very suburban, a matter of our valuing comfort over excitement.

Late that evening, at dinner, we pass plates left and right, spooning out chicken sagwala and basmati rice, laughing at our commotion and sudden hunger. The restaurant is an Indian place with red carpet and dim lighting. The smell of curry and coriander steams from the kitchen. It's one of Jon and Michelle's favorites—*cheap,* they tell us, but awfully good. It's not far from the SUNY campus where Jon works.

He seems like a decent man—handsome, mostly kindhearted. He has a small goatee and I can easily imagine him in a college auditorium, a large Manet projected on the wall, coeds in the darkened front row. He's the sort who would attract a line during office hours.

"The uniform," Allen says. "My god, professor, it's the weekend and you're still in uniform."

Jon looks down at his green turtleneck, then tugs at the lapel of his sports coat.

"It's comfortable," he says.

Michelle blushes and stares at her plate.

There is a new Allen in the room. The man I have been living with, the sculptor who is never out of bed until noon, who forgets to shave, is now lively and joking, the person leading conversation. Seeing Michelle after all these years has lit something in him. He loves the tartness of the chutney, makes contented sounds when he downs the lamb. He pours out wineglass after wineglass, happy he convinced Jon to try a new merlot. He keeps telling Michelle how great she looks. I can see the evening turning into one of Allen's "Top Ten Meals"—the mental list he maintains of just such occasions. And it is all very good, extremely good, but I'm the relative newcomer here and can't get the full effect. I think you have to really know the people you're eating with for the great meal. There has to be a mix of emotions to take flavor to the next level, the one beyond taste alone. There has to be something happy going on.

It's almost ten when we get the bill. We've ordered sherbet to wash things down, cool off our tongues, and the check lies near Allen's wrist. I nod at the conversation, listening to Jon talk about an old art professor and his "revisionist Marxist crap." He's trying to be funny, but it's playing flat. Underneath the table, I open my wallet, my fingers pulling out the crisp, clean bills from an ATM. When I have five of them, I reach forward and tap Allen's knee.

He pretends not to notice. He's telling Jon about our booth neighbors, the man who ran away after the five-hundred-dollar quote.

"I think he told the rest of the crowd," Allen says. "It was like the well dried up."

"It wasn't that bad, was it?" Michelle asks.

"I did get a lot of reading done. And Philip, Philip got to readjust the fabric swaths all day."

I tap his knee again and Allen feels the money. He pushes it away. I should just give up. I should realize I am hurting him. But my own stubbornness gets in the way, my overwhelming need to help him save face in front of his old friends. I push again. He frowns this time and shoves back. I push forward. I have a fleeting sense of how stupid this must look: two grown men arm wrestling underneath a dinner table, each of them trying to show nothing above. Allen is better at it. He gives my hand a sudden twist and when I jerk away my wrist hits the table leg. The money flutters to the floor and Michelle looks down at her ankles.

"Philip's playing footsie," Allen tells her.

Jon pulls out a credit card. "This," he says graciously, "is on us." Michelle rushes in with a flurry of questions about Allen's studio. I know he's eyeing me and can actually feel him staring while Jon signs the check. But Michelle keeps up with the questions. She is suddenly charming, animated, her voice cajoling Allen into answers and distraction. On our drive home, as Allen grows quiet, she starts pointing out Albany's landmarks. When we pass the large concrete concert hall above the convention center, she says, "And you already know about the Egg, Allen. You've seen it from underground." She frowns melodramatically. "Please, don't hold our architecture against us." Like me, Michelle is one of those people who maintains order, who gets physically ill when there is argument and discord. But when we get home, it's the children who come to the rescue.

Last night's relative calm was deceiving. The old Victorian is already a house that teeters on anarchy—a parrot screeching in the kitchen, ballet tights hanging from the banister, toys scattered on the floor—and the young and very inexperienced baby-sitter has altered

the mix by giving the kids too much dessert and not enough maca-
roni. Laura and Porter are flying around the living room, their tiny
shoes pounding like the hooves of wild animals.

"Play with us! Dance with us!" Laura yells.

Like a good uncle, I comply.

We put on a BeauSoleil album, hot Cajun music, and our dance
skitters to the violin and washboard. I don't know where the energy
comes from. Memories of New Orleans. The pink of Laura's face.
The sound of *thump, thump, thump* as we move across the floor. It
doesn't matter. My jeans and cowboy boots feel right. The sweat
along my arms feels right. I spin.

"We'll never get them into bed," Jon says.

Allen shakes his head. "You'll never get *him* off the dance floor."

After two more fast numbers a waltz comes on and Laura settles
to the couch. She kicks with her feet a little, trying to keep time.
She's breathing heavily and her cheeks look round and flushed.
Porter is sitting on the floor, his eyes still red at the edges. His hair is
sweaty and matted above his ears. The sugar high has bottomed out.

I feel like joining them, like sinking to the ground myself, but
then Allen is in front of me, an arm around my waist, his left hand
taking my right, and I feel him moving to the music. He starts with
one-two-three footwork, his hand swaying, and I follow. It's muscle
memory, automatic response. When he pulls me closer, I can feel the
heat of my face reflected in his.

Laura tries to stifle a gaping yawn.

Then her parents join us and we become four dancers, two pairs
waltzing, the light throwing shadows at our feet. Michelle has a hand
on the back of Jon's neck and I catch her staring at us, a faint longing in her eyes. It's not Allen she's looking at—it's us, Allen and me
together. I can tell she's feeling something, some essence of her life
long ago. The children are falling asleep, but we don't stop. Our fig-

ures glide around the couch and coffee table, moving late, late into the night.

The next day is a series of small disasters. First thing, just as we pull into the plaza parking garage, Allen spills coffee down his shirt. Then, about ten or so, a microphone whines and a woman on the main stage tells us that Albany's Adult Poetry League will be reading. We haven't noticed the sound system before—the large black and gray speakers sitting only twenty yards away—but now they boom with the first poem:

> *Love is an untamed bird*
> *A flight of feather and wind…*

Allen glares over the top of his travel book. He doesn't have to say it. I know what he's thinking. He goes back to reading about Prague. The poet, a small man with a ponytail, gets flustered by the noise in the convention hall. Voices rise to meet the amplified sound. The polite quiet of moments before has dissolved into an irritated murmur.

The man reads louder:

> *A Dove? NO! SOME OTHER FOWL!*
> *A RAVEN. That's what you are.*

I put my head on the table and shake it from side to side.

"It's not your fault," Allen says.

"It is, actually."

"Well, okay," he says. "But you're trying, Philip. It's nice to know you're trying."

"Really?" I say, not even raising my head.

"Really," he answers.

Not long after that, when we're both getting hungry, Allen begins to hurriedly pat down all his pockets. "Oh, shit," he says. We ask the church ladies to watch our booth and we take the elevator to the basement. The keys are lying on the darkened front seat, locked inside the rental car.

"I am such an idiot," Allen says.

"No," I say. "You're a brilliant man who is very, very distracted."

The church ladies come through. One of them, Emmy, has a cell phone and calls her husband. He uses a tool called a Slim-Jim to open the car door. It all feels vaguely illegal and I find myself looking around the parking garage, then avoiding cops as we walk back to our booth. We thank Emmy and her friend and insist on buying a birdhouse. It seems like the least we can do.

There's a new poet up on stage, a woman reading about her body.

> *I touch myself*
> *I touch my breast, my vagina.*

Allen and I give Emmy a worried glance.

"Good for her," Emmy says. "Good for her for talking about her vagina."

Around us, the other exhibitors begin taking down banners, closing up shop, and I start to do the same. But for no good reason except to torture himself, Allen decides he wants to go to the Festival awards ceremony. I try to talk him out of it. It's almost two o'clock, we still need to get our things at the Prentices', and there's an eight-hour drive ahead of us. Allen is insistent.

The ceremony takes place in a large room with stacking chairs, and the man who wins the grand prize is a local artist, a swarthy, friendly looking fellow in extra-large jeans and suspenders. He paints landscapes—snow-covered, moonlit barn scenes. His canvases are not particularly large, but there is a lot of detail in the boards and shingles. He often puts a fallow landscape in the background, a deer or a pheasant slinking in the dead brown grass in the foreground.

There is always a yellow light coming from inside the barn—late-night milking or something. He's known for this: his yellow light on the snow.

"Just shoot me," Allen says. "Please."

At the Prentices', Michelle tells us that she's actually met the barn painter—Albany is a small town that way. He gives art talks to local churches and schools, always has a booth at the summer fairs.

"A politician," Allen says.

"Don't be bitter," I tell him.

"I'm not bitter," Allen says. "I'm never bitter."

"Then don't go calling people names."

"I didn't say he was Newt Gingrich," Allen says. "I didn't get *personal*."

There are screams from the living room and we rush in to find Porter and Laura fighting over a book. Michelle tells both of them to cool it and threatens a time-out. Her voice is louder than I've heard it before and has an edge of motherly irritation. It seems to scare Porter more than Laura. She starts pointing at him.

"He...he..."

"I don't want to hear it," Michelle says.

Allen kneels down so his head is level with Laura's. He asks if she wants to help him pack.

"No," she says, clutching the book, and the tears start in full. "I don't want you to go," she says. "Don't." She runs from the room and charges up the stairs. A door slams. Porter sits on the carpet and looks slightly confused. He gives me a half-hearted shrug. He knows I'm only a transient. He knows he doesn't have to explain anything.

It is Jon who surprises me. He's been upstairs working on his book—something about Greek theater and art—but now we hear him talking to Laura, the sound low and soothing. And when I go upstairs to pack, I see Jon in Porter's room. He's gotten Laura to lie on the cot she used the night before. He's stroking the top of her head, barely touching her hair, and Laura has closed her eyes. The tears have stopped. He's telling her a story about a winged god, perhaps one from his book, perhaps one that just sounds real enough for the moment. The effect is the same either way. By the time our suitcases are ready, Laura is asleep.

Before Jon comes downstairs, Allen gives Michelle a quick hug. "Secretly," he says, "I had sort of hoped to see you a little miserable." He smiles at his own impertinence. "I mean, it's such a long way, and you go and turn out to be such a happy disappointment."

"Oh," Michelle answers, and she flushes. "You're too much. You're both too much." She reaches for me. "Uncle Philip," she says.

It is hours later, when we're driving down the New Jersey Turnpike, that I finally feel myself settle. I am in stocking feet, have the heat turned down low, a thermos of Michelle's coffee lying beside me. The rental is running smooth and the cars have thinned enough that we all seem to be gliding along, a calmness settling across the lanes. I nudge the cruise control up to seventy-two, leave one hand on the wheel, check the cup holder for loose change.

The car has gotten so dark I can barely see Allen's face, and when he grows silent for several miles, I am afraid that he is crying. I don't know where the feeling comes from. The weekend. The show. The life waiting for us in Alexandria, our home. A sense, I guess, of just how fleeting his touch was the night before, that our dance was one of those moments when you feel really good about something, and then it sort of slips on you, drifts away. I wonder if the kindness we share is more a matter of habit—our years together—than love.

When a truck's headlights sweep across Allen's face, I see that he is not crying at all, that he's only drifted off. His head is against the backrest, his breathing deep and regular. A leg twitches. Once again,

I have misinterpreted everything. The mistake seems terribly signifi-
cant, a moment I will want to remember as the years go by. And yet
I already understand that simpler things will overwhelm it, fall into
place long after this stretch of highway is past. There will be Laura's
stars, her flushed cheeks as we danced. The way Porter sat sweaty and
frowning on the floor. Michelle's hand against Jon's neck—and the
look she gave the two of us. And I worry that some day, perhaps not
all that far in the future, I will stop short on a sidewalk and mutter
to myself about trying to give Allen money. I will see those twenties
skimming on air. Old love sneaks up on you like that. And I will
stand there on the concrete, coats and umbrellas swirling around me,
and know, in a way I cannot with Allen sitting beside me, that this
moment, this passing in the dark, is already behind us, gone.

KIRA SALAK

University of Missouri-Columbia

BEHEADINGS

What I see before anything else, is space. The unadulterated space of central Cambodia, which gives me the sense of having arrived at the end of something. I look away from the window and wait for the other passengers to get off the plane. Everyone else has come to Siem Reap accompanied by friends or family members, and they stare at me, the lone woman in no hurry. What they don't know is that I consider this just another place, another destination, one of so many in this world.

The last time I heard from David, nearly four years ago when I was back in Chicago, he'd written to tell me that Cambodia is "clean." He explained what I already knew: at least 1.7 million people dead from Pol Pot's scourge, a fourth of the total population. *All the bad karma has washed over this place,* he wrote. *It's annihilated past sins. This is the cleanest place on earth.*

Cambodia, a "clean" place. That alone told me that this was just another one of my brother's escapes. He'd become a Buddhist. I wasn't surprised by his new incarnation, and Cambodia? Well, why not. It sounded as good a place as any. He didn't have to worry about the American authorities pursuing him in a country where the Khmer Rouge was still actively collecting foreigners' heads. Hell—I doubted even his own ghosts would have the courage to follow him there, particularly when there were so many others to compete with. Nearly two million, give or take. A country aching in sin. Cambodia had always depressed the hell out of me, even though—as the Associated Press knew—I didn't usually care where I went, as long as it wasn't home. To me, Phnom Penh always looks like it's been bombed. Crumbling buildings, shit in the streets, child beggars who've had their legs blown off. My first time there, it took me a week to discover that all of this tragedy was normal—it actually represented a country at peace.

Out the window, I see a crowd of young men with their American hand-me-down T-shirts from aid organizations, making them billboards for Nike and the University of Virginia. They sit on mopeds in the airport parking lot, waiting for someone like me, the rare and foolhardy "rich tourist" willing to brave Pol Pot and beheadings for a single glimpse of the fabled kingdom of Angkor Wat lying outside of town. Supposedly it's more incredible than the Pyramids; if only I were here for the sightseeing. If only this time I didn't have to find David wherever he's hiding in this land of lotus pools and killing fields, where a fourth of the population greets you from mass graves.

I leave the plane and walk across the tarmac. Already sweating, I put on my baseball cap and sunglasses. In a paddy adjacent to the airport building a water buffalo chews its cud, watching me, its jaw unhitching from side to side like the arm of a record player. I stop to watch it and try to imagine the afternoon when my brother arrived at this very airport. I picture this same animal chewing away, gazing at him with its Buddha eyes, casting no judgment.

I claim my bag and pause at the airport doors to stare outside. A few disinterested palm trees sag along one side of the parking area, their yellow fronds clattering in the wind. I've never had reason to come to this part of Cambodia before. I walk outside, leaving my sunglasses off for a moment. The moto drivers soon surround me, assailing me with offers to drive me into town. They want my U.S. dollars, the hard currency that is more widely used here than the Cambodian riel.

A young man practically runs me over, pulling up and beckoning me from his moto. It is always the same tedious script.

"C'est bon marché, Madame."

"I'm not French," I say.

"Cheap for you. Ten dollars."

"Two dollars."

"No profit for me. Okay, six dollars."

"Two dollars or forget it."

We stare at each other in silence. I cross my arms and wait.

"Okay, okay." He pats the seat behind him. "You come. Two dollars. But no profit for me."

He balances my bag on his handlebars, and I sit behind him. The motorbike putters out of the parking lot and down the narrow asphalt road toward town. No trees anywhere now, just the flat green rice paddies and blue sky and a horizon at 360 degrees.

I shut my eyes and sigh, the wind whipping hair from beneath my baseball cap and sending it flying about my face. I think of my mother, ninety pounds in a hospital bed, dying. Whenever she's upset she mumbles in Czech, as if her mother tongue knows her pain better, can express it more accurately to the world. "I want to see David," she said in Czech, delirious from the morphine. She held my hand, blue eyes focused on mine, her face wrinkled and sallow beyond her sixty years. A dying face. And nothing I could do.

"Matka," I said, my Czech sounding foreign and reluctant as it came out, "David's gone. Remember?" But I'd already decided that somehow I would bring him back.

I have to remind myself how he used to be. My brother was the kind of boy who needed to bury any dead thing he found—overturned beetles, roadkill squirrels, wilted azaleas. When our father died from a sudden heart attack, David screamed during the entire wake because he wasn't allowed to bury Dad alongside the baby robins and drowned earthworms in his backyard cemetery. He was only eight; I was thirteen. I spent the whole wake trying to get him to shut up—even threatened him with Dad's ghost returning to punish him.

"Dad will come after *you*," he snapped. "You're the one not crying."

You can't afford to be sensitive, I thought. Not with life the way it is—sudden heart attacks, people getting old, dying. I didn't want David to know about any of that. I was determined to keep him innocent, Dad's death his only lesson in life. And for a while, life *was* good to him. He was a precocious child, extroverted and charming—very much my opposite. My parents took out a second mortgage to send him to the best private elementary school in the Chicago suburbs, a school for "the gifted"—kids with a minimum IQ of 130. David was already well into algebra when my father died, a boy genius for whom everyone had great expectations.

"Do you go to Angkor Wat?" the moto driver asks me over the noise of the tiny engine.

"What?" I open my eyes.

He glances over his shoulder at me. "Do you go to Angkor, Miss?"

"I don't know."

He laughs. Why else would I be in Siem Reap? But my thoughts aren't even in Cambodia anymore, let alone on Angkor Wat.

"I give you good price," the young man is saying. "Ten dollar for day. I take you, Angkor Wat."

The driver readjusts my bag on the handlebars, sending us zigzagging across the road.

"You're going to kill us," I yell over the sound of the engine.

"Ten dollar for Angkor Wat, okay for you?"

He's got me thinking about the story on the AP wire about the Frenchwoman who was shot here last week. It was in all the papers. Travel advisories against going to Siem Reap. "What about the Khmer Rouge? A woman was shot."

"Yes, but she go too far. Not safe, place she go. I know safe place."

I watch the rice paddies drift by, the sun streaking the water between the new seedlings. The color of young rice plants must be the purest green on earth. An intoxicating green.

"Do you know an American named David?" I ask him. "He lives in town."

"No. I never see this man."

But he answers too fast, too easily.

"He's got brown hair, blue eyes," I say. "He's a Buddhist student. I think he lives in a temple somewhere."

"No. I never see this man."

An old woman, hunched and walking by the side of the road, her red sarong torn and stained, stops and gazes somberly at us as we speed by. I look over my shoulder at her. She hasn't moved. Her sad eyes remind me of my mother's. Eyes that know too much, that can't bear the knowing.

My mother was nine when her own parents, Czech dissidents, were sent to their deaths in a Nazi camp. Her aunt ended up taking her to America after the war, to Cicero, Illinois, the closest to Prague you could get in such a strange and prosperous place. Still, my mother made every effort to grow up an all-American girl; she did such a good job that by the time she was an adult, all that remained of the Old Country was the faintest rough roll to her *R*'s. In every other way, she reinvented herself. Her life was one great part to play in the name of normalcy. No more pain. No more suffering. She wanted things to be Good. A devout Catholic, she prayed every day, with the fervor of Jews I've seen nodding before the Western Wall.

Hard, then, to go on remembering, but I have no choice. I remember. The police cars arrived at our door on a Saturday night. I had just graduated from college and was home for the summer. I was upstairs unpacking clothes and trying to picture myself in New York City and Columbia's School of Journalism in the fall. David was eighteen, a senior in high school, gone with my mother's car. Gone all day, past his evening curfew. Gone well into the night. The flashing lights from the cruisers, the firm, unfamiliar knock on the front door—all of these things combined into a single moment of crushing terror. I pictured blood, hospital beds, horrible talks with funeral home directors feigning sympathy. I heard the slow beeping of a machine monitoring vital signs. As I stumbled from my room to the front door, my mother already stood on the stoop, speaking in a low voice with a policeman, an old acquaintance of my father's.

"What happened?" I asked her.

They were both silent.

I turned to the cop and yelled for an explanation. He took a step back. Another policeman looked at me solemnly from one of the squad cars.

"David has had an accident," my mother said.

"What happened? Is he okay?"

The policeman watched me from the stoop, his eyes looking tired. Profoundly tired. So sick of delivering bad news.

"David is all right—but someone has been killed." Now the tears rolled down my mother's face. "This man says that David killed a little boy . . . with the car. Killed him."

The little boy was Jeremy Randall Parker. Age four. I can never forget the name: Jeremy Randall Parker. Services for Jeremy Randall Parker. Of 1201 Windhaven Court. David Marzek held for driving while under the influence and manslaughter in the death of Jeremy Randall Parker. About to begin preschool at Manning Elementary, La Grange, Illinois. *Jeremy Randall Parker.*

According to the papers, it happened this way: David was driving down an alley behind some houses, well over the posted speed limit of five miles an hour. He had had some beer at a friend's house and his blood-alcohol level had reached the point of illegal intoxication. Little Jeremy was playing inside a large washing machine box, and David, thinking the box was empty, accelerated to run it over. When he felt the bumping sensation, he immediately stopped and got out of the car. A moment later he was running to a nearby house to call 911. An ambulance came and the boy was rushed to the hospital. Jeremy died en route. Time of death, 5:38 P.M. CST.

After my mother paid David's bail and brought him home from the police station, he stopped speaking and eating. That same evening he put a knife to his arms and wrists and carved himself up so thoroughly that by the time my mother discovered him, he was unconscious. He was rushed to the hospital. Afterward, he took up residence in the state mental ward. They restrained his arms. He was fed intravenously and counseled by psychiatrists. Doctors performed a kind of medicinal alchemy until a concoction was found that doped him up enough to curb his self-mutilation impulses and bring back his voice.

"It was an accident" was their mantra to him. "You didn't mean to do it."

I was there once, standing just outside the door, listening to one doctor's recitations, when David's voice, low, foreign sounding, snarled out, "What the fuck do you know?"

And silence. Because they didn't know. How could they? All those doctors had gone to school, gotten their Ph.D.s, thought they were experts in the human soul. But David had killed someone. It wasn't a reparable thing. Jeremy Randall Parker could never come back.

The moped lurches.

"Can you slow down?" I yell.

He does.

I breathe deeply, feeling the adrenaline pulse through my body. I look out again at the incredible blinding green of the rice paddies. Considering all that's happened to this country, I don't understand how it can be so beautiful.

"What do you think of Pol Pot," I ask the young man's back. "Do you like Pol Pot?"

Over the sound of the engine: "Yes, of course."

I'm not surprised. I push my sunglasses higher on my nose and stare at the back of his neck, at the slice of dark brown skin above the top of his Bulls T-shirt.

"Why?"

"He kill clever people. Clever people steal from poor people."

"Oh."

"All clever people dead. If people doctor, dead. People teacher, dead. People rich, dead. This is good thing for Kampuchea."

I remember an old Slavic fairy tale my mother used to read to me called "Vasilissa the Beautiful." An evil witch, planning to kill a young girl, discourages the child from asking too many questions. "If you know too much," the witch warns, "you'll grow old too soon."

As we slow down at a crossroads to wait for a truck to pass, I know I can't be near this man anymore. I hop off the moped and grab my bag from the handlebars.

"What is problem?" he demands.

I throw a dollar at him. "Fuck off."

I walk into downtown Siem Reap, and I'm relieved to see that it hardly resembles Phnom Penh. Rather, it looks tired and ready for sleep. There is no urgency here, no sense of chaos. The air doesn't smell sickly pungent from garbage rotting in the streets. Instead, it smells fresh, like after a rain. Whitewashed, mildew-stained buildings languish in the sun. On the side roads, a few colonial-style houses sit as evidence of France's old Indochine empire, shaded by giant trees. Moto drivers wait in groups on the side of the main drag, watching me pass, perhaps hoping I'll hail one of them. But I like the walk. It gives me a pleasant sense of direction, purpose.

I'm not worried yet about finding David—if I can dig up Dinka warlords in the Sudan for interviews, I'm sure I can find Siem Reap's only American Buddhist novice. Yet I can't figure out how to convince him to come home. You'd think it'd be enough, our mother's dying, but if he were to come home, he'd have to face all the legal responsibilities of his actions. After he was discharged from the hospital, he went to court. My mother spent a fortune of Dad's insurance money on the bond and a decent lawyer for him, and the judge ended up suspending his sentence for manslaughter, fining him heavily, and requiring him to stay in the state by putting him on probation for years. David would avoid prison. It seemed a blessing.

I started at Columbia, and I found myself occupied by my studies. For a while I forgot about what happened to David.

My mother told me about the continued fallout, though. Shortly after the six-month anniversary of the accident, David broke the conditions of his probation by driving my mother's car, without a license, to the Fox River. He'd parked, then hiked along the river with a pick ax and towel. It had been one of the coldest days on record for the Chicago suburbs, three degrees below zero, windchill factor in the negative double digits. I can imagine some of the tree limbs so weighted with ice that they'd broken and were dangling despondently over the river. I can picture David debating all of this, stopping every now and then to feel the river's icy surface with his fingertips. Perhaps he was conscious of the silence of the snow, the sense of a world so deeply caught in winter that the green spring is unimaginable. And here in this place, he stopped finally. He heaved his backpack to the ground, brushed snow from the ice, and started to chop himself a hole. The hole needed to be large, because he would have to dive into it four times—naked.

This came out of the shrink's report. It's not clear how many times he actually got in and out of the water. I was told that David, once again in the state hospital, kept mumbling an old Algonquian phrase. A shrink got the translation out of him—"See the great warrior, I will make him rise." Apparently David had dug up some information at the Newberry Library in Chicago about an old Shawnee manhood ritual. Teenage boys wanting to be reborn into men with honor and virtue underwent an arduous sort of baptism by jumping into a river four times in the middle of winter. On the fourth plunge, the boy dived down to the bottom of the river to grab a handful of silt that would be sewn inside his *pa-waw-ka* pouch, a magical charm of protection that he wore around his neck. Only the bravest, strongest of them attempted it on the very coldest days of winter, achieving a more potent reward. Wearing the *pa-waw-ka*, the new warrior was blessed and became immune to malign forces. All the evil in the world could no longer hurt him.

David had wanted the hardest test, of course. He would have died if a man hadn't driven by and noticed him, naked and floundering in the river. As it was, he was rushed to the hospital with a severe case of hypothermia and barely a pulse.

When I heard about it, I quit school and flew back from New York. Someone needed to knock some sense into David, and if the shrinks or my mother couldn't (and obviously they couldn't), then I would. My brother needed me.

I head toward Siem Reap's post office, the return address on David's last letter, which arrived a year ago. There's a chance someone might remember him, know where he's living. The post office is a small building that resembles a run-down warehouse, with a staff of dozing employees seated behind an ancient window stained with fly carcasses and fingerprint smears. I show the employees my press credentials to let them know I'm serious. Using the manager as interpreter, I tell them I'm looking for an American. I give his name and physical description.

The woman at the counter shrugs. Another man says many of the Buddhist monks live in the temples by Angkor, but he's not sure if there's a white man among them.

As I head to a guesthouse nearby, I stop in a couple of government offices and some stores along the road to make inquiries about David. My Cambodian is terrible; we speak in either French, English, or Japanese—whichever tourist language they've learned. I have to coax the French out of some of the older staff, as they still hesitate to use words that would have sent "clever," educated people straight to the killing fields. They all tell me they've seen no foreigners in Buddhist robes.

I give up. For now. I'll head to Angkor tomorrow. I get a room at a place called the Mahogany Guesthouse and have dinner in the rooftop restaurant. A group of young backpackers sits nearby, an outspoken American man bragging to them that no matter where he's traveled, he's drunk the water everywhere and has never gotten sick.

"Only people with weaker constitutions get dysentery," he's saying. "It has to do with the *constitution*."

I order a beer and take out David's letter. I don't open it yet, but study the envelope made of thin airmail paper. My beer comes and I take a long sip, wondering if David had someone else go into town to mail his letters for him. I take out the letter now and stare at the handwriting. Small, printed script. Calm script that's barely familiar. I used to have trouble reading his handwriting as it traveled and wound about, looking more like Arabic than English.

> *Dear Chris,*
>
> *I finally got your letter about Mom. (The post office in town had it for months.) I know why you're upset. You think I've just run away from everything. And I know you think I need to own up to what you call my "responsibility" for what happened. I can't figure out how to get you to understand that I'm not running from anything anymore.*
>
> *I've thought about what you wrote, how Mom is getting worse and needs to see me. It's not that I don't care about her, or you. Believe me, I wish I could see her but if I return to the States, they'll never let me come back here, and I've found something here that sustains me. I've found the virtuous path, the Noble Eightfold Path and have entered the Sangha.*

I put down the letter and sigh. I've read it over a hundred times, but it always feels new. I have trouble knowing where my brother's sincerity ends and his indoctrination begins. This seems like a milder version of his *pa-waw-ka* ritual back at the Fox River—yet another attempt to obliterate the guilt.

I'm starting to think that David is too much of a coward to come home. I think he believes that if he stays away from his problems long enough, they'll vanish. I've met expatriates like that living in remote corners of the world—burned-out alcoholic men in grimy bungalows with local mistresses fussing about them. Sometimes they're useful if you're following a story, need tips on how to handle a situation, but there's an odorless stench about them. Maybe they killed someone, made a bad business deal—you never find out what. I just don't want David to turn out like that, burned out, drugged out on some West African beach, abandoned by the world.

I sip my beer. An Indian man sets up a microphone in a corner of the room and starts singing a Bob Dylan song. The backpacker clique next door passes around a joint and sways to the music. The American man offers it to me and I shake my head.

"Where are you from?" he asks.

"Chicago."

"Seen Angkor Wat?"

"Tomorrow."

The other backpackers turn their attention to me.

"We're going to try to hire an army escort so we can see Banteay Srei. If you want to pitch in some money, you can come with."

They're talking about the distant temple where the Frenchwoman was shot last week. The Angkor Wat area is too heavily guarded by government forces for the Khmer Rouge to get close to it, but Banteay Srei, all alone in the countryside, is fair game. It is always described as "too beautiful for words." And it had better be, for people to risk their lives to see it.

"You won't be able to get an escort there," I tell them. "The place is off-limits. The Khmer Rouge are still all over."

"We're going to try. We're hiring some soldiers."

"Look," I say, "I'm a reporter, and they won't even let *me* near the place. I did some asking around today, and the situation is still bad."

They glance at each other. Why should I care? Let them go, let them *try* to go. The Frenchwoman had an armed escort, and she was still shot. But they're so young, like my brother. I feel responsible for them.

"If you end up going," I say, "stay inside the buildings as much as possible. Don't let anyone get a fix on you."

"'Get a fix'?" one girl asks.

I feel exhausted. "Snipers."

They glance at each other again. The American remembers the joint and checks to see whether it needs to be relit.

"Cashed," he says.

I turn back to David's letter, to the part that starts to get crazy.

> *I've written to Mom already to tell her how I feel, and I think she understands. You're the only one I can't seem to reach. It's just that for the first time since what happened, I've found peace in the Glorious Root-Guru, the Blessed One, Avalokiteshvara. Every day I pray that I and all sentient beings will reach the Blissful Realm. I pray that the Root and Lineal Gurus will bless me with Resolution in order to reach this end. May they bless me with Emptiness.*
> *Chris, I love you and Mom, always.*
> *—David*

"The Glorious Root-Guru," I say, trying out the words. The back-packers look at me, thinking I'm talking to them.

The Indian man starts singing a Steve Winwood song, "Can't Find My Way Home." It's time to go to bed. I head down to my room on the second floor and open the door with my key. None of these rooms has windows, and only the tired light from the hallway seeps in beneath my door as I close it behind me. I don't turn on a light. Don't want a light. From one of the rooms down the hall, I can hear the dull pattering of Cambodian voices coming from a radio or TV set. Tonight, I miss silence.

I collapse onto the bed, smelling the dust rising from the sheets. It seems amazing that I may actually see my brother tomorrow. The last time I saw him, in the hospital, they called him a "critical case," his *pa-waw-ka* rite an "attempted suicide"—they always had a marvelous way of disguising things with words. I understood everything for what it was, though. He was trying desperately to pay for the death he'd caused, and it seemed inevitable that both my mother and I would also have to pay: We would be forced to watch him suffer, unable to help.

I was finally allowed to visit him a few weeks after the incident at the river. I remember all the security in the hospital and the visitors' area: steel doors opening up into a large, unassuming lounge area with wood-paneled walls and fluffy, friendly couches, counselors offering obligatory smiles. David was smart, though, would have noticed how all the friendly objects had been chosen with the patients' self-preservation in mind, nothing able to be removed or used as a weapon.

I waited in the lounge, facing an overhead television with the volume turned off, basketball players running around on the screen, in and out of my consciousness. I must have been frowning; a man with glasses and mustache hesitated before coming into the room. He smelled like aftershave lotion, was trim and professional in a button-up blue shirt and tie.

"Christine Marzek?" he asked.

I crossed my legs and nodded. "Chris."

"I'm Dr. Moran, David's doctor." He shook my hand. "You look like you'd rather be somewhere else."

"Yeah." I studied him: in his early thirties, probably fresh out of some doctoral program and in his first real job—*David* was his first real job. My hands were shaking and I ordered them to stop.

"So you're his big sister?" he asked, smiling.

"Yeah." My voice was quaking, and he acknowledged it with a flicker of his eyes. "How is he? When is someone going to help him?"

He sighed and pulled up a chair. "It'll take some time."

"This must be part of it, part of the deal," I said.

"What deal?"

I looked at him. "His deal with the universe. His penance for killing a person."

Dr. Moran studied me for a moment. He had moist eyes, assumed compassion.

"I'm not sure he's being punished by anyone," he said gently. "He's too busy punishing himself."

"You ought to be a priest," I said.

He blinked in curiosity.

"You're so eager to save people. You know, there's nothing you can do for my brother. How do you reverse what he did? How do you make up for it? Can Prozac bring people back from the dead? My mother goes to church three times a day now. She can't talk about anything without quoting the Bible. All I ever hear about is god-damn redemption and salvation, redemption and salvation. Drives me crazy."

"This must be hard for you."

I sighed and recrossed my legs, glaring at the TV. Tiny men were throwing a ball back and forth to each other.

"We can talk about it, if you want." He crossed his fingers and waited, but I didn't say anything. "Look—I can't promise any quick fixes. But I do suggest that—"

"My brother's brilliant. He excelled at *every*thing." My voice was too loud. I shut up and stared at the TV again.

"These things take time."

I laughed at his silly optimism. If I couldn't get over it, then how was David supposed to?

He studied me in silence. Finally: "Your mother said you've dropped out of grad school to come back here."

"Yeah."

"She's worried about you. Do you plan on returning?"

"I don't know."

He leaned forward and looked at me, waiting. When my eyes finally met his, he said, "Your mother's concerned about you, Chris. You should go back to school. How many more lives have to be messed up over this?"

I rolled my eyes, my hands shaking again. "You don't even know me."

"Okay," he said, leaning back.

"I just want to see David."

They brought him in. To take one look at him was to know that he would never again be the little brother I'd grown up with, whom I'd taught to read and write and recognize the constellations. Five years older than David, I remembered holding his newborn self in my arms. I remembered the delicate vulnerability of his tiny fingers, the softness of his skin. The first time my mother had tried to hand him to me, I'd run off in terror. I hadn't wanted the responsibility. What if I dropped him? Ruined him in some way?

David was thin now, pale, with limp, shoulder-length brown hair. In my memories—those intractable memories—he was still athletic looking, had a runner's sinewy body and broad shoulders. He was still the wrestler who'd won State, the National Merit Scholar, the grinning, mischievous young scientist whose project on electromagnetism had won him first in Nationals.

But I tried to focus on the present: David, wearing a stained white T-shirt and blue sweatpants, smelling like disinfectant soap. He had a dragging walk, like some crazy person's. His eyes wandered about the room as if he were a baby trying to fix on things and understand their purpose. When he sat down in the chair next to mine, the orderly accompanying him—a large, strong man—took a seat in a far corner of the room and locked his gaze on the TV screen. He was here with us because David had been caught with a pen he'd stolen, hurting himself.

I wasn't sure what to say at first. I tried laughing. "This place is a pit, isn't it?"

No response. He was working at the cuticles on his fingers, peeling off pieces of skin. I glanced briefly at the long pinkish scars covering his hands and arms.

We'd never been a hugging kind of family, but I hugged him. I took his heavy body into my arms and held it. He felt bony, frail, his arms remaining at his side. When I caught the orderly glancing at us, I cupped the back of David's head in my hand.

"You have to get over it," I whispered into his ear. "You have to."

No response. I'd been warned that he often refused to speak, that his voice had to be coaxed out of him.

"Talk to me."

Nothing.

Here was something I couldn't solve. David had done this to himself, and I couldn't think of a cure.

Holding David tighter, I looked across the room. The sun was slanting in, lighting up the end of a blue couch. I focused on the light as it hit one landmark after another—the next cushion on the couch, the edge of a floor tile. The onslaught of light was barely perceptible, yet soon the entire end of the room was blinding me.

I motioned to the window and the orderly got up to pull the curtains. Then I heard a sound. From between David's legs, a stream of urine rolled off the vinyl chair and trickled to the floor.

Eventually I went back to New York. There was nothing I could do. My mother called me periodically to say that he was getting better, that his therapy was working. Finally, after nearly a year, they discharged him under outpatient supervision. My mother took care of him, making sure that he stayed doped up and visited his doctors. In the meantime there were more court dates and talk about whether he should go to prison for breaking the conditions of his probation and driving my mother's car. It seemed as if the craziness would never end.

Yet, he'd gotten out of the hospital. I didn't believe it until I actually spoke to him on the phone. His voice was soft, hesitant; he sounded like a child keeping secrets. When he asked me for money, I didn't think anything of it. All I wanted to do was help him. I had a few thousand dollars saved up, and I sent it all, believing that he really wanted to get his GED and apply to college. But a few days after he got my check, he disappeared. It was a serious matter—he had broken the outpatient agreement with the hospital and the courts. The police had a warrant out for his arrest; if they caught him, he'd go to prison for sure. Then I received a postcard from Mexico. All it said was, "I'm sorry."

I knew David wouldn't be coming back.

I leave my guesthouse as the sun rises, determined to find my brother. The stray cats and dogs claim the mornings here, sniffing about the closed-up food stalls of the central market and the piles of garbage stacked along the streets. The closed stores and empty streets remind me of Skopje, Macedonia, where, on my way to cover the war in Bosnia, I panicked and wouldn't leave the train station because of the steel shutters pulled down over the storefronts outside. In the Sudan and Mozambique, shuttered stores meant impending chaos: rebel advances, women being raped, male children conscripted into ragtag rebel armies. They meant destruction—with me in the middle of it. Again.

Yet, I asked for this life. Originally, I'd studied broadcast journalism, but after David's trouble, it seemed meaningless. I began studying international affairs with the idea of becoming a foreign correspondent and getting away from home. A year went by and I didn't hear a thing from David. Then I got a postcard from Varanasi, India, with no message on it. But Varanasi told me everything I needed to know. I wondered if the Brahmans of that holy city were teaching him anything. I wondered if they'd convince him to come home and deal with the consequences of his actions.

I graduated and accepted a job with the Associated Press. I'd be a stringer, covering international news. They needed people to work in their foreign bureaus, people who didn't care where they went or what they did. Pretty soon I was off on my own, freelancing in places like Khartoum and Mogadishu. As a war photographer told me, "The shitholes of the world always provide the best stories—if you can get yourself out of them." David might have said my karma was good, though he couldn't have known how much I tempted the world. How much I hated it for its senseless parceling out of benevolence and pain.

I start walking down a street, taking deep breaths. Moto drivers materialize from the alleyways to ask me whether I need a driver to take me to Angkor Wat. I look at each person, not knowing whom to choose. Whenever possible, people and things need to *feel* right.

Across the street, I see an old man in a gray cap and wrinkled white shirt. His face is drawn, somber. He leans against a beat-up blue motorbike, watching the young men swarm around me.

I quickly cross the street. He looks at me with quiet surprise as I get on the back of his bike.

"Angkor Wat?" he asks.

"Yes."

We start driving along the river and through downtown, building after building shuttered in the dawn. The air is cool, still. Almost cold. Yet with the rising sun I can feel the midday heat beginning its offensive.

The driver leans over to tell me his name is Ga. "Muslim," he says, pointing at himself. Then he cuts a finger across his throat. "Pol Pot."

The Cambodian Cham Muslims were Pol Pot's pet project. They were among the first people to be slaughtered, along with most of the country's Buddhist monks. Ga is a rarity. The last of his kind.

"Mother, father, brother, sister—" he cuts a finger across his throat as he drives, then points ahead toward the Angkor temple complex. "Sras Srang."

The mass graves of Sras Srang, in the midst of the most popular of the Angkor ruins.

"Me," he says. Then he points at his ankle and shakes it like there's a chain around it. "Khmer Rouge. Understand?"

"Yes."

We drive on in silence. On the way out of town, I see a small Buddhist temple and ask Ga to stop so I can inquire about David. No one is inside when we enter. There is an old stone Buddha without a head, surrounded by brass bowls, prayer flags, rice offerings. A single stick of incense burns from a bowl before the altar, giving off a thick, sweet scent.

I point to the headless Buddha. "Khmer Rouge?" I ask Ga.

He nods emphatically. "Kampuchea is bad, bad country. No good, Kampuchea."

I put my own chin on the neck of the Buddha, linking my hands with those of the statue. Ga stares at me, perplexed.

"Is Banteay Srei beautiful?" I ask him, remembering the temple where the Frenchwoman was shot.

"Yes, yes." He looks at me, his eyes moist. "You want see? I can take."

I move away from the Buddha. "You mean, *go* there?"

"Yes. Go."

"Oh god—it's too dangerous." I laugh.

"No, no." He pulls the red-checkered scarf from his neck and puts it around my hair. "You hide." He tucks my hair under it. "Okay. You Kampuchea girl."

"Too dangerous for *you,* then."

He shrugs, his face drawn. Perhaps he's not scared of anything anymore.

A monk in an orange robe appears from the back of the temple and slowly approaches us. He winks a hello to me and I bow to him. I ask in French if he's seen a young American man named David, living at any of the temples in town.

He grins and answers in English. "Yes, yes. Yesterday I see him by the Bayon temple. By Angkor."

"Is he all right?"

The monk looks at me, perplexed by my question. "Of course," he says.

We return to Siem Reap, to the French Cultural Center in town so I can call my mother and give her the good news—that I know where

David is, that he's all right and hopefully I'll be bringing him home. It takes the manager twenty minutes to put the call through, and I keep waiting, hands wringing, wanting to tell Matka that after six years, she'll be seeing David again.

The manager hands me the phone at last, and it's my great-aunt on the other end of the line. Her voice sounds fuzzy from the bad connection, her heavy Czech accent further obscuring her words. I have to ask her to repeat what she says, and when she does, and when I think I understand, I lean back against the wall, closing my eyes.

"Will she come out of it?" I ask.

Silence. "They don't think so."

My knowledge of comas is from the movies, where coming out of one is always a convenient act of divine intervention—and I know that real life is never convenient. I ask my aunt in Czech to tell my mother that I've found David and he's coming home. We lose the connection.

I pay the manager for the call and go to the bathroom. Leaning my head against the mirror, I avoid looking at myself. I know I should have come here earlier, when Matka was healthier. I shouldn't have waited so damn long. I bang my head against the mirror.

I go out to the veranda of the French Cultural Center and order a glass of scotch. When it comes, I drink it down and order another. A couple of French businessmen, overdressed for Siem Reap in shirts and ties, glance at me with curiosity.

Maybe I *didn't* come here for Matka. *I* was the one who wanted to bring David back. Without Matka and David, whom do I have left? What connections? What reason to go home?

I finish my scotch and see that Ga is waiting for me across the street, gray cap pulled down. When our eyes meet, he offers me a smile. I try to smile back, but it feels sloppy on me.

I pay for the drinks and walk over to him. I steady my voice as I speak. I want to know if he'll take me to Banteay Srei, after all. I want to see something beautiful.

It's a long ride. Ga dresses me up like a Khmer villager, red-checkered scarf hiding my hair, one of his wife's handwoven silk sarongs around my waist. The rice paddies trail by on either side—sharp, brilliant-colored fields, an enormous sea of green. Farmers tend to the tiny seedlings, glancing up as we speed by. Small villages of raised, thatch-roofed huts appear at intervals. I hide my face in the small of Ga's back, taking peeks at them. Even the poorest families have lotus pools in front of their huts, sacred pink and red flowers spreading out across the surface of the water, their color a sanctuary for my gaze.

David used to talk about going to Brazil just to see the giant macaws, those rainbow-colored parrots. He used to be obsessed with color. I once bought him a New Guinea Birdwing butterfly with blue-green satin wings, and he hung it over his bed as if it were a cross.

"I'm going to the Amazon and New Guinea," he'd said to Matka.

"I know you will," she said.

But he never did make it there. Probably never will. It doesn't make sense to want anything. Everything is a matter of what you're allowed to have. Thy will be done, Matka used to say. Reminds me of being in the Middle East. People unable to speak to me about the future without saying *Insha'allah*—God willing—their eyes directed toward the sky.

No one has noticed yet that I'm not Cambodian. And this, too, feels like a gift. Something I'm allowed to have. I wonder when the generosity will end. The Khmer Rouge have already collected twelve foreigners' heads in the past three years, each one bringing international notoriety and news coverage. Young aid workers were taken while trying to rid the land of its mines. Then there were some foolhardy backpackers looking for a good story to tell people back home. And of course the Frenchwoman last week, with her army escorts and their AK-47s.

None of it enough.

We do about fifteen miles per hour now, the road dusty and full of potholes. Ga points ahead. In the distance, in the midst of a large patch of jungle, I can see what looks like a small pyramid. Banteay Srei. We drive closer until we reach a thatch enclosure, some kind of barn. Ga stops and turns off the engine, parking the bike inside. From a distance, we're only peasants getting out of the sun. I must be content to view the temple from afar or not at all. I understand why Ga insisted that I stay by the road; approaching Banteay Srei, having any obvious interest in it whatsoever, will endanger my life. The only way I can see the beauty is to pretend I don't see it at all.

A few old village men drive a water buffalo toward a nearby village, glancing at us as they pass. Their eyes widen when they see my blue eyes and white skin, and they mutter something to Ga and shake their heads. He shushes them and shoos them on.

Alone, I walk up the road, clutching the scarf beneath my chin and stuffing some stray hairs behind my ears. I take a peek at the temple. It was constructed over one thousand years ago but is so well-preserved that it looks as if it were finished yesterday.

It's made of sandstone, a central tower rising in the middle. I've never seen such a place: The carved stone looks animated, even from this distance. Smiling, full-breasted women gaze out from porticoes guarded by coiling serpents. Flowering filigree winds and trails about columns and covers the walls like vines. On the arches, elephants parade before Siva, the Destroyer, seated on his throne above his minions.

Ga whistles to me from the side of the building, telling me I've gone too far, that I should come back.

I head across the moat, toward the entrance to the temple. It's guarded by human-sized men with snarling lion heads. They kneel on one leg before the entrance to the temple, their heads cracked open by the Khmer Rouge. I pause before them for a moment. They dare me to go on. I head up the stone steps and into a courtyard. Tiny figures flutter about the walls and gaze out at me from the filigreed buttresses and archways, looking curious, or perhaps scared. I glance up at the cobra-headed *nagas,* all scowling at me, then out at the surrounding jungle. I see no one, but that doesn't mean no one is there. In the distance, by the barn, Ga is waving at me, urging me to come back.

I see a spread of dried blood on the stone floor of the courtyard. It must be where the Frenchwoman was shot. The rain hasn't come since last week, and there hasn't been anyone brave enough to wash up the blood. I walk to the spot and wait. I pull off my scarf, revealing my blond hair, and wait. This is how it happens. A decision is made. Fate or bad luck. My mother would call it fate. All of it, fate. The will of God.

Ga waves his arms wildly at me.

Siva, the Destroyer. Vishnu, the Redeemer. They are the reason for this temple.

But no shot comes.

I head back the way I came, through the courtyard and down the steps past the lion-headed guardians. I slowly make my way across the stone bridge and over the moat to the safety and anonymity of the dirt road. The lion-headed figures look small and helpless from this distance.

I walk over to Ga. He is already starting his motorbike. He shakes his head at me.

"Not safe," he says, pointing at Banteay Srei. "Bad place."

I replace my head scarf and get on the back of his bike without a word.

There are tears in his eyes. "Bad place."

On the way to the Bayon temple, to find David, I ask Ga to stop. He pulls over without a word and turns off the moped's engine. We are in the middle of an ancient bridge bordered by giant, beheaded figures. I walk to the side of the bridge, gazing down at the waters of a wide moat, heavy with algae and duckweed. If I find my brother, I'm not sure what I'll say. My mother's in a coma, and half of me wants to yell at David, demand to know what kind of life he thinks he can have here.

Ga joins me, gazing down at the murky waters, and I watch him. He was imprisoned, probably tortured, and I wonder what he thinks when he sees these beheaded figures all over his country. I want to give this man thousands of dollars, make him a rich man, convince him that there is such a thing as a kind God and a benevolent universe.

We look out at the ancient moat, jungle pressing in on both sides. At the end of this bridge stands a giant stone turret topped with four faces of Avalokiteshvara, the Buddha of Compassion. Here is David's "root-guru," his bodhisattva. Each face looks in a different direction and smiles serenely. The bodhisattvas intrigue me. According to Buddhism, they were on the verge of reaching nirvana but refused to go to it. They opted to return to the world of suffering so that they might offer their assistance to other beings. For one thousand years, these sublime faces have gazed down at the world. At the great Khmer civilization rising before them. At the invading Thai hordes. At the abandoned city of Angkor, left to the jungle until a French explorer discovered it again in the 1860s. And then, not so very long ago, directly beneath their gaze, at the soldiers of the Khmer Rouge driving Siem Reap's undesirables over the moat, to mass graves prepared among the temple ruins. Perhaps Ga's father came this way. Perhaps his brother, or his sisters. The faces would have gazed down with half-open eyes, blessing all who came before them, judging no one.

"Do you like this place?" I ask Ga.

He shrugs.

"But do you...Your family..." I cut a finger across my throat and point down the bridge.

He picks up some pebbles from the ground and beckons. Placing the pebbles on the stone bridge, he looks at me, then flicks one off.

"Brother," he says.

He knocks off a second.

"Sister number one." And a third. "Sister number two."

Two more stones leave for his parents. And a few more for other family members and friends. Finally, he holds up what is left of the pile of stones, a small handful now, and these he pockets. "Mine," he says. He taps his pocket. "Mine."

I nod.

But he shakes his head in frustration and points to my shorts. I pull out the empty pocket.

"I haven't really—"

He grabs my wrist and hands me his pocketful of stones. "Yours." He looks me in the eye until I realize I'm supposed to pocket them. "Yours."

The Bayon is directly ahead, at the end of a long road bordered by jungle. At first glance, it looks like a large pile of rubble. Giant carved stones lie haphazardly in the grass, and Cambodian children in ripped T-shirts climb them. As we approach, little girls lift younger siblings to their hips and run to the road. They surround me, begging for riel.

As I pass out bills, I see a couple of Buddhist novices in white robes sitting in the ruins, muttering mantras. I'm thinking one of them might be David, so I approach them, but they turn out to be Cambodian women. When I give them David's name, say "American," they nod their heads and point at the Bayon temple.

Looking for some way to enter the temple, I climb up a steep stone stairway. It ends at a dim corridor that winds into alcoves where beheaded Buddha statues rest in smoky candlelight. Monks in orange robes sit alone or in pairs before the statues, praying with their alms bowls before them. I search every dark chamber, confronting one headless Buddha after another in the confusing, labyrinth-like passageways.

All of the Buddha statues in this temple have been beheaded. I know from being in Phnom Penh that it's almost impossible to find a Buddha anywhere in this country that hasn't been decapitated. There must have been so many heads to take off, and the Khmer Rouge must have done something with them. I want to know where they are. I want to find them. I swear, I could devote my life to putting those heads back on.

David isn't anywhere. There is no one in any white robe. I sit on the stone steps. From the walls carved faces beam down on me from several angles, some from high above, others great and auspicious before me. I can't stop looking at them—they're whispering to me. Kind reassurances, such beautiful words. I tell them I'm afraid to leave this place. I tell them about my brother, and how he killed a young boy. I tell them my father died and my mother is dying. I tell them about the woman I knew in Sarajevo who kept her little girl in a bomb shelter for a year, only to finally let her out and see her get blown apart. So much, I can't tell it all. The ravaged villages I saw in Mozambique, the anguish in refugees' eyes—I've lost track of it all.

The faces know all of this already, and they whisper beautiful things. Some have pieces of their cheeks missing, their eyes, the crowns on their heads, from Khmer Rouge target practice. They guide me into the inner sanctuary, the tower of stone at the center of the temple. I walk up the steps, the light growing dim. Incense smoke catches on sunbeams and wafts out through shafts of stone into the sky. In an alcove, a headless Buddha rests among bright red prayer flags, lit by a single candle. A Buddhist monk in an orange robe sits in front in the near darkness, holding his *mala* in his hands and counting off one bead after the next, eyes closed, lips moving. He doesn't notice me as I walk by him; only the candle's flame marks my passage.

There is a faint light in the darkness ahead, and I feel my way along the stones to the spot. It's a tiny patch of light, and when I stand in it and look up, I see that fifty feet above, at the very top of the tower, the sunlight falls in. Smoke spirals up toward it, past the enormous stones, and I'm certain—I can't explain how—that my mother has just died.

I hear the mantra of the monk, a low, even humming, and discover that I've been crying. The tears have soaked the front of my shirt, and now the cool air of this inner chamber makes me shiver. I turn around and glance at the monk, trying to make out his face. His eyebrows and hair are shaved off, and that, along with his placid expression, makes him look innocent, as if he were a child. I'm envious of the radiance of his face, how it resembles the giant faces outside. I watch how effortlessly his lips move. How gracefully his head bows. And now, as he leans forward, the light illuminates his hands and his prayer beads and glows on a series of pale pink scars that wind down his arms.

I fall back against the stone wall. Whispers assail me, repeating my brother's name over and over. Kneeling down, I can feel the stones in my pocket pinching my skin. I want to see if his lips will stop moving. I want to know if the mantra will end. Minutes go by. He doesn't stop. An hour. Another hour. The incense smoke finds me, curls about me, its scent lingering on my skin. I can't wait any longer. There must be some way to leave without disturbing him.

AMANDA DAVIS

Wesleyan Writers Conference

⤬

LOUISIANA LOSES ITS CRICKET HUM

We who were not there cannot possibly understand how they came like flies: swarming up all of a sudden and buzzing over the horizon, thickening the sky with their heavy shadows. We were playing poker at Jimmy's—beers sweating, fans going round and round, the sound of pool clicking the moments by. Everyone admits it: We all felt the air chill. The dense Louisiana air disappeared and an icy breeze sliced through.

Andy said *Damn,* threw his cards on the table, and headed for the jukebox: full house and James Brown.

I felt it like cold fingers crawling up the back of my neck. *Something is happening all right,* but I just folded quietly and waited to see how the chips lay.

We did not deny that something was happening, but we didn't let it thwart our game. I was down twenty-seven dollars and Jerry was up at least twice that. My gut burned from bar food and the hair on the back of my neck prickled and danced. I wondered who or what we'd invoked, but I didn't see any of it—deep in my liquidy bubble the world warbled on in its usual uneven trajectory, leaning this way and that, odd as ever.

But out there. If you were out there you might have seen it. Luther Binge said he saw the livestock and children proceed single file: the cows and chickens marching in a straight line, the kids frozen in prayer. *Been watching too much television,* I thought, but who was I to say? Of course I wasn't out there. I was swimming in my own inebriated world, muddling things further with the smooth darkness of booze. I was losing at poker, down a hand in life. I was waiting to be swept away by something, but hiding in Jimmy's bar so it couldn't find me if it wanted to.

There was nothing unusual about that night. It started like they always did. We gathered one by one and bought each other drinks. Shots of bourbon and sweaty beer chasers. We swaggered and lurched around until we had enough for cards and then we gathered around the table in the back—like any night—and dealt ourselves a hand, tossing insults like they were the petals of flowers, that loosely, that softly.

I should have been home.

Later Mamie Dixon described them like insects, said she thought the sky was full of giant wasps. I can't imagine a more terrifying sight but she says, *No,* says, *They were beautiful, really.*

But that was the summer of days I closed the restaurant early and came home late, afraid to look Ellie in the eyes if she was up. I wanted nothing to come between me and the inevitable fact of her departure, which I felt lurking on the horizon like the evening's dull hum. I drank until I had buried the soupiness of things—that the elements of my life had remained the same for as long as I could remember, that we made sense only up to a point, that something very wrong was happening all around me, something unnamable and steady. Rolling upon me with the unshakable nature of time and history, streaming generations all coming one after the other like a rush of water, like a flood of humanity.

And like this I was overcome.

At Jimmy's we didn't talk this way. Alan racked and I shot and the sound of me connecting, of me scattering balls to all the corners of that green felt earth was as satisfying as anything I knew. Icy cold beer and music that made our heads nod, our hips swing and grunt in agreement. I never knew then what I needed to know. I never knew that misery leaks like a terrible viscous thing. I never knew the toxins I could spread, nor the stain my unhappiness could create. I never knew what left me lurching toward emptiness, a skeptic looking for proof of abandonment.

I remember coming home after, walking the path to my house. It was dark, all the streetlights blown out, though what worried me was not the blank night sky or the feeling that something had just been there, but the dark of my house. That's what worried me. Each step closer I got, the clench on my stomach tightened until at the porch steps I felt myself shaking and knew if I went in I wouldn't like what I'd find: kitchen light out and Ellie not there.

I slept under pine trees out near Hubert Hall's yard. I always found I moved toward his house when something went wrong. Found his lawn the best place to sleep off a drunk. It seemed to me they led a graced life, Hubert and Betsy and their four perfect children. Their plants flourished, their windows shined. I doubted they had cavities, or rashes, or any other side effects of life, any one of them.

We had no kids. Though Ellie tried fertility tests at one point, what was wrong with us was less nature and more will. How could I bring a baby into a world I felt deteriorating? How could I say I loved someone if I believed that cataclysmic things would find us? Ellie tried to drag me to church with her but I wouldn't go. *I don't believe,* I told her. *What's the point?* She looked away then, out the window or up at the ceiling. *Who you asking for help?* I muttered, but when she asked what I'd said, I mumbled, *Nothing.*

I woke to ants crawling on my face and the peeping whispers of the twin Hall boys, blond and saucer-eyed, poking my legs. I rose and brushed myself free, creaking with the stiffness of a night spent on the ground. The air was light, the day warm. The open sunlight seemed like a redemption of everything, as if to prove something dark couldn't fly to a land as lovely as ours.

Blinking in the light, I made my slow way up the slope to my house. There were brass bands playing in the back of my head and there was Ellie, rocking on the porch. One look at her face told me everything was different, but I chose to ignore that. I smiled like any other day and sat beside her on the swing.

We tossed gently, back and forth, through the cacophony of living things calling to each other. If I could have held the moment in my palm it would have been a shiny bead, precious, carried everywhere for good luck. Off in the distance I saw Len Belton mowing his lawn. Ellie put her head on my shoulder and closed her eyes. We still hadn't spoken. I pushed off a little on the porch and we swung back and forth.

And I knew. Her whole body was tense, anxiety crackled in her like lightning. I could feel it coming off her in waves and it turned everything in me cold.

There's something I have to tell you, Ellie said.

I smiled, a stiff jerk of the lips, but held my breath and couldn't speak. *Something is very very wrong,* she said.

In front of us spread the landscape of our lives: the slope of the hill down our yard to the cul-de-sac. The Halls' house to the left of us, the Wintersons' to the right. Off in the distance was the spire of the First Congregational Church of the Lord and beyond that Jimmy's bar. There was a school farther up the road, people, lives. There was the restaurant I managed, the pool we swam in, the library that lent me ideas. There were trees—pine, willow, oak—flowers, honeysuckle, bees. All of it spread from the axis of us into a swirl of life here on earth at that moment. All of it.

I know you know it, she said. *You slept outside, seems like you're aware of something, but we have to* talk *now, Kenny. We have to.*

It's funny how knowing everything is about to up and tumble away from you turns the world rich, nauseating colors. Background sounds rise up and roar at you, sink down and envelop you. I felt it all like a gasp for air.

UFOs, I said. *What happened last night?*

It's not what happened last night, she said. *It's a lot bigger than that.*

I still had my arm around her and her head rested on my shoulder. *No,* I whispered and kissed her on the forehead. *We can work it out, El. We always do.*

She sat up and curled herself into a little ball on the other end of the swing, which jerked from side to side.

I don't think so, she said. *Really.*

I couldn't look at her. The sky threatened to fall down. Trees tried to pull up their roots.

You're just confused.

I don't want to be your wife anymore, Kenny, she said and undid ten years like they were nothing more than ribbon.

You don't mean that, I said and stood up. The sky had darkened, the wind picked up.

But it tumbled out of her, black and thick: *I don't want to wake up to hear you showering, don't want to find your hairs in the bathroom, your laundry mixed in with mine. I don't want to hear you late-night stumbling drunk or watch you reading book after book and still managing the stupid restaurant.*

I couldn't breathe, but I don't exactly remember what happened next. She was gone when I came to, lying on the porch. She must have stepped over me to leave. I heard the last thing she said, though: *I'm in love with someone else.*

I couldn't quite bear to go inside, so I sat on the steps while the rain threatened to come. Nothing felt like it belonged to me. Jay Winterson came out his back door with a garbage bag. He waved and started up the hill.

Hear about the visitors? he hollered.

I nodded but my throat felt tiny.

Rona says the kids were frozen stiff. She wants them to draw me pictures, he yelled, scratching the place where his hair was thinning. *Wants the kids to draw the whole thing. Keeps saying, show Daddy! Show Daddy what it's all about.*

I didn't see a thing, Jay, I shouted back. My voice cracked.

He laughed and scratched his head again. *Andy phoned earlier. Said Gloria was all packed and missing when he got up this morning.*

He shifted from one foot to the other, took a deep breath before spitting it out. *You think whatever it was is coming back?*

I stared at him as wind began to whip at the trees of our neighborhood.

I'm at a loss here, I told him.

What? he called. It was getting harder to hear over the weather. He was fifteen feet away with a bag of trash hollering to me. I waited for fire to sweep through or the earth to open up like a bottomless cavern and swallow us all, but it just began, gently, to rain.

Ellie's left me, Jay, I called down. *I think I'd better go inside.*

I rose unsteadily and reached for the railing. Jay looked uneasy and took a step back.

Aw, Kenny, he said. *Aw,* and he stood there rocking back and forth on his heels, hands stuffed in his pockets like a grade school kid.

Hey listen, you call us if you need anything, he finally shouted and turned to go.

None of it mattered, none of it. I could have been a better this or that, I could have spread myself through the world in a more generous manner. I could have loved Ellie with all of me but she still might have left. The silence of my life was thorough and deafening. I watched him walk away and wished for something in me to erupt.

I was in the wrong place when it happened is all. They had to come back. I wanted them to sweep through our town again and freeze whoever they needed to get to me. I wanted them to shatter everything I knew so I would wake wherever I woke with my world new and pink and fresh. I sat in the dim gray kitchen while the rain beat down and wished, with all the hope and whiskey I had left, for the force of their anger, the size of their hate; for them to come back and land on my house.

I went back out on the porch. The rain had picked up and it blew in sheets now. Trees bent, the sky was the eerie yellow-gray of southern storms. I stood on the steps rocking back and forth. *Return!* I hollered into the whirling wind. *Come back, you cowardly bastards!* I was weeping then, wet and empty. How I must look to them: a small drunk man sobbing on a tiny porch. *You!* I begged with everything I had, as loud as I could. *How can you expect us to pray to you?*

ZOEY BYRD

Hollins University

OF CABBAGES

The day my husband came home and saw the two hundred cabbages piled up in the courtyard against the wall was in October, I think, or September, and the cabbages were napa. Since his death, I've looked in the produce departments of several American grocery stores for the exact name to check and make sure. Sometimes names will change or a new variety will be introduced. I know it was definitely October, or maybe it was November, anyway, months before the F-4 crash but close enough that I associate these cabbages with his passing. Babies are born in a cabbage patch, but we didn't have a chance to have a baby. We were going to wait until we got back to the States. This I remember too well.

It was no big deal—we were going to spend a year in Korea. I wasn't even supposed to be in Korea. I wasn't "sponsored" by the Air Force. Korea was a one-year hardship tour—an unaccompanied tour—meaning the Air Force wouldn't pay for a spouse to move there. I can't recall the exact details. Maybe we were to stay longer for some reason. At any rate, it seemed we would be there forever. We had big plans, too—Hong Kong, Singapore, Sydney. We were going to travel to warm places with lots of water—exotic port cities, the more civilized ones. No rickshas, tuk-tuks, or jeepneys for us. We would travel in style.

I don't know why my husband didn't join the Navy if he loved the water so much. He had grown up in Santa Barbara, parasailing off the coast. Something about water, something about air, I don't know what.

Damn those cabbages, I think, as if they are responsible and will continue to be responsible for everything I cannot control in my life. *Bae chu,* the *ajuma,* our landlady, called them. I had pointed at the cabbages upon their arrival and demanded of her, "What in the world?"

"Bae chu," she said, with a wave of her hand to shoo me off. She didn't speak English. She was busy supervising the unloading. Another day in this strange place, I thought. I couldn't wait to hear what my husband would say when he got home. It would be something good. Korea was chock-full of the unexpected. I could just lie on my floor all day and never be bored.

Our living arrangement with the *ajuma* was temporary. It had been my idea. I didn't want to live in a Korean hotel outside the main gate while we waited for our real apartment to become vacant. I wanted to sleep on a heated *ondol* floor and feel as if I were alone with my husband in a foreign place. I didn't want to be close to the Air Force base. It wouldn't be romantic. We hadn't had time for a honeymoon trip; we'd gotten married so fast. I wanted to be married to him, not to the military.

So we rented a one-room deal in the back of the *ajuma's* house. We had a private entrance at the rear. The house was far enough from the base that I felt safely distanced from the clubs in the ville and the bargirls with their black raccoon eyes. I was afraid they were going to steal something from me. At the time I'd agreed to take the room, I wasn't aware that being on that edge of town put us at the end of the flight line; I could hear the fighters launching every morning. At first I worried about the noise, but after a while I didn't notice. The times when I did, I did so deliberately, listening for my husband, feeling he was in a safe place once the roar of the jets faded, meaning that the aircraft were up in the air.

"*Bae chu,*" I said out loud and the *ajuma* said, "Yesss," hissing back at me like an American. I sat on the stoop to our door and watched the debacle of the cabbage delivery and thought something was definitely going on here. It was *kim chang* time in Korea, the season of kimchi-making, when the housewives received their loads of cabbages, garlic, red peppers, and scallions and began the process of making enough kimchi to last through the winter. But I wouldn't find this out until later. I was still learning.

A month before, right after we moved in, I told my husband I'd discovered something very odd up on the roof.

"Let's do a recce," he said, meaning a reconnaissance mission in which we'd go take a look, check things out. So we went up to the roof where the *ajuma* had the enameled, black clay pots lined up. It felt as if we'd been transported back to biblical times—a flat roof where events took place, revelations occurred or not, and people came together to eat, sleep, and look out at the surroundings, or into the sky. The possibilities were limitless on a flat, solid roof.

My husband held my hand, something he rarely did in public and never did in a military environment. He had an aversion to PDA, public display of affection. But there on the roof, in the middle of it all with a view of the expanse that we lived in, we couldn't have been more alone.

"And you say I never take you anywhere," he said.

"I say, 'We never go anywhere,'" I corrected him.

"It looks like the remains of the Kim clan," he said, referring to the clay urns. They were waist high, and stoic-looking in their darkness.

"Stop it," I said. "The landlady will hear you."

"She doesn't speak English. We're only more noise."

He started singing "Up on the Roof," an oldie but a goodie, and I went to the clay urns and began to lift one lid after another, peering in and inspecting the contents. At first I was nervous, thinking it was possible they held the ashes of an ancestor or two. But no, what they contained was edible. It was food. "Soy sauce," I said, lifting the lid of an urn full of a black frothy liquid. Then: "Here's bean paste something or other." It was brown and thick. Lifting the lid of another, I announced, "This is that red pepper paste." All those things were fermenting. My husband, however, couldn't bear to look. Fermentation didn't appeal to him.

"I've seen enough," he said, meaning he'd seen enough since the day we stepped off the plane at Kimpo and smelled the night soil. We'd arrived after dark, landing in a smoggy Seoul. We couldn't see a thing, but it was spring and the rice fields were being planted. The pungent smell of human waste greeted us. The cab driver who drove us from Seoul to the base, an hour and a half away, reeked of garlic and fish. He chain-smoked the whole way because he knew we were military, and he had no reason to treat us like guests. On the radio he listened to music—a woman crying out what sounded like a long complaint. It was their folk music, I'd later learn.

"Wait. There's more," I protested to my husband as we stood on the roof. I wanted to see what the other urns contained, but he pulled me away, over to the edge, where we looked out on the other square houses with their frosted plastic windows and faux brick walls. Each house had the same walled-in courtyard where the housewives did it all—washed, cooked, and cleaned. A massive tangle of phone wires and electric wires ran haphazardly from pole to pole, connecting the homes, the stores, the eating places, and the bars. There were no lawns or trees.

"Can you believe we live like this?" my husband said.

Before I could respond, a pair of fighters launched from the base. The roar of their afterburners filled the air. It was loud and offensive. We both looked up.

"What the hell?" he said, checking his watch. Something was going on. Something good, he said, which to me meant something not so good. And he was missing it. He had a late report time.

I put my arms around his waist and held on. I tried to look at the fighters and care, but they seemed small and insignificant as I watched their gray bodies shoot into the sky. I couldn't see or feel what my husband did. Years later, when I'd hear fighters launch like that, it would disturb and excite me at the same time—something good, something bad—but at that moment on the roof, all that mattered was being together, surveying the tiny ville we lived in and knowing it was our home.

My husband continued to look up, but I looked down. It was a disconcerting view. A motorbike raced dangerously through an alley to deliver goods. A stray toddler wandered out of a doorway. A hand pulled the child back. Women all over the ville worked stooped over in their courtyards. Their backs were being ruined slowly by the labor they had been born into as women, as housewives. With their bare hands they washed clothes and picked through rice. It was life right in our faces. Korea was chaotic, but it had an order imposed on it, a predictability in which anything could happen. The smell of kerosene and charcoal heaters stank up the air while a film of yellow dust blew in from the Manchurian plains and settled onto windowsills. We were truly in a foreign place.

"The clay pots," I said to my husband. "We'll remember this."

"I won't remember a damn thing, honey," he said. "You'd better remember for me."

"Okay, I'll try."

That night as we lay side by side in the futon I whispered into his ear, "Koreans don't cremate. They bury their dead in hillside graves." In a book I'd found at the base library, I'd discovered a picture of an ancestral gravesite. The individual graves were mounds of earth that looked like full-term pregnancies dotting the terrain.

"I've seen them," my husband said.

"Where?"

"On takeoff."

"How can you see them?"

"They stick out like sore thumbs."

The day of the cabbage delivery was like any other day—I was waiting for my husband. It was late afternoon by the time he got home. I expected him much later, but there he was, walking in the door like I didn't know what. We were supposed to take off our shoes before we came in, but he never did.

"What the hell's with all the cabbage?" he said. "You know I hate cabbage."

"There was a sale," I said. I didn't look up at him. I was lying on the heated floor reading a *Good Housekeeping* magazine that my mother had sent from Dallas, as if I couldn't buy it on base in the Stars and Stripes bookstore. Sometimes she sent *Ladies' Home Journal* but mostly *Good Housekeeping;* it was the more Republican of the two. She liked to feel she had control of the situation, me in a foreign country with an Air Force man. She wished I had married a boy from Midland or Dallas and stayed home. My mother thought Californians were corrupt.

"That's it. We're moving," my husband announced.

I listened to him unzipping something. Then I heard the sound of Velcro ripping. It was true we never ate coleslaw or sauerkraut—those were picnic foods—but I hadn't known he disliked cabbage.

"It's the *ajuma*'s cabbage and this mess on the floor is just me. I'm getting the laundry ready for tomorrow," I said. Earlier that day, I had started to sort our clothes but hadn't gotten past dumping them on the floor. At noon, I walked to base to check our mail and then ducked into the base library to look for information on cabbages. On the way home, I cut through the Korean market and watched the eels swimming in large tubs of salt water, wondering how the women cooked them. I didn't buy anything, but my day had been complete.

"Tomorrow, you say? Good idea. We'll move tomorrow." He was rummaging through the wardrobe, our only piece of furniture. He pretended not to hear me, but I knew he'd caught every word.

"Listen," I said, because I had an idea about our taking leave in the spring. I'd read a travel article on Saipan in *Good Housekeeping*. It was a small article, tucked into the back pages of the magazine—as if the magazine's editors didn't want good housekeepers to become overly fixated on tropical vacations. The writer of the article had used the word *azure* to describe the color of the water off Saipan. Not aquamarine or turquoise—the tropical variations of blue that came to mind—but *azure*. The tiny photograph that accompanied the article captured this azure. It looked like blue curaçao. With a bottle of vodka and some white tequila, I'd thought, I could mix a Blue Shark in it.

I glanced up at my husband and he smiled at me. He had changed into running clothes. He couldn't sit still for even a second. I watched him as if he were a television I'd just flipped on. One channel, many channels—he was always changing, changing his clothes.

"I'm listening," he said, setting his watch, preparing to run.

"Are you?" I said.

"Time's up. Give me a kiss." And I did. I stood up still holding the *Good Housekeeping* in one hand. Hello, good-bye—we were always killing two birds with one stone it seemed. There was a certain conservation of resources in our relationship, and it appealed to me. On the outside our life looked messy—clothes strewn everywhere, cabbage piled high in the courtyard, odd hours kept, weekends that were just another two days blowing by, and meals late, half-cooked, or never eaten. But in our intimate moments together, we wasted nothing.

"I'll tell you later," I said, "and you'll like it."

He raised his eyebrows and headed for the door. When he opened the door he stopped—or something stopped him. It was the cabbages. They were still there, and would be for a couple of days until the *ajuma* got organized and enlisted the aid of her female relatives and friends who would help her. *Kim chang* was a community effort. I'd read all about it at the library. I peered around my husband's shoulder at the magnitude of the cabbage wall. It was like seeing the ocean for the first time. Stark white cabbage stalks with pale leafy ends. How could he not love it?

"This is bad," he said. "This is real bad."

"They look different in this light," I said. It was late afternoon, and through the autumn haze the sunlight illuminated the courtyard from a soft angle. "So solitary. Like a pale green sea." I wanted to prep him for the trip to Saipan. Eventually I would introduce the concept of *azure* to him.

"I disagree," he said. He was intimidated by the cabbage. I tried to think of a vegetable I disliked as intensely but there weren't any that came to mind.

"It'll be okay in a few days," I said.

"We're moving. This is a sign." He didn't like where we were living. It had nothing to do with the cabbages, really.

I waited, but he didn't budge. He took my hand and we stood in the frame of the doorway, staring out at the cabbage wall as if waiting for a wave to break. It was one of those moments in which he was leaving and I was staying, and we stood together, on the precipice of what I can only call our mortality, because it felt that way in the afternoon light.

"We'll go for a walk after dinner," I told him. "You'll see. Every courtyard has a wall piled high with cabbages. It's that time of year."

"All right," he said. He gave my hand a quick squeeze before dashing out the door, past the wall. He flipped the latch on the iron gate and bounded into the alley. The gate clanged shut—not a prison sound as I would later hear all Korean gates to be, but a friendly home sound, the coming-and-going sound, the hello–good-bye sound.

That night in bed, I forgot to tell him what I'd read at the library about cabbage. I was fixated on Saipan.

"Azure," I said, as if giving him a quiz.

"That's blue."

"Where?"

"At twenty thousand feet. It's the blue that bites you. It's not dark, however," he explained, and I wondered if we were talking about the same thing. I tried to see him and his aircraft shooting through wisps of clouds to get to that blue. He had another life up there that I caught glimpses of in the minor annoyances of the life we led on the ground. Things got in the way on the ground—the cabbages, the iron gates, the narrow alleys, broken-up sidewalks, the motorbikes, the dirt, the piles of garbage. The taxis honked, the buses screeched their brakes, and both spewed exhaust copiously into the air.

"What about the ocean?" I asked, still on the topic of azure.

"The Yellow Sea or the Sea of Japan?" he said, referring to the bodies of water that surrounded Korea.

"Saipan," I said, cutting right to the point.

"Didn't we bomb the hell out of it in World War Two?"

"I hope not." It wouldn't seem the place for a vacation if that were true.

"Saipan?" he said. "We leveled it. Hellcats, Avengers, five-hundred-pound bombs. Strafing. Piece of cake." He yawned, and I realized he wouldn't be awake much longer.

"Saipan is in the *Guinness Book of World Records* as having the world's most equable temperature. It averages eighty-one degrees Fahrenheit year-round." I'd read the blurb from *Good Housekeeping* so many times I'd memorized it.

"Put it on our travel list, then," he said, and just like that he was sound asleep.

In the morning he stepped outside to check the weather, and I heard him say, "Those damn cabbages are still there," and I said something like, "I didn't know you hated them so," and he said, "I didn't until they amassed at our door. This place is history. That's one thing I can guarantee."

I have a recurring dream in which my husband is running out in the desert, someplace like Texas or Arizona, where the big, bright skies are best for flying. I hear him call out my name, wanting me to come with him. When I say *No, I can't,* because that's what you're supposed to say to the dead who beckon you to follow them in dreams (*Be polite and firm as if speaking to a child,* the experts on coping recommend), the landscape turns into Korea and there he goes. He runs past the end of the flight line and through the rice paddies, where the scorch mark from the F-4 crash is still visible. He's not wearing his watch. He goes down a dusty road, over a small hill, and past an enclave of farmhouses with their blue-tiled roofs. He runs as if flying, while all around him, spread out as far as the eye can see, lie fields of cabbages. I see him running—I see all of this—but I'm not with him and he's not calling to me anymore. Then, all of a sudden, he is transformed into an impala—the most graceful of the African antelopes—and begins leaping across the savannas of Tanzania. He sports the long, lyre-shaped horns like a crown. I hold my breath. Eventually he reaches the Indian Ocean and I watch him bound across the water. *Where the hell does he think he's going? Madagascar?* He's so agile. I try to call out to him to stop, but my voice won't make the necessary sound. He just gets farther and farther away from me until I wake up in a panic, unsure of where I am, but knowing exactly where I've been. That was our marriage. It went by so fast, and yet in my mind it covered all that ground. From what I can see, where I lost him was in the cabbages. It's that simple.

What I never got around to telling my husband is that Chinese cabbage is not a true cabbage. It's a member of the mustard family. But the whole damn world calls it cabbage. It's called *bae chu* in Korean and *bok choy* in Chinese. But *bok choy* in Chinese refers to all leafy-headed vegetables, and the varieties are endless: *joy choy, siew choy, ching-chiang choy, lie choy, mei qing choy.* In American supermarkets, I never see anyone buy the cabbage that's labeled *bok choy;* it always looks thin and limp, the dark green leaves loose and floppy. It must sit there for days, an uncertain future ahead of it—waiting— as mists of water spray down on it at timed intervals. What's called napa—*wong bok* in Chinese—also goes by the name of celery cabbage, and that's what the Koreans use to make kimchi. It sits fat and happy on the produce shelves, glowing in its pale green sweetness under the fluorescent lighting. I think more people buy it. I buy it as if I'm a pilgrim snatching up temple trinkets at a tourist kiosk, trying to replace what was wrongfully taken from me. China Pride, China Flash, All Autumn, China Doll, Marquis, Cha Cha, China Express, Nerva, Blues, Tango—all varieties of napa. The possibilities are endless. These are the facts, and I guess I spell it out to try to explain exactly where I've been and just how complex it is.

Korea—where the hell is that? people have asked, or better yet, simply, *Why?*

Korea is an insignificant country, after all—divided, cold; a sore thumb of a peninsula. The Koreans plant their cabbage crop around the middle of August for an October or November harvest. The cooler temperatures contribute to the sweetness in the stalks. The country people still wrap the black kimchi pots in straw and bury them in the ground, up to their necks. This prevents freezing, and it keeps the kimchi refrigerated. They place a stone on top of the cabbage to keep it from exploding, and then they put that clay lid on top. After a month or two, the pickled vegetable is ready to eat. It's important to do this right. Fermentation—the fiery heat of the red pepper, the stinging smell of the garlic, the liquid brine mixing with the anchovy paste, foaming, bubbling, gurgling up—gives the kimchi its bite. It's a staple that for centuries has kept the Koreans, the descendants of Mongols, alive, warm, and secure all winter long. Safe, buried in the ground, fizzing, ticking. All that cabbage. It makes me think of everything I ever waited for and everything that remains hidden from me on this peninsula, this land of the morning calm that the peasants still call *Chosun*—an old, but hopeful name, as if they, too, will someday regain what was wrongfully taken from them.

There's a Korean saying that a man can live without a wife, but he can't live without his kimchi. It's that serious.

As expected, my husband and I left our *ajuma* and moved into a modern apartment with a bedroom, a living room, a kitchen, and a bathroom. It was always the plan. We had a small patio in the back. It was civilized. At the base exchange we bought a television, a VCR, and a stereo. We were on the first floor of a house, but no one lived upstairs for some reason, and of course, there was a wall around the house with an even bigger iron gate that enclosed our bare courtyard. We were closer to base. It was more convenient, but I missed the coziness of our one-room place, and I missed the *ajuma* laughing at me. The day before we moved, she had shooed me away when I tried to help her and the other women with the kimchi-making. Armed with cleavers, they were splitting the cabbages in half on the cold pavement, and then putting the halves into large garbage cans to soak in salt water. When I picked up a cleaver, the *ajuma* took it away from me, saying, *Aigu, aigu-na. Good grief.* I, the bad housekeeper, the inept foreign lady, had no place in their domain.

A year later, however, alone and living in Seoul, I'd see exactly how the Korean women made the kimchi. I lingered in an alleyway one morning near my apartment, motionless before a mountain of cabbages. All I could think was, *I just want to help.* Laughing, an *ajuma* motioned for me to come closer, and offered a cleaver so I could try. It wasn't easy, but after several attempts I was able to whack a cabbage in half with one swift chop. It felt as if I'd split the world in half, causing the two sides to fall away from each other. No magazine or book could tell you what it felt like.

"This place is history," my husband said for the umpteenth time on the day we moved. We'd packed our suitcases for our new apartment and were about to leave our *ajuma* behind in the courtyard pounding garlic cloves into a pulp with the biggest mortar and pestle I'd ever seen. The mortar was the size of a birdbath, but deeper, hollowed out, and the pestle was like a fat, marble baseball bat.

"No kidding," I said to my husband. He took my hand and pulled me through the iron gate. I didn't want to leave.

"We're out of here," he said.

"Of course we are," I said, giving in. Some things were inevitable.

That night as we lay in a bed, not a futon, I told him that Koreans and garlic went back as far as prehistoric times, and what did he think about that? How could something like garlic be so old? I'd never heard anything so crazy.

I wanted to stay up all night and talk. The new house made me nervous and it seemed we should christen it by not going to sleep, but by staying awake as long as possible. I told him that on Lunar New Year's eve, Korean parents kept their children up as late as possible; it meant that the parents would live a long time. The whole purpose of the New Year's celebration was to make as much noise as possible. All the din and hoopla was said to chase evil spirits away.

I went on to ask him if, as a child, he hadn't ever spent the night with a cousin or two, staying up late, battling sleep, scaring each other with tales of ghosts and monsters. He knew about pushing the envelope, after all, and going beyond the physical limitations of the body. It was no big deal, right? I gently nudged him, signaling that it was his turn to talk.

"Garlic?" he said. His voice was barely audible. He had an early morning ahead of him. He was fading fast.

"Garlic," I said back, a little too loudly. I wanted to keep him awake. I told him I guessed some things like garlic—the simplest and most insignificant things—had no ending. Wasn't it always that way? I started to give him a list of everything I could think of that

had stubbornly endured time—garlic, cockroaches, barnacles, sand...
but by then his eyes were closed and he was sound asleep. Out like a
light, as usual.

Before drifting off after him, I flipped through the back pages of
my magazine to find that travel article on Saipan. We'd eventually
make it there, but that's a whole other story.

"Azure," I whispered, scaring myself a little. It made me think of
sharks swimming beneath the sea and jets flying beyond the clouds.
Both were gray bodies that moved wordlessly through a blue ele-
ment. I looked at my husband sleeping, and he seemed to frown. I
smiled and turned out the light. Something about air, something
about water—I would never know what. But at that moment, it had
nothing to do with the cabbages, I could see. Nothing at all.

WHITNEY DAVIS

Syracuse University

❧

THE SHARP LIGHT OF TRESPASSERS

The rivers of my America ran as flat blue lines on maps, overshadowed by thicker red lines marking freeways, interchanges, and interstates. No teacher ever taught us about the Pocahontas River. Where it begins, where it ends, what is negotiated.

In Northern New Jersey the name is not Pocahontas; waters originate under the name Ramapo River. Farther south, toward Central Jersey, through Lincoln Park, Pequannock, and the city of Paterson, the Ramapo turns into the Whippany River, which parallels highway after highway and sits flush with a monster paper products company. It must find its way into pulp tanks, collect itself sifting wood and waste, only to be shot out again through blurting pipes buried just beneath the ground. As the Whippany, its waters move among the Oranges (cities South, East, and West), Maplewood to Stirling where they swing a hip westward toward Pennsylvania, into Madison County. In Madison, the Whippany River, for a short run behind the

George Millhauser Projects and a few small pedestrian parks, wears the face of Pocahontas.

On the map, the Pocahontas joins again and again and again, and I lose her in the veins of America. It appears, though, that all these tributaries of various names have the energy to reach east to the port city of Perth Amboy—a sea town that greets, day and night, the broad body of the Atlantic Ocean.

How I became a keeper of these facts is clearly just the geography of a girlhood. We just happened to move to a street that backed up to where a portion of her body lay. Poor people and even people like us, pretending they weren't poor, lived on the Pocahontas side of town.

Our mother moved us from New York City to Madison in the spring after her graduation from nursing school, desiring to be closer to our grandmother (our sitter) and Madison Memorial where she'd secured a job. Our new house, as new as we could have known, was a two-family in a block that was not black, as my grandmother pointed out, and not white, which would have made a better but less impressive address. In the preceding years property closest to town, where renters could find Victorians divided into large drafty apartments, had turned over to immigrants—Latinos and Latinas. The streets were mostly spoken in Spanish. The population was made up of Colombians, some El Salvadorans, and a few fragmented families from Honduras—we were all fragmented, popped apart by possibility.

My grandmother had us calling all our neighbors Puerto Ricans. She'd always made a life in a middle- to working-class African American neighborhoods, but those were either full or faded away south. Most of those families from her day had split into the "haves" and the "nots"—north to high horse country and south to public housing (George Millhauser projects).

————

Reg and I ran like disobedient dogs straight for the property line in the backyard. What we sat at the edge of the grass were the limitations of land, a place where gravity and water had worked the earth down, worked a river or at least a muddy bed. We were presented with the wearing away of humus, soil, leaves, and long fur-topped weeds exposing the dusty bone of earth, a path. A path in our minds meant we were to go, get beyond the yard, because other people had. The path headed on a diagonal, downward through a frail wood of mostly broken back trees until it was severed at the bottom by a chain-link fence. Someone had already taken tool to chain, ripped and rolled it back enough for a person to move through, a large person if they wanted. Green and brown beer bottles, broken and whole, shone like unnatural stones along the fence, on the bank, in steel-colored water. Reg and I made ritual the picking up of bottles, curiously punishing ourselves by smelling the stench of dark soil and rotten brew before heaving them hard onto wet rocks. We never thought much of the inebriated night owls who came to the woods to drink while we sat in the house eating our dinners in front of the TV.

For a while we chose the path and the water over the corner store, over smart-mouthed kids hanging by the swings, over bikes thrown under the porch. Those first few months the water level never rose more than three or four feet, and in parts there was just barely enough stream to cover a lone, stuck sneaker or runaway tire. It was an open mouth for objects refused. We raised to one another, with pioneer spirit, the building of a bridge. Our pinnacle piece was going to be a rusting shopping cart, an emerging silver monument to the Stop & Shop. We walked the bank for what *we* called miles, as dogs in various yards strained at their leads, furiously announcing the coming of trespassers. We were Explorers, Fortuneseekers, Traveling Negroes from New York—often accompanied by our slight white neighbor, Warner. We asked him the day we met him on the front porch, in the cruel way kids do, why he was weak, rawboned. His sister, Desiree, stepped up, claiming he was born premature, but our mother whispered his limbs, his shrunken chest looked more like he'd suffered the effects of fetal alcohol syndrome. Our mother, the nurse, now had license to diagnose the world. Tell *me,* I said as I lay on my back on the living room floor, why I feel the way I feel.

Warner and Desiree were clearly cared for, though, wanted by their cautious mother, who at first look also appeared to lack the proportions of solidity. However, their circumstances proved her a woman with endurance; any other might have long since lost the kids to the County. Warner had been growing in the other side of our house for several years and had never tried the path, not until we started down it. Reg followed me, sliding in his soleless sneakers. No one could have convinced us before we moved that a whiteboy would be waiting there, shiny faced—not quite a full moon in a dark sky. Warner was waiting for us to show him how to make use of the yard and the dull, drywood porch we called headquarters.

But by the time that first spring ended, going down to the gnat-dancing, dry riverbed seemed mostly a waste of time and the trash by the bank no longer seemed full. Summer was on us, and from the time we woke up hot with humidity sunken into our sheets we complained there was nothing to do. Our grandmother was not about making a nest. "You can't complain about nothing in here. Get outside, complain all you want to the concrete." The heat burned out the lawns; it made playing in the street like doing weary work on the devil's unrelenting land.

So Reg, Warner, Desiree, and I opted to leave the two-family with towels around our necks, as if caring for South American pythons. We walked in sweaty shoes and socks, because our mother always insisted on both, to Lincoln Park, where they had a public pool. Actually, on most occasions Reg and I tried to slip out on our own. We preferred the deep end and Desiree and Warner could not swim—nobody told them to try. They just bobbed, screamed, and paddled in the shallow end. Our larger concern, though, was kids from the projects who preyed on them, trying to dunk their fair heads until they coughed chlorine. Alone we had a better chance of swimming unassaulted. The majority of those kids had brown bodies like ours, but they had never seen us before. They were clear the first day: "You think you all that." We had no other choice but to believe them. There was no point in explaining that we'd be walking to the same bus stop come cool, that we, too, would be standing cold, sleepy-eyed on the curb. We were the same kids waiting for pops in the shadow of the same clunker of a truck, pulling damp dollars or coins from our sneakers: We were all waiting for the same sweet thing; even though the picture on the side revealed ten different ice-cream choices, you knew the middle-aged guy inside only had one kind.

Nobody got what they wanted. I wanted to cannonball, run and jump high and hard, breaking the surface, but that was against Lincoln Park pool rules.

If they wanted to fight, we would fight. Reg could fight his hands off. What else could we do? We had white friends. We wore slick, new bathing suits. Most of them sagged in oversized hand-me-downs, boys and girls in rough-edged shorts, water-logged underwear.

We learned that in our neighborhood, on afternoons when we could get a good count of Latinos and a few white kids from the Piedmont Condos, we could hide-and-seek in the yard or play another version, "Bloody Murder," on the street. We'd muscle someone's hose from its place by the side of their house like it was a strange animal, only controlled by its neck. We sprayed and sprayed, screamed and sprayed, even when the rusted mouth dry-coughed from the pressure of our hands. Older kids, teenagers, strangers on ten-speeds clicked, clicked down our block, while we stood in the middle of the road, admiring with our arms crossed.

"Where did you get that bike? Them sneakers, that phat hat, jacket, game watch, name ring, gold tooth? What kind of people are your people . . . with those eyes, that kinda hair? That your sister? Ya'll don't look anything alike."

Late on a day when all that talk had headed nowhere, our grandmother parted the curtains and caught at least five of us trooping the path to the Pocahontas. She came out into the yard, her frank voice quick from years of dealing with bad behavior (when my uncle Sonnyboy was sixteen he threw her color TV through the plate glass window; she called the cops, let them cuff him up). With stiff throats Reg and I looked toward the house and wished we were standing in the deepest, densest lick of earth—where we'd be sure to be counted with the day's survivors.

Survive we did that day from the shadow of our deeds, but it was only because the minute my mother walked in the door our grandmother started the story by saying, "Your two and the whiteboy were going into the woods with a gang of Puerto Ricans." Our mother was not dealing with her ignorance and right there cut our sentence from a beating down to a warning, before she could throw her coat to the chair.

She diagnosed our grandmother loudly. "You have lazy synapses . . . loose mouth muscles, Mama." We watched her from our place in front of the TV. She pulled chicken from the freezer and held it under hot water. She shook her head, her hair still in a smooth bun. She did not want to hear another word about her neighborhood.

I heard her slam the back door the next morning before her shift. Through our bedroom window I saw her pose at the property line—

white dress, white shoes, sheer white hose showing brown legs, holding her red nails hard around her hips. It wasn't like our mother to survey a situation. She'd just say, Don't. Don't *you* and *you* go near the car, that part of the park, those kids, that dog, the X-rated movie channel, don't ever touch *any* of my things again. That is how I remember her, in stern white, working white, a uniformed servant to some tragic hour, to some faraway siren sound.

Maybe she, too, had not heard of waters old, entrenched, and hiding in her part of the world.

We stayed away from the embankment and the water for at least two years. Even when our cousins came from Brooklyn and we had nothing to do but show off our suburbia. We showed them our tire-swing, the tree it was attached to, our porch, and the shy white kids attached to that.

Reg was ten and I was eleven, almost twelve, when two Latino boys came to the front door asking for Reg's ransom. Desiree and I were playing out a doll-drama inside. The smirking boys ordered me, in the diluted English of our brownbodied streets, to get Coca-Cola and chips or my brother was going to get dragged to the piranha in the river. While I wanted to play along, bring them into my mother's kitchen while Desiree and I pretended we didn't want them in there, near us, I couldn't—the mention of the river caught me. Rainy autumn weather had once again stirred childhood curiosity. There had been a swelling, coercive movement visible from the ridge and I knew they wanted to find a way to shove each other around down there.

"No you don't," I said swearing past them toward the side yard. If my brother got even one shoelace in the water, my mother would lose control. I ran out and around to the side of the house where I found Reg and Warner standing in the woods, hands on their heads, elbows out. They'd been hustled between two large boulders that made the boundaries of their prison. Two more boys held sticks on them in case one tried to sprint toward the side door. When Reg saw me he smiled, the smile of a fool, foolish enough to play a game with prisons and punishments.

"You so stupid," I said.

If you are just Reg and Warner, outnumbered, you don't play games where there is capturing and rules made up by fourteen-year-old Puerto Ricans from Columbia who lived south of South Crown Street.

When I got back into the house Desiree had taken it upon herself to change the fashions of the dolls. Her doll was wearing my doll's Rollergirl hot pants and halter top and mine was wearing a house-dress her mother had made from scrap fabric. At first I said, "I don't think so, Desiree." Then I said I didn't care. I dealt out all the story lines anyway. The Cinderella always overcomes her troubles. She gets to go to the ball and lay down in the cut-open Kleenex box with a half-naked Ken—we'd long since lost his surf shorts.

But later that same day in October, Reg did hit the water. Twenty minutes before our mother was to be home. I'm sure he fell fast, Warner looking on. The older boys had gone and the two of them, feeling somehow above what was previously forbidden, feeling desperate to raze the boredom, went down to pitch rocks, play Tarzan, play Castaway Island . . . whatever. Reg came to the door wet as midwinter. I sucked him through, pulling him down, stretching and straining him across the floor in an effort to strip him of his hardening cords, knowing my mother was not the kind of woman to isolate blame. We hid his soiled clothes, hid the events of the day, because often "sorry" doesn't do. Reg toweled his face in the bathroom and I combed from the back of his head specks of leaf, a green silk curling into his hair.

After dinner Reg didn't want to stay up with me.

I walked home from school alone the next day because Reg stayed in bed with a fever. When the fever didn't break in a day my mother took him in.

Every day after that I walked home alone from the plain public school, because my brother Reg went to a special school for the blind. Bacteria, *Staphylococcus,* with the capacity for rapid growth and reproduction, my mother had said, expanded and joined together to form longer *Staphylococci,* in ears, nose—in mass in the throat. But it was the fever that took down his sight.

I hated my grandmother because the way she told me that day it happened was worse than the truth we grew to live with. She knew how to use the solid part of bitterness: "Black things find their way to black people." That day I walked away from her face. I walked the mile to the hospital, cutting coatless, mad-faced through the projects. I went into Madison Memorial Emergency Room and up to the desk, where I told the nurse on duty I had something important to say about Reggie Harrow. I thought they needed to know he had fallen in the river a few days back.

"What river?" another nurse passing by wanted to hear.

Maybe there was an antidote, a dark fluid shot to clear the clouds. I cried . . . it seemed a good time to yell, too. I made the women swear they wouldn't tell my mother. I don't know why I thought they wouldn't. She was working somewhere on one of those floors and I was making a hard mark in her colleagues' minds. It just seemed the best place to confess the truth, in the sterile light of the emergency room where they know how to build you back, but my moment called emergency had long since evaporated. I thought for years the

Pocahontas River was a reason. Maybe she'd been waiting for someone to get caught facedown—so she could whisper her regret, black into their eyes.

"Bacteria long to be on us," my mother said. She could think of a million reasons why I was not to focus on the cause.

"Reg," she'd said, moving her head from side to side, "Reg let his hands drift over every imaginable source."

He loved to feel the trying of a livething, flipping to fly from the closed cup of his hand.

LIDIJA S. CANOVIC

University of North Texas

Bats

In the morning Slavko tells his sister they have bats. It's the first thing he's said to her in months. He doesn't say he plans to shoot them. She shrugs and walks off into the kitchen. He watches her empty a plastic bag full of overripe, almost rotting tomatoes into the tin sink, then goes back to the anteroom. Even with the water running, he can still hear her old voice, an internal buzzing sound gnawing at him. He can't make out the words, but he knows what she's thinking— they are all God's creatures. He doesn't care. He takes the Moskovka gun from the wall and sets it in his lap, brushing the dust off the year carved into its heel: 1893. He waits for a sound in the weak light of the large votive candle that glows beneath the icon of the Mother of God with Three Hands. He hears nothing.

He first heard the flapping of wings the night before when he was in bed. He thought it was only a frightened insect, a large night moth perhaps. Then something hit the ceiling and he heard nothing at all. From the sliver of light that pushed past the sides of the drawn red canvas blinds, he noticed a patch on the ceiling, right next to the dusty glass chandelier. He saw the patch was a small animal. It lifted its wings and flew over to the top of the old oak chiffonier that stood in the darkened corner of the living room.

The Moskovka is his father's gun from the First War. Slavko has never used it. His hands were always too weak for hunting and he wasn't any war's soldier. When he was younger and still living in the country in Bajina Bašta, just across the river from Bosnia, children came up to him and said, Hey, *Deda,* tell us a war story. He didn't know any. He lied and said he didn't remember the war, then showed them the gun. It was his only connection with the war and with his father, who died at thirty-six from a mortar wound in the head. That was on a Sunday in April of 1914, almost eighty years ago. Every Sunday afternoon Slavko cleans the Moskovka, and he never lets anyone touch it.

One night in a dream his sister pulled the gun off the wall mount and hit his jaw with the steel butt plate, breaking his teeth. They rattled in his mouth like dice. It was the following day that he stopped talking to her.

Slavko, his sister says when she speaks to him, you're a jackass. She snatches the second half of the daily *Politika* he reads only for the obituaries. He hopes he will recognize someone's name, but sees only pictures of young men. Who in God's name are you looking for? she asks. They're all dead, all the people you've ever known. It's our time, too. Even the century has grown weary of us.

Later, she combs his hair back with her fingers as if he were her husband. She brings him chicken soup. Since the dream, however, he believes he has no teeth. His dreams have replaced his memory. He twirls his tongue over his gums and feels nothing but smooth skin. He can't taste anything. He believes it is her way of telling him he has nothing to live for, because he's old and useless, so he calls her useless, too. Your cooking is of no use to me, he tells her, but she keeps doing it. She cooks *sarmas* with vine leaves and moussaka with withered clumps of egg yolks. Everything tastes like paper in his mouth.

When she goes to the kitchen to wash the dishes, he tells her he hates her. If you die tomorrow, he says when she turns the faucet on, I won't call anyone for days. I'll just keep you here. I want to watch you rot.

She turns the water down and glances at him through the door. You can read the first half of the newspaper, she says.

He wonders if they have been like this since they were born. He doesn't remember her young. She says they had the same mother and same father, but he doesn't remember that either. He does remember a girl, about ten years old, a warm body placed into his bed when he got back from work, and there was a war then, but he doesn't remember which one.

She reminds him. Remember Bajina Bašta, she says.

He nods. He knows he was born there, but doesn't know when. He sees a whitewashed house, the swift blue Drina, a broken butter churn, and a slaughtered lamb lying on black grass. It must have been years ago that they left. Maybe he was young then, but the reflection in the mirror tells him he must be eighty now. His mouth looks like a dark, inverted flower, crumpled and withered and caving in.

Last night, when he heard the whirring of the bats and her breathing in the other bed, he made lists of things he wanted to shoot. The mirror. The glass of water she keeps by her bedside that glows pink with her dentures. Her chin. The building they live in. He dreamed of finding that vulnerable spot that carries the weight of all the walls. He knows the building must have one, since it looks so much like a crate anyway. If he found that spot, one bullet would be enough to crack it open like a walnut.

He pulls the bolt out of the Moskovka. Its chamber is hollow, but he has a small box of bullets in case he needs them, tucked on a shelf behind the New Testament. She doesn't want him to keep the bullets there. How do you think Jesus' words could be written in red if a path hadn't been cleared for him by these? he asks, waving the box in front of her eyes. The bullets clang against each other in the box.

He isn't sure if he'll be able to fire the Moskovka, since it hasn't been cleaned in so long, so he goes out to the terrace to get a bottle of sunflower oil. The bottle is among his "war rations." He might have missed all the wars, but he's ready now: rows of canned beans, peas, and corn stacked on the small wooden shelves. Broken plastic cords twisted around a spool. A year's worth of newspapers covered in clumps of dust, tied with a piece of rope, the lettering washed out from the spring rains. A box of Biljana laundry detergent. On the floor, a sack of flour full of moth larvae and four large cans of powdered milk with rust flaking off the lids.

She tells him the bats are looking for insects that have gathered there. It's just a pile of junk, she says.

He wants to tell her she will be grateful for this junk when another war comes, but he says nothing.

Slavko stayed awake listening to the bats. He knew there must be at least two, probably a male and a female, and he imagined more hatching in the chiffonier. He didn't move under his thick blanket in order to hear them better. They hit the ceiling and sometimes the chandelier, their wings chopping across the room like the helicopters passing overhead.

He fell asleep and dreamed that her body was lifeless, made of only two bones, a thigh bone and an arm, the top of the thigh bone like a small, rounded head. He carried her as if she were a child and looked for a place to bury the bones. People he saw through his window, the ones with their big drooling hounds, passed by and he worried the dogs would dig her back up, so he went to the botanical garden. Its name, Botanička Bašta, reminded him of his hometown, Bajina Bašta, and he wanted to take her home and bury her somewhere beneath the bell tower. With his hands he dug a shallow grave for her, scooping out the damp black soil with his dry fingers.

He woke briefly. The branches of the oak in front of the window whipped the sides of the building all night long. She had left the red canvas blinds spooled at the top of the window, and the shadows of the branches raked across the ceiling in the half-light, wrapping themselves around the ceiling and the side wall as if they were trying to trap him. He closed his eyes and continued digging.

In the morning, his fingernails were dirty with earth and he spent an hour cleaning them out.

The bats are quiet in the daylight, hiding in her musty laundry. He sets the gun on the bed and goes through the stacks of pressed hand towels and folded handkerchiefs. He tells her to wash them again, in hot water this time.

The iron isn't working since you tried to cut its cord for your war rations, she says. She locks the doors of the chiffonier, tells him she's expecting guests and needs the towels.

You're nothing but a useless bag of flesh breathing my air, he wants to tell her, but everything between them has already been said. To utter the words is simply a waste of energy.

He moves on to the next plan, darkening the room with the blinds to coax the bats out.

She's cooking again. From the kitchen he hears the radio crackling the introductory music to "Two White Doves," her favorite, a show that plays Old Town songs. She is humming, and a few words escape her mouth. Where are you, my white dove, she sings, her voice a young girl's.

He cleans the gun in the half-light, pouring rancid sunflower oil into an old pair of underwear, the elastic fuzzing up on the sides. He brushes the surface of the barrel, then takes a warped toothbrush to clean the inside. Tiny black clumps fall out, as if it hasn't been cleaned in a long time.

The whirring sound brushes by his ear again. He jolts the gun upright and hits the bat in flight, knocking it down onto the commode. The bat stays sprawled on the lacquered surface, then tries to pick up its wings. A few drops of oil have splashed on the top and the bat's feet drag across them. He grabs the tall candle and starts hitting the bat. The candle breaks in half, but he continues hitting. The bat stops writhing and tilts its head back. Its head is like a small black dog's.

She walks into the room. What's that noise? she asks. She turns on the light. The carpet is covered with broken bits of wax.

He is holding the bat in his hand. He rips its wings, and they feel like garbage bags between his fingers.

Christ, she says. Mother of God. She crosses herself and covers her open mouth.

The bat's head curls up between his thumb and index finger. Don't go calling Christ, he says. Christ can't help you now.

In the afternoon he finds another bat in the bathroom drinking toilet water. Every time it slips on the porcelain surface, it starts flapping its wings. He shuts the door quickly and goes to get the gun.

She is in the kitchen again, preparing paprikaš. The house smells of overcooked tomatoes.

Where are you going? she asks him.

There's another one in the toilet bowl, he says.

She drops the ladle and wipes her hands on a small wet towel. Leave it alone, she says.

He pushes her aside and goes to get the Moskovka. He can hear her opening and slamming the bathroom door. He takes the gun off the wall mount. He opens the chamber and finds it empty—he's sure he loaded it this morning. His hands are shaking and he can't slot his fingers into the trigger. Frustrated, he throws the gun on her bed and goes back to the bathroom.

She is standing on a stool and reaching to close the window. There, she says. All gone.

He lifts the toilet seat and finds it empty. He looks at the floor. Several pairs of wrinkled shoes are piled on top of each other in the corner. What bad luck. In the country, that's like burying someone in the ground, covering up his shoe with yours. They should be lined up neatly, one beside the other. He kneels down to move them.

The bat's gone, she says, louder this time, as if he hasn't heard her. So don't bother looking for it in the shoes.

His knees are pressed against the cold cement floor as he holds up a pair of shoes, figuring out where to place it.

All right, you stupid *budalo*. Look for yourself, she says and walks back to the kitchen.

The shoes are all the same, so he can't line them up by size. There isn't any space on the floor. He tucks several pairs next to each other, but the last pair has to be put on top of the rest. He sighs and struggles to get up, pushing weight on his knuckles to straighten out his legs.

In the mirror, the face of an old man frightens him. The man's eyes are bright blue, so rounded they are almost falling out. He is wearing a gray button-up pullover that has been patched in several places from moth bites. The man doesn't look away, and neither does he. They stand there together, sizing each other up.

Look at you, the man says. Sorting out other people's shoes.

He looks down and then back up. The man is still there, staring at him.

Look at what you've become, the man says.

He doesn't reply. He's not sure what the shoes have to do with anything.

Remember Bajina Bašta, the man says.

His father's gun hanging on a white wall. A slaughtered lamb lying on black grass. That's all he remembers. He turns to leave.

There's a bat in your head. You can't remember anything, the man in the mirror says just as he goes out the door.

In the early evening, he hears noises coming from the anteroom. A man's voice, then hers. They are talking quietly. He opens the door to find out who it is and sees a middle-aged man holding a small sack of flour.

Good afternoon, Slavko, the man says.

She goes over to hug the man, and her arm curls around his waist and disappears behind his broad back. Standing next to each other, they look like mother and son, the same twisted lips and large eyes. Milan's here, she says. Do you remember Milan?

We don't need flour, he says. We have plenty out on the terrace. He walks back into the living room, closing the door behind him. He sits in the armchair in the corner, sets the Moskovka on her bed, and waits.

He used to sleep in the kitchen, where the window faces the street instead of the courtyard. A traffic light is tucked behind the edge of a building on the street where buses passed. At night it blinked at him through the trees. He had never seen a traffic light before. At night it bled red light onto his ceiling. He moved to this room, and now he sleeps in a narrow bed next to hers.

He moves toward the door to hear what they are saying. He can't make out the words. He hears the man say something that sounds like "I walk plank of water," and then she answers back, "No knife bring summer." They must be spies speaking in a secret language. He wants to know what they are saying, but he can't crack the code. He wonders if they are lovers, if that's who she was cooking the rotting tomatoes for.

He remembers being in a field of wheat, the sun cracking the clumps of earth around him. He is pretending to be asleep, but a bee keeps swirling over his fingers, dripping with tomato juice. He waves the bee off. The ground below him molds itself to his back, absorbing his sweat. A hat covers his face, and through the tiny holes in the criss-crossed straw he sees her lying on the wet soil by the river, her bare arms covered in freckles from the sun. She is giggling. She motions to a man lying beside her to come closer. The man unbuttons her white blouse, the one she wears to work in the field, and slips his dark hand onto her breast. She grabs his wrist to stop him. He might not be asleep yet, she tells the man. Slavko, she says. He looks at her face through the holes. It is serious. Slavko, she repeats, a little louder this time.

The man, too, turns around to look at him. His face is like Milan's, only younger. See, he's asleep, the man says and buries his face into the nape of her neck, where the light brown plait begins.

The bees will sting him, she says as the man takes off her blouse. He opens it up and reveals a sliver of sweat dripping between her breasts and down to her belly. Because of the sunlight, the sliver looks like a knife blade.

When the man's body covers her, she looks over his shoulder at the pile of crushed red tomatoes lying beside Slavko's motionless fingers.

———

He pulls the door open with his fingers to hear them better.

Where is the gun now? he hears Milan say.

Her reply is muffled.

He's a lunatic, Milan says. And you don't have to stand for it. We'll put him in a home.

He can't hear her reply.

That fucking war, Milan says. Tell me where the gun is.

No, she says. He can hardly stand it here, son. Leave him be. He's not going to hurt anybody.

He'll hurt *you*, Milan says. He doesn't know what he's doing. Does he remember anything?

I talked to God today, she says, and God told me to take him home. He can't live here like this anymore. He never goes out on the street. He's afraid of everything, of passing cars, of people shouting. One night he was sobbing in bed because he said there was blood on the ceiling from the traffic lights. He needs to go home, son.

What home? Christ, have you lost your mind, too? There is nothing there anymore. The house is blown to pieces. It's just a pile of rubble now.

He hears banging, as if someone has slammed a glass of water down on the table.

Maybe if he saw the field in front of the house, she says.

God, there is no use talking to you, is there? I told you it's all ruined. The barn's gone. I talked to Milena and she said her husband saw dead cows lying in a pile out by the Perišićs' field. They were being hauled away by tractors.

Gospode Bože. Save us from this.

I'm just saying there is nothing to go back to there.

She is crying. Can't you at least go and see if there's anything that can be salvaged? The clock? Mama had some books, some photo albums—

A book with a broken spine, pages of smooth gray cardboard, photographs of a dozen women, some sitting down, some standing behind them, wearing white dresses, their eyes pale and frozen, one of them his mother, full breasts, weak smile, the photograph covered with thin paper, like mist, like milk.

Me? Milan shouts. Are you crazy? That's not my goddamn war. Don't yell, she says, hushing him. He doesn't know.

You haven't told him yet?

Son, he doesn't remember why he's here and I won't tell him. It has only been three months.

He'll find out from the papers, Milan says. And then what will you do? If he's crazy enough to run around the apartment shooting bats, imagine what he'd do if he knew that.

He won't find out. I steal the *Politika* from him every day. Then I tell him he can read the first half, but you know what he's like. If I tell him to do it, he won't. He just reads the obituaries and he doesn't know why there are only young people in them.

Milan sighs. Christ, what an insane family.

All he did was kill a bat, she says. Leave him be. It's his last war.

He moves away from the door. He can hear the whirring sound of wings in his head, as if a spool of film has been tugged out of a news-reel projector. A war, he thinks. He can see soldiers moving in the night, crawling on their bellies through the marshes and fields. The soldiers' faces are his family's: his father, his grandfather, his brothers. At first he can see them clearly, but then their eyes become obscured by bats' wings. He takes the Moskovka from her bed and grabs the bullets to load it, then walks into the anteroom. Milan is sitting on the old couch, leaning forward so the wild strawberry slatko in his spoon won't drip on the floor. She is crouched in the corner on a chair. She gets up when he opens the door.

Where are you going? she asks.

Move the hell out of my way, he says.

She grabs the gun. Please, Slavko, I'm begging you, leave the gun.

He shoves her, and she falls back onto the chair.

You, he turns to Milan, still seated on the couch, watching in disbelief. If it's not your war, it's not your land, he says and spits on the red carpet in front of Milan's shoes.

He opens the door to the stairwell. He has never seen the stone steps before, or maybe he just doesn't remember. He hears her old voice shouting behind him as he starts down. His legs are light, and at the bottom of each flight he jumps over the last stair. The heel of the Moskovka bangs against his thigh. A woman on the third floor cracks open her door, then sees him with his gun and slams it shut again. City people, he laughs. They're afraid of everything.

He opens the thick glass door of the entrance into the front yard. The street behind the gate isn't big, but he doesn't remember ever seeing it. It is late afternoon. A few small children are on the corner playing *lastiš*, the white elastic band stretched behind their ankles. Across the street he sees a faded brick building, the plaster from the walls peeling off in thin sheets. Behind that building he sees another, behind it another, and another, for kilometers it seems. On the busy cross street he sees a bus drive by, leaning to its side from the weight of the people standing by the door. It lets out a snake of black air as it pulls over. He opens the wire gate and steps down onto the pavement.

Watch your step, he says.

Then he remembers. It is her voice telling him those words, holding onto his arm as he treads carefully on the smooth cement. Watch your step, she says. This isn't the cobble road you're used to. He nods but wants to cry. The tears come only on the inside, and he swallows them like spit.

———

He sees the farmhouse, the barn farther south, and the sun piercing the haystacks. His father's gravestone is in the backyard. He remembers the hollow sound that bounces off the walls as he walks through the rooms. He is alone. He eats tomato broth, because that's the only thing he has and knows how to cook. As he scoops out the dry *knedla* dumplings made of water and flour, he hears a breaking sound and a bullet shell falls onto the wooden floor. He looks up and sees it has pushed through the wall. He gets down beneath the table and that's where the soldiers find him.

Hey, *Deda,* one says, what are you cooking? Where's your family? Why are you still here?

He doesn't know what to tell them.

A few days later, through the rear window of a car, he watches the white house disappear behind a line of oaks.

Belgrade—he remembers now. The White Town. Not a patch of grass, and where is the Danube? The trees rustle above him. Their branches intertwine above the street. The Moskovka is cold against his body. He hears another whirring and thinks it must be the bats flying among the dried leaves, like small soldiers protecting their piece of land. He looks up, and the trees are like a web above him, trapping the sky.

ROOMPA BHATTACHARYYA

Wayne State University

Loss

There is some sort of weight on her face—a searing, relentless pressure hurting her eyelids, heavy against her nose and mouth. It occurs to her that she cannot breathe, that she should panic, that she should struggle. Twisting her head, sensing the scream rising like bile in her throat, she realizes suddenly that she is free. She can breathe; she can see.

"Avanti?"

She sits up abruptly on the sofa and the light hits her eyes full force, like the back of a hand.

"Oh, sweetie, I'm so sorry. You were stirring and I thought you were already awake." Fran's plump pink face, hovering above her, wrinkles with concern.

"No, no, it's okay." Avanti tries to smile; she knows the woman means well. Anyway, she prefers Fran's overly solicitous ministrations to those of the local Indian women, who have brought armloads of

Tupperwared food and now huddle in pensive, whispering groups, having come to pay their respects. She can hear the hushed drone of female voices from the kitchen now, and the awful, familiar shame washes over her again.

"Are you hungry? I made you some soup—it's vegetable, don't worry!" Fran emits the awkward "aar-aar-aar" Avanti has come to recognize as laughter. She continues to be amazed at how ill at ease Fran seems around her. Yet she is the only one of the neighbors who has offered any sort of support.

"Thank you," Avanti tells her, though she knows she will not eat it. Jiten Da, she notices, is still seated in the corner by the kitchen, his hands neatly folded in the lap of his tailored black trousers. It has been odd for her to address him and some of the other men with the honorific for "older brother," as they are all more than old enough to be her father—indeed, Jiten Da could be her grandfather. Avanti watches him watching her for a moment, a brief moment, before lowering her eyes. Like his wife and the other women, she senses that he, too, is a bit frightened by her. She drops her head into her hands, then grimaces as she slides off the sofa, slowly, as if it hurts. She is exhausted, of course, but she is also well aware that he is still scrutinizing her.

Fran is still talking. "...and that nice Mrs. Batra stopped by. She brought those roses right over there." Her hand flutters in the direction of the door, where Avanti vaguely notes a scattering of red amid a heap of green tissue paper. "Although red roses—" Fran's thin mouth twists with slight distaste, but she almost immediately smiles and pats Avanti's shoulder. "Well, everyone's different, that's what I always say. It's the thought that counts, right?"

Avanti wants very much now to get away from her. "I'm going to take a shower," she says, darting off before the woman can respond. Glancing back once as she hurries up the stairs, she sees Fran standing

alone in the middle of the living room, chafing her hands, a bemused, uncomfortable smile straining her lips. Avanti knows from
experience that Fran will try to fit in, interrupting the buzzing Bengali conversations with her seal-like laughter, obliviously blathering
on as the others nod politely and sneak knowing, rueful looks at one
another. That Fran is eager to ingratiate herself with the Indians who
have been by these last two days is clear, but why she acts this way is
beyond Avanti.

Two days. Avanti is unsure why she has stopped in front of the
bedroom. She slept there last night—a long, undisturbed sleep. She
has not cried since the funeral this morning. She has only cried,
she realizes, around the others, letting them smooth her hair, rub her
back, murmur soothingly in her ear.

The heavy, dark-suited man at the crematorium had stared in awe
at the vast crowd of onlookers, confusion marring his look of practiced serenity. "You're the wife?" he asked Avanti. "Are these other
relatives?"

She could not speak. She stared at the sleek casket, her upper lip
beading with sweat from the warm crush of people and the heat em-
anating through the wall of the crematorium. She imagined the
flames, roaring and soothing, relieving the body of the burdens that
had destroyed it—a contained, benevolent hell.

"We are her family. She needs us to be here," Jiten Da informed
the man before gesturing to the women clustered like soldiers around
Avanti. "Don't let her see."

Avanti found herself enveloped in firm, maternal arms, her face
wedged against a fleshy neck smelling of baby powder and mustard
seed. She faintly heard the soft click of the gate closing behind the
casket, and at long last she was allowed to return home. They still,
however, refuse to take seriously her requests to be alone.

"She's so young," Ila Bose said yesterday while Avanti pretended to nap on the sofa. "It's too much for her; they were only married just over a year, together here for only eight months. What if . . . well, she shouldn't be alone."

Avanti cannot tell these women, all of whom are her mother's age, how desperately she needs to be by herself, to allow this terrible numbness to engulf her fully. She is exhausted by her pretenses of heartache, but she is also curious to know what will happen. She does not know exactly why she is grieving, not yet. She knows how she should feel, but is not certain yet that she does at all.

Slowly, painfully, as if it is forty-eight hours ago, as if this time she knows what to expect, she steps inside the room. Down the hall, in the bathroom, water rushes through unseen pipes; a tinkle of laughter drifts in from downstairs. She lies back on the bed, their bed. The elaborate overhead light fixture hangs loosely, most of the glass broken by the police officer who cut the rope. Two of the curved, gilded arms are bent downward, grotesquely, as if beckoning to her.

Noise. That was her first impression of America. And size. The KLM terminal was a vast expanse of white walls and blue carpet. A calm, confident female voice announced a flight number on the overhead loudspeaker. Avanti had braced herself for the swarms of white faces, the glare of bright lights, the modern surroundings, but not for the feeling of helplessness, the absolute terror.

Rahul touched her arm. "We have to get our bags." It was as if they were meeting again for the first time, afraid to speak, afraid to smile. She clutched her purse with both hands, remembering the wistful look on her aunt's face as she handed Avanti that purse before the wedding and proudly announced that it was from the most expensive store in Calcutta. Avanti stood motionless for a moment, the smooth maroon leather dampening under her palms, as Rahul strode off into the crowd. She remained rooted in place until he paused in midstep, turning back to gaze at her quizzically before gesturing for her to follow.

"Are you all right?" he asked as she approached.

She nodded mutely, suddenly aware of the breadth of his shoulders, of how much taller than she he was. Sitting in the yellow plastic seat, watching as he effortlessly hoisted their suitcases off the conveyor belt, Avanti felt relief wash over her like a slow, warm wind. She was married to this man—this man who had so deftly booked their tickets, found their connecting flights, asked for extra pillows on the plane—and she loved him, truly, loved him so much there was an ache in her chest.

Her father had liked him immediately—he keenly admired the work ethic and determination of the Indians who had left to forge new lives in Europe and the States. Her mother had been hesitant at first, and inconsolable after the wedding; she didn't want her oldest daughter a twenty-four-hour plane ride away, even if it was in America. Her sister Anu had pointed out his height—at least six feet—and concluded that living in America made one taller. Avanti had liked his smooth, strong jaw, his quick smile, his rumbling laugh.

"I saw you at the Mitra wedding last week, Avanti." Rahul's mother had smiled generously, obviously pleased with herself, as the two families sat awkwardly sipping tea. "Bina Mitra gave me your father's telephone number—even though I think she had her eye on you for her nephew! But I promised Rahul I would inquire only about the prettiest girls..."

Everyone had chuckled politely. Embarrassed but not surprised at the woman's candor, Avanti struggled briefly to respond without sounding conceited or uninterested. Luckily, the parents had started

comparing medical histories and astrological ⟨
nibbled on a biscuit and sneaked furtive glances

"So you do speak English well, then?" he ha
adults tactfully left them alone for a little while

"Yes, although I'm sure not as well as you," ~~Avanti answered~~
consciously. She had never spoken to one of them before, the much-
lauded Non-Resident Indians. And he was different, palpably so,
from the Indian boys she knew.

"Oh, you speak very well," he assured her.

A hundred questions had surged through her, but she swallowed
them back, clamping shut her trembling jaw as she waited for Rahul
to speak again. He had paused a moment to peer out the window, his
eyes narrowing pensively before glancing back toward Avanti. Her
face had grown warm as she forced herself to meet his dark gaze, worried that she had tensed her mouth in an unbecoming way.

"This is so awkward, don't you think?" he had asked suddenly. "I
always wondered how it would feel, meeting someone like this, asking each other questions..." As the burning in Avanti's cheeks became almost painful, an odd thought flitted unbidden through her
mind: Why had Rahul returned to India to find a bride? Many other
NRIs married women from their adopted countries. Avanti had seen
several such couples shopping in the posh New Market district.
None of the men had been particularly impressive, but all radiated
that faint, peculiar sort of disdain that marked them as expatriate
rather than foreign-born Indians. The wives had seemed to blend together as well. They may have been English or German, Canadian or
American, but they seemed uniformly pale and unreal, clutching
their handbags and honey-colored children close at their sides. Rahul,
Avanti realized, must have chosen to follow custom and let his parents search out potential wives. Her sister and friends had been
right—she was very, very lucky.

meetings later a date had been set; she saw him alone twice ore the wedding. No one ever asked her if she wanted to move to the United States, but she, too, had taken it for granted that she did.

There wasn't much of anything to see outside as the taxi pulled away from the airport, just a labyrinth of lights and stark gray buildings against the blue night. Rahul tentatively slipped an arm around her and they sat, silently, stiffly, until they reached home.

Avanti wanted so intensely to lean into his chest, to tell him how she felt, to hear his response. She could see the words, the right words, behind her closed eyes—she could taste them in her throat, soft and yearning, trapped and tingling.

She remained quiet later that night, listening to the new, chenille-covered bed gently creak under their combined weight. Staring straight above her, unblinking, Avanti watched a wayward moonbeam glance off the overhead chandelier—a momentary shimmer—and suddenly Rahul's face covered hers, the sweat from his forehead stinging her eyes. She shut them quickly, guiltily, as his jaw clenched and quivered against her cheek, as the sharp corner of his hip burrowed into hers, as his moist palms slid over the ridge of her collarbone, the swell of her breasts. She waited as he heaved himself off of her, marveling that she could elicit in him such shuddering gasps, her flesh trembling as cold air swept the places where his body had been. Rahul's back loomed before her, casting vague shadows on the far wall, rising and falling with his slowly steadying breaths, and still she waited.

Rahul told Avanti she could start her master's degree whenever she felt ready, but the crisp, impatient voice at the admissions office unnerved her, and she decided to postpone it for some time. As it was, she was uncertain how she would commute to the campus. She was afraid of learning how to drive, and she sensed that, fortunately for her, it had not even occurred to Rahul to teach her. She tried to imagine herself in a classroom, surrounded by pale, speculative, staring faces. Once proud of her mastery of English—having been educated in English medium schools, she found it came to her almost as easily as Bengali—she now felt her tongue thicken with shame whenever she was forced to speak to an American. She could hardly bear the almost imperceptible shift in the eyes of the supermarket clerk, or the way the television repairman leaned forward and cocked his head, as if not only confused by Avanti's accent but unable to hear her as well.

Three days after Avanti's arrival, Fran materialized on the front porch minutes after Rahul had left for the hospital. Armed with a plastic-wrapped plate of sugar cookies, Fran knocked and peered through the window until Avanti could make herself open the door.

"Oh, there you are!" Fran's hazel eyes creased in a broad smile, her voice breathless, nervous.

Avanti had no desire to see Fran's home, but unable to manage a polite refusal, she found herself following the woman to the cheerful, mauve-shuttered house across the street. She sat at the polished dining table, nodding mutely, taking tiny sips of bland tea, as Fran chatted on ("And you know my doctor is Indian! Isn't that something? First my doctor, now my neighbors...". Avanti gazed around the room, her thumb rubbing the pastel ducks embroidered on the place mats, her eyes skimming the icy cut of the crystal in the china cabinet. In the ornate mirror on the far wall, she watched her reflection: a dark, rigid, curiously shrinking blur.

The small house Rahul had bought as a surprise for her was more of a revelation. She had been warned that there were no servants in the United States, that all of the housework and cooking would be her responsibility, but it was an adjustment nevertheless. She had been well trained, however, during the four-month wait for her visa after the wedding, under the watchful eye of her mother-in-law.

Rahul was on call most nights, as he had been denied the surgical residency he wanted and was instead working in the emergency room. Avanti was awed by her husband's job, unable to think of anything to say when she saw him in the mornings, unshaven and still dressed in scrubs. He seemed exhausted all of the time, gulping down without comment the curries she knew were too salty and the rice she could tell was undercooked. Once he brought home three Lata Mangeshkar CDs for her, and the memory of how he patted her hair as she opened the bag warmed Avanti for weeks afterward. Rahul never listened to the CDs himself.

He introduced her to the local Bengali community that very first weekend. She wore a green-and-gold sari her sister had picked out for her and some of her wedding jewelry—much too fancy, Avanti realized quickly, for a simple get-together at the Banerjees' house.

She felt herself drawn to the young woman discreetly setting the table, the only other person not engaged in conversation at the party. Sandhya Banerjee was exactly her age, having recently graduated from college—"electrical engineering," her proud father bragged— and she smiled at Avanti warmly as they were introduced. From across the room Avanti studied the other girl's copper-streaked hair and tall figure, slim as a flame, clad in fitted black pants and a turtleneck sweater. Could she understand? Would she, too, know this vague, nameless unease? Perhaps the chasm between them was still too great. Perhaps Sandhya saw Avanti only as a new family acquaintance, and an overdressed, heavily accented one at that. Of course, maybe they would actually become friends; maybe Sandhya could introduce Avanti to some new people, take her shopping, and advise her on how to become American enough for Rahul.

Avanti waited, hoping for the right moment, but a car honked outside immediately after dinner and Sandhya rushed out, her heels clicking against the kitchen tiles.

"Oh, Sandy has an American boyfriend, you know," her mother said, following Avanti's eyes. "Michael. His father is an oncologist."

Avanti listened to the car sizzle off into the rainy night and sank deeper into the plush sofa, forcing her focus back to the women seated around her.

"It's so obvious you're a new bride," Reshma Biswas told her, her loose-fleshed hand patting Avanti's. "Don't worry. We know exactly what you're going through."

Yet the other women remained distant from her, even those close to her age. Rahul would leave her at the door of these parties, heading off to the living room and the TV and the other men, while she was relegated to the kitchen with the other women. She tried her best to join the lilting, amused conversations, but generally offered to help the hostesses heat the *thorkari* or roll the rotis instead. She would carry trays into the living room, shyly handing cups of tea to the men. Rahul was always hunched alone in the corner of the sofa, his gaze riveted on the television, taking a moment to acknowledge her with a faint quirk of his eyebrows as he took the cup from her hand. They spent most weekends this way—Rahul in one room, Avanti in another, silently driving home together afterward.

"Are you happy?" he asked her abruptly one morning. She had lit a stick of incense and the faint, sweet smoke drifted around the kitchen, circling her, warming her.

"What?" Avanti had heard him, of course, but was shocked, even offended, by the question. She watched him fearfully, in pulses, unable to manage more than fleeting darts of her eyes.

"Happy." He stood at the window, facing away from her, hands on his hips, staring out into the blinding glare of day. "Are you happy?"

There was, she understood, only one answer she could give. "Yes."

Avanti did not see his back stiffen, his jaw compress, but she sensed something hard and vast spread between them suddenly. It did not occur to her to ask him the same question. Rahul's contentment was a given—as was hers. Wasn't it? She concentrated on the tiny orange glow on the tip of the incense—a hint of heat, a vague flame.

Rahul stayed at the window a moment longer, nodding slightly, before stomping across the kitchen and slamming the door violently. Avanti ate her breakfast alone, wondering what to say if he raised the subject another time. But she wasn't forced to decide; he never mentioned it again.

The phone shrills, and Jiten Da's deep baritone booms in greeting, as if from within a locked vault. From the living room, Avanti cannot distinguish his words but can hear the sudden higher pitch, the quickened pace. She wedges herself into the crease of the sofa, willing her body to disappear.

"Avanti, I think it's your mother," Ila Di whispers loudly. The others become silent, staring at her.

Avanti tries to understand this. What could she possibly have to say to her mother now? She stumbles into the kitchen, feeling the other women's gazes slide over her like a thousand tiny fingers. Jiten Da holds the phone out to her as if it is burning. She waits as the others slowly, self-consciously file out of the room.

"Ma."

"Avanti!" As she expected, her mother is crying. Fear, abrupt and incomprehensible, blazes through her stomach like a wraith.

"Ma, right now I—"

"What's going on? How could you not call us? We have to hear this terrible thing from Rahul's family?"

Avanti closes her eyes. The familiar emptiness encompasses her again, swallowing her whole. She grips the phone in her hand, willing herself to be rigid. She can see herself start to shake, to flail helplessly back and forth, her body escaping whatever hold she still has over it.

"What happened? Why did Rahul do this to himself, Avanti, why?"

He didn't do this to himself, Avanti thinks with absolute certainty. He did this to me. She can hear her father's voice in the background, hushing her mother's sobs.

"What are you going to do, Avanti? You must come home!"

Her mouth trembles, but to her own horror she is screaming, not sobbing, her throat scorching with the effort. "I don't care! I don't know! I don't care what happens to me now!"

Avanti is gasping, falling against the wall, the floor sliding up toward her face. As she lies there, waiting for her shuddering breaths to cease, waiting for the thudding of her heart to slow, she discovers with a jolt that she cannot hear anything else. The phone in her hand is silent; the rest of the house is still. All at once she hears the shuffle of feet, the repeated slams of the front door. She becomes aware, gradually, of the hum of the dial tone, the rumble of car engines outside, of her own steady breathing. She stares at the ceiling, imagining the room, their bedroom, directly overhead. She is entirely alone in the house now.

PATRICK RYAN

San Francisco State University

Before Las Blancas

I drove most of that first day. I could smell him on my fingers, hours after we'd done it. Down a stretch of road marked HURRICANE EVAC-UATION ROUTE, he told me he was getting pimples again, that's what kind of young he meant. "I could spell out your name on my face," he said. "Hell, the middle of my nose. I haven't gotten zits like this in ten years."

We pulled off the road four times and reached down deep into our pants, jacked one another off and told each other *te amo, te amo* because we had just learned how to say it. I watched the pimples grow one at a time. There was no stopping them. But I was still thirteen, and Neil could never be thirteen again no matter how many pimples he had. We both knew it. He had big legs that stretched out like magnolia roots into the bottom of the car like he was never going to leave it; and, after we passed Gonzales, Baton Rouge, Henderson, I could tell the trip would take its toll on him even if he was only twenty-eight. The top of his head poured sweat like a leaky faucet, all his worries about us and being in love with me, but I smelled like a stinkbug, that's what he said.

Qué lindo eres, we practiced together. Finding "beautiful" in our phrase book under sightseeing, meeting friends, useful expressions. Outside, Louisiana sped by us like cop cars and fat mosquitoes. Neil's freckled arms and legs peeled from his sunburn in that passenger seat with seven slashes from Aubrey Clyde's pocketknife, but it seemed like he was shedding more than skin: his New Zealand woods, his tour guide job. We shared all the clothes I'd been able to muster out of my closet and none of the clothes he brought with him from Auckland. My Bermuda shorts reached down to the middle of his biscuit-colored thighs. My biggest T-shirt hugged his chest like shrink-wrap. His big duffel bag, full of my PE uniforms and Dickies, plopped back and forth in the back of our El Dorado but neither one of us opened it. The less clothes the better. Neil was sorry he hadn't brought sunblock though.

"When we hit seventy-seven we can sail for a day and a half," he said. "Clear through, no cops, no RVs, right on through to Las Blancas. Just you and me—but look at this shitter, right smack on the inside of my ear. It's crazy. That's what kind of young I mean."

And it was me who made him young again. My mom said I had some creepy kind of magic in me that I wouldn't know how to use until I was fifty and had gray hairs on my chin. But that didn't keep me from wishing. Thinking how there'd be no hitches if we were both teenagers. If he were Aubrey Clyde or the other way around. Besides it seemed so strange to me that a man could love a kid. Especially me with my long ears and puny butt. But here he was rotting away on the inside like a big cavity, and all that was for me.

"We're not even in Texas yet, silly," I told him. He was skipping towns like smooth rocks. We wouldn't be on Highway 77 for a day and a half. Santa Teresa was another day past that from what I could figure on the map.

"It's like Clevedon but flat," he said.

He looked out past the edge of the road and ignored my driving, all what I was saying. Alder and cypress trees, wet sun belly flopping into the Atchafalaya swamp, locusts singing and maybe some tree frogs, too. He told me out in New Zealand he'd flown a genuine World War II Dakota over country just like this except for a thousand hills and how the Hunua popped up out of nowhere and then there'd be lakes and waterfalls the color of avocados and limes that took the breath out of him. Mountains that made you fear the cold even though it was blazing hot. Neil said he'd take me there and we'd fly that plane, live out a secret life without judge and jury. Just us and the Dakota and maybe a dog. That's how we could get away.

"But is it legal?" I asked. Keeping under seventy. Loving that I was behind the wheel of a real car. Both our seat belts were on. We didn't want to be stopped. No trouble. No getting sidetracked. It didn't matter that I didn't have a driver's license; we'd decided from the beginning that we weren't going to be pulled over for squat-shit. My mom wouldn't be home from Florida until Friday. Three full days for her to not start any of her phone-call ruckus. Then we'd be in Mexico by Saturday.

"I have no idea," he said. "Not even a clue."

He was Scotch taping playing cards up on the dashboard; I guessed it was solitaire but I wondered if it was something else. "Hey, *¿Te puedo dar un beso?*" He taped up the three of clubs. "It means 'Can I kiss you?'"

"*¿Te puedo dar un beso?*" I said twice. "Maybe, but you gotta let me drive the car every day." He ran those beautiful hands over my legs.

He had twelve or thirteen cards taped up and I pressed on the gas a little too hard, but that didn't matter. No cops were around for miles. He could have done whatever he wanted with me. I wouldn't have stopped him.

When we passed a Dairy Queen somewhere close to a place called Mermentau, I remembered I hadn't fed the bird. But Neil said not to worry about it, birds could go for days without solid food. I smelled him on my fingers again and now he smelled like the skin of a rattlesnake. I'd never even seen a rattlesnake until we left New Orleans that morning and pulled onto the road and then got a flat outside of La Place.

"Okay," I said. "But if it dies..."

The flat tire didn't slow us down much. I was pretty sure I knew how to change a tire; Aubrey Clyde's brother worked on cars all day Saturdays and I'd watch both of them get greasy black changing tires and pulling out carburetors and revving up engines too loud. I fixed the flat myself, without a hassle, too, while Neil pissed in the woods and chopped the head off a rattlesnake that snuck up to the car. Holding the wet crowbar over his shoulder, Neil said he'd killed two dozen snakes in his life, but never a rattlesnake.

"Have you ever killed a cockroach?" I asked him now. I'd heard cockroaches lived through hell and back, but I figured there weren't any roaches in New Zealand. People from other places always freaked out when they saw them. I don't like snakes though. I was proud of myself for not being scared. I didn't see it when it was alive. It was curled tightly around itself like some kind of spring.

"They eat cockroaches in India," he told me. "Bet you didn't know that. Just like we eat raisins or peanuts. Imagine that."

"My mom compares everything to cooking," I said.

We passed a truck full of cattle. For two miles everything smelled like shit.

"Christ, you're so beautiful," he told me. "Has anyone ever told you that? That you're so fucking beautiful?"

I didn't know if I should believe him. Maybe he saw beauty differently than anyone else in the world and then what would that matter? Aubrey Clyde said I was just an average-looking kid with a big brain, but he was drunk as an ant when he said that. But Neil said it to me a hundred times a day. He'd look at my butt when I was peeing or take a picture of me when I was just waking up from a nap and say it again and again.

"You," I said to him now. "You tell me that too much."

We were well past Rayne, a little town without any public toilets, and I tried to pay attention to the road signs: Kootsie's Cajun Dance Hall was back there, the rice festival was three days away on this next exit: Crowley-Eunice. *Qué lindo eres* was bouncing from one end of my brain to the other because I wanted to say it to him perfectly this time, roll it off my tongue like a peach. The water came right up to the highway around there, pea-soup green and webbed with pipelines and frogs maybe. Frogs were everywhere in Acadia Parish. On all the signs. Fried, baked, blackened. That and rice. I looked at him straight in the eye and said, "I like you, too, you know. The way you look. You're a handsome guy," all in English. Pimples and big knees stuck out of his shorts. Besides the fact that I hadn't been with any other men in my life, so what did I really know? And then I put my eyes back on the road and watched for coons because I couldn't just steer around a coon; I'd have to lay it down flat and that took coordination.

What I knew before all of this running away was that I was an explorer. I dreamt about everything I could do before I was eighteen, not the least of which was falling in love. Once I even made a doll that looked like Aubrey and wrote my name over the doll's heart and kept it in my closet for three days to make him love me back.

My mom was throwing her annual crawfish boil when my eyes first caught Neil. All of her PBS employees were there, and some of my aunts and uncles, too. I blew away from the thick crowd in our backyard like the smoke from the big metal tubs and spent the night by the back shed. I watched my toes wiggling in the damp grass to see if they'd grown any bigger and asked myself where I could find something on me that I didn't already know. My legs have sixteen hairs that are black. Twenty-eight that are gold.

I'd thought: This is the year I'll discover a new planet, or fly to New York to meet Woody Allen, or kiss Aubrey Clyde in his bed when he doesn't expect it. That's what I thought, but now all of those things seemed silly compared to this trip to Las Blancas.

"Evan, eh? That's a great name," was how Neil introduced himself. "Not quite as boring as Neil." Then he set up camp beside me with a plate of food and a beer. I already knew who he was. He'd arrived from Auckland a few hours before with his gear, cameras and big lights, black bags with silver rods sticking out of them. My mom had invited him to stay with us for a while. He was a tour guide in New Zealand and made documentaries about weird food, but I'd only seen one of his films and it was about pogo sticks in Japan.

"Mom says you live in the mountains," I said to him. He was sweating and smiling big. The heat from the boil reached us by the shed. I sat there in my shorts and bare feet and smelled the crawdads, the Zatarain's; it made us all smell like real Cajuns.

"Well," he told me. "I've got electricity. I'm not a nature freak."

All night we ate little red potatoes with our hands and tried to guess who was drunk and who was stoned. "Your aunt Beth is whacked, I'd put cash on it," he'd say. He smelled like onions, too. I laughed at everything, and he laughed because I laughed. We watched the cockroaches scutter back and forth along the sides of my house, into potted plants, off the sides of wooden planks, into thin crannies on the porch. And all my mom's friends, all the other people mingling in front of us seemed just as creepy.

The party went on as long as my mom could force a drop of juice out of it. When the mosquitoes came out in full force, the petered-out men poured their beers into plastic cups and limped out the side gate. Neil and I were so close that our calves were touching and his big smile made me feel safe. My mind reeled with ideas for the two of us. He could let me tag along on his shoots or let me bring Aubrey Clyde over to be in one of his films. He could show me how to work a camera. I could see why my mom liked him. They'd shared a bungalow in Naples for a week, and she fell in love with him like she always falls in love with men who drink wine and live in other countries. But I could see why she still liked him now, even though she wasn't in Italy and swooning over everyone with an accent. If there's anything that makes my mom like a man, it's getting what she wants. She's the decision-maker, and Neil was as happy-go-lucky as they come.

"You're a crazy little kid," he told me.

After everything was over and the house was in a coma, I watched him make up the living room couch with the spare sheets. His lips were cracked, his shirt was untucked and the ends wrinkled. "Night-ee-o," he said, and then he winked at me and went to sleep. That's all, just like that. I knew he wasn't anything like Aubrey Clyde—but the way he looked at me that night, the way he'd shut up and just watch whatever I was doing. Under the bull's horn my mother bought in Spain, I stood on my toes so the wood floor didn't creak and grinned like I'd just gotten my first kiss. The blinds in the living room, hanging over the big picture window that was put in after I was born, were wide open, and I walked over and shut them. I wondered if I could find my way back without tripping. The shades were still swinging back and forth, ten, eleven times, and Neil was wet with moonlight. He was a little star on the couch for me to follow.

When I woke up the next morning, Neil and the sheets he'd covered himself with were gone; the backyard was raked and cleaned. I found his bags stashed in a corner of the hallway. He came looking for me in the afternoon and the next five days went by faster than I could grow up—or just about. By the end of that week, Neil and I were joined at the hip. My mom would leave for work in the morning, and Neil would creep into my bedroom with a guilty grin. We did it right there, with the door open and the bird chirping in the kitchen. It was all so amazing, like he just fell out of the sky for me.

Now the rain came in big splats, like the world was spitting on us, and the windshield was dirty from driving through mud puddles by the time we got to Welsh. Neil drove and I sat with my feet over the air conditioner vents, legs spread like a caught pig. We'd hooked a make-do tarp, some packing material from his cameras, over the back of the El Dorado so his bag didn't get wet, but I could hear water sloshing back and forth anyway. The gray clouds went jet-black.

"Aren't you gonna miss school?" he asked me. My big toe was over the ace of spades. I'd thought about school when I was talking to Aubrey this morning and just had that nagging sense of not belonging there anymore, not being part of that world.

"Why would I?" I told him. "I'll learn everything from you. You know more than my teachers. Or I'll read some books."

He didn't say anything right away. I knew this was the first time he'd thought of me and school. But I was right. I was learning a new language and history was all written down. All I'd have to do was hole myself up in some library, whether it be Mexico or not, and read till I had it all memorized. "Well, books can't teach you math though. Not real math," he said. Then he was thinking to himself. He sucked on his teeth. "So how 'bout this," and his face lit up. "I can teach you three or four days a week. Just what I know. You're already learning Spanish. Then I can hook you up with someone who's really a teacher once we—once we know where we are. Maybe my friend Pedro will even know someone."

I tried to count the zits on his face, pushed my feet through the hot mess on the car floor—the rest of the playing cards, chewed-up cups, wet Kleenex. Both of us got quiet when miles up ahead sun scratched into the bottom of the sky. Big white fingers that reminded us "Hey, things could work out." No matter how fast we drove though, we couldn't get out of the rain. Pellets the size of peanuts, trees that looked like velvet cutouts on a greeting card. The start of a flood. It made me feel like I could drown any second. I didn't know if I'd told him that. That I couldn't swim.

"And the man's as blind as a bat, Evie," he said to me out of the blue.

"Pedro? The Mexico man?" I asked him.

"Blind as a bat," he said again. "We could make out in front of him and all that'd give it away would be the slurping."

It really did seem logical then. He was so sure that we could hide out in the back room of this stranger's house until we got a boat back to New Zealand. A blind man—what more could we ask for?

I'd never thought about running away until Robbie Berkowitz died. Not that I was so upset or even close friends with the kid, but because I saw Aubrey Clyde for who he really was and then I knew that him and I would never be what I wanted. There wasn't much in New Orleans that I cared for, besides being some help for my mom. So when Neil said he was thinking of going to Mexico, just as a side-trip, then maybe boating back to New Zealand, I'd already gotten the idea in my head.

"You wanna be with me that bad?" he asked me.

We had just fucked in my mom's bed, watching nasty videos he bought at Second Skin. I was amazed each time I came inside of him.

We were rubbing our feet against each other trying to make static. "I wanna chew on your toes," he told me. "Every day, okay?"

He kept saying it didn't make any sense to him—us. As though we made sense to me. My mom had already left for Florida, Southern Cooks United something or other. I wanted to fuck him everywhere, in the back shed, in the attic 'cause it got so hot up there. That made sense to me. "Why do you wanna be with me so bad?" he asked me again. We pulled the sheets off of us. Ran into the kitchen and made peanut butter sandwiches.

"I don't know. You're fun to be with," I told him. "And you like me." It was that easy. Hours went by like that, discovering what we could, comparing our bodies as if we were science experiments. Neil set up a big camera and filmed me making funny faces and eating carrots.

"Well, you could be my assistant. We'll get a car. Go along the coast. I have a friend in Las Blancas with a great little shack. He makes crab cages."

"I'm not talking about just a trip," I told him.

He got a funny look in his eye and said, "What do ya mean?"

"I mean why don't we go away, and I can live with you. We can go back to New Zealand and do stuff like this."

I didn't tell Neil about how I loved Aubrey Clyde. It didn't seem so important. It was my secret, so I'd know I left something behind. Kind of my sacrifice for Neil. I don't think he figured it out even meeting Aubrey. "You got weird friends," was all he said.

Getting a car was why we went to Aubrey Clyde's house. The '82 El Dorado was the third car in his dad's cracked-up driveway, backed in between a toolshed and an old Nova on cement blocks. His brother told us he'd sell us the El Dorado for four hundred bucks and gave his word the car would make it to Mexico three times and back.

We both saw the monster, Neil and me, and laughed like we were the only ones who could see past the bad powder blue paint job. The only ones who knew what an El Dorado with a bent tailpipe could be used for. It was magical; enough for me. The sun was peaking over the top of the shed—it carved the car into two pieces and made it hard to see anything but the oiled grass under us, but it was still perfect. "Solid piece of machinery though. A real muscle car," Aubrey's brother told us, pointed to the hood and then kicked the front tire with his boot to prove it. "I rebuilt the engine myself."

Neil gave me a wink, and I went inside the house with Aubrey, back to his little room on the left. "Your cousin's got a big nose," he said. "Where's he from—France or something?"

"No, he's an Aussie," I told him. "That's my dad's side of the family. But listen. Me and Neil. We're taking a trip."

"Whatcha talkin' about?" Aubrey wanted to know. He was taller than last summer, the summer he used to spend nights at my house because he drank too much. He stretched out on the mattress, shirt hiked up so I could see the small of his back, the flesh-of-an-apple-colored skin.

Aubrey Clyde was an albino if I'd ever seen one. Skin as white as papier-mâché or maybe snow, but I'd never seen real snow. He rolled his own cigarettes in the boys' bathroom and blew the smoke into the toilet bowl between his legs. "If you flush while you exhale, the smoke'll go down the pipes," he said. I'd never smoked one of his cigarettes so I didn't know the truth. I just sat in the stall next to his and listened to his feet, long beautiful things that ran faster than I ever could. Some days he wore corduroys that rode up higher than his socks, and those days it took everything in the world not to reach down, pull at the little hairs that grew on his calves, and kiss him there. I'd smell the tobacco. He'd hand me one underneath the stall, the skinny wet thing, and I'd run it under my nose. I saved seven cigarettes that Aubrey Clyde rolled. I brought them with me to Aubrey's. I was going to give them back. Or maybe smoke one with him.

"My brother's giving me his Buick next year. Think I could make it to California in three days?" He lost my train of thought and found his own. I watched his legs swing up and down, crash on the bed.

"We have to go pick up my mom," I said. "She's stranded in Little Rock. Her car broke down."

I don't know where it came from, but I stuck with it.

"Arkansas, huh? She must be pretty pissed," he said.

"Yeah, really pissed. She's got the flu, too."

"So why can't your mom just take a plane?" he asked.

I laughed at him 'cause I was nervous as hell. "She's got the flu," I said. "Don't you know anything? Her whole head would explode." Then I stuck my head out the window to watch Neil start up the El Dorado. All of a sudden I realized I wouldn't be able to tell Aubrey everything. None of this would make any sense to him, and even if it did—well, Aubrey wouldn't keep it to himself.

Three hundred miles away from that driveway, Neil and I tried to make sense of the road. Fog like a whole sea covered the rice fields on both sides of the highway. The car was wet even though it wasn't raining anymore, and Neil had wiped the windshield with one of my dirty T-shirts. It looked as if the moon was bigger here than in New Orleans. Made everything eerie. Everything the same grayish color, even a muskrat that dodged out of the path of our El Dorado, tail catching up with its head, and scurried into the grass.

"Hola, mi nombre es Señor Evan." Our book was getting worn-out, too damp. *"Su casa es muy grande."* I practiced my Spanish even though I couldn't see too well in the dark. It got my mind off this strange world. I wanted to be able to order a Coke, get a hotel room, not let Neil worry about us looking like criminals, runaway weirdos. The words got blurry quick. On the little map that came along with

the book, I only saw Spain and cities like Córdoba, Barcelona, and Madrid. Where's Mexico? San Fernando? This Francisco Villa where they shot game and hunted wildlife in the trees behind the mountains, close to the sea. *"Tengo dinero. ¿Donde está el cuarto de baño, por favor?"*

"What does that mean?" Neil asked me. "Let me guess: 'You have eyes like Don Juan.' Or, 'Where's the Alamo?'"

I didn't answer him. I just giggled and thought about sex.

Near dusk, we pulled into a rest stop somewhere near Lake Charles. A big clearing, like a baseball stadium in the middle of jungle. Two big cranes, instead of trees, and an orange cement truck sat quietly out past a wired fence and a whitewashed electric generator.

A foul heat dribbled down on us—air like Crisco. I missed the air conditioner. Missed the wind when we blew across Louisiana.

"Twenty minutes, 'kay? And maybe a little nap," Neil told me.

I'd never seen a rest stop with a whole slew of hiking trails, tiny worn-out routes. Dogs ran off and disappeared in black bushes. We took our pillows out and dusted them off, got rid of cracker crumbs and pine needles, shook them over the green state garbage cans. Neil looked beat. He fell into his pillow and didn't want to wash his face or rinse his mouth out. "Just stay in the well-lit places, got me?"

When I walked into *el cuarto de baño,* all the silver mirrors like the side of a scratchy coffee Thermos, two men as fat as whales were finishing up at the urinals. I waited by the little sink and washed my hands over and over. The evening felt as hot as pavement.

"I got something else for you to wash," the bigger one said to me. His friend ran a fat blue comb through his hair and said, "Keep it up, Joey. One day someone's gonna have a gun and you're gonna make a wisecrack and BLAM—"

I heard someone's footsteps. At first glance, I would've bet it was Aubrey Clyde; this Mexican kid who ran in and put his head under the air blower, made me ignore the two men, wet raven-black hair.

Not the color of Aubrey's skin—Aubrey was whiter than paper, but the shape of him. Maybe someone ran a pencil around Aubrey, made a copy, and mailed him to me right here.

I brushed my teeth and kept the cap in my hand the whole time. "Your dad's looking for you," he said to me.

The backs of his legs were dirty and bruised up like peaches. A little girl was screaming at the door, "Momma's gonna bust your butt. You betta give it back, Jorge!"

"He's not my dad," I told him. "He's my brother."

The two big men walked out laughing. I didn't want to go outside yet.

"You betta get a raincoat, Frisca. Momma's sleeping anyway!" The Mexican boy pulled a little doll out of his pants and pushed me out of the way with his skinny hips. *"¡Perdón! pequeño hermano.* I just need to fill this up, *apruebe?"*

He held it under the faucet, pulled the rubber head off, and filled the whole thing with water. "I wouldn't brush my teeth in there," he said. "It's limy. And he looks like your dad, *cabrito. Mi hermano* is eighteen." Then he ran out wagging his doll back and forth.

I spit everything out. That crazy silver mirror: deformed, strung out, leaner, taller, was this what I'd look like when I grew up? *Su nombre es Señor Neil. Mi nombre es Señor Evan.* Neil was someone who could be my dad, or close enough. Or maybe not really but the way he looked today, getting pimples like measles, sweating gallons out every one of his big pores. Not that it mattered when it came to how much he loved me. I could tell how much he loved me by the way his hands worked me over. Eased me into anything he wanted.

When I walked outside, Neil wasn't waiting by the bathroom. I stuffed my toothbrush into my pocket and saw just about the most beautiful sight I'd ever seen on that road. Behind all the kids playing, the Mexican kid who looked like Aubrey swinging that doll around. It was freaking tremendous: arrows of light pointed down, perfectly still, from the one domed streetlight arched over the parking lot to the wet grass-covered picnic area, between the little squirts of sink water. It wasn't even the moon, but it fell down out of nowhere like the insides of angels.

I missed Aubrey because of the kid. I missed what he'd be telling me—making fun of those short-shorts, making jokes about Texans. I wanted to run and get Neil. Show him how the kid looked like a bronze statue pointing somewhere. I didn't know where, just somewhere in the opposite direction from where we were going. I wanted to tell him about Aubrey Clyde finally. But by the time I got to the car, it was all gone.

We crossed the state line near midnight, and Texas didn't seem any different from Lake Charles or Sulphur. I had my ideas of cowboys in tight jeans with prickly brown faces, but we only passed an oil tanker and a yellow minivan with a sleepy, white-enough family inside. Then, five miles or so past the line, all the streetlights were off, maybe someone timed them wrong, except for one—this solitary pole with a flickering yellow bulb. Our headlights lit up the others as we approached. The legs of a metal giant ready to step over our El Dorado.

"Kinda spooky," Neil said. He still looked dog-tired. "Think it's aliens?"

I smiled over at him, huddled into my own seat with my feet stirring in those playing cards he'd left on the car floor, my arms folded across my chest. He was driving now. I didn't like to drive at night. I couldn't tell when I was falling asleep, and I'd probably run off into a ditch and kill both of us. *Ocho, nueve, diez,* I counted in Spanish. *Dieciocho, diecinueve, veinte.* Nothing would keep me awake.

"Do you wanna get a hotel?" he asked.

I didn't believe in aliens, but I looked up at the sky anyway. There must have been a million stars up there, and I could see them all without the streetlights. The moon was settled over a highway sign: steep grade or something like that. I was tired, and a bed sounded like heaven; the perfect medicine for us both. *¿Dónde está los hoteles? Dónde está—*.

"Are you falling asleep, too?" I asked him.

"No," he said. "I could keep driving. I could keep going."

Then the lights lit up the roadway again. The first one ran toward us as if God were handing us a candle. Neil's face was dolloped with little red bumps. One hundred and one zits, we'd begun to call them.

"I'm falling asleep," I told him, held my hands over my eyes.

"I just thought maybe we could rest—and think a little clearer in the morning. See what Texas looks like." I knew it looked the same as Louisiana. "I wanna lay in your arms," he added. "Naked again. Pretend it's home. New Zealand winter."

I imagined his body the way I felt it the first night, a few days after we'd met, and how I heard my mom wheezing in the other room, and kissed his stomach between her bedtime noises. Maybe he wasn't thinking. I drove with the idea that cops were right behind us. That we were on the brink of being caught at every intersection, every exit. I told him no. No, we couldn't get a hotel.

"Okay—your choice," he said.

I was quiet. Maybe he wasn't so headstrong. Hadn't thought this all out. Maybe those pimples weren't the half of it. I rolled down the window and looked up again and the wind was warm. Like when I rode the roller coaster at Pontchartrain Beach, dreaming of Aubrey Clyde's calves, and for two minutes there was no way to keep the hair on your head still. That kind of fast. That kind of warm.

Robbie Berkowitz died on a wet morning that smelled like dirty diapers because the garbagemen were late. Robbie was umpiring as best he could with his bad vision. I don't know why we put him back there. He should've been in right field. He wore fat glasses that curled around his big ears and the jock boys always bullied him. They'd shove him up against the walls of the stairways, lick one of their fingers, and smear his glasses with wet V's.

The word *fag* slipped out of another boy's mouth, and it sounded like a crazy chant. "Let's see if Robbie the fag can catch," and when Aubrey Clyde was up to bat, they laughed and held their hips like old, wasted soldiers. Waited and scrutinized Robbie with their black asphalt eyes. Aubrey ran, and he threw the bat like he always did, even though it was against the rules, but this time it hit Robbie Berkowitz square in the head. Knocked him flat back against the steel cage and left him there. A loud *thwack*. A thwack that you could tell was too loud, so thick that it had reached inside his head and pulled out something.

"What's wrong with that fag?" Aubrey didn't see right away—not the blood, out of Robbie's nose and even his ears. A squawking red that didn't come from that dent in his head where the bat hit him, but someplace deeper.

"Shit, he's bleedin'—all over," he said. Everyone else rooted themselves to where they were. We couldn't talk like Aubrey was talking. That blood was filling up our mouths.

Then Robbie's foot wiggled back and forth, spazzing out, like he was cumming or tapping out some kooky rhythm. And I knew it was bad. Someone said, "His head's cracked. His head's cracked wide open."

The day of the wake, Aubrey, Tina Marcelo, and me took the bus back from Leitz-Eagan together. We snuck into Aubrey's house 'cause his mom was narcoleptic. I got comfortable on the bed. Aubrey was sitting on his dad's old rocker with Tina on his lap. She was licking his neck with her little pink tongue and putting her fingers in his ears. *Don't you know I'm still sitting here,* I wanted to say. But we were all acting like weirdos. None of us had seen a dead body before.

Tina had wide hips. I watched Aubrey quiver underneath her. I knew he couldn't keep her on his skinny legs forever. "I'm so bummed," she kept saying. She was pressing up against him with a stoned sad look. Whispering in his ears, "Do me, do me," and I laughed a little. She said, "Do me, do me," and then she fell off his lap and hit her chin on the arm of the rocker and started bleeding from her top lip.

Aubrey said, "Girl, get a towel. You're gonna need a Band-Aid." He was laughing at her.

"Your mom's white trash," she said back. I don't know why she was mad at him. She said she had to go home 'cause Aubrey didn't even have a Band-Aid big enough to fit a pinprick. She was having her little breakdown. Her eyes were wet, and she was wearing makeup, so it was obvious.

After Tina left, Aubrey said her name twice and giggled.

"Damn, she's got it bad." He put on one of his Beastie Boys CDs. "You kissed a girl yet?" he asked me.

"I don't know," I said back, then realized that didn't make sense.

"What are you—high or something? You've never even kissed your dog, huh boy?"

I was about to say yes. He turned the music up.

He slouched and dug his fists down into his pockets. His dress-up jeans were too tight. Like they were two or three years old. He played with himself. I could tell he was half hard. He leaned forward.

"You wanna play around some?" he asked. "Like you did that night?"

I guessed he meant the night I kissed him when he was asleep. I didn't want to ask. I figured he was teasing. I moved down to the foot of his bed so our knees were almost touching.

"You ever let a guy piss on you?" he asked.

He was breathing so quick that I could hear it over the stereo. Of all the things he could have said, I wasn't expecting that kind of thing. He got up, unzipped his pants, and poked his dick in my face. It was big. Fat. He jiggled it and made me kiss the tip.

"I'm going to piss all over your face, okay?"

I didn't know what to answer.

"Okay," I said. And he pretended to let go with it. Laughed like he was high on something.

"Freak," he called me. "Why are you my friend?"

Then I kissed his belly, and he punched me in the face, but I knew he could've punched me harder. It didn't even give me a black eye. Still—from then on I felt different about Aubrey Clyde. Before, I'd always thought he could fall in love with me, too, just as easy. One day he'd say, "Sure, I've always thought about it." Or, "I couldn't stand not having you around."

In the morning, Neil and me faced a green world with our El Dorado, as if looking at Texas through an earth-sized filter, big sheet of tinted glass. Neil called it a toxic sky, sat up in the passenger seat moaning, "Goddamn my mouth. Canker sores now. I'm getting every freakin' case in the book." He pulled down his bottom lip till it was touching his chin so I could see the white ugly crater. "This is not making me feel young again."

"Looks painful," I said. I was just waking up; he was ready to hit the sack. "My mom used to put iodine on mine—the red stuff."

He spat out the window. Nothing was around. No exits, no houses, just trees. "Yell if you see a drugstore in the bushes."

Morning came and went as quiet as we were quiet. Neil stretched his long body out on the passenger seat, even put a leg out the window, and napped off and on. When he did talk he went on about this road being too busy and that road being too far out of the way and how we could find a little house somewhere in Mexico with a couple of dark-skinned Mexican women who didn't speak English making us churros and scrambled eggs, or we could build a roof over the back of the El Dorado and camp in it for a few weeks. Twelve feet of half-inch-thick plywood. Some varnish and a few gold ornaments like you find at flea markets. That's what he said, but it was the way he said it.

"We just need to get wherever we're going quick, okay? This running is—I don't know—it's hell on you and heller on me."

"Nothing bad's happening," I said. I wanted him to know.

"Bad is a sliding-scale term, Evie."

I could've done something about Neil and his canker sores, pimples, and bad feelings; I could've used my magic, wished him into a normal man again. But I didn't know how. My mom was right; it all took practice, years of it. A whole twenty-four hours ran by us: Beaumont, Wharton, Refugio, and by then the car smelled like a steel factory and sweatshop all in one. I said to him that it wouldn't be such a good idea to kiss anymore, at least not on the mouth. Not until the canker sores got better and he could eat salty foods again, not until he didn't have all that pain.

Crazy as the half-car/half-house idea was, I would've went along with it in a heartbeat. It seemed pretty okay to me. But Neil didn't seem right. That's what I thought then—okay, string up chili pepper lights around the whole car, fit a futon mattress in the back, hook up a minigrill to the cigarette lighter. But he didn't know what he was really talking about, no logic to any of it. All these desperado plans didn't add up to anything but being scared silly. What we'd said in the beginning was Mexico would be a few weeks at most. Then New Zealand and his wild woods. I thought: Maybe the best thing to do would be to go back home—all the way home. Or even go my own way, head for California, then get Aubrey to come and save me.

"Sure are quiet today, aren't you?" He pulled his leg out of the window and then picked up his playing cards. "I'm sorry, kiddo," he said to me after a while. Maybe he knew what I was thinking. "You're right. Definitely. What more could I ask for?"

Then past Olmito the El Dorado burped like an old dying beast. That's what Neil said, a burp, because it groaned and spit a little smoke out. I kept driving. I didn't know anything about cars. "The hell was that?" was what Neil said, and the speed-limit signs, the billboards, the white daisy weeds outside came at us slower and slower until we were dead on the road. For a half mile we pushed the car— it seemed bigger and heavier—to a run-down gas station on the left side of the highway. SALT POND a sign read. "And there'll probably be no freaking mechanic either!" Neil yelled. The day was hotter than all of June—I felt it.

The gas station crept out of a mess of alder trees, looked ready to be pulled back in any second. Once we got the car into the parking lot, Neil pressed his hands into the back pockets of those little shorts and huffed loudly. His face was redder than if he had a sunburn, a nasty red that started in the ears then worked its way around the front, right into his mouth then unleashed like a fury. He told me, "Evie, find a damn curb and just stay away from me for a while." His eyes got big and froze. He knew what he'd said. I saw the shame wash over his face.

I wondered how far we were from Mexico, how many miles to Las Blancas. *¿Qué dirección a Santa Teresa?* Neil was at rope's end. Had his shoulders up to his ears and his skin was blotchy. Three hours later all I'd had to eat was cold tamales. Neil didn't eat at all. He stood in front of the El Dorado, begged it to work again, and waited. *Ningún mecánico, ningún aceite,* the lady behind the counter didn't speak English. If we could make it to Brownsville, the border, there was a giant service station there. *Un montón de aceite,* and Joey *el mecánico.*

"Well, there's a guy inside—says he broke down, too," Neil said to me. He slammed the hood closed. "I think he knows someone, and there's a chance he can get a couple of tow trucks out here."

"Great," I told him. I sat on the curb. He went back inside, arms swinging looser than a ripped cord. I heard another man inside say, "You gotta get yourself a better insurance plan, mister. Saves your ass like a pretty parachute." Cars passed like fast ocean waves. I could've imagined that's where I was—just by putting my head down. Fat doodle bugs crisscrossed next to my feet, and two dogs wrestled with each other in the mud next to the pay phone. One of them ran over to me in a crazy heat, a chunky Boston terrier that sniffed up a trail of plump hot raisins on the ground, until his wet nose found my shoes.

"Hey, fella," I said. Dogs have these eyes that make you want to roll over, too. I scratched under his corn chip ears and smiled. "I know what you're thinking. But what if I never get to kiss someone again?"

He was hyper as a jackrabbit, curly tail going this way and that way. "Go on," I said. "Go play."

I don't know what got into me, a bad-tasting throb in my neck, what possessed me to walk over to the pay phone and pull out all my quarters. But once I had the receiver, there was no backing out. My legs were shaking so bad I had to crouch down and reach up for the numbers.

"Evan?" I laughed when Aubrey said my name. "Goddamn you tricky little fucker, your mom's been calling here like a crazy woman."

She'd come back early. I could see her running up and down the hallways, looking at the dead bird, no son. I don't think she could have imagined the whole caboose, what we'd done—everything.

"Why'd you lie to me about her, dude? She's having one of her fits."

I could see the salt pond from the booth, shaped like a broken tooth. I stared at it. "I'm in Nebraska, Aubrey. Honest."

"Nebraska?" he laughed at me.

I was ready to spill it all out—Neil, the El Dorado breaking down, the pimples. Instead, I hung up and walked out of the booth like I hadn't even made a phone call. I tried to keep Aubrey's high-pitched white trash voice as far away as that smell of rattlesnake, the revving engine in his front yard, maybe even Robbie Berkowitz.

When Neil came out again, he'd decided we'd push the car to Brownsville and there'd be a mechanic somewhere along the way. He said, "It's a real big city, don't you think? To be on the border." His face was a map of where we needed to go. He looked defeated. We'd rest for another hour or two here. Juanita, the lady at the register, said her boyfriend was bringing fresh burritos over later. My eyes were burning from the smell of the condiment chilies she was cutting, and Aubrey Clyde's voice was in my ears for good. I couldn't get him out of my head. Him just worried about me lying to him and about my mom's fits. How crazy was that? I thought maybe I should've told him about sex—about Neil and I doing it four times a day up until yesterday night. Or made up some story about being kidnapped. I wanted to take it out on Neil—let it fly out 'cause it was stuck in my gut.

We stayed until dusk, the quickest nightfall I'd ever seen. Neil said we needed to talk. "You know, Evie," he said. "I know I've said this and all, but—I really love my mountains and New Zealand and all." We watched Juanita spinning a knife around on the deli case. The Mexican woman drank one Pepsi after another. "I've built a whole life there. Showing people my land and making them woozy when they see orange hills or whatever it is we're flying over." We both stared out in front of us, as if we were driving for real. "There's no feeling like it—taking them up in my Dakota, out over the water. But the first time! The first time I flew a plane—it was like putting one foot into heaven."

A big truck pulled out of the parking lot and scattered white dust everywhere. I listened to the sound of little rocks cracking. "I had a woman with me. Wanted to learn just as bad as I did. I think maybe she had three kids and a husband. Imagine that. And we took this little plane up and after seven minutes I could swear someone pulled the air out from under us. An air pocket maybe—and neither one of us knew what to do really—I mean we'd trained for this kinda thing, but—well what are you going to do when you're dropping down like a missile? We must've dove three hundred, four hundred feet and almost hit a mountaintop. A pretty one, but rocky. Hard."

His eyes were on the tip of my nose, like I had his lines written out there, went back and forth between both my eyes, never sure which one was looking at him right then. I thought maybe he was crying. "We got to the ground and just sat there in the plane. 'What in God's name was it?' kinda thing that went over us. That's what we were thinking. And it was a parachute, some old parachute sitting in the back of the plane flew out and opened up and caught itself on the tail and *wham!*"

I thought I should hold his hand, but I didn't move. We were both sleepy, soft around the brain. He kept talking, said "The woman— she got a fear of heights after that, didn't want to fly, couldn't go through with the rest of the class. And I—I don't know, maybe I wouldn't have either if I thought I had any other choices. But I couldn't go back to my family."

Another big truck came through our parking lot, a little Volvo with whitewash wheels after it. I asked him, "Why? What's your mom like?"

"My mom?" he said, and he yelped it like he wasn't sober.

Five minutes we were quiet as the alder trees, no wind coming off the pond. I guessed he didn't want to talk about his family. I wanted to touch him, so I rubbed his leg up and down, right up to his crotch. "Well," I said. "I wanna fly with you."

He got real stiff, held his breath. "Evie," he said. Then cried like there was a whole ocean in his chest. That quick. I didn't know if I'd said something wrong. I thought about the old plane falling down from the sky. I thought about me learning Spanish without him. His head still as a crow and tears rolling down both sides of his red cheeks, he said, "I'm sorry, Evie, I'm so freakin' sorry." Over and over again. I scooted closer to him and put my arm around his back. Patted him and told him I'd be there for him. He could count on me. All the way to this place called New Zealand.

"I can't bring you back, Evie. We can't go. We can't."

I didn't understand him at first. Between his sobs and the racket of those trucks grinding off the road, blowing by us and moving our car like it was a kite, none of it made any sense. But gradually I understood what he was saying. It was all about New Zealand, home, and all I knew how to do was get out of the car and keep my mouth shut. I curled up in the back of our El Dorado.

The next morning I woke up without my socks on. I'd slept the whole night barefoot and without a blanket in the back of the El Dorado. The morning sky washed over everything, and I sat up watching the sun hang waist high in thick grizzled air. I didn't see Neil, not a sign of him.

I clenched my toes in my hands and warmed them. Even though it was already hot, already burning leaves off the elm trees, something kept me cold, and I didn't know what it was. My legs stretched out in front of me like useless wings, and bigger than the last time I looked at them.

I saw the ticket when I walked around the car and shook the dirt off my shorts. It was laying on the front seat next to fifty-five bucks and a bag of chips. I didn't know what it was—I guess I knew it was a ticket, but I didn't know who it was for or what it meant. Honest, the first thought I had was to try the car. See if it worked again and drive it off. Leave Neil wherever he had wandered off to and make it back to Lafayette to stay with my dad. I'd wear a cap and sunglasses and no one would pull me over 'cause I was already looking older, could let the hair above my lip grow into a little mustache.

There was only one ticket. One-way back to New Orleans. And there was a scribbled-fast note on a napkin saying Greyhound passed in front of Olmito about a quarter mile from here at 10:30. Then in tiny writing: I love you.

I looked around and thought he was filming me. Playing a joke on me. There was a hole in my heart down to the center of the world— China, New Zealand. I ran to the salt pond, felt the chalk stones pushing into the soles of my feet while I climbed over the little levee. I wanted him to be there, sitting by the water waiting for me. Wanted to tell him we were both crazy, that it felt good when he loved me.

The water was gray as moon, almost black close to the shore and then spotted, whiter and whiter as it ran out to nowhere—moving haze on the other side. The clouds ran as fast as cars. I thought I saw a man standing waist deep in the pond; with long arms, white as all the salt. I ran up to the water and almost leaped in with all my clothes still on, but it was only a whitewashed metal post, bent up and close to falling over. Some device to anchor fishing boats or catch crabs—I didn't know. What I knew was, it wasn't Neil. The arms were a gull's wings, and as my toes touched the water, the bird flew away.

ANTOINE WILSON

University of Iowa

❧

HOME, JAMES, AND
DON'T SPARE THE HORSES

The taxi left me at the Perrins' gate, enormous wooden doors flanked by stone walls, set ten yards back from the dark ribbon of Pacific Coast Highway. The marine layer hung thick in the night air, a mist redolent with salt, kelp, and rotting fish. Cars emerged from a glowing white nimbus, passed, and disappeared, twin red dots in the distance. Drivers stared at me, at my silhouette in the security lights, the lone carless human on this stretch of highway.

I straightened my tie, checked my jacket for wrinkles, pressed the buzzer. I was fifteen minutes early and would have waited at the gate if it weren't so cold. My legs, especially, were feeling cold in my father's old suit: long at the wrists, short at the ankles. I should have had it tailored, but I had only been in Los Angeles two weeks, and most of that time I'd spent preparing for my first Southern California gallery show.

I'd had a few solo shows in Albuquerque, and some of my work had been in a group show in New York, but I'd sold only a few pieces. Then a friend of a friend of a gallery owner in New Mexico helped me land a solo show at Irus Projects in Santa Monica. From the start, this gallery seemed destined for failure. Russ Matsumura ("I Russ," he introduced himself) believed himself a revolutionary and refused to pay rent on the gallery. He was in the process of being evicted from his seventh location. He'd named his gallery after Irus, giant beggar and protector of Penelope's suitors. Lest I feel like a lost cause, the friend of a friend of the gallery owner in New Mexico called me often to assure me that Russ was well connected.

He was. Through Russ I made many artist friends: Kylie built little mirror-boxes; Johan dipped dumbbells in colored wax; Sam videotaped himself digging enormous holes with enormous equipment; Callie stitched voodoo dolls, on commission; Alfredo made hair shirts from athletic wear.

I took pictures at night, on the outskirts of big cities, using only ambient light.

I was welcomed into their circle.

Three hours before my opening, the gallery's power was shut off. Russ left, presumably to call the power company. (The gallery had no phone. Russ made all calls on an illegally cloned cell phone, but it hadn't been working since that morning.) I sat behind the makeshift bar and watched the room—no larger than a two-car garage, with low ceilings—fade from yellow to orange to night. I waited in the dark, sipping at a cup of three-dollar red. I suppose I could have gone across the street and stood under the streetlamp, but I'm accustomed to sitting in the dark.

Wrapped in a sleeping bag, shivering from the cold, under a sliver of moon in the New Mexico desert. Hasselblad on the tripod, shutter timed at 25 ASA: five minutes, ten minutes, fifteen minutes, and so on, up to a half hour. Taking a picture in darkness, an image of a succulent leaf: a green thing, barely green under amber haze of city glow, under blue highlight of moon. I sipped from a thermos of soup, thought of nothing. Beef broth, pasta nests, and no ideas: If I ever had a formula for making art, that was it.

The room lit up. Russ had pulled his truck up to the front of the gallery. He shut the lights, cut the engine. He entered carrying a crate. He reached into the crate, grabbed something. I heard a click, then a whir. The flashlight in his hand cast a dim yellow beam, then went out. Another click, another whir, and the yellow beam came back on.

"They're Russian," he said. "No batteries required. We'll hand them out at the door."

I picked one up, squeezed it, made my own dim yellow beam. I pointed it at Russ's face. He smiled. I pumped the flashlight a few more times on my way out the door. Then I threw it onto the railroad tracks and headed home.

The show was an enormous success. Well reviewed. Sold two pieces. Russ blacked out the gallery windows so people could see the work in the dark during the day. He asked me to stay away from the gallery. People were calling me *reclusive, nocturnal, ascetic.* Apparently, my absence from the opening had created a buzz. Enough of a buzz to incline Maurice (say "Morris") Perrin to summon me to one of his soirees.

"Maurice," Russ informed me, "*makes* artists."

I pictured a stable of art kids, cigarettes and ouzo around someone else's pool.

The speaker next to the buzzer clicked, and someone with a Spanish accent said: "Yes?"

"Graham Witt for Mr. Perrin," I said. There was a pause.

"Drive in, Mr. Witt."

The gates opened automatically, ponderously. I imagined a trap-door in slow motion. The driveway dropped toward the promise of a house: a copse of palm trees, illumination.

Russ had told me what he knew about Maurice: He was an icono-clast in his field, which was some type of banking; he conceived of his soirees as oases of high culture in the intellectual desert of Los Angeles; he encouraged his friends to purchase work by his stable of pet artists; and he harbored a desperate urge to be an artist himself.

I tried to connect these facts to the man who stood before me. In-deed, he had the severe cheekbones and gaunt otherworldliness I'd seen in some artists. And he was one of the tallest people I'd ever seen, probably closer to seven feet than six. A disproportionate num-ber of frustrated would-be artists are very tall people.

"Lose the tie and jacket," he said. He opened a closet in the entry, handed me a hanger. He moved slowly and deliberately, as if glass-boned. I put my tie in my jacket pocket, my jacket on the hanger, the hanger in the closet.

"Button," he said.

I undid the top button of my shirt.

"Good," he said. He leaned back on his heels. "Now untuck."

I untucked my shirt.

"Very good," he said. He tousled my hair. "Perfect. Can you come back in half an hour?"

There was no way to tell if he was being serious. His patient, closed-mouth smile betrayed nothing.

"A half hour?" I asked.

"Yes," he said. "We're not quite ready here."

"I suppose. But I've got no car."

"Then you should tell me to go fuck myself."

I didn't say anything. He smiled broadly now, with teeth.

"Say it," he said. "Tell me to go fuck myself."

"I *can* go away for a half hour."

"Tell me to go fuck myself or you can go away for good."

"Go fuck yourself," I said.

"Hah!" He clapped his hands together. "*Perfect!*"

I didn't know what to say. He pushed open a door to the side of the entry.

"You can wait in here," he said, ushering me in with his hand.

"Thank you, sir."

"Graham."

"Yes?"

"Politeness keeps us from the prize." He winked and shut the door.

The room into which I'd been ushered was square, with elaborate parquet flooring. It smelled, inexplicably, of cauliflower. The paintings in the room were older than the artwork in the entry, and not as good. The Rouault stood out from the other paintings, most of which were by minor Postimpressionists. There was a black grand piano in one corner, and a stack of folding chairs against the wall. The tassels on the piano bench cushion matched the tassels on the curtains, and the pattern of the curtains matched the shade on the standing lamp. The mantel, devoid of photos, held only a bust of Beethoven and an old mandolin. A room suited to its purpose: the overdetermined dream of a small-minded decorator.

A latch clicked in the corner of the room and in walked a young woman, bony and pale. Batlike, too—she moved very quickly and did not notice me right away. She reached for a folding chair at the top of the stack, pulled it down, and unfolded it, all without any sign of struggle: She was stronger than she looked. As she reached up for a second chair, she scanned the room absentmindedly. She marked my presence, and without any show of surprise, rolled her eyes at me.

"My horrible father," she said under her breath.

"I'm sorry?"

She inspected me a moment, breathing through her nose. She struck me as beautiful, but possessed a peculiar set of features, the sum of which could not account for this impression of beauty: Her eyes were too far apart (with bulgy eyeballs), her lips thin, her cheekbones hard and uneven. She wore a silver frog charm tight around her neck, behind which the skin of her throat seemed almost translucent, marmoreal.

"You're an artist?" she asked.

"Yes," I said. "Graham Witt."

"Lydia Perrin," she said. "My horrible father has *no* idea."

"May I help you with the chairs?" I asked.

She sat, crossed her legs, pointed at the stack. "Line them up facing the piano."

I unfolded chairs. She ran her hands through her hair as she talked.

"My father invites artists here a lot, you know."

I nodded.

"Young male artists, because he thinks that's how I'm going to get over Gio. He has *no* idea. Gio and I were engaged."

She waited until I nodded, then continued.

"My father thinks I tried to kill myself because Gio left me. But that wasn't it at all. Can you keep a secret?"

"Sure," I said. I started on the second row of chairs.

"You'd better keep it or I could get killed." Here, she spat the whole thing out, in monotone, as if by rote. "I met Gio at a Pace/Wildenstein opening in Beverly Hills and we fell in love. Gio—my little fuzzy-wuzzy. We got an apartment and got engaged, too. We had this great apartment in Venice. California, not Italy. But then we ran out of money, and I had a problem that I needed money for. If you know what I mean. And Gio liked to spend a lot of money. Gio got this idea because he had friends in the Mafia who would give him money for art. They were like the art dealers of the Mafia. Gio said we should take a drawing from my father's house and replace it with a fake—Gio's a really great artist, he made great fakes, they fooled everyone—and then he could sell the real thing to his Mafia friends. I thought it would be fun, and I wanted to get back at my father, too, but that's another story."

I had most of the chairs lined up by now, so I sat down to listen to her story, but she stopped.

"Aren't you going to finish the chairs?"

I resumed setting up chairs, and she resumed her story.

"Gio replaced a drawing with a fake and stole the real one and we got good money for it. So then he went wild and started doing it to everything he could get his hands on. Then he made a lot of money. I told him he had to stop, you know."

I nodded.

"Because he was stealing all of my father's artwork, and I had already gotten back at my father enough. Gio told me he would have me killed if I told anyone. He had never hit me or threatened me before but I thought for sure that if I talked he would have me killed. It would be easy, he said, with Mafia friends."

"Your fiancé threatened to have you killed?"

"He did."

I nodded.

"So he kept stealing stuff and replacing it with fakes, and I think the fakes got worse and worse, but nobody noticed. And that's when I swallowed a bottle of pills and Gio called 911 and left me for good. I told my parents that we broke up and that's why I tried to kill myself."

"Mm-hmm."

"My parents made me move home, and that's why I live with them. And they think that I'm depressed because I don't have Gio and they bring artists here to cheer me up. Papa thinks I want another artist boy. But I can't stand to live here, I can't! Look on all the walls! Nobody sees it but me!"

She crossed her arms to signal that she'd finished.

"That's quite a story," I said. I had a chair in my hands. If Maurice had walked in at that moment, I might have thrown it at him. I left it half-folded and walked around the room. The Rouault, indeed, looked a little funny now, its lines shaky and hesitant. "Lydia," I said, inspecting the surface of the canvas, "is this one of them? One of Gio's?"

"All of them are Gio's," she mumbled.

I turned around. She was seated with her arms at her sides, eyes closed, like an abandoned marionette. "Lydia?" I approached her.

The door opened behind me, and there stood Maurice, in a tuxedo.

"Ready to mingle?" he asked.

"Your daughter," I said. "Is she asleep?"

"She's preparing—she'll be playing for us later on. We'd better leave her to concentrate." He stepped into the entry hall, and I followed.

A dozen or so of Maurice's friends, in evening wear and tuxedos, mingled in the living room, sipping drinks, laughing falsely, wiping flecks of appetizer from their spouses' lips. When Maurice and I entered, everyone stopped what they were doing and looked at us.

Maurice gave a mock bow and said: "This, my friends, is the artist Graham Witt. Graham Witt," he extended his arm, "these are my friends."

To my horror, they applauded.

Behind them stood a giant window, which during the day might have offered views of Catalina, but at night, with no lights outside, acted as a mirror. In this mirror, above these dozen heads, I saw the reflection of the painting that hung over *our* heads in this high-ceilinged room: a swimming-pool Hockney. Even in the reflection it looked like a fake.

Mrs. Perrin took my arm and led me to the bar. She looked remarkably like her daughter, but sculpted in fat instead of bone. As if her daughter had not been born, but had one day stepped out of her, fully formed. She wore pearl earrings and a pearl necklace, and her hair was exquisitely coiffed.

"We don't have ouzo," she said. "Will anisette do?"

"With water," I said. "No ice."

"Yes, sir," she said, eyebrow raised.

"Look, Mrs. Perrin. I know why I'm here, and I'm not happy about it. So if you don't mind, I'm just going to have this drink and go home."

"That would be a shame," she said, twirling an ear-pearl. "You've got a roomful of people, all interested in your work. And *I'm* a huge fan. Tolerated that horrid little gallery."

I chugged the anisette. Several people had moved in closer to initiate introductions. Whiskey breath from under yellowing mustache, his tiny wife; a slim fop in ascot and glasses, his huge wife.

"Your work," Mrs. Perrin continued, "has a certain *Japanese* simplicity."

"Yes," said Yellow Mustache, "have you spent time in Japan?"

"Do you meditate?" asked Slim Fop.

"Enough," I said. "We all know this isn't about my work."

"Ahh, the temperament," someone mumbled behind me.

"Maurice," I called. He stood across the room, discussing the merits of a (clearly bunk) de Kooning with two guests. He turned his head toward me, nodded. "Can you call them off? I've had enough of this charade."

Those standing around me were offended, and deeply satisfied at having been so deeply offended. Maurice rushed over, apologized on my behalf, pulled me aside.

"You're doing a great job," he said.

"This is humiliating," I said. "I thought you'd brought me out here because you were interested in my work, but now that I know why I'm really here I can't go through with this."

"I *am* interested in your work, Graham. But one's work is not everything." He winked.

"This is bullshit. I'm not your gigolo. I'm leaving."

Maurice leaned down to me, whispered in my ear. "Say it louder," he said.

Maurice's guests wanted to know, without question, he said, that they were in the presence of a real artist. They wanted a little abuse. I told Yellow Mustache that he didn't know anything about art. He didn't insult me back. He didn't hit me. He smiled painfully, asked me to tell him a thing or two about my theories. I told him I didn't have any theories. I had insomnia and a camera.

Yellow Mustache may have been deferring to my authority, but when I mentioned to Slim Fop and his huge wife the limited possibilities of their sexual union, I got a polite chuckle and nod instead of a drink in my face or an order to hit the road. I had, for the night, carte blanche. I let rip audible farts and received shy smiles of appreciation.

I patted Mrs. Perrin on the rump as she walked past me. "Firmer than I thought it would be," I said.

She grabbed me by the ear and whispered into my other ear, "You're a *perfect* asshole, Graham." Then she kissed me on the cheek before walking off to mingle.

Carte blanche got boring quickly, and I was sure there were limits somewhere that I wasn't willing to test. I stood in front of the giant picture window and looked into the blackness where the ocean should have been. After my eyes adjusted, I could see a few lights out on the water, but the night wasn't clear enough for Catalina.

I focused my eyes on the reflection in the window. Minglers mingling, some watching me, waiting for my next move. They were enjoying themselves more than I was. I sipped at my seventh anisette and wondered why I was there, other than to placate Lydia. (Where was Lydia?)

Who were these people? The men all wore tuxedos. I looked like I'd slept in my clothes. The women all wore jewelry. Reflected tennis bracelets, rings, necklaces, pins, and watches glimmered, cast darting bits of light across the sea. Maurice hovered in the distance, where Catalina should have been.

"Can't you see what's happening here?" I turned around. Everyone in the room looked at me as if intermission had just ended. "You want me to act crazy, Maurice? You think you're getting something real?"

Several guests smiled smiles of pure anticipation. This was the main event: the artist's tantrum.

"You want real?" I walked to the wall and pulled down a small Giacometti sketch, a male bust, ballpoint pen on paper, framed in cherry, sandwiched between two panes of glass. "This is just pretend," I said. I brought down the Giacometti on the corner of the coffee table, shattering the glass, tearing the drawing, and slicing my palm.

No one made a sound. I felt my drunkenness fall away, and everything suddenly became clear. I had stopped the charade. My hand bled onto the carpet.

Maurice began to clap. "Bravo," he said, and soon everyone was clapping.

I ran into the kitchen to wash and bandage my hand. I wrapped the cut with paper towels, then noticed, in the corner of the kitchen, by a door that probably led to maid's quarters or a laundry room, a ceramic cat bowl, hand painted. Beside a smudged calico cat with crossed eyes there was a name, painted in childlike lettering: GIO.

I found Maurice leading everyone into the music room.

"Not now, Graham. Lydia's about to begin."

"This can't wait," I said.

"*She* can't wait," he said.

Lydia floated in through the back door, wearing a capelike garment, and sat at the piano.

I took a chair at the back of the room, wondering if the Giacometti I'd destroyed had been real after all. If so, it was probably worth thirty thousand dollars. Gio. Perhaps she'd named her cat after her old fiancé. I was panicking, I told myself. I looked at the Rouault. Definitely bad. Yes, I thought, she must have named the cat after the guy. What else?

Yet there was something about the way Lydia looked seated behind the grand piano, like a child hanging onto the edge of a floating dock.

The piece opened with hurried, muted chords that grew progressively louder and were then joined by a simple trilling theme (echoing high and low). It rose to a quick crescendo. The theme's recapitulation followed, with twice as many notes. Lydia's fingers glided over the keys, smoothly, confidently; she played as if she were absent, letting the music do the work. The piece plunged into a series of ascending jazzlike chords, then emerged into a restrained, patient, classical theme. Whereas from the opening I had felt like a dalmatian threading through the legs of galloping horses, suddenly I was watching horses and carriage from a height, and their velocity didn't seem so great from my new perspective. As the first movement proceeded through its series of frustrated climaxes, I grew less aware that Lydia sat before me, playing. The sound shut down my other senses, one by one, until I felt utterly transported, hanging on every note.

The second movement was devastating: Everything stopped; all that had come before was cleared away. Lethargic, almost silent chords, and a three-note tra-la-la evoked a city of rubble, with no one left to rebuild it. The tra-la-la sounded like a call for help, with the final la a loss of hope, a surrender. Between these repetitions of tra-la-la came a number of full rests. The piano would stop vibrating for a moment, and it felt as if someone had sucked all of the air from the room. Lydia came alive for each tra-la-la. Her face, blank through the first movement, was now tight with concentration, though this part was technically much easier. She clenched her teeth, and the tendons in her neck stood out. Near the end of the almost four-minute section (the introduction to the rondo, it turned out), she hit the tra-la-la so hard, the flowers on the piano shuddered. These were single notes. The final note of the introduction was a single tra, and it was shattering—no trace remained of Lydia's cold absence and reserve. She put everything, emotionally and physically, into the act of hitting that one note, and it reverberated through the room, a dissonant, unmoored, solitary cry.

In the next moment, she began the rondo and was gone again—absent, letting the music do the work, calm and composed, as if she'd been playing the rondo all night, its simple, classical theme evoking images of sunlight and billowing curtains. She remained like this through the end of the piece. She finished, we applauded, and she bowed—utterly without affect.

"What was that piece?" Slim Fop asked Maurice, as Lydia started to wander out.

"Beethoven," Maurice said. "I don't remember the opus number."

But Lydia heard the question, too, and approached Slim Fop. Suddenly, she was animated again, waving her hands as she spoke. "The piece was written by a beggar in Italy, during the Second World War," she said, "under Mussolini, and he was a Jew in hiding, and he was found out and killed by Hitler, but the music he had written got smuggled out by some underworld friends of his. Then people, to protect the music, said that they'd been written by Beethoven, but they were by a composer named Giovanni, who was just an Italian beggar who died penniless." She took a deep breath through her nose, raised her eyebrows. "He wrote beautiful music—"

"Lydia, sweetheart, let's go to bed," said Mrs. Perrin. She took her daughter by the arm. Side by side, they looked even more alike, as if they were sisters rather than mother and daughter. Mrs. Perrin led Lydia out and everyone stood in silence. Slim Fop's wife looked at him scornfully for his faux pas.

Maurice lifted his head (he'd been staring at his feet). "Opus fifty-something. Waldheim? Waldstein Sonata? I don't remember. Beethoven."

When Mrs. Perrin returned, she said: "Let's all go into the gallery and see Mr. Witt's picture."

Maurice stopped me in the entry. My heart began to pound. "Maurice, sir," I said, "I'm sorry."

"Never apologize," he said.

"Your daughter—"

"She plays the piano beautifully," he interrupted.

"Yes."

He nodded several times. "We're very careful with her," he said.

"Maurice, I've got to go back in there and apologize to your guests."

He didn't say anything, just looked at me as if looking right through me.

"I've ruined the evening," I said.

He hit my shoulder with the side of his fist. "You *made* the evening. By the end of the week your show will be sold out." He reached into the closet, handed me my jacket. "Now, we can't have you in here while they're looking at your work. That's your MO. You'd better go home." He put his hand on my head. "Keep it up and you're going to be huge, kid."

"I ruined your Giacometti."

He smiled, shrugged. "It's insured."

I stepped out the door, past a row of black Mercedes and BMWs, past a Volvo or two, up the long driveway to the Pacific Coast Highway. I had just destroyed a minor piece by a major artist.

I walked toward Santa Monica. I tried to hitchhike, but my right hand was bandaged and looked horrible. I had to keep it in my pocket, while putting out my left thumb. Unless I craned my head around, I had my back to traffic. People didn't even slow down to look at me. I kept my thumb out but knew I'd have to walk at least as far as the MTA stop, wherever that was.

The marine layer had dissipated somewhat; straggling mist clung to the streetlamps. Someone's mail littered the side of the road. Bits of paper on the shoulder as far as I could see. I flipped each piece over with my foot as I came to it. Coupon circulars, utility bills, computer catalogs, a lawyer's bill, a greeting card—some torn, some intact—spaced at thirty- and forty-foot intervals.

A car slowed behind me, and I turned around to look. A black Mercedes pulled alongside. The driver honked the horn. Some of Maurice's guests. They waved and smiled and drove on. Then it happened with a Volvo, then one of the BMWs. I put out my thumb. They just waved and smiled.

SUSANNA DANIEL

University of Iowa

❧

WE ARE CARTOGRAPHERS

We arrived at Stiltsville late Friday afternoon and spent the evening on the porch, discussing survival. "Seventy-five percent of the world is water," said my husband, Dennis, to our daughter, Margo, who was fifteen. Margo had her feet on the porch rail and was picking at her toenails. Dennis said, "Would you know what to do if you were lost at sea?"

The Stilthouse, where we spent most weekends, was a wooden house built on pilings in Biscayne Bay. It stood five miles from shore amid a dozen similar structures. From the Stilthouse, downtown Miami resembled a foggy sequence of many-sized blue bottles; the evening skyline gave off faint stars of light. Black water heaved beneath us. To the south was the WHRC radio tower and to the west was Soldier Key. Beyond Soldier Key were forty-eight miles of open sea, then the Bahamas.

Margo said, "We have enough food here to ration for weeks. And enough water. Water's important." Beside Margo sat her friend Beverly. Beverly was an athletic girl with small eyes, broad shoulders, and a head of lovely brown curls. She was slapping at mosquitoes with a magazine.

"You're not stranded here at the house," Dennis said. "You're lost at sea. You're stranded out there." He pointed into the black.

"Do I have a boat?" Margo said.

"A raft," said Dennis.

"A radio?"

"No radio."

Margo scanned the horizon—the Everglades to the left, Cape Florida to the right. We sat beyond the edge of a continent. "What else do I have?" she said.

"That's the first thing you do—assess your resources," said Dennis. I looked at his profile, into the dark spaces between unruly thatches of eyebrow. I thought, Give her a blanket. Give her a flare. Then I thought, Give her nothing. Make her strong. "You have two life jackets," said Dennis. "Orange ones. The raft is partially inflated and you're alone."

Dennis lifts these scenarios from camping manuals and field guides. He quotes from them at the dinner table: *You can tell a manta ray from two sharks swimming side by side because the ray's fins will submerge at the same time.* What interests me is the idea of the family functioning independently, like the Swiss Family Robinson. It seems that what we lack most in this modern world is the ability to depend on others. I miss baby Margo, who could not feed herself.

"That's all I've got?" Margo said.

"You're a goner," said Beverly.

"Not if I relax. The first thing I do is relax."

"You also have a bucket," said Dennis. "It's morning, summer. Getting hotter by the minute."

"What am I wearing?"

Dennis took a swallow of his beer. "What you're wearing now," he said. She was wearing a T-shirt and denim shorts. Her ankles were slender and tan. "But pants."

"She'll burn up," said Beverly.

"Right-o, Beverly. Okay, Margo, you have one of those yellow raincoats your mother wears." I thought of desalinization pills, anti-exposure suits, patch and first-aid kits. Margo, drifting on some bit of blue ocean. Margo, dehydrating.

I said, "What happens to the body when it dehydrates?" Across water, voices soar. The Davidsons' Stilthouse was eighty yards off; they could probably hear every word we said.

"Your pee turns bright yellow," Beverly said.

"You get dizzy," said Margo.

The boat fenders squeaked. It occurred to me that every purpose has a material suited to that purpose. Like rubber for fenders, because it floats and holds air and won't break. Wood for docks because it's strong and weathers well. Fiberglass for the boat because it's light and easy to maintain. That is survival. Choosing what to make and how to make it and what to make it from—it is all survival.

"Margo," said Dennis. "You have two orange life vests, a half-inflated raft, a yellow raincoat, and a bucket."

"The bucket's for bailing," Margo said.

"Check. What else can you use it for?"

"I don't know. But I'll use the raincoat as a tarp, for shade."

Dennis made a sound like a buzzer on a game show. "You'll need that to protect from exposure. Use your pants as a canopy."

"But I was thinking of using my pants for a sail."

"What's the use of a sail? Do you know where you're going?"

"I'm going to shore."

"You don't know where shore is. Besides, you're way out—it's best to stay put. Use the bucket for drag."

I said, "Meantime, cover up."

"And keep a log," said Dennis. "What should you log?"

Margo said, "I know—the time, which I can guess by looking at the sun, the weather—"

"And your condition," said Dennis. "Are you hurt? Are you bleeding? Does your head hurt?"

"If I'm bleeding, I'll attract sharks."

"Bleed in the boat."

I said, "What does she eat?"

"She's in the ocean, sweetheart," Dennis said. "She'll eat fish."

Once, Dennis said that to survive one must overcome the need for comfort and maintain the will to live. Dennis is convinced that our daughter—who at the slightest whine of hunger can step into the kitchen to find fruit, milk, leftovers—must understand these things.

"What if they're poisonous?" Margo asked.

"Chances are they aren't," said Dennis. "Not in the middle of the Atlantic."

I said, "You know how to tell? Cowfish, they're poisonous, they have spotty flesh. And porcupine fish and thorn fish have spines. Don't eat anything with spines. Spines are warnings."

"Your mother's right," said Dennis. "Those fish are clearly not edible. Also, don't eat fish that blow up like balloons. You'll know it's poisonous if it tastes like—"

"Pepper," I said.

"Right-o. And in that case, puke your guts out. Anything that looks like bass or grouper, you can eat. But eat it fast so it doesn't go bad."

I said, "Otherwise, you have to dry it out and salt it. But then you lose the fish's water."

"If it goes bad, puke it up," Dennis said.

I said, "But you don't want to do too much vomiting. You'll need your water."

"Knock out the fish against the side of the raft," said Dennis. "Cut out the gills and the blood vessels along the backbone, like your mother and I do when we cook fish here."

"I have a knife?" said Margo.

Dennis looked at her. "Margo, you always have a knife." For Dennis, this is true. He keeps a knife in the glove box, his desk at work, the bedside table.

"Okay, I scale it and then I skin it," said Margo.

"You don't have to skin it," Dennis said.

"Fine," said Margo. "I think I've got it."

Bedtime was early at Stiltsville. Each night, Margo and I towed mattresses onto the porch that faced the radio tower. Dennis preferred to sleep inside, out of the wind. Margo didn't have a history of tossing and turning, but I always wedged my mattress between hers and the porch railing just in case. Years ago, when we shared the Stilthouse with the Moores, Tommy Moore fell off the porch into the shallow water, landing on barnacle-covered I beams that had been left there when the house was built. When they helped him out minutes later, Tommy's legs were ribboned with red gashes. It never occurred to us— the adults, the decision-makers—to have those I beams removed. We never thought to kill the electric eel that lived in an oil drum under the dock, either, until the other Moore son, Warren, dove down with a mask and a machete and sliced off the eel's head. For weeks the severed head dried atop a piling, untouched by the pelicans that bother our lobster traps, until I was sick of its raisin eyes and bald head, and I knocked it into the water with the back of my hand.

There were dangers at Stiltsville; accidents happened. But it was our little island. On an island, there is the illusion that all disasters can be averted, all enemies accounted for.

In the morning, Dennis took Margo and Beverly snorkeling in No-Name Cove while I cooked bacon, hash browns, grits with butter. When they returned, the girls skipped upstairs before Dennis cut the engine. They were dripping wet, in bathing suits.

"Mom," Margo said, gulping orange juice, "Beverly found the coolest whatchamacallit."

"It's white," said Beverly.

"Let's see," I said.

In Beverly's palm was a sea urchin the size of a golf ball. The sea urchins near the dock are eggplant-colored and large as a man's fist. This one was pearl white. I turned it over in my hand.

"Girls, it's drying out," I said. It is easy to forget that some things from the sea—clams, sponges, coral—are alive. "It needs water."

I rushed down the stairs. Dennis met me halfway but I pushed past him to the swimming ladder. New barnacles scratched at my bare feet. I tilted my palm in the water and the sea urchin drifted away on its side. I watched it go, then looked up into the amused face of my husband and the embarrassed face of my daughter. I wanted to tell Margo not to worry so much, but who was I to say it, after coming to the rescue of a sea urchin?

I stepped out of the water and into a towel Dennis spread for me. "Sorry, kiddo," I said to Margo, meaning sorry for the embarrassment. To Dennis, I said, "Do crustaceans make albinos?"

"I think everything makes albinos," he said.

After breakfast, we fished off the dock. Margo gave up early, but Beverly caught a too-small fish, then unhooked it herself and threw it back. "Gross," Margo said when Beverly offered her hands to smell. They got towels and headphones and magazines and camped on the eastern square of the dock, where the boat and its lines wouldn't cast shadows. Dennis began fooling with the boat bilge, which was sticking. He'd donned his Stiltsville uniform: threadbare pajama bottoms and no shirt. His back was pink and freckled. Every year we go to the dermatologist, who tells us to stay out of the sun. "How can we stay out of the sun?" Dennis says agreeably. "We live on the water." He winks at me, as if our life, our lifestyle, were an inside joke. I wondered when it would be time to take Margo with us. It was probably already time.

I changed into shorts and settled into a rocking chair on the porch. Something itched at me—first a mosquito, then something unnamable. "Babe!" Dennis called. He was at the stern of the boat, wiping at his neck with a towel.

"You got the wrench?"

"In the generator room," I called down to him.

He cupped his ear.

"The generator room!"

He spread two open palms. My husband, when he wants to be, is a mouse plunked down in a maze.

I grabbed chips and soda for the girls and a beer for Dennis and headed downstairs, stopping for the wrench on the way. Dennis had me hold nuts and washers while he tightened the propeller shaft on the starboard engine. "How long since that one's been cleaned?" I asked. He said, "Too long," and gave me a kiss. It was a blessing that Dennis had the boat to occupy him; otherwise, he tends to manufacture diversions. One slow afternoon at home, he washed the dog with my ten-dollar salon shampoo. Another time, I had the flu and he decided to sterilize everything I'd touched. He rifled through cabinets looking for rubbing alcohol. When he couldn't find any, he took an old bottle of cologne and started spraying things. "Ninety percent alcohol," he boasted. He was particularly concerned about the telephone receiver. I refused to answer the smelly phone for days.

Instead of returning upstairs, I backed into the downstairs hammock and lay there fingering the ropes above my head. I watched the girls enjoy their music and magazines and my husband enjoy his boat. I sank into a nap. The afternoon passed without conversation and without a meal.

The air felt like evening and smelled of hamburger when I woke. The girls weren't on the dock but their towels were, rumpled by wind.

"Margo!"

Her voice came from the second floor. "What?"

"Your stuff is still down here!"

No reply.

"It's going to go in the water!"

Footsteps thunked across the wood above my head. My sleepy body was too dense to lift. Margo appeared on the stairs. She glanced at me as she passed, saying, "Dinner in ten." One of the best things about Stiltsville was grilling burgers for dinner, which meant Dennis cooked and Margo made potato salad. I dropped my legs to the floor, thinking about slicing tomatoes and onions, washing lettuce.

After dinner we watched the sun set. Stretches of silence were launched, sliced by a word or two, and launched again.

"Cumulus?" Margo pointed.

"Stratocumulus," said Dennis.

"I think those are cirrus," Beverly said.

"Stratocumulus," said Dennis.

The girls went downstairs. I washed my face, tasting brine, and Dennis went to bed. I put out three mattresses and collapsed on the one closest to the porch railing. I was going to shout for the girls to come get ready for bed when above the light smacking of the tides, I heard Margo's voice: "The North Star."

"Mmm-hmm," Beverly said, her voice muffled.

"All the other stars circle around it," said Margo.

Links in the hammock chain creaked. Beverly said something that sounded like, "Show me."

Inside their voices prowled conspiracy and intimacy and something I couldn't name. I scooted on my belly until my ears were over the side of the porch. I was right above them. Someone at the Davidsons' Stilthouse said, "No, the other one," and the words somersaulted across the water. Margo said something about never going anywhere without a map.

Beverly said, "You're my map," and my daughter said, "Ah."

From the silence and the way my stomach felt inside it—all knotted lines and clenched teeth—I understood that they were kissing.

Then Margo was speaking again. "Know where your map and compass are at all times," she said. It was from a pamphlet Dennis had brought to the dinner table weeks earlier: *Tips for Persons Traveling in Groups.*

"Mmm," said Beverly.

Tips for Persons Traveling in Groups said that if the person in your troop, on your boat, or in your aircraft with the maps and compass is killed, it is essential to obtain these things off the corpse. I'd rerouted the conversation into plans to go camping.

"My dad gave me a compass for my birthday," Margo said.

Beverly said, "Show me again," and I braced myself.

"It's straight out from the center of Cassiopeia. It's in line with the two stars at the end of Ursa Major."

"The Big Dipper," said Beverly, and Margo said, "It's the last star in Ursa Minor."

"The Little Dipper."

"That's hard to see . . ." Margo's voice trailed off.

"Does this feel good?" asked Beverly.

When Margo was a baby, she slept in the room across the hall.
Her sleep made me nervous. Each night when her crying whimpered
to silence, I lay in my bed and counted to 100. If she hadn't started
up again, I brought my feet to the floor and stepped—toes, ball,
heel, pause—to the edge of the bedroom carpet. I opened the door.
The wooden hall floor buckled under weight, so I reached for the
nursery's doorjamb, tipped forward, and scissored one leg over the
hallway as if it were a moat thick with angry crocodiles.

I thought of those nights as I rose from my mattress and made my
way to the stairs, careful not to make noise. I pretended my eyes were
on the tips of my toes and tried to gauge whether, if I took a step or
two down, the girls could see me from where they were lying in the
hammock. I decided on three steps, to be safe.

I closed my eyes and willed it untrue. Across the water came a
man's voice: "Damn it, Kathy."

The hammock shifted and settled into a soft swing. "Like this?"
said Beverly.

I crouched until I was eye-level with my shins. I almost lost my
balance. I saw four bare legs—two thin and two thick—and the
hems of two pairs of shorts. The slender legs lay straight, knees up
and feet flexed. One thick leg was knee-down between them.

"I'm pretty good at this," Beverly said.

Margo's shorts appeared. Beverly had a thumb in the open zipper.
Her hand moved up and out of sight again but the shorts remained,
loose around Margo's knees. Margo made a sound of pleasure. Or the
imitation of a sound of pleasure.

Margo said, "Harder." Then, "Oh god." Across the flats, Marcus

Davidson was lecturing his daughter, Kathy, about having forgotten to bring something from home. Either he hadn't noticed that voices carry more easily over water, or he didn't care. Where was Julia Davidson, Kathy's mother?

"Are you close?" said Beverly.

When Margo was six we took her skiing—her first time—at Beech Mountain. She buried her face in my jacket and cried all the way up the lift. At the top, Dennis tried to reason with her but she wouldn't listen. I said, "Let's put her in ski school," but Dennis told me to stay out of it. I said, "Dennis, she's scared. This isn't working." He positioned Margo at the top of the slope and held her shoulders as she squirmed. Then he pushed her.

Margo, an excellent skier, has developed Dennis's fear of fear.

It occurred to me, as I listened to my daughter's heavy breaths, that she is a person who forever will try new things until she is no longer afraid.

Margo said, "Right there, don't stop, you've got it." Then she groaned, and was silent.

I reversed up the stairs and lay on the mattress farthest from the ledge. Margo would sleep next to me, which left the vulnerable mattress for Beverly. Marcus Davidson said, "Forget it. It's not worth it," and the radio towers blinked thirty-nine times before the girls came to bed.

The next day I left breakfast on the kitchen counter and hollered, as I went down the stairs, that I was going to walk the flats. Dennis was shaving and the girls were still in bed. The tide was so low that bristles of shaving plants were sticking out of the water on the flats, drying in the sun. I could have walked to the Davidsons' and told them to keep their squabbles to themselves.

"Mom!" Margo yelled.

I stepped out of the generator room, where we kept old shoes for walking in the water. "What?"

"Wait up. We're coming with you."

"Hurry up."

I didn't wait. I chose a pair of ballet slippers that Alma Moore donated years earlier and kept on my T-shirt so my shoulders wouldn't burn. I swam away from the dock until my feet touched bottom. Then I walked as quickly as I could while taking care not to step on sea cucumber, brain coral, starfish, or anything else that lived. The girls were sitting on the dock, lacing shoes. They looked like any pair of teenagers—eager and sunburned and oblivious. Margo waved and they climbed down the swim ladder.

Beverly had never walked on the flats. "Is that a snail?" she asked.

"Conch," Margo said. "Don't touch. It'll cut you if you scare it."

"The shell or the thing inside?"

"The thing inside."

We walked in circles around each other. Our footsteps clouded the water.

"Is that a sponge?" Beverly said.

"That's a red beard sponge," said Margo.

"Can I pick it up?"

"Mom, can you touch a red beard sponge?"

"No," I said.

"No," said Margo.

"Why not?" said Beverly. "It just looks like a sponge."

"Why not, Mom?"

"Some sponges have tiny needles you can't see." Beverly looked skeptical. "They'll leave silica under your skin," I said. "You'll get open sores that fester." I hoped *fester* was a scary word.

Beverly moved on. Margo said, "Mom, are there maps of this bay?"

"Sure."

"I want one," she said.

"Ask your father."

We turned to watch a ray skim past. Margo's hair, wet-black, fell in loose waves past her neck. I was amazed by the slope of her shoulders in the sunlight. Then I thought of the night before, and for the first time in my life, had to look away from my daughter.

"What kind is it?" Beverly said.

"Leopard," said Margo and I.

They spent that afternoon reading magazines and chatting on the porch. I drank two beers in the kitchen and listened for echoes of their intimacy. I heard none. They were girls, mostly and merely. They listened to music, snapped at each other, complained of boredom. They finished four sodas each and three bags of chips. Margo said Mr. Somebody—a teacher they would have next year—looked like a frog and Beverly said he was sexy. I put down the knife I was using to slice celery. "He's too old," Margo said but Beverly disagreed. Margo said, "Jimmy is sexy," and Beverly said, "Jimmy's cute, but he's not sexy." Then she explained the difference.

Nailed to the wood paneling in the Stilthouse kitchen was a hurricane-tracking map that had been there forever. Beetle-sized blue and red magnets (blue for watch, red for warning) were clustered in one corner. We hadn't had a hurricane since Hugo two years earlier, which tore several two-by-fours from the Stilthouse roof and a dozen shingles from our house in Miami. Tropical storms brew constantly from May to September (that weekend they were tracking one in the West Indies) but they have so many ways of falling apart. They diffuse over the continental reef like bullies losing nerve, or rub up against cold snaps and disperse like bubbles in tepid bathwater. Sometimes they just disappear. Angry radar spirals dissolve and the screen goes black.

We did not know then that within the year, our Stilthouse (survivor of Agnes, Gilbert, and Hugo) would be blown away by Andrew, the century's most successful storm. Our little family would find itself unmoored. We would fill weekends with sundry diversions—trips to the Keys and bland Florida beach towns like Sanibel and Jupiter, places full of strip malls and brunch specials. We would boat the bay and the Miami River, destinationless. Once or twice, we would anchor where our Stilthouse had stood. We would dive the spot like any wreck, searching for bed frames, shutters, shoes. Treasures of an era. We would use channel markers instead of Stilthouses to navigate homeward. We would feel loss and lost, and only then would I understand: This is what it means to be part of a family. There are no maps and the territory changes. We are explorers, traveling in groups.

Beverly closed up the windows while Margo and I hauled bags downstairs. A cockroach crawled out of a kitchen drawer and I trapped it in one hand, walked to the porch, and pitched it into the water.

"How do those things get out here?" said Margo.

"They come with us," I said, lifting a cooler into her arms. She took a step toward the stairs and tripped on the linoleum, then caught herself.

"Is it too heavy?" I said. I reached to take the cooler, but she held onto it.

"It's fine," she said, turning away. I listened to her footsteps on the stairs, then looked at the floor for what had tripped her. There was nothing there. For a split second, the world seemed rigged with invisible dangers: She could slip and hit her head on a cleat, or fall off the boat into the propellers. But I knew that the real threats were things I would never envision, and prayed that she was armed.

Dennis had some trouble with the starboard engine, but by the time everything was on the dock and the house was closed, he'd gone swimming. He backstroked away from us, grinning. "Last chance for a few weeks," he shouted.

Margo stood at the prow of the boat in her swimsuit, then stepped over the rail. She turned around so she was facing the boat. "Careful," I said. She shook out her hair and brought her arms to her sides. Then her arms shot up, her knees bent, and she dove backward into the air. She hit the water hands first and surfaced facing the boat. Dennis, treading water, hooted and Beverly and I clapped. Margo swam to her father and Beverly stared down at the water where Margo had dived. Blue bubbles wrestled to the surface.

Margo kicked, spraying Dennis, and he splashed her back. To him, she was still a girl on whom life had made no impression. But I knew she'd begun to sample what life had to offer, and that soon she would encounter limits. I told myself that this was just my mother-thinking, that maybe it only seems as if the possibilities narrow as we grow older and more experienced.

"Are you going in?" I asked Beverly. She shook her head. Her breasts under her T-shirt were almost as large as mine. I wanted to ask if she was in a C-cup but instead I said, "Looking forward to getting back?" I didn't understand the look she gave me but then I did: It was the first question I'd asked her since eavesdropping. We live— Beverly, me, the adults she knows, the teenagers I know—in a world where adults communicate with children by asking about their lives and thoughts and hopes. We are genuinely interested or we pretend to be. My behavior had been rude.

Beverly shrugged. "I like it here," she said. I looked at her. She had a solid, square body and a flat stomach. An uncommon body. The parts of a woman that taper didn't taper on her. She lacked neck and waist, her ankles were as thick as her knees. But she wasn't ugly or even masculine; she was just unfinished. I tried to finish her in my head. I decided she would not get taller, but eventually her waist would segue from her hips. She would get sick of all that gorgeous hair and cut it off. Then years later, she'd have regrets and grow it out, but it would come back different. She'd move to the northeast and populate her sex life with men, mostly, plus a few women. Then the balance would shift, until she no longer slept with men at all. She would never be beautiful and would always fall in love with beautiful women. Women who are effortlessly feminine, who are strong and sometimes cruel, who are mostly practical and almost always hetero-sexual—women like Margo.

"How are your folks, Beverly?"

"Fine."

"School okay?"

"Fine."

"Do you still play basketball?"

"I made the team. I tried to get Margo to try out but she wouldn't."

"She's doing drama this year. That's probably why."

Beverly nodded. I wanted to heave her into the water. I wanted to slap her face and watch it redden.

"You guys are really lucky to have this place," she said.

I wanted to put my arms around her, to breathe through her hair. I wanted to tell her not to touch girls like my daughter, but if she was going to, to be careful. I wanted to tell her how to follow through.

"Don't cut your hair," I said. "You're going to want to one day, but don't. It's lovely. It's you."

"I won't," she said, but she had no idea.

MATTHEW PITT

New York University

The Mean

Twenty after four on Tuesdays, the chimps went berserk. Their mayhem followed an arc (source, midpoint, apogee, to trace it on a rose compass). First the troop would pet at the safety glass lightly, as though consoling it. Then they'd prowl the perimeter of their cage, feet and knuckles skimming concrete. This was a warning—it meant their hearts were getting hotter, meant they were close to getting mean. They took it out on the bars. The chimps rattled the iron, clamping down, wailing to be let in on whatever secret it was outside they could smell and hear but not see. Sometimes the head zookeeper would forget to put up their toys. That was when Tuesdays howled. The primates would hurl Wiffle balls, spinning tops, rattles, and building blocks at the bars. The noises were echinate, arrhythmic, and relentless. The chimps wouldn't let up for hours.

By then, Charles Shales and his high school students had killed their joints, cached their pipes, and vacated the hideout. By then they'd left the Milwaukee Zoo, gathered their paraphernalia, having taken pains not to leave behind any trace of their festivities under the scaffolding behind the Monkey House; they trusted the harsh winter winds to scatter the scent of drugs by morning, and the chimps' memory of the commotion to dull and fade. The group would ask Shales if he wanted to hang with them, but Shales would decline.

He'd have to come home and get his head unclouded in a hurry. Shales would have work to do in preparation for tomorrow's remedial algebra classes—maybe, say, a hundred papers to grade on the associative property—with a blue pencil and a bag of salt and vinegar potato chips as his only anchors. The high from the joints would be all but dried, just a small static gristle scatting somewhere in his head. But the pain wouldn't be back yet; that was the main thing. He figured he could barrel through most of his stack before the pain supplanted the pleasure.

After washing the skunk and zoo from his hands, Shales would pop in live tapes of Liddy's band, Some Assault. Would listen for her crisp drumwork, urgent four counts, and harmony vocal. He would bend over and tap his fingers against the speakers, head bobbing. The band was confident, brash, numinous.

They sounded—just as rock should—like polished hell.

The first ten papers Shales read would actually be fine. But then he'd come to some kid who argued, say, that the associative property made every integer negative, once what was outside the parenthesis multiplied with the numbers inside of it. But this kid wouldn't call the process multiplication; he'd call it "claiming." He'd write for his sample problem: $1 (4 + 1) = -5$, and then explain his reasoning: *"When the first one is claimed by the four and the other one, it's all bad.*

The first number is now a minus, and so's the second. Whatever number's are inside the parenth thesis have control over the other number. No matter how much bigger that other number is." And Shales would check the kid's name on the front of the paper and wince. "You're wrong in every way," Shales would write, "but you show your work well." He'd draw a C. Then a twinge would kick up, just beneath the skin. He would try not to look at the clock, mentally punishing himself when he took two glances in the same minute, wondering when Liddy would be finished with her show, when she'd slip into his room and climb in his bed.

Wednesdays they held faculty luncheons at the high school. These were designed for teachers to relay disturbing student behavior, or to reveal any intimate grievances the students had confided. Usually everyone just swallowed their cafeteria food and left. The only real issue they wanted to discuss was, "Higher wages or we walk!" But they gave wide berth to *that* subject; the district superintendent was always in attendance, ass pressed against the radiator. Shales imagined that, at the first sign of teachers talking contract negotiations, the superintendent would press some button with his butt warning the governor and, that night, a midnight law would be pushed through the Wisconsin legislature declaring faculty luncheons off-limits to everyone but students.

After lunch Shales spotted Mary grading quizzes by the water fountain. He darted through the crowd to stand by her. "Hey Charlie," Mary said, picking sesame seeds from her undersized yellow sweater. "It's been many bells since we've been together."

Shales affirmed. The motor in the drinking fountain turned over. The other teachers filed out from the lounge, dumping their food trays. The smell of burned chicken patties wafted up from the trash can just inside the door. Shales and Mary stood without saying anything. When Shales had first moved to Milwaukee, Mary had made overtures of friendship, had checked up on him. Since he'd gotten sick, most of their interactions consisted of long, desiccated silences.

"So," she finally asked, "how's your weekend shaping?"

"Oh, I can't think about that on a Wednesday." Any time other than the current moment felt far off to him. The weekend was an aeon from now; yesterday's high, the Pleistocene era.

She pointed to his eyes, which he must have forgotten to dab with Visine. "Looks to me like your weekend's already begun."

"Student papers. Can't get enough of the little geniuses. What about you? Are you doing something, going to a show?"

"No more movies for a while," Mary laughed. "Not with 'the Spoiler' lurking."

"The Spoiler" was what the newspapers called Vondra Popeil. She had been haunting the Milwaukee Cineplex since midsummer, gaining notoriety and ire for standing outside the main doors and giving away the resolution to every new movie. "They get married, have two children. It's van Heuk who wrote the ransom note. Penny dies courageously, her mother gives up crack, they leave it open for a sequel." Since she was purchasing tickets to the movies, the police couldn't pick up the Spoiler for trespassing.

"It's too bad, too," Mary said, as if answering a question. "I could use more stories without endings. If she'd only cover my eyes and ears *before* each picture ended, I'd laud her with lilies." Mary was an English teacher, and Shales loved her turns of phrase. He loved how she could get words to do what she wanted—she probably didn't see it this way, but she'd tapped into a formula. She could create a little beauty with her metaphors and rhythms, a beauty that seemed to intercept the misery of time. In her own way she was preventing endings.

———

On the Thursday before the last Tuesday, Liddy came over to Shales's apartment after a bad practice. She was wearing a tank top with an iron-on peanut butter cup on the front. "I can't do this much longer." She clutched her hands, folded her knuckles—this was to work out the tension in her fingers. She gripped the drumsticks too tight, always too tight. "Charlie," she said, "you can only tell your friends they suck so many times before it puts the friendships in jeopardy... Maybe I should just give up and join the marching band."

He thought of her group, five of them, a prime number, indivisible. Then again, so was one. "If you join the marching band, I could come watch you play. In fact I'd get paid for it. But honestly? I hate pep rallies and the marching band gives me chiggers."

Liddy laughed and pulled off her shirt. Her breasts were rosy, the skin hot. She placed her arms around Shales, still holding the shirt. He could feel the fabric and the drying sweat on his neck. This was normal, he told himself, her coming over and peeling off her clothes. His listening to her discuss her career as a rock star while his cells tore one another to pieces like feral dogs. "So do you really want to do that? Quit? Don't you want the band to reach its full potential?"

"I am the full potential," she declared, rolling into bed. "My beat's the only good thing about us." She swallowed six pills, three shapes, four colors. Shales had asked her once why she never smoked with him. "Where you're going's good for you," she'd said. "I need something higher."

"So what was the problem tonight?" Shales asked. "Same as always?" Liddy thought the guitarist played like one of those solo-hogging dinosaurs from the seventies. "Jilt's really getting to you. I've seen the way you look at him the day after a show. Like he's stolen your best friend or your diary."

"I don't have a best friend," Liddy said. She darkened the room by pulling the sides of the pillow over her face. "Or a diary." She placed her hand in Shales's, into his grading hand, and let it lie. His lesson plans fanned out onto the floor. She'd be asleep inside of two minutes. It wasn't like before, though before wasn't so long ago: They wouldn't have sex, probably never would again, and this suited Shales, because when they did have sex he felt he had something to live for. It wasn't that it was so good, or exciting. It was that it was irrevocable. No matter where Liddy went, what records she sold, or what shelters she wound up scurrying in and out of, she would remember him inside of her.

"It's not like Jilt's not replaceable," Liddy said, more asleep than not. "It's his stash we can't replace. If he wasn't connecting us he'd be gone. I mean it, if what he was giving us wasn't helping you, he'd be a fucking antique."

She poked out from under the pillow when she heard Shales set the alarm clock. "Three hours' sleep. Can't you let me stay the whole night for once?" Shales ignored her bait. He wasn't going to get drawn into this argument again. They had agreed to these terms: She could stay over, but they had to get her out of Shales's apartment before first light, before his neighbors rose for the day.

Friday morning before the last Tuesday. The oncologist greeted Shales warmly, not a good sign. His crinkled midwestern accent was based on inverse proportion: The more dire things had become, the less urgent his inflection. It's metastatic, he said. It has spread to the liver. Does he want to be put on a list for something experimental? Or does he want to double the chemotherapy? No. To both.

The doctor's voice glazed over—grew so calm Shales wondered if he should expect to die this very moment. Shales has had breast cancer for nine months. He has been given an LHRH, administered cyproterone acetate; tamoxifen; chemo in tandem with CAMs; and of course the antacids, Alka-Seltzer, Tums, false trails leading nowhere.

The only things that haven't let him down are the fat joints and the short nights with the seventeen-year-old stray who plays drums in bars. The seventeen-year-old he just dropped off, who by now is behind the McDonald's Dumpster puffing meth, killing hours until the school bus comes.

That night Shales went to the Cineplex; *Hit and Run* was showing. He could smell chocolate being munched, could hear parents brushing Kleenex below their kids' leaky noses. He turned and looked directly into the projector. By then *Hit and Run* had thoroughly annoyed Shales. Some facile load of bullshit he could've guessed even if the Spoiler hadn't screamed it in his ear earlier, where the rich girl and boy live fickle lives but learn about themselves thanks to the drifter they accidentally hit while driving their convertible; where the gentry falls on hard spiritual times but is repaired, ultimately, by this poor drifter who shows them how much they've been neglecting. When the end credits scroll, the gentry is more compassionate and the unemployed man has become the gentry's new caretaker, and there is a sense of justice, a sense that light rewards the lost.

The reels of his own plot were what Shales wanted to pick through, anyway.

On Reel 1 was Liddy—thin girl with dark-dyed hair, wet-looking like a tarmac after a rainstorm, knobby elbows, pale pink gums, small teeth that were sharp and told a story, tight stomach, trace of fat at the hips, wrists wrapped in white tape. The day of the first semester final exam, she'd worn a jacket with the McDonald's logo, a Taco Bell T-shirt, and a Jack in the Box necklace. She kept her bangs out of her face with a hairpin shaped like a carrot that had come from a juice bar. Shales approached her as he passed out ScanTrons. "I like the accessorizing." "Thanks, Mr. Shales." He had been Mr. Shales to her then. She had been the girl who kept dropping her pencil during the exam. Playing him for a fool, dipping down for quick peeks at a cheat sheet pressed between her sock and her boot. He told Liddy to stay after class. That was when she first called him Charlie.

Their conversation was initially gummy and awkward. I wasn't scheming, man. You were just dropping your pencil? Just dropping it. I drum, Liddy said. Beat skins. It takes a few days to recover feeling in my hands after shows. Against better judgment, Shales gave her the floor. She explained how good it felt, splitting time, or resurrecting it, as though it were dead, with booze and X buzzing in her at one on a school night. And Shales must have grown concerned and told her to go see a doctor, or at least the school nurse, about her hands. Then he must have slipped and mentioned himself. Mentioned, in passing, everything. He must have felt exhausted keeping secrets, must have been drawn to the prospect of giving away his secret, unburdening himself of it. Or, he was looking for another identity to climb into. He told Liddy he'd pass her if she wrote an essay defining the mean. She agreed and clasped his hand, and told him she was sorry about the cancer, Charlie, and there's something I can do for you, if you want.

Next Reel: Liddy gets on Shales's bad side. She doesn't show for a conference. He looks over her essay as the light outside weakens. Winter comes early in Wisconsin. She clearly has problems explaining math concepts in print. She thinks the mean is the number that occurs most in a given set. She's fairly bright, and he doesn't want to fail her, so he agrees to let her explain it to him orally. But she doesn't show, making Shales late for chemo. Shales decides on humiliation tactics. He takes out a Rolodex and calls Liddy's parents. A nightclub manager answers. He is amused to be speaking with a math teacher and is mentally recording every word Shales says for later tonight, when he'll retell it over a few cold ones. Liddy's the little wispy piece, yeah? Yeah, I think you've been had, teach. I may have three or four kids running around I don't know about, but Liddy ain't one of them. Parents? Don't think she's got 'em, truthfully. I think one died and the other dropped her. Beyond this I don't know, and since I'm not social fucking services I don't need to know, yeah?

Third Reel: Liddy walks in during conference hour the next day. High. Got my days confused, she giggles. I heard you spoke to Mom and Pop, and my uncle Jack Daniels. She giggles. I played last night and my head is still on nap time, so I guess you can flunk me. But Charlie, I really don't care. Last night we played great. I played great. I pounded so hard I couldn't say if it was the sticks cracking in two or my arms. She giggles. I'm no student. Fuck school, I'm a student of life. Too much life. Shales listens and nods, not with the consternation he thought he'd feel. The girl has guile, noise, and not a prayer of living past thirty at the rate she's going. She's his hero. She has talent—although most of that talent is anger, and will burn away as she forgets the family she is angry at. Liddy sighs: Am I expelled, Charlie? He rips her essay in two. I'll be dead inside a year, he says. That's an extreme. You live like Dionysus, that, too, is an extreme. The mean is balance. The mean is when both of us are sleeping. Any questions? Liddy says no, and Shales prints an A on her hand, on the spot where the stamp for last night's club is rubbing away. She pushes close to him and draws sticky, sweet breath on his face. I told you I would help you and I mean it. Can you smell this, taste this? This is what I'm good for. Prepare yourself, she whispers, for a little peace.

Shales found himself in the Cineplex parking lot, warming his Buick. He had no idea when he'd left the movie theater, or if *Hit and Run* was over yet. The heater churned, biting into the accumulated sheet of frost. What if the Spoiler had approached him years ago, offering to tell him the ending he was living now? What if she'd told him that right out of engineering school he'd be designing Apache rotors to be peddled off to unconscionable regimes in shaky state-sponsored auctions? Or told Shales that eventually he'd muster the courage to quit that job and leave California, where medicinal marijuana was allowed, for Wisconsin, where it wasn't, but only then would his body fall apart? Would he have believed her?

But there was no one to tell him the state of things, only X rays and biopsies . . . he was getting ahead of himself. Trying to finish the problem without showing his work. An equation was just a story condensed into one sentence, or a narrative in reverse. With a narrative, a reader waded through rows of flowery words hoping to come away with one core truth—with equations, a reader picked over the core truth, and then revised it, plugging in factors and numerals, deciphering, extrapolating, justifying its presence to make sure it belonged at all.

Reel 4 was Shales in transition, resigned to his desperation, letting it take charge. Reel 4 was when his view of life reversed: until now he'd been a disciple of moderation. He had tried to exist in the mean: meaning balance, meaning restraint, meaning a lapse in judgment in one thing—say junk food—could be remedied only by a stricter regimen in a corresponding situation—say ten minutes longer on the stationary bike. But as the pain intensified, all that sentiment broke down. Shales sought out extremes. He told himself he was still sticking to his philosophy; it was just that his body was so wracked and torn apart he had to respond in kind; the more apocryphal the sources the better. Shales tried support groups—a half dozen, until he forgot which building and which night and which of his peers were in remission and which metastatic. He sought out a therapist but couldn't afford it. He tried acupressure, shark cartilage, gin, and Dramamine, tried to take up the clarinet again, tried a whorehouse for the first time since the Army, tried mistletoe (which actually did keep him sedate through mild pain . . . could be just the act of chewing, or the unofficial theorem that enough shit flung results in some of it sticking). Then there was that night he drove over to Madison—on a recommendation—and was buzzed into a warehouse with an awful draft. Shales didn't remember it all, but the process involved having his head swaddled in a tunic, and resting his chin inside what amounted to a large rubber band suspended from the ceiling. He felt hands; they smelled of camphor; he heard chanting in French. All the while Liddy and her offer were looming, dilating, looking less crazy.

So the deal went down. Liddy arranged to be caught with a note in class. Shales pretended to catch her and confiscate the note. The note was from Jilt, the guy who had the stuff, and it contained the details of the deal. *Meet at 2 sharp. You dick us you die. You squeal you die. You late you lose. Milwaukee Zoo. Monkey House. By the bush's. Don't look like a teacher. But don't look like a teacher trying not to look like one.* Shales tried to catch Liddy's eye to confirm these strange directives, but she refused to look up from her desk. Shales left school before noon, feigning nausea in fourth period. He was sure it was a setup. He wondered if he should buy a gun at Wal-Mart. But he wound up bringing nothing but the hundred, in twenties, specified in Jilt's note. Oh, and wide-ruled paper, in case they had nothing to roll the pot into. Shales took back roads to avoid being seen, long and vacant roads in the industrial zone, Devore Drive, Jackson Circle Park, past the old cinema where he and Mary—before he got diagnosed—used to watch films together, past the alley behind the Pink Rink, closed now six years, and so on and on.

It was bitterly cold but the sun was bright and feisty. He realized why this spot had been chosen. Sheets of blue tarp covered cranes and bulldozers: Construction was under way on the Monkey House, and the grounds were closed to the public. The area was abandoned. Shales stood in one spot, just behind a pile of pallets. His brow was moist and he felt more nervous than he ever had before a CT scan, or lying naked on tissue paper in some featureless examining room in Oncology. As he waited he watched his squat shadow lengthen in front of him, flatten, as though the sun were beating it submissively into the concrete.

The kids showed precisely four hours later, two hours late. They walked not toward Shales but past him. He didn't turn to mark their progress. A minute of silence passed, another, another. Finally he was sent for. Liddy emerged, took his hand, and led Shales beneath the temporary scaffolding in back of the Monkey House.

No one seemed happy to see him. Of course, he was the variable in this equation. They had all done pot before. They had been doing pot four, five, six years: as tagalongs to older brothers, at school dances to relieve the awkward roaming in the gymnasium, in bathrooms, in basements, in bed, taking a hit to help them relax before big exams. They had built this routine at the zoo—it was their textbook—and they were wary of allowing intruders in on the magic, especially middle-aged teachers in sweater vests. But Liddy had vouched for Shales and had, apparently, sweet-toothed Jilt.

Then Jilt reached for his inside jacket pocket, shoulders wide like he was baring his chest for the world. As he made these motions the group gathered round. Since there'd been nothing in the way of formal introductions, Shales listened closely for names: he knew Liddy and Jilt, Mikey had dropped out of his class the year before, there was the guy in back not speaking or being spoken to, and another one, either Claude or Claw, Shales wasn't sure which.

"You score kind?"

"Shit. Naw. DeJuan tells me like ten seconds ago he won't deal us out no more. Shit is that?"

"Shit."

"He try to up the piece's price?"

"Naw naw, check it out. DeJuan's a pussy, simple as that. Told me he cut out on school, cut out on dealing, all so he could work on his game at the yard. On his game — he's five foot seven. Can work on his game all damn decade, he's still gonna wind up just another unemployed nigger with a crossover dribble."

The quiet one, the one in back, looked at Shales for the slightest fraction of a second, to see if Shales was cool. Shales was cool. Shales was fighting pressure that was bench-pressing against his organs. He was cool with anything that would take that away.

"So then where'd you get the shit? Secondhand?"

"Would I fuck you like that? The shit is à la Ray's brother."

The dim thin eyelids rose. "Ray's brother?"

Mikey held his arms triumphantly overhead, bent at the elbows. "Touchdown!"

"Yeah yeah, but smoke good. Proceeds from this afternoon will contribute to posting bail. Ray's brother got DEA'd hard."

"Shitting?"

Jilt shook his head. "Real. They spun him, spun his house for six and a quarter. Spun dry."

There was a moment of silence to mourn the loss of Ray's brother to the Milwaukee penal system. Then the quiet kid approached his old teacher. "Shit Shales, this is your lucky day!"

The kid took a hit off something, and Shales stopped sweating. It was the first time in fifteen minutes they'd addressed him, and he figured if he didn't speak now, they'd forget he was here. "I don't know if you've been filled in on . . . what you've been filled in on. But I really want to try some of that . . . I'd pay . . . name your price."

"Name my price what *I* got?" The kid moaned ruthlessly. "Well now, let's see . . ."

"Kyle!" Liddy screamed. "He's a first-time customer. Just like anybody else. First-timers are always right; don't be a fuck."

Shales turned to Liddy, trying to beg her off. "But this is what I want."

Mikey grabbed Kyle's joint. "No, see, Shales, time to get schooled. This shit is just that, shit. What you want is what my man Jilt's got under the jacket. I'll translate it to math terms. Kyle's joint is addition and subtraction. Any penny you pay for that weak-ass, beaned, grown-in-a-tub shit is a penny too much. Kyle knows that, but Kyle knows he can't get high off anything anymore, and he just smokes for the recreation. What's in Jilt's jacket is logarithms and cosines. Hard-to-fucking-get."

"See what you want," summed up Claude or Claw, "is the kind."

Again Shales looked to Liddy for guidance, and got none. "I'm sorry. A kind? Kind of what? Kind of brand?"

"No," said Jilt, impatient at how long it was taking to hammer home the lesson, "the Kind." He pulled out the first bag and held it to his nose. "The Kind. You can't think about it this much or the shit won't feel good when you finally get around to doing it."

"Well, I have the money, old twenties, pre-1990, like your outline said. So can I buy some and..."

"We're waiting," Jilt said, checking his watch. "You should wait, too. You've waited this far for your hit. You might as well wait for 4:20."

"What's 4:20?"

The boys snickered, embracing the power of slang knowledge. "It's a special time. A minute we all hold dear." Later Liddy would clarify: 4:20 was ceremonial, teatime for stoners. Then she would step in before Mikey could take Shales's money to test the alleged Kind, and make sure they weren't beaning Shales. Liddy was his protein and his protector that first Tuesday.

Shales doesn't really remember the details anymore of the actual smoking; time wasn't passing, just sensation. Like the first time he'd had the courage to suck up all the way, and it was like he was breathing a garden. Or how Liddy's hair glinted under the sun, a color that couldn't have existed except in magazines or under black light—waxen, mordant magenta. The sight of mechanical lungs Mikey produced from his backpack—"This is how you use a bong, man"—and how the smoke from the Kind he paid for waved feebly through the bong's chamber, like the hands of a man tentatively poking ahead in a pitch-dark cave. Shales's lower jaw muscles fibrillated between hits. He pinched his skin for the friction. The magic had come: It was now dullness in Shales's skull, not pain in his stomach, claiming authority. The dark pearled eyes of reconnoitering seagulls, settling on the zoo grass, a stopover on their way to Lake Michigan—the birds stood at their stations, tensed, and took slow, deliberate steps toward the humans, eyes surveying the sub-rosa scene point to point like Secret Service agents—filling him at once with both paranoia and peace. Come to get him. The monkeys hitching up their noses and moaning from within the cage. Come to get him.

After a few hits Shales decided to let himself into the conversation. The gang was talking about pranks—pulling the wool over authority's eyes, getting one's way despite the system, all that kid shit that was really cool. He would play it cool, too; he wouldn't just start in. He'd just add a few *uh-huh*s or *right*s now and then, until the others were comfortable with his presence. Then it hit him. No one was talking. They were busy smoking, or inspecting each other's skin for veins, or doing these things and looking at Shales. It was him; he had been the only one talking all along.

So it didn't bother anybody when Shales just started a new story, the one he'd been planning to tell while busy listening to, and trying to politely interrupt, himself: "So I mean, just because someone's good with numbers doesn't mean they won't fuck with you. You know that Catherine the Great's math tutor, guy was Swiss, Euler,

Leonhard Euler? Euler once tricked all these wealthy, erudite Court philosophers into accepting the validity of a higher power. Know how? Just wrote $(x + y)^2 = x^2 + 2xy + y^2$ on a blackboard, drew a line beneath it, and added 'Therefore God Exists.'" Shales drew in more smoke; the old stuff was clinging to his throat. "So I guess what I'm saying," he said, giving everyone a moment to rein in their laughter, "is that this is really nice."

After Catherine the Great he was in. The procession of Tuesdays followed. The kids were inquisitive, asking questions no one else in Shales's life had, or would. What was the Hemo-Vac like? Did it actually suck up blood? Why aren't you bald? How much time do you have? They began making sure he had better shit than the rest of them. They dropped their cost. Everyone wanted Shales's last hit of the day to be off their joint—they wanted something to remember him by. Shales knew all this—but he was getting more to smoke in the deal so he let it slide.

Besides, he was participating in the nostalgia, too. Watching how the boys stood, like cantilevered sculptures, one bent at the waist trying to cup a flame, another's legs sailing wide apart. Jilt, getting funnier and more confident each week. Liddy was different. She was still beautiful but in the way of worn brick, not so much for her strength now as for her strength then. On the last Tuesday she was wearing houndstooth pants and Shales's Space Camp sweatshirt, wasn't doing much at all, just packing on the vein leading to her elbow. It vaguely disturbed Shales that he couldn't bring himself to tell Liddy to stop. But she wasn't his kid anymore.

It was closer to say he was theirs. Now, it was closer to say this. They spoiled him. Mikey blocked the January, then February, now March, winds; Kyle patrolled the grounds more often—as the days lengthened, and the construction crew started putting in more appearances—so Shales didn't have to look over his shoulder. Jilt, like a grandfather, always had something special in his jacket pocket for Shales. The Tuesday episodes were feeling less like drug transactions and more like holiday reunions with family. Shales gave them updates on his treatment; the others stood and smoked and shot up, rapt, listening to him.

And Shales was astounded by their game of numbers. 1011, 808... Mikey can't make it today. Oh wow, why? 611. They'd picked up the codes of offenses from cops that had busted them, or friends of theirs. Rote memorization impressed Shales; he had a soft spot for attempts at order. Actually, he was prepared to call the group quite smart. They didn't possess dented vocabularies, just...specialized ones, for the benefit of their own comprehension only, all ties to classical expression severed.

"We gotta get nake sometime, baby," said Jilt to Liddy. He was playing with her, of course. By now everyone in the group except Claw (it *was* Claw) had slept with Liddy. Jilt was trying to get under her skin, but the only thing that could these days was the syringe— and bad shows, and when she heard Shales vomit from a bathroom or behind the forsythia that lined the Monkey House. Anyway the teasing was for Shales's benefit, too, to deflect the awkward silences. He was close to finished. He looked beaten even when grinning. His decline was clear to them all—maybe even to Shales a little less than the others. They blew out smoke but without much verve. You could hear the monkeys groom each other and hum through their flat noses.

Then Jilt said, "Man, we want to get something out." Shales looked up from Claw's bong. The circle tightened. Jilt cleared his throat and reached into his pocket. He pulled out a sheet of paper, looked it over, and glared. His ever-present smile went into hiatus. "It's wet."

Kyle: "What?" Jilt: "The page, dipshit! The page we wrote for Shales at lunch. It's fucking soggy!" Kyle: "Don't look at me." Jilt: "Who should I look at? Who else had to take a hit while we were writing and forgot to dump out his bongwater before he put the bong in my fucking pocket?" Liddy: "So just say it, Jilt. Say it to Charlie." A pause, because Jilt was collecting himself and one of the chimps had unraveled a hose and was whipping it into the safety glass. Quiet. Jilt: "Fuck. I forget every damn word." So they offered to walk around without Shales for a while and try to come up with a new page, but Shales did not want to be left without them.

"In this problem, solve for y."

Shales stepped back from the blackboard the following morning, wiping chalk dust from his hands. He let silence take over. He watched the second hand on the hall clock sweep past twelve. He gave the integers time to sink in. Not one of the kids made a move for pencil or calculator. When he called on students for the answer in a minute, the faces would be blank and stiff, as though a military superior had entered the classroom. That was all just fine. Shales was rapt with two girls sitting in front. They were smacking gum— grounds for detention according to the rule he had floated months ago, when he cared about such distractions. The taller of the two girls had constructed a fortune-teller, one of those pinwheel-shaped puppets. She picked a number and used that number to guide her friend's fate, concerning who would ask whom to the spring dance. Shales couldn't stop watching. They'd written the names of two boys, Billy and Ryan, on all eight of the fortune flaps, and it was clear they had crushes on both boys. The whole thing riled him. Who were they kidding, giggling deliriously when they drew one of the boys' names? As if they were playing with chance, as if they had no idea how things were going to turn out. They were stacking the odds and pretending there was still something at stake. Look at them. Fingernail polish the color of grime, infantile light in their eyes. Giggling at their good luck. That's not probability. It's a mirage.

Shales insisted on the Wednesday matinee. But neither he nor Mary were dressed for the Cineplex, which was kept uncomfortably underheated. So Shales draped his arm around Mary like a stole. She let his fingers nibble below her left shoulder. Mary looked around. The screen was frightful and enormous. Though this was the movie everyone was hyping, and this was its premiere, hardly anyone was watching with them. Morning weekday shows were always this sparse, apparently: About ten ushers sprawled out along the back row, watching as spectators, and they seemed to be so comfortable as to forget they wore Velcro cummerbunds, or that their fingers were artificially buttered.

Shales and Mary stepped into the lobby. Shales took a long look at Mary, waiting for her review. "Well, you know, it wasn't bad," she offered. "But if I'm going to get fired for insubordination, I expect an instant classic." Shales thrust his hands into his pants, scanning the lobby. He seemed intense but in control. Not like the man who'd appeared in her classroom just hours before, who'd called Mary out of her room with a whisper. Who'd said he needed help, needed her, could she grab her coat and leave with him, right now? She could drive his car, he'd said, providing keys. There was no question of her not going: She could imagine him seized with pain on Highway 94, car sliding over the yellow stripes, the road slippery with ribboned snow, on the way to Racine.

But then in his car he told her the pain was clearing. It comes, it goes. Shales asked if she would instead take him to the Cineplex, to the matinee premiere of *Princely Sum*. And it was a good movie, just not what she'd expected. "What has that actress been in?" Mary asked. "Where have I seen her before?"

"Where is she?" asked Shales, stepping outside.

"That's what I mean. She absolutely rings a bell, but I don't know from where..." Mary looked up. Shales had stormed over to the box office window: He was screaming at someone there, a woman who had just bought a ticket. He was making wild, circling gestures with his arms, and his shirt collar fluttered as he wagged his index finger at her face. The woman cowered before Shales, ticket wrung in her hand. Mary stepped forward, peering into the confrontation. "You dumb bitch," Shales said. "Listen good. Here's how it goes, here's how it ends. He doesn't get the girl. Okay? And when he slips into the coma? Slipping into the coma was the best thing he ever did."

The Spoiler stood quietly. Her face seemed tight below the nose, as though she were having difficulty clearing her throat. Her lips parted slowly, unspooling. Her ticket for the next show dropped from her hand and blew down the walkway. She chased after it.

Mary watched the Spoiler try in vain to snatch the ticket off the ground. But each time she had caught up to it, it spilled forward in the breeze, tumbling just beyond her tightened fist. Mary approached Shales, gazing at him: His teeth were clenched, his breathing abbreviated and heavy. Mary touched his hand—it was as if his heat had all coiled there. She began to laugh. Shales turned toward her, startled by her amusement. "What, what?" she asked. "What do you want, for me to send you to the principal? It was enterprising revenge!"

Shales wondered if he should let go of her hand. If he did, she would ask him to take her back to school. But if he didn't, he could prolong his day with her a little more. A pair of brakes squealed just then. An elderly couple had pulled their car over to the curb. They were studying the marquee, straining to read the show times, hashing out what to see, whether they would see anything. Mary called out to them: "It's safe to go in, in case you're wondering. No one's going to ruin your ending. We have this guy to thank for that."

Shales smiled. "Yeah. I mean, that's not why I came here." Mary studied her ticket stub as if appraising its future worth. "You have to believe that. Whew. For a guy with nothing left, I feel pretty clear."

"Well bravo, and I mean that. But your summary was shaky, Charlie. What were you watching in there? He did get the girl."

Not the one he thought he would, and not the way he thought he'd get her. But somebody should be getting something in the picture. Shales did the math. He considered his will, funeral arrangements, not yet finalized. It wasn't like it wasn't his body to do with as he wished. He didn't have to put his family's concerns before his, just because that was the standard thing. Fuck the visitation. He wanted to be broken down, become something else. He could have himself placed in an urn, to be signed for and picked up and carried off by Liddy. She could take his remains behind the forsythia at the zoo to smoke up the ash, suck up a high, some clutch of pleasure to trap momentarily between her teeth and throat, letting him escape, ring by ring, through the lips.

CONTRIBUTORS

ROOMPA BHATTACHARYYA is a graduate of Wayne State University and lives in suburban Detroit. She is the winner of the Tompkins Award for Short Fiction and has received a Cranbrook Writers Guild scholarship. "Loss" is her first published work.

ZOEY BYRD holds an MA in English and Creative Writing from Hollins University, where "Of Cabbages" won the Andrew James Purdy Prize for Short Fiction. She is currently at work on a novel.

LIDIJA S. CANOVIC was born in Belgrade, Yugoslavia, grew up in Africa, and is now working toward a degree in Texas. She completed her MFA at Minnesota State University, Mankato, and is currently working on a collection of short stories set in the war-torn former Yugoslavia.

SUSANNA DANIEL was born and raised in Miami, Florida, though she now lives and writes in colder climates. She is a graduate of Columbia University and the writing program at the University of Iowa, and is at work on a collection of short fiction set in South Florida. She is currently a writing fellow at the Wisconsin Institute for Creative Writing.

AMANDA DAVIS lives in Brooklyn and is the author of a collection of stories, *Circling the Drain* (Rob Weisbach/William Morrow, 1999). Her fiction, nonfiction, and reviews have appeared in *Story, Seventeen, McSweeney's, Esquire, BookForum,* and *Black Book.* She is currently at work on a novel, *Faith Duckle,* to be published by Harper-Collins in 2002.

WHITNEY DAVIS, a graduate of William Smith College, recently earned her MFA in Fiction from Syracuse University, where she was also a Fellow in the African American Studies department. She is finishing her first collection of stories.

ERIN FLANAGAN's short stories have appeared in *The Baltimore Review* and *Colorado Review.* She has been awarded a work-study scholarship at the Bread Loaf Writers'

Conference and is currently managing editor of *Prairie Schooner* and a Ph.D. student at the University of Nebraska, Lincoln.

HA-YUN JUNG was born in Seoul, Korea, where she lived most of her life. Her stories have appeared in *StoryQuarterly* and *Prairie Schooner.* A recent graduate of the MA Program in Writing and Publishing at Emerson College, Jung is also a translator and is at work on a collection of contemporary Korean fiction translated into English. She is currently the Carol Houck Smith Fiction Fellow at the Wisconsin Institute for Creative Writing.

JEB LIVINGOOD teaches at the University of Virginia, where he is the faculty advisor for *Meridian.* His fiction and essays have appeared in *Yemassee, The Texas Review, C-ville,* and *The Hollins Critic.*

CHRISTINA MILLETTI received her MFA from Brown University in 1996. She is currently a Presidential Fellow at the University at Albany, SUNY, where she is writing her dissertation on women experimental writers. Her fiction has appeared in *The Chicago Review* and *13th Moon.* The New York Foundation of the Arts recently awarded her a Thayer Fellowship to complete her novel-in-progress, *Room in the Hotel America.*

JULIE ORRINGER grew up in New Orleans and Ann Arbor and now lives in San Francisco. She is a Truman Capote Fellow in the Stegner Program at Stanford University, where she is working on a collection of stories. She received her BA from Cornell University and her MFA from the Iowa Writers' Workshop. Her stories have appeared in *The Paris Review, The Yale Review, Ploughshares,* and *Pushcart Prize XXV,* and she has received the Smart Family Foundation Award and *The Paris Review* Discovery Prize.

MATTHEW PITT earned his MFA at New York University, where he was a *New York Times* Fellow in Fiction. His work has recently appeared in, and won awards from, *Confrontation, Prism International, New York Stories,* and the *St. Louis Post-Dispatch.* Now living in Brooklyn, he is at work on a story collection, a novel, and a complex origami project.

PATRICK RYAN was born in New Orleans in 1970. His short stories have appeared in *Men on Men 2000, The James White Review,* and *Harrington Gay Men's Fiction Quarterly,* among others. He is a graduate of the MFA Program in Creative Writing at San Francisco State University.

KIRA SALAK received an MFA from the University of Arizona, and spent two years after graduation living in Japan. Currently she is enrolled in the University of Missouri-Columbia's Ph.D. program in Creative Writing. Her travel memoir, *The Four Corners,* will be published by Counterpoint/Perseus Books in fall 2001. The book recounts her experiences in Mozambique during its civil war, as well as a solo journey she took across Papua New Guinea as she attempted to retrace the route of British explorer Ivan Champion (the first person to successfully cross the island in 1927).

LYSLEY A. TENORIO was the 1999–2000 James McCreight Fiction Fellow at the Wisconsin Institute for Creative Writing at the University of Wisconsin. He is currently a Wallace Stegner Fellow at Stanford University. His work has appeared in *The Atlantic Monthly* and *Ploughshares.*

TIMOTHY A. WESTMORELAND studied and taught astronomy at the University of Texas at Arlington before becoming a writer. He completed his MFA at the University of Massachusetts at Amherst. His fiction has appeared in *Scribner's Best of the Fiction Workshops 1998, Quarterly West, Indiana Review,* and other places. His collection of stories, *Good as Any,* and his novel, *Gathering,* are forthcoming from Harcourt.

ANTOINE WILSON was the 2000–2001 Carol Houck Smith Fellow at the Wisconsin Institute for Creative Writing. Born in Montréal, Quebec, he received an MFA in 2000 from the University of Iowa. His story "Photog!" is forthcoming in *StoryQuarterly,* and he is currently working on a novel.

PARTICIPANTS

United States

Advanced Fiction Workshop with
Carol Edgarian & Tom Jenks
P.O. Box 29272
San Francisco, CA 94129
415/346-4477

American University
MFA Program in Creative Writing
Department of Literature
4400 Massachusetts Avenue N.W.
Washington, DC 20036
202/885-2990

Arizona State University
Creative Writing Program
Department of Literature
Tempe, AZ 85287
480/965-3528

The Asian American Writers'
Workshop
16 West 32nd Street
Suite 10A
New York, NY 10001
212/494-0061

Bennington College
Writing Seminars
Bennington, VT 05201
802/440-4452

Boston University
Creative Writing Program
236 Bay State Road
Boston, MA 02215
617/353-2510

Bowling Green State University
Creative Writing Program
Department of English
Bowling Green, OH 43403
419/372-8370

The Bread Loaf Writers' Conference
Middlebury College
Middlebury, VT 05753
802/443-5286

Brooklyn College
MFA Program in Creative Writing
Department of English
2900 Bedford Avenue
Brooklyn, NY 11210
718/951-5195

Brown University
Program in Creative Writing
Box 1852
Providence, RI 02912
401/863-3260

California State University,
Long Beach
MFA in Creative Writing
Department of English
1250 Bellflower Boulevard
Long Beach, CA 90840-2403
562/985-4225

California State University,
Northridge
Department of English
18111 Nordhoff Street
Northridge, CA 91330-8248
818/677-3431

California State University,
Sacramento
Creative Writing
Department of English
6000 J Street
Sacramento, CA 95819
916/278-6586

Chapman University
Department of English and
Comparative Literature
1 University Drive
Orange, CA 92866
714/997-6750

Colorado State University
Creative Writing Program
Department of English
359 Eddy Building
Fort Collins, CO 80523-1773
970/491-6428

Columbia College, Chicago
Fiction Writing Department
600 South Michigan Avenue
Chicago, IL 60605
312/344-7611

Columbia University
Writing Division
School of the Arts
Dodge Hall
2960 Broadway, Room 400
New York, NY 10027-6902
212/854-4391

DePaul University
MA in Writing Program
Department of English
802 West Belden Avenue
Chicago, IL 60614
773/325-7485

Eastern Washington University
Creative Writing Program
MS #1
705 West First Avenue
Spokane, WA 99201-3909
509/623-4221

Emerson College
MFA in Creative Writing
120 Boylston Street
Boston, MA 02116-1596
617/824-8750

Fine Arts Work Center in
Provincetown
24 Pearl Street
Provincetown, MA 02657
508/487-8678

Florida International University
MFA Program in Creative Writing
Department of English
Biscayne Bay Campus
3000 N.E. 151st Street
North Miami, FL 33181
305/919-5857

Florida State University
Department of English
Tallahassee, FL 32306-1580
850/644-4230

George Mason University
Creative Writing Program
MS 3E4
Fairfax, VA 22030
703/993-1185

Hollins University
Creative Writing Program
P.O. Box 9677
Roanoke, VA 24020-1677
540/362-6317

Hunter College
MFA Program in Creative Writing
English Department
695 Park Avenue
New York, NY 10021
212/772-5164

Indiana University
Creative Writing Program
Ballantine Hall 442
1020 East Kirkwood Avenue
Bloomington, IN 47405
812/855-8224

Johns Hopkins University
The Writing Seminars
135 Gilman Hall
3400 North Charles Street
Baltimore, MD 21218-2690
410/516-7563

Johns Hopkins University, Part-Time
Graduate Writing Program
1776 Massachusetts Avenue N.W.
Suite 100
Washington, DC 20036
202/452-1123

Kansas State University
Creative Writing Program
Department of English
106 Denison Hall
Manhattan, KS 66506
785/532-6716

The Loft Literary Center,
Mentor Series Program
Suite 200, Open Book
1011 Washington Avenue South
Minneapolis, MN 55414-1246
612/215-2575

Louisiana State University
English Department
213 Allen
Baton Rouge, LA 70803
225/388-2236

Loyola Marymount University
Department of English
University Hall
One LMU Drive, Suite 3800
Los Angeles, CA 90045-2659
310/338-3018

Manhattanville College
Master of Arts in Writing
2900 Purchase Street
Purchase, NY 10577
914/694-3425

McNeese State University
Program in Creative Writing
P.O. Box 92655
Lake Charles, LA 70609
337/475-5326

Miami University
MA Program in Creative Writing
Department of English
356 Bachelor Hall
Oxford, OH 45056
513/529-5221

Minnesota State University, Mankato
English Department, AH 230
Mankato, MN 56001
507/389-2117

Mississippi State University
Drawer E
Department of English
Mississippi State, MS 39762
662/325-3644

Naropa Institute
2130 Arapahoe Avenue
Boulder, CO 80302-6697
303/546-3540

New Mexico State University
Department of English
Box 30001, Department 3E
Las Cruces, NM 88003-8001
505/646-3931

The New School
Office of Education Advising and
Admissions
66 West 12th Street
New York, NY 10011
212/229-5630

New York University
Graduate Program in Creative
Writing
19 University Place
New York, NY 10003
212/998-8816

Northeastern University
Department of English
406 Homes Hall
Boston, MA 02115-5000
617/373-2512

Ohio State University
Creative Writing Program
Department of English
421 Denney Hall
164 West 17th Avenue
Columbus, OH 43210-1370
614/292-2242

Open Road Writing Workshops
P.O. Box 386
Amherst, MA 01004
413/259-1865

Pennsylvania State University
MFA in Creative Writing
Department of English
S. 144 Burrowes Building
University Park, PA 16802
814/863-3069

PEN Prison Writing Committee
PEN American Center
568 Broadway
New York, NY 10012
212/334-1660

Saint Mary's College of California
MFA Program in Creative Writing
P.O. Box 4686
Moraga, CA 94575-4686
925/631-4088

San Diego State University
MFA Program
Department of English and
Comparative Literature
5500 Campanile Drive
San Diego, CA 92182-8140
619/594-5443

San Francisco State University
Creative Writing Department
College of Humanities
1600 Holloway Avenue
San Francisco, CA 94132-4162
415/338-1891

Sarah Lawrence College
Office of Graduate Studies
1 Mead Way
Bronxville, NY 10708-5999
914/337-0700

Sewanee Writers' Conference
735 University Avenue
Sewanee, TN 37383-1000
931/598-1141

Sonoma State University
Department of English
1801 East Cotati Avenue
Rohnert Park, CA 94928-3609
707/664-2140

Southampton College/Long Island
University
MFA Program in English & Writing
English Department
239 Montauk Highway
Southampton, NY 11968
631/287-8420

Southwest Texas State University
MFA Program in Creative Writing
Department of English
601 University Drive
Flowers Hall
San Marcos, TX 78666
512/245-2163

The Squaw Valley Community of
Writers
10626 Banner Lava Cap
Nevada City, CA 95959
530/274-8551

Stanford University
Creative Writing Program
Department of English
Stanford, CA 94305-2087
650/725-1208

Syracuse University
Program in Creative Writing
Department of English
401 Hall of Languages
Syracuse, NY 13244-1170
315/443-2174

Temple University
Creative Writing Program
Anderson Hall, 10th Floor
Philadelphia, PA 19122
215/204-1796

University at Albany, SUNY
The Graduate Program in English
Studies
English Department
Humanities Building
Albany, NY 12222
518/442-4055

University of Alabama
Program in Creative Writing
Department of English
P.O. Box 870244
Tuscaloosa, AL 35487-0244
205/348-0766

University of Alaska, Anchorage
Department of Creative Writing &
Literary Arts
3211 Providence Drive
Anchorage, AK 99508-8348
907/786-4330

University of Alaska, Fairbanks
Program in Creative Writing
Department of English
P.O. Box 755720
Fairbanks, AK 99775-5720
907/474-7193

University of Arizona
Creative Writing Program
Department of English
Modern Languages Bldg. #67
Tucson, AZ 85721-0067
520/621-3880

University of Arkansas
Program in Creative Writing
Department of English
333 Kimpel Hall
Fayetteville, AR 72701
501/575-7355

University of California, Davis
Graduate Creative Writing Program
Department of English
Davis, CA 95616
530/752-2281

University of California, Irvine
MFA Program in Writing
Department of English &
Comparative Literature
435 Humanities Instructional Bldg.
Irvine, CA 92697-2650
949/824-6718

University of Central Florida
Graduate Program in Creative
Writing
Department of English
P.O. Box 161346
Orlando, FL 32816-1346
407/823-2212

University of Cincinnati
Creative Writing Program
Department of English &
Comparative Literature
ML 69
Cincinnati, OH 45221-0069
513/556-3946

University of Colorado at Boulder
Creative Writing Program
Department of English
Campus Box 226
Boulder, CO 80309-0226
303/492-7381

University of Denver
Creative Writing Program
Department of English
2140 South Race Street
Denver, CO 80210
303/871-2266

University of Florida
Creative Writing Program
Department of English
P.O. Box 117730
Gainesville, FL 32611-7310
352/392-6650

University of Georgia
Creative Writing Program
English Department
Park Hall 102
Athens, GA 30602-6205
706/542-2659

University of Hawaii
Creative Writing Program
English Department
1733 Donaghho Road
Honolulu, HI 96822
808/956-8801

University of Houston
Creative Writing Program
Department of English
Houston, TX 77204-3012
713/743-3015

University of Idaho
Creative Writing Program
Department of English
Moscow, ID 83843-1102
208/885-6156

University of Illinois at Chicago
Program for Writers
Department of English MC/162
601 South Morgan Street
Chicago, IL 60607-7120
312/413-2229

University of Iowa
Program in Creative Writing
102 Dey House
507 North Clinton Street
Iowa City, IA 52242
319/335-0416

University of Louisiana at Lafayette
Creative Writing Concentration
Department of English
P.O. Box 44691
Lafayette, LA 70504-4691
337/482-6906

University of Maine
Master's in English Program
5752 Neville Hall
Orono, ME 04469-5752
207/581-3822

University of Maryland
Creative Writing Program
Department of English
4140 Susquehanna Hall
College Park, MD 20742
301/405-3820

University of Massachusetts, Amherst
MFA Program in English
Bartlett Hall
Box 30515
Amherst, MA 01003-0515
413/545-0643

University of Michigan
MFA Program in Creative Writing
Department of English
3187 Angell Hall
Ann Arbor, MI 48109-1003
734/763-4139

University of Minnesota
MFA Program in Creative Writing
Department of English
207 Church Street, SE
Minneapolis, MN 55455
612/625-6366

University of Missouri-Columbia
Program in Creative Writing
Department of English
107 Tate Hall
Columbia, MO 65211
573/882-6421

University of Missouri-St. Louis
Master of Fine Arts in Creative
Writing Program
Department of English
8001 Natural Bridge Road
St. Louis, MO 63121
314/516-6845

University of Montana
Creative Writing Program
Department of English
Missoula, MT 59812-1013
406/243-5231

University of Nebraska, Lincoln
Creative Writing Program
Department of English
202 Andrews Hall
Lincoln, NE 68588-0333
402/472-3191

University of Nevada, Las Vegas
MFA in Creative Writing
Department of English
4505 South Maryland Parkway
Las Vegas, NV 89154-5011
702/895-3533

University of New Orleans
Creative Writing Workshop
College of Liberal Arts
Lakefront
New Orleans, LA 70148
504/280-7454

University of North Carolina,
Greensboro
MFA Writing Program
P.O. Box 26170
Greensboro, NC 27402-6170
336/334-5459

University of North Dakota
Creative Writing Program
Department of English
P.O. Box 7209
Grand Forks, ND 58202
701/777-3321

University of North Texas
Department of English
P.O. Box 311307
Denton, TX 76203-1307
940/565-2050

University of Notre Dame
Creative Writing Program
355 O'Shaughnessy Hall
Notre Dame, IN 46556-0368
219/631-5639

University of Oregon
Program in Creative Writing
Box 5243
Eugene, OR 97403-5243
541/346-3944

University of San Francisco
Master of Arts in Writing Program
Program Office, Lone Mountain 340
2130 Fulton Street
San Francisco, CA 94117-1080
415/422-2382

University of South Carolina
MFA Program
Department of English
Columbia, SC 29208
803/777-5063

University of Southern Mississippi
Center for Writers
Box 5144 USM
Hattiesburg, MS 39406-5144
601/266-4321

University of Texas at Austin
Creative Writing Program in English
Calhoun Hall 210
Austin, TX 78712-1164
512/475-6356

University of Texas,
Michener Center for Writers
J. Frank Dobie House
702 East Dean Keeton Street
Austin, TX 78705
512/471-1601

University of Utah
Creative Writing Program
255 South Central Campus Drive
Room 3500
Salt Lake City, UT 84112
801/581-7131

University of Virginia
Creative Writing Program
Department of English
P.O. Box 400121
Charlottesville, VA 22904-4121
804/924-6675

University of Washington
Creative Writing Program
Box 354330
Seattle, WA 98195
206/543-9865

University of Wisconsin-Milwaukee
Creative Writing Program
Department of English
Box 413
Milwaukee, WI 53201
414/229-4243

University of Wyoming
Writing Program
Department of English
P.O. Box 3353
Laramie, WY 82071
307/766-6452

Unterberg Poetry Center/Writing
Program
92nd Street Y
1395 Lexington Avenue
New York, NY 10128
212/415-5754

Vermont College
Master of Fine Arts in Writing
Montpelier, VT 05602
802/828-8840

Virginia Commonwealth University
MFA in Creative Writing Program
Department of English
P.O. Box 842005
Richmond, VA 23284-2005
804/828-1329

Warren Wilson College
MFA Program for Writers
P.O. Box 9000
Asheville, NC 28815-9000
828/298-3325

Washington University
Writing Program
Department of English
Campus Box 1122
One Brookings Drive
St. Louis, MO 63130-4899
314/935-5190

Wayne State University
Creative Writing Program
English Department
Detroit, MI 48202
313/577-2450

The Wesleyan Writers Conference
Wesleyan University
Middletown, CT 06459
860/685-3604

West Virginia University
Creative Writing Program
Department of English
P.O. Box 6269
Morgantown, WV 26506-6269
304/293-3107

Western Illinois University
Department of English and
Journalism
Macomb, IL 61455-1390
309/298-1103

Western Michigan University
Graduate Program in Creative
Writing
Department of English
Kalamazoo, MI 49008-5092
616/387-2572

Wichita State University
MFA in Creative Writing
1845 North Fairmount
Wichita, KS 67260-0014
316/978-3130

Wisconsin Institute for Creative
Writing
University of Wisconsin-Madison
Department of English
Helen C. White Hall
Madison, WI 53706
608/263-3800

Woodland Pattern Book Center
720 East Locust
Milwaukee, WI 53212
414/263-5001

The Writer's Voice of the
West Side YMCA
5 West 63rd Street
New York, NY 10023
212/875-4124

The Writers Workshop
Kenyon College
Gambie, OH 43022
740/427-5207

Canada

The Banff Centre for the Arts
Writing & Publishing
Box 1020-34
107 Tunnel Mountain Drive
Banff, AB T0L 0C0
403/762-6278

Booming Ground Writers'
Community
Buchanan E-462, 1866 Main Hall
University of British Columbia
Vancouver, BC V6T 1Z1
604/822-2469

The Humber School for Writers
205 Humber College Boulevard
Humber College
Toronto, ON M9W 5L7
416/675-5084

Sage Hill Writing Experience
Box 1731
Saskatoon, SK S7K 3S1
306/652-7395

University of British Columbia
Creative Writing Program
Buchanan E462-1866 Main Mall
Vancouver, BC V6T 1Z1
604/822-0699

University of Calgary
English Department
Creative Writing Program
Calgary, AB T2N 1N4
403/220-5470

University of New Brunswick
Department of English
Box 4400
Fredericton, NB E3B 5A3
506/453-4676

University of Victoria
Department of Writing
P.O. Box 1700, STN CSC
Victoria, BC V8W 2Y2
250/721-7306